SEX, GHOSTS, AND GUMSHOES

Bob Gunn

Llumina Press

Copyright 2004 Robert K. Gunn

All rights reserved. No part of this publication may be reproduced or transmitted in any form or by any means electronic or mechanical, including photocopy, recording, or any information storage and retrieval system, without permission in writing from both the copyright owner and the publisher.

Requests for permission to make copies of any part of this work should be mailed to Permissions Department, Llumina Press, PO Box 772246, Coral Springs, FL 33077-2246

ISBN: 1-59526-346-2
Printed in the United States of America by Llumina Press

Table of Contents

Chapter One
The Rise and the Fall — 5

Chapter Two
Hell Hath no Fury — 22

Chapter Three
A Haunting Experience — 39

Chapter Four
Girls will be Girls — 54

Chapter Five
Beauty and the Ghost — 77

Chapter Six
Fools Rush In — 102

Chapter Seven
A Book Store by any other Name — 124

Chapter Eight
Just a little Patience and Fortitude — 143

Chapter Nine
All that and a Piece of Chocolate Cake — 164

Chapter Ten
When Pigs Fly — 187

Chapter Eleven
Rollin' on the River — 207

Chapter Twelve
Seams that Drive Men Wild — 228

Chapter Thirteen
Sugar and Spice but not so Nice — 249

Chapter Fourteen
A Date with a Lady   270

Epilogue
A Grand Opening   284

CHAPTER 1

THE RISE AND THE FALL
NOVEMBER 1933

Kerby Brewster was a dead-ringer for the young Cary Grant. From the charming smile to the dimpled chin, the lean but muscular acrobat's body to the slight English accent, Kerby was a mirror image of the actor. Even his age, twenty-nine in 1933, matched that of Grant.

Cary Grant had released no fewer than thirteen films between the beginning of 1932 and the end of 1933. But it wasn't until he caught the eye of Mae West, who told him to, "Come on up and see me some time," in the movie *She Done Him Wrong* that the public really started to notice Grant. After the release of the film in January 1933, rarely a day went by that someone, usually an attractive young woman, didn't stop Kerby to ask for an autograph. Kerby didn't mind. To the contrary, he found it an effortless way to meet members of the opposite sex, not that Kerby Brewster needed any help in that regard. Kerby loved the ladies, and the ladies loved being loved by Kerby. He learned at what some might consider a too early age how to make a woman happy, and while he lasted, Kerby Brewster did his best to put a smile on as many female faces as possible.

Like his likeness, Kerby was born in a working class suburb of London, England. His family had immigrated to Manhattan's West Side in 1914, when Kerby was only ten years old. They lived in the same infamous tenement house at 39th Street and 10th Avenue that a *New York Times* reporter referred to as "Hell's Kitchen," in a neighborhood that the same reporter called the "lowest and filthiest in the city." It was that reporter's description of the tenement house that Kerby would later call home that resulted in the area at 39th Street between 9th and 10th Avenues becoming known as Hell's Kitchen. It wasn't until later that the name was expanded to include the surrounding streets.

Aside from the general despair of the neighborhood in which Kerby lived, he also found himself smack in the middle of an Irish immigrant community that had little love for the English. In the early part of the twentieth century, Hell's Kitchen was owned and operated by Irish street gangs with names like the "Dead Rabbits," the "Gorillas," and the "Gophers," who earned their name from their practice of holing up in basements and cellars. The gangs were led by legendary criminals like "Mallet Murphy," who was famous for using a mallet as his weapon of choice; "One Lung Curran," who gained fame for taking a cop's frock overcoat right off the officer's back; and "Battle Annie Walsh," also known as "The Queen of Hell's Kitchen," who was the most feared female brick hurler of the age.

As a result of growing up in the notorious Hell's Kitchen, Kerby grew quick on his feet and even faster with his fists at a very early age. He also developed a charm and wit that matched the quickness of his hands and feet. Kerby was usually ready to face pretty much any problem head on, but he was nobody's fool. He recognized discretion as the better part of valor. If the opposition were too big or too many, Kerby felt no shame in running from it. If there was no avenue of escape, Kerby's vocal chords went to work. His mother used to say, "Kerby could talk the peel off of an Irish potato if he had to." But it wasn't potatoes that Kerby loved peeling.

It was almost as if Kerby's way with the ladies had been thrust upon him. Born naturally handsome, Kerby had his first experience with the finer sex when he was still a very young man, some might even say a boy. As would prove to be the case on most occasions thereafter, that introduction to life's greatest pleasure happened through almost no effort on Kerby's part. That first experience would lead to an education in pleasing the opposite sex that most young men, and women for that matter, wish could be made a part of the mandatory school curriculum.

♥ ♨ ♣

It was a brisk and gusty Fall morning, and young Kerby Brewster was finishing up an errand he was running for a neighborhood bookmaker, delivering an envelope to a grocery store on the Upper East Side of Manhattan. After handing the envelope over to the lucky grocer, Kerby spotted the shapeliest pair of legs he had ever seen. The legs belonged to a blonde who had her back to Kerby. She was walking slowly down a grocery aisle, balanced on a pair of spiky, black heels. Kerby followed the heels of the blonde's shoes up to the thick, black seams of her stockings. He eyed the seams up as far as he could, to a point just above the hollow in the back of the blonde's knees, where the seams ended at the hemline of a glistening black fur coat. In his young mind, Kerby imagined the seams running higher up the blonde's legs and ending at a pair of silky, white thighs.

The fur coat swayed back and forth and the fur itself shimmered as the blonde strolled down the aisle, her hips switching naturally with each step. At the top of her coat, the lady's long blonde hair flowed down her back and contrasted sharply with the shiny black fur. It was while Kerby was eyeing the blonde's hair glimmering on the back of her head that she turned suddenly and their eyes met. Her face was even more beautiful than Kerby had imagined it might be while she had her back to him. She was maybe twenty-five years old. She smiled wickedly at Kerby when she caught him staring at her. Embarrassed, he turned for the door and started to exit, but it was too late. He didn't know it, but young Kerby Brewster had just been added to the blonde's shopping list.

"Hold on there," the blonde hollered, as Kerby took his first step out into the sunlight.

Kerby turned and stared at the woman who stood with her right hand resting on her right hip which was thrust out seductively. In her left hand was a basket brimming with groceries that seemed to be weighing down her left side.

"Think you could give me a hand carrying these groceries home?" the blonde asked, still smiling devilishly. "I'll make it worth your while."

"Uh . . . sure." Kerby responded innocently, and then he stood nearby as the grocer bagged the blonde's goods and she paid him. The two exited the store with Kerby carrying a single bag that was none too heavy.

"It's been a long night," the blonde explained. "I'm beat. I'm just getting home from a night out, but I needed a few things, and I don't want to have to come back out once I'm home. You understand, don't you?"

"Sure," Kerby answered. "No problem. I'm done for the day anyway."

"Oh no, you're not," the blonde said flirtatiously, but Kerby had no idea what she meant.

Soon a doorman was letting the pair into an upscale apartment building on Lexington Avenue. They rode an elevator up to the seventh floor in complete silence. When they exited the elevator, the blonde directed Kerby to the door of her apartment. She unlocked the door while he stood waiting. Once inside the lavishly furnished apartment, the woman directed Kerby into a small kitchen area.

"Just put the bag on the table, sweetie," the blonde instructed Kerby.

As Kerby reached out to put the bag down, he felt the blonde's breath on the back of his neck and then her arms reaching around his waist. Before Kerby knew it, his pants were around his ankles, and the blonde was lowering his under shorts. Kerby wasn't sure what was happening, but he was content to let it run its course. He never uttered a word. In a matter of seconds, young Kerby Brewster was standing stark naked in the blonde's kitchen with his back to the table, his slightly turgid manhood on full display. The blonde stood in the doorway of a spacious, dimly lit living room, smiling as she eyed Kerby up and down, obviously enjoying her view. She was still in her fur coat, black nylons, and black high heels.

Without saying a word, the blonde took Kerby's hand and led him into the living room. Kerby was still content to see where this was all going, but he started to feel a tad embarrassed that the blonde remained dressed for a snowstorm while he was as naked as a monkey. He was hoping that she would take off her clothes and allow him to see her in all of her glory, but the blonde did not oblige as she instructed Kerby to lie on a plush couch in the living room. Kerby didn't mind so much the fact that the blonde had kept her fur coat on when she leaned over his prone body, and he felt the fur lightly brushing against his naked skin. It tingled him wherever it touched.

Soon the blonde was kneeling on the floor alongside Kerby, running her long red fingernails slowly, but somewhat harshly, down his chest. It hurt slightly at first, but Kerby ultimately decided that it felt good. When the blonde's nails got below Kerby's navel, his slightly solid member suddenly shot up straight as if it were spring loaded. The blonde looked down at Kerby's pride and joy as if it had startled her and then she smiled up at him. He lay frozen with excitement, intimidated by the blonde's beauty and experience and feeling incredibly vulnerable at the fact that he was totally nude and now obviously excited and she was still fully clothed and in complete control.

The blonde raised herself over Kerby again and started to gently kiss his forehead in various spots, her fur coat again lightly brushing his body. Her soft kisses worked their way from his forehead down to each of his eyelids and then down to his nose. She kissed him behind his right ear, and Kerby could feel the warmth of her breath on his neck. He liked it. The blonde moved to his mouth and repeatedly darted her tongue between his lips, but she teased him by withdrawing it every time Kerby tried to touch her tongue with his. The blonde was in charge, and she would decide when and if their tongues would meet.

When the blonde was through taunting his mouth, she moved down to his neck and then his chest before her soft kisses turned to bites. The blonde bit each of Kerby's nipples just hard enough to hurt before she shifted back, kissing each nipple lightly and then working her kisses down the center of his chest to his belly. She paused after kissing his navel and stared down at his engorged organ again, which was now throbbing as if there were something inside trying to burst out.

Kerby worried that he might explode before the blonde even reached his manhood. He breathed a sigh of relief when she turned her attention back downward and expressed her oral affections directly on it. In a matter of seconds, Kerby felt as if he was about to let loose, but the blonde stopped at just that moment, pulled back and allowed him to relax for a second before she started again. She teased Kerby for minutes that seemed like hours, repeatedly bringing him to the edge and then stopping as if she were having some silent communication with his member and it was letting her know when it was ready to finish.

Finally, the blonde let Kerby erupt. For a second, he felt bigger and better than he had ever felt before in his life, then he looked down at his rapidly deflating penis and felt spent. *What about her?* the naive Kerby wondered as the blonde crept back up his body and nuzzled under his neck with kisses as if she were about to start all over again.

"I'm really sorry, lady, but it looks as if I've had it," Kerby noted, looking down at his now flaccid organ which was resting on his scrotum as if it were taking a nap.

"I don't think so," she responded.

The blonde stood up alongside the couch, her pelvis eye level with the supine and apparently exhausted young man. She opened her fur coat for the first time, and Kerby saw that she was completely nude underneath, except for a black lace garter belt that was attached to her black nylons. Kerby found his face inches away from the blonde's thoroughly waxed vulva, a vision that would come back to him in dreams for the rest of his life.

"Still think you're through?" the blonde teased, glancing down at Kerby's manhood, which had jumped back to attention without his even realizing it.

"I guess not," a relieved Kerby replied, after following the blonde's eyes down to his groin and realizing that he was back in business.

The blonde straddled Kerby's head with her silken thighs, and Kerby looked up to find that her flush labia were slightly parted, and she was glistening inside. Kerby had never even seen the female treasure before, other than pictures, yet here he was with a view generally reserved for certain kinds of doctors. Further up, Kerby saw the blonde's flat white belly just above the black lace of her garter belt, then her perfectly symmetrical breasts sweeping downward toward him before jutting up to swollen, ruby-red nipples that pointed outward and upward.

As Kerby brought his face up between her thighs, the blonde arched her back and moaned lightly, then she straightened up just as quickly when Kerby started licking at her sweetness as if it were an all-day-sucker.

"Not like that, sweetie. Pretend that it's the wing of a butterfly and you're licking honey off it," the blonde instructed.

As Kerby went back to work, the blonde continued to sit upright and directed him in his efforts. She instructed him on where to put his tongue, how to get it there and what to do with it when he got it there. Kerby listened carefully to every word the blonde uttered and followed obediently, occasionally looking up to see what reaction he was getting. If the blonde arched her back or moaned, Kerby knew he was where he belonged and doing what he was supposed to be doing, whether or not she told him so.

Eventually, the blonde moved down Kerby's body and slid him inside of her. Kerby almost exploded on contact with the hot wetness inside the blonde's womanhood, but he held back. In time, the blonde worked him with her groin in the same way that she had with her mouth. She squeezed and thrust until Kerby was on the verge of completion, but each time she stopped just before sending him over the edge, then after a brief respite she started all over again. The blonde instructed Kerby the whole time, until his organ was so acquainted with her internal anatomy that it seemed to know on its own where it was supposed to go, how hard it was supposed to go there and how long it was supposed to hang around before moving elsewhere.

When they were finished, the blonde fell forward onto Kerby's chest and slept for a while with her legs draped loosely around his sides. Kerby could still feel her inner warmth on his lower belly. There was no way that Kerby was going to sleep after what he had just experienced for the first time in his young life, but he didn't have the heart to wake the blonde. *It might not be the right thing to do,* Kerby thought to himself as he lay motionless, smiling like the cat who just ate the parakeet the entire time that the blonde slept. Kerby Brewster would not need any religious rite of passage to make him feel like he had reached manhood. The blonde had just taken him there.

When the blonde woke up, the two bathed together, and she continued to instruct Kerby on what to touch and how to touch it. Kerby sucked the information up like the sponge that he used to lightly dab every inch of her body. By the end of their time together, Kerby felt as if he had completed a crash course on female anatomy.

As the blonde ushered Kerby out of the apartment, she forced a handful of crumbled bills into his palm. "I'm not done with your education just yet, but the next time I see you I want you to be dressed a little better. Take this and get yourself some decent clothes."

As Kerby made his way down the hallway to the elevator, the blonde asked where Kerby hung out and assured him that he would be seeing her again. On the way home, Kerby did just as he had been instructed, stopped at a haberdasher and bought himself some new threads.

A week hadn't gone by before the blonde showed up in Hell's Kitchen in a chauffeur driven limousine. Kerby was feeling awfully good about himself, wearing his new outfit, when she pulled up. He wasn't in the limousine for more than thirty seconds before the blonde had the outfit off him, and she was on the floor of the car between his legs. When the blonde had finished satisfying Kerby, and then instructing him on how to satisfy her, they went shopping, and she bought him a designer suit, shirt, and tie, which she picked out with no input from him. Then she took him to an expensive midtown restaurant and instructed him on table manners while they ate. The blonde, who still had not asked Kerby his name and had not offered hers, was not only intent on having Kerby satisfy her sexually, she wanted him to meet her standards in every respect.

Kerby's education in making a woman happy lasted for over a year, with the blonde making regular, unannounced visits to Hell's Kitchen whenever she got an itch that needed to be scratched. Kerby had no complaints. He enjoyed every minute he had spent with the blonde and appreciated every second that he was with her, everything that she taught him, everything that she had bought him, and everything that she did for him. The blonde never promised Kerby anything, and, in fact, forewarned him that the day would come when she would stop showing up and he would never see her again. "But by the time I'm through with you, women will be lining up to take my place," the blonde assured him. She was right.

Several weeks had passed without the blonde showing up in Hell's Kitchen, and Kerby knew that his time with her was over. A short time later he found out why and for the first time learned her true name. One morning, Kerby opened his newspaper to the "Society Page" and there she was. Her name was Helen Rose, a stage actress and burlesque star who, according to the press release, had just wed a big-time movie producer who was taking her to Hollywood to turn her into a star. Kerby wished her well and then turned his attention to trying out his new skills on anything wearing a skirt. There was no shortage of takers.

As a result of his newfound talents and refinement, Kerby Brewster was a unique blend, at times a suave and debonair ladies man, at others a barroom brawler who continued to hone his skills in that regard through no real choice of his own. By the time he was twenty, Kerby had worked his way through a long list of women who liked the way that he treated them out of the bedroom, and loved the way that he treated them in the bedroom. To most of the young and sexually inexperienced ladies in his life, Kerby seemed to know more about their bodies than they did. They did not know or care how he came by his knowledge, it only mattered that Kerby be willing to share his talents with them.

Kerby also gained the grudging respect of the men in his life. By his twentieth birthday, he was quite close to the same Irishmen that he had battled throughout his teen years. A group of them took the police exam together, and before he turned twenty-one, Kerby was walking a beat wearing the distinguished looking blue uniform of the New York City Police Department. He looked as handsome and dapper in his uniform as he did in the expensive, tailor-made suits he wore when off duty. Women loved him either way.

By twenty-five years of age, Kerby had used his brains, bravery, and wit to rapidly work his way up the ladder to a detective position in the Homicide Division. Kerby was extremely good at his job, but by the time he was twenty-nine years old, he had grown bored with the politics and limitations of the department. He decided to strike out on his own by getting a Private Detective's License and opening his own office. He opened an office on East 33rd Street and Second Avenue, and business was good almost immediately, though mostly from suspicious husbands and wives who wanted to know whether their spouses were cheating on them.

♥ ⚔ ♣

Yeah, both personal and business lives were sweet for Kerby Brewster in November 1933, as he sat with his back to his desk and his heels resting on the sill of his window, staring out at the recently built Empire State Building just down the street from his office. Kerby was thinking that the Empire State Building reminded him of something when he heard heels tapping on the ceramic tile floor of the hallway outside of his office. He sensed that the heels were coming in his direction, but he waited until he heard the rap of knuckles on the frosted glass window of his office door before he dropped his feet from the windowsill and turned his attention to the office entrance.

"It's open," Kerby shouted, and then he waited, wondering what the legs on the heels would look like.

When the door opened, Kerby was not disappointed. To the contrary, the woman that walked through the doorway was one of the most beautiful women that Kerby had ever seen. Tall and built, with legs that stretched forever and breasts that seemed to be too big for her body, Kerby recognized the lady immediately from pictures that he had seen in the newspapers. It was Renata D'arcy, the wife of Irish Pat D'arcy, one of the wealthiest men in the country and the most ruthless man in New York City. Renata's newspaper pictures did not do her justice. Aside from her voluptuous body, her face was perfect in every respect. Of Italian, Irish decent, Renata had long auburn hair that framed a perfectly smooth olive complexion and turquoise eyes. Her nose was tiny and sat atop full red lips that seemed constantly puckered as if always longing to be kissed.

"Mr. Brewster, my name is Renata D'arcy-- ," she began before Kerby cut her short.

"I know who you are Mrs. D'arcy. I think most New Yorkers do," Kerby interrupted, making his way around the desk and assisting Renata in taking off her coat. After hanging her coat up and sliding a chair underneath her, Kerby made his way back behind the desk and sat down opposite Renata.

"How can I help you, Mrs. D'arcy?" Kerby asked nervously, hoping that Renata D'arcy was not going to be one of his typical clients. Kerby did not want Irish Pat D'arcy as an enemy, nobody in their right mind did. Kerby had no intention of getting involved in an investigation that might in any way raise the ire of Irish Pat.

Irish Pat D'arcy had risen from the same Hell's Kitchen streets on which Kerby was raised. By all outward appearances, Irish Pat was a legitimate businessman. He owned several construction companies and could have made a very good living from them alone had he chosen to. His companies had built and were continuing to build numerous brownstones on the Upper East Side of Manhattan, not to mention a few of the city's new office buildings. But everyone who was anyone knew that the main purpose of Irish Pat's construction companies was to give him a way in which to clean the money that he made from his real business.

Irish Pat was a bootlegger. He owned nearly a hundred large speedboats that were based in the Miami area and ran day and night to Cuba and Jamaica for rum and other liquors. Irish Pat controlled most of the illegal distribution of liquors on the East Coast and personally owned a large number of speakeasies from Miami, Florida to New Port, Rhode Island. You didn't own a speakeasy in Manhattan unless you had Irish Pat's permission.

Kerby was also well aware of Irish Pat's reputation for ruthlessness. He had most of the New York City Police Department on his payroll. Irish Pat was not someone to be messed with, especially not now, since prohibition was about to be ended, and Irish Pat's very lucrative bootlegging business was about to come to a close. Irish Pat was in particularly mean spirits.

Renata D'arcy said exactly what Kerby did not want to hear. "Mr. Brewster, I have reason to believe that my husband is being unfaithful. I mean, Patrick has always cheated, everyone knows that, but I believe that this is different. She's not one of his bimbos, not a one-night-stand. She's someone special to him. Someone for whom he may be prepared to leave me. Before that happens, I want to know who she is. I want pictures of them together, incriminating pictures. I'm sure you know what I mean. If Patrick decides to end our marriage, I want to be able to prove adultery. I want to drag him and her through the mud and take him for every penny that I can."

"What makes you think I'm the man for this job, Mrs. D'arcy? Your husband is a very powerful man, and I've only been at this for a short while. Why me?" Kerby wondered.

"Actually, it's the fact that your operation is new and my husband is very powerful that attracted me to you. You see, Patrick has done business with most of the established private investigators in the state. I couldn't risk going to someone with whom he might already have a relationship. You're fresh, no chance that Patrick has used you for anything yet. More important, my assumption is that you're hungry too. If you're just getting off the ground, I assume that you can use the capital. Get me what I want Mr. Brewster, and I will make it well worth your efforts. I will make you a very wealthy man. Finally, Mr. Brewster, I wouldn't be telling you the entire truth if I didn't admit that I am very familiar with your reputation, most women in the city are. I thought that you might be more willing than others to help out a lady in distress."

"I'd really like to help you Mrs. D'arcy, for a lot of reasons, but I'm afraid this is out of my league," Kerby declined apologetically.

"I'm not an easy woman to say *no* to Mr. Brewster," Renata persisted, reaching into her purse with both hands, pulling out a thick wad of bills and tossing them onto the desk right under Kerby's nose. It was more money than Kerby had ever seen at one time in his life.

"I wasn't kidding when I said I would make you a rich man, Mr. Brewster. I fully understand the risks that you will be taking if you agree to accept this job. There's $200,000 in that bundle that's yours if you take the job and get me what I'm looking for."

The actual sight of the money caused Kerby to have second thoughts about taking on Irish Pat D'arcy, but he was still hesitant, very hesitant. In order to buy time and think it through, Kerby excused himself to use the men's room down the hall. Standing at the urinal, Kerby weighed his options. If he took the job, he would probably never want for anything in his life. On the other hand, if he took the job, the only other thing he would probably need in his life would be a coffin. *Just not worth the risk*, Kerby concluded. When he got back to his office he would explain nicely to Renata D'arcy that he would really like to help her, but it was just too dangerous.

When Kerby opened the door to his office upon his return, Renata was facing the door, standing with her behind resting on Kerby's desk. She was bare-ass naked, except for a pair of red patent leather heels.

"I told you I was familiar with your reputation, Mr. Brewster. I also warned you that I am not an easy woman to refuse," Renata cooed seductively, while parting her legs ever so slightly.

How tough can Irish Pat D'arcy be? Kerby thought to himself as he made his way to Renata and pressed his lips to hers, at the same time reaching behind her with his right hand and sweeping his desk clean.

Kerby placed his hands around Renata's waist and gently raised her into a sitting position on his desk before he eased her torso back so that she was laying on the desk with her legs hanging off. He then reached down, gently removed her shoes, took each of her feet into each of his hands and raised them so that her heels were resting on the edge of his desk with her legs parted. Then he sealed the deal by lowering his face to her waiting pudenda. Renata moaned her consent to the contract.

As he watched Renata D'arcy exit his office, Kerby knew that his penis had just entered into an agreement that his brain had told him was a bad idea, even given the money that had been offered. He also realized that there was no point in fretting it any further. Given the way that the contract had been finalized, there could be no reneging now.

Kerby decided he would go right to work on the D'arcy case and try to get it over with as quickly as possible. After all, there was the possibility that Irish Pat did not have a special mistress. With Renata as his wife, why would he? Kerby was hopeful that he would be able to report back to Renata that her fears were unfounded. Then he might keep a good percentage of the money and return the rest.

With the wad of bills tucked under his arm, Kerby kicked his leather executive chair to the corner of his office and climbed on top of it. Then he removed a tile from the ceiling in the corner of his office, reached up into the ceiling with the bills in both hands and placed them into an open metal safe that he had built into the ceiling when he first opened the office. Kerby shut the safe, spun the tumblers and jumped down.

That same evening, Kerby planned to make the rounds of all the speakeasies in Manhattan. He knew them all. He had been to each and every one of them at one time or another and had seen Irish Pat in one or another of them on many occasions. If Irish Pat wasn't at any of them, Kerby thought he might at least start questioning acquaintances regarding whether any of them had seen Irish Pat with a new woman on his arm who appeared to be something more than the one-nighters for which he was well known.

♥ 🗡 ♟

Kerby dressed in his black formal wear and black bow tie, customary for a night out in the thirties, and he headed downtown to the Wall Street area. He worked his way uptown, stopping at each speakeasy he knew of on his way. Kerby had hit perhaps seven different joints without sighting Irish Pat before he stopped at a place on the waterfront on the East River, just down the street from his own office. By the time he found himself knocking on the door of the waterfront speakeasy, Kerby was already feeling the effects of one too many drinks that he had consumed during the earlier stops. The only information that he had been able to gather was from a friend that he ran into at his first stop. The friend told him that he had seen Irish Pat being awfully cozy with a raven-haired beauty the previous evening.

At Kerby's knock, a small window in the door to the speakeasy opened and a brutish face appeared. Even though he had been to the place several times before, Kerby expected a series of questions from the brute before being allowed to enter. He was surprised when the guy opened the door without the standard quiz. Kerby was even more surprised when the guy, whose body was as menacing as his face, smiled at him and addressed him by name.

"Mr. Brewster, how nice to see you this evening, sir," the bruiser said, leading Kerby into the place by his arm and offering to take his overcoat.

This is not a good sign, Kerby thought to himself as he began to make his way past several crowded tables in the raucous club, heading toward the bar on the other side of the room. Before Kerby was halfway across the speakeasy, the bruiser returned from hanging up Kerby's coat and called him back.

"Right this way, Mr. Brewster. We've reserved a place for you in the VIP room this evening, sir," the bruiser said, before leading a stunned Kerby toward a door at the end of a narrow corridor.

The VIP room turned out to be a small office, furnished with a desk, a leather couch and several wooden armed chairs. A distinguished looking Irish Pat D'arcy sat behind the desk, appearing none too pleased. Two large henchmen sat on the leather couch but rose immediately as Kerby and the brute entered the room. The henchmen took up positions on either side of the door as the bruiser led Kerby to a chair in front of Irish Pat's desk, forcefully sat Kerby down and stood directly behind him.

A slight smile crossed Irish Pat's face just before he spoke. "I am not a man to mince my words, Mr. Brewster. I did not get where I am today by being coy. I will tell you right up front that I don't tolerate people sticking their noses in my business, especially my personal business. Now, before you deny anything, let me forewarn you that Renata does not go anywhere nor do anything without my knowing about it. So, I know that you two had a little meeting this afternoon. I also know that already this evening you have been to every one of my clubs from here to Wall Street and that you have asked various people questions about my personal business at each and every one of those clubs. Now again, before you explain yourself, Mr. Brewster, and try to give me a reason not to kill you, let me warn you not to lie to me. If I determine that one utterance out of your mouth is a lie, you can consider yourself a dead man."

Kerby knew from Irish Pat's reputation that he was not bluffing when he said he would kill Kerby if he lied to him. He also felt certain that Irish Pat already knew exactly what he had been hired to do. Kerby decided that in this instance honesty would be the best policy and perhaps even save his life. He reluctantly related to Irish Pat exactly what Renata had hired him for.

When Kerby was finished, Irish Pat looked pleased. "That was very good, Mr. Brewster. I have determined that every word that you just spoke was truth, and I am going to forgive you your mistake in agreeing to take this job, that is, assuming that you assure me that you are going to discontinue your investigation and return to me any money my wife may have given you as an advance. Did my lovely wife give you an advance, Mr. Brewster?"

Kerby hadn't counted the money, but he had no doubt that the number Renata had given him was accurate. He also had no doubt that Irish Pat already knew exactly how much money Renata had given him. Kerby admitted that amount to Irish Pat and assured him that the money would be returned in the morning.

"You are a rare honest man, Mr. Brewster, and your honesty has saved your life tonight," Irish Pat smiled as he gestured for the bruiser to lead Kerby to the exit.

Kerby breathed easier as the bruiser reached for the door, but Kerby lost his breath for a second when Irish Pat asked one final question. "Mr. Brewster, did you have sex with my wife?"

Kerby was ready to be honest about pretty much anything if it would get him out of that office alive, but he sensed that there was no right answer to this question. If he lied, and Irish Pat knew about the sex, Irish Pat would certainly kill him. If Kerby told the truth about having had sex with Renata D'arcy, Irish Pat would have to defend his honor, especially if the truth came out in front of his underlings. Whichever path he chose, Kerby knew that there was a good chance it would lead him to a cemetery for his own funeral. He weighed his options quickly and decided on risking the lie.

There was, of course, a real possibility that Irish Pat did not know about the sex, after all, how could he? But that was not the deciding factor for Kerby. The deciding factor was a strange one. Kerby had a strict rule about kissing and telling. He never discussed or bragged about his sexual encounters; he never really needed to. But in Kerby's mind it went much deeper than that. To him there was something important about preserving a woman's honor when it came to that sort of thing.

Kerby turned to face Irish Pat who remained seated behind his desk.

"No, Mr. D'arcy," Kerby said emphatically. "I've only met with your wife on one occasion, in my office this afternoon, and I did not engage in sex with her."

"That, Mr. Brewster, is a very costly lie," a disgruntled Irish Pat replied, looking toward a door to his right, which opened at his glance as if he had some psychokinetic power. A badly bruised and battered Renata D'arcy was led into the room, her beautiful turquoise eyes barely visible through slits in the puffs of black and purple that surrounded them.

"You see, Mr. Brewster, my beautiful wife has already confessed her transgression with you, and as a result of her honesty and remorsefulness I am going to spare her life. Not so for you, Mr. Brewster," Irish Pat said through a sardonic grin.

At the sight of Renata's battered face, Kerby forgot about the risk to his own life. His adrenalin began to pump and his heart rate quickened, as it always did when he knew that his hands were his only way out. Before the last word was out of Irish Pat's mouth, Kerby spun and dug his right fist into the bruiser's gut. As the big guy doubled over, Kerby hit him in the side of his head with a hook from the same right hand. The bruiser toppled sideways to the floor. Kerby moved with such speed that before any of the other henchmen in the room could react, he was flying headlong over the desk at a disbelieving Irish Pat.

On impact, Irish Pat's chair flipped backwards, and Irish Pat flew out of it, landing flat on his back. Kerby landed on top of Irish Pat who was screaming for help from his bodyguards. As the other henchmen in the room raced toward the fray, Kerby drew his right hand back and crunched it down into Irish Pat's face. Irish Pat's nose flattened on impact and blood flew in every direction, as if Kerby had squished a tomato under his fist. Kerby got off two more good blows, fracturing the orbit around Irish Pat's left eye with a shot from his left hand and then shattering Irish Pat's right cheekbone with a shot from his right hand. Then Kerby felt the butt end of a handgun come down on the back of his head. Things went black, and Kerby fell forward onto Irish Pat's shattered face.

When Kerby came to, he was seated in one of the chairs in front of Irish Pat's desk. His wrists were secured tightly to each of the arms. His mouth was gagged. Kerby could feel the cold circular steel of the barrel of a gun pressed to the back of his neck. Standing in front of Kerby was Irish Pat D'arcy holding a bloody white towel to his face. Blood dripped from the towel into a puddle on the floor between Irish

Pat's feet. The bruiser and the other henchmen stood behind Kerby. Renata D'arcy was no longer in the room.

"Can't I do him now, boss?" the bruiser pleaded. "I'll blow his brains out and bring him right down to the river and dump the body."

"No," Irish Pat grunted through the towel, in a garbled, hardly intelligible voice. "Too noisy, there are still people out there, and he's not going into the river. I want to make sure that his body is never seen again. Go to the icebox and get a pick. That should be quiet enough."

The bruiser left the room, went to the icebox behind the bar, and took out a long, thin, tubular icepick. While they waited for him to return, Irish Pat instructed the remaining henchmen on what to do with Kerby's body once it was lifeless. "We're laying the foundation for a brownstone up on East 80th Street tomorrow. By midmorning the cornerstones will be going in. I want his dead body in the concrete for the foundation right beneath one of the cornerstones. That should ensure that nobody ever finds him."

Kerby was thinking about how upset his very religious mother would be at not having a body to bury in hallowed ground when he heard the door to the office open and then slam shut. As he listened to the footsteps of the brute drawing closer, with the understanding that his too short life was about to come to an end, Kerby thought, W*hat the hell!* Then he swung the pointed toe of the black patent leather shoe on his right foot up with all of his might, catching Irish Pat directly between his legs. As Irish Pat bent to reach for his jewels, Kerby let loose a second kick that met Irish Pat's face as it came down, breaking his jaw on impact.

Irish Pat's head snapped upward before he dropped face first to the floor at Kerby's feet. Kerby drew his right foot up to stomp Irish Pat's mangled face into the floor, but before he could do so, he felt the point of the ice pick as it penetrated the back of his head at the base of his skull.

Once the ice pick pierced through the skin, it wasn't terribly painful, just a sense of pressure as the thin tube slid up into Kerby's brain. There was no pain at all in the brain itself, but Kerby's thoughts started going haywire the deeper the pick went into his head. First he saw flashes of white light, then streaks of color. Then he saw Helen Rose above him, straddling his head with her smooth, white thighs. Kerby looked up into her glistening womanhood and felt himself being drawn upward into it. As Kerby entered the sweetness of Helen Rose, everything went black.

♥ 🚫 👤

The following morning, Kerby Brewster's body, wrapped in a black tarpaulin, was laid to rest in the concrete foundation of a brownstone being built at 180 East 80th Street between Park and Lexington Avenues on the Upper East Side of Manhattan. His grave marker would be the cornerstone for the right front of the building.

CHAPTER 2

HELL HATH NO FURY
JUNE 1999

The tall girl stood with her back pressed against the panel between the doors of the bathroom stalls. She was distraught. "That bastard! I can't believe he did this to me! I swear I could kill him!" she howled.

The short girl was directly opposite the tall girl, leaning against one of the porcelain sinks. She was not sympathetic. "I'm not one to say I told you so, but I warned you! I warned you! I warned you! They're all scum. There is not one of them out there that can be trusted. They're all looking for one thing and one thing only," she snapped.

"I thought he was different," the tall girl explained.

"Different? He is the prototypical self-absorbed jock. Not to mention that he may be the biggest air-head in the bunch. The fucking kid thinks New Jersey is the capital of New York. I mean, how much dumber can you get than that?" the short girl countered.

"I thought I could change him," the tall girl continued.

"That is sooo typical and sooo naive. If you found a Neanderthal roaming the streets of New York City you'd be more likely to have success civilizing him than you would a teenage boy, and it doesn't get any better when they get older either. My mother says that men just naturally suffer from arrested development. They never get beyond the sex-crazed insipidness of their teenage years. They never grow up emotionally. They can never be changed, and they should never be trusted, not one of them. They're all disgusting little perverts," the short girl argued.

"But he was so cute, and he could be so sweet. He told me he loved me. I never would have given up my virginity to him if I thought that was all he was after. Heaven knows, I never would have let him put it in my mouth, no matter how much he begged. I can't tell you how much it upsets me to think that I am nothing more than another notch on that stupid son-of-a-bitch's bed post.

"I know that he's told everyone too. You should see the smirks I'm getting from every senior boy I pass in the halls, and that big breasted little slut that he's going back out with now, you should see how she looks at me. I'll bet you that he told her too. It just makes me feel so cheap and dirty. I swear to you, if he were here right now, I would kill his ass," the tall one snarled.

"If you want to commit the perfect murder, you don't do it by killing someone who has just given you the motivation. If you were to kill *him* now, the police would be knocking at your door before the end of the day. But if you were to just pick one at random, no one would ever suspect you, or rather us. I mean . . . of course . . . I'd help you do it," the short one noted, staring at the tall one and waiting for a reaction.

"Pick one what at random? Help me do what? the tall one wondered, with a befuddled look.

"Pick a boy to exact your revenge on, to murder. I mean it's the whole gender that sucks. The rest of them are no different from him. What difference does it make whether you get your revenge on him or someone else just like him? We could get rid of some other stupid little arrogant jock and spare some other girls the humiliation that he just put you through. If it were up to me, I'd round them all up and kill them all. With sperm banks and artificial insemination, who needs them? Keep the male children alive long enough to milk them and then get rid of them too. I bet the world would be a whole lot better place without them. There would probably never be another war," the short one continued, and then she waited for a response from the tall one, but none was forthcoming. The tall one just stared pensively.

"Well? What do you think? I say we should do it, assert our superiority, commit the perfect murder. We're way more intelligent than the stupid male cops who would be trying to catch us. We would get away with it, no sweat," the short girl finished.

"You're not kidding, are you?" the tall one finally responded.

"No, I'm not kidding," the short one answered flatly. "The freaky little perverts have certainly killed enough of us throughout the ages. Think of all of the serial killers and rapist murderers throughout history, and all of the innocent women who have been degraded, killed, and mutilated just so that the little sex freaks would have something to think about while they pleasured themselves. It's about time some us women started evening up the score. Don't you think?"

"I have to get back to class. Let's finish this conversation later," the tall one answered, but she had already made up her mind. She was ready to do it. Plotting the perfect murder would be an interesting mental challenge. It would definitely be exciting carrying it out, and the way she was feeling at that moment, she had little doubt that one fewer male would be no great loss to the world.

The tall girl was Nikita Bach, known to her friends as Niki, the second smartest person in NYHSST, the New York High School of Science and Technology. She was a beautiful, blonde teenager with the look of a runway model, long legs and small but incredibly perky breasts, the kind that only a teenager has. Despite the fact that she was attractive and had legs that most men would die for, Niki Bach had rarely dated throughout her high school years. Her height was one disadvantage. At 5'11" in her stocking feet, she was taller than most of the boys in the school. Her superior intelligence, which she loved flaunting, didn't help matters either. It intimidated most of the boys she knew. But the thing that really seemed to scare boys off was that Niki was an impeccable dresser who dressed way older than her age. In designer suits, high heels, and lots of makeup, Niki Bach just seemed too worldly and sophisticated for the jeans and sneaker wearing boys with whom she went to school.

The short girl was Jeannie McCloone, the smartest person in NYHSST. She and Niki had been best friends since preschool. They lived in the same apartment building on Central Park West, just north of the Museum of Natural History. Jean lived just one floor below Niki, and given the flimsiness of the ceiling that separated their apartments, they had no secrets from one another, whether they liked it or not.

The two hit it off at an early age. Though each was envious of certain characteristics that the other possessed, they were not in any way resentful. Each had learned early on to accept the fact that the other was superior, and always would be superior, in certain respects. Niki found out before they had reached third grade that, try as she might, she would never be Jean's intellectual equal. Niki was plenty smart and worked incredibly hard at her academics, in part just to stay close to Jean, but when it came to intelligence, Niki was and always would be second best. Jean had a photographic memory and a superior mind that Niki realized she could never match.

Jean envied Niki's attractiveness and runway model's body as well as her sophisticated style. Niki had a presence about her that Jean knew she could never equal. Jean was not a homely girl, nor was she excessively short or fat. It was just that appearance-wise there was nothing special about her. Slightly below average in height and a touch overweight, Jean looked short and chunky when next to Niki, which she was most of the time. Jean had mousy, brown, flyaway hair that she was constantly trying to keep out of her face and off of the glasses that sat atop her somewhat thick nose. She was no match for Niki's natural blonde hair, powder blue eyes, and perfect little nose. Initially, Jean also did her best to try to match Niki stitch for stitch clothes-wise, but the same clothes just did not hang on Jean the way they did on Niki. Jean eventually gave up competing in that regard, resorting to a typical collegiate style of dress to match her personality.

♥ ☥ ♣

"Let's do it!" Niki exclaimed, before Jean had fully opened the door to her apartment later that evening.

"I knew you'd go for it. I've already started developing a plan and making a list of the things we'll need," Jean responded excitedly as Niki crossed the threshold into the apartment. "I probably shouldn't admit to this, but the truth is I've fantasized lots of times about doing this," Jean confessed.

Niki was as comfortable in Jean's apartment as she was upstairs in her own. She practically lived there. Jean's mother and father were divorced, and Jean lived alone with her mother. Niki had only a vague recollection of Jean's father. He left when Jean was only ten years old and no one had seen or heard from him since. Niki remembered that Jean was crazy about her dad when she was little and devastated when he left, but now she seethed at the mere mention of him.

Jean's mom was a very smart woman, a surgical oncologist at Sloan Kettering Hospital. She was rarely home. When she was not at the hospital or at her office, she spent most of her time at a girlfriend's apartment. Mom and the girlfriend used to spend a lot more time at Jean's, until Jean walked into mom's bedroom one night and caught the two stark naked on the bed in the throes of lovemaking. Jean raced right upstairs and tearfully confided everything she had seen to Niki.

It seems that mom had her head at one end of the bed, and the girlfriend had her head at the other. They were connected at their groins by an unusually large rubber sex toy. Needless to say, it was a traumatic moment for Jean, who was only thirteen at the time. It was several days before she could even face her mother again. But the truth was that in recent years Jean and Niki had wondered out loud to each what the sex toy might feel like.

"I say we pick an underclass man, maybe a junior or a sophomore. Somebody with whom people would not expect us to associate. Of course, he'll have to be a jock. Getting him alone will be no problem.

We'll just make him think that he's about to get lucky. We could ask him if he'd like to experience something kinky. These jocks have such overblown egos that he'll never suspect a thing. He'll think he's doing us a favor. Naturally, you'll have to be the primary bait," Jean plotted.

"Sizemore, Peter Sizemore, he's a sophomore who starts on the varsity football and basketball teams. He already thinks he's God's gift to the girls in this school. We can tell him how wonderful he is and ask him whether he's ever had two girls at the same time. He'll be in his fucking glory," Niki laughed.

"Where do we take him? Mom's never home, but it would be way too risky to bring him up here. How would we get him out past the doorman once we do him? And there will be blood. I mean it won't be very exciting if we just poison him. We have to cut him. I already have two of mom's scalpels hidden away."

"My dad has a warehouse in Staten Island on the Kill Van Kull. He stores some of the furs that he imports there before they're moved to Manhattan or sold to retailers. It's a very secret place, hush, hush, in the middle of nowhere, you know, because of what he keeps there. Only a handful of people know about the place. No one goes there without dad's okay, and he's in Moscow dealing for sables or minks or something. He won't be back for a month. I know where the key is, and like I said, it's right on the water. We can get rid of the body right there."

Before he changed his surname to Bach, Niki's father's name was Bachuta. He was a fur importer, born in Moscow, who made a very lucrative living importing sable and mink from Russia. Niki liked her father's business, not only because of the lifestyle it afforded her, but because it required him to be away from home most of the time. When he was home, Niki's dad spent most of his time drinking iced vodka and slapping her mother around.

Niki's mom was a gifted violinist who was much younger than her father. He had brought her back from Russia on one of his trips, and he treated her as if she were part of his merchandise. Though he never raised his hand to Niki, he regularly accused her mom of cheating on him while he was away, accusations that were not true, and Niki had witnessed her father punch her mom right in the face on a number of occasions. She hated him for it and barely spoke to him when he was in town.

"We're on then," Jean trumpeted. "It's just a matter of when."

"This weekend. It has to be before the graduation ceremony. I want to do it as soon as possible, while I still have the bad taste in my mouth.

If I wait too long, I may chicken out. I'll set it up for Saturday, June 24th, a week before the graduation ceremony. He'll go for it in a *New York minute*. My only concern is how we are going to overpower him when we get him where we want him. He is an athlete after all, a real fucking muscle-head."

"No problem, a couple of beers and a few of these and he'll be out like a light until we've got him secured," Jean explained, pulling out a handful of little white pills from her pocket. "Mom keeps a stash of all kinds of tranquilizers and painkillers. One of the perks of the profession, you know. We can tell him they're uppers or something to keep his stamina up because we plan to give him a real workout. I'll pick up electrical tape and nylon cord tomorrow to tie him up with once he's out. We can bring him out of it once he's immobilized, so that he knows what's going on when we do the dirty deed."

♥☒♣

Peter Sizemore bought every word of it, just as the girls expected he would. He was one of the few boys in school who was eye to eye with Niki height-wise, even when she wore heels. She told him she had been watching him since he was a freshman and thought that he was irresistible in his basketball shorts. She had to have him before the year was over, she told him. She would be leaving for college soon, she noted, and she couldn't bear the thought of going away without letting him know her true feelings and being with him, at least, once.

Peter's jaw dropped when Niki told him that as an added incentive, and to prove that she was really crazy about him, she would bring along a friend, Jeannie McCloone. Peter had only a vague idea who Jean was. *Kind of a plain-Jane, egghead type*, he thought, *but not that bad and definitely doable*. After all, she was only to be the icing on the cake. *Two girls at once*, he thought, *every man's dream*. He couldn't wait to tell his buddies, but that would have to come later. Niki made Peter promise that he would not utter a word about it until the summer was over and she had left for college. She knew how guys liked to brag, she said, and that was okay, but she didn't want her reputation being ruined before the upcoming graduation ceremony. Soon she would be off to college and Peter could tell whomever he liked. A small price to pay in return for the fantasy she was providing, Peter decided. He would keep his mouth shut.

On Saturday morning, Jean got her mom's okay to use the car. She loaded the trunk with nylon cord, electrical tape, cleaning fluids, two mops, a bunch of towels and sponges, two flashlights, a change of clothes for her and Niki, and four cinder blocks. She put the tranquilizers as well as a bunch of similar looking vitamins into her purse with the scalpels. Later she took a twelve-pack of beer from the refrigerator, put the beers into a cooler filled with ice and placed the cooler into the back seat of the car. Her adrenalin flowed the entire time. She couldn't remember the last time that she had felt so excited, so alive.

Niki had arranged to pick Peter Sizemore up on a quiet road in Central Park to ensure that no one would see him getting into the car with them. When they pulled over to the side of the road, with Jean driving and Niki in the back seat, Sizemore started pounding his chest with both fists and howling like a gorilla trying to scare away a threat.

"Fucking typical!" Jean exclaimed out of the side of her mouth before Niki opened the back door to the car and Sizemore slid in next to her.

"What's up ladies? You girls ready to have your worlds rocked?" Sizemore asked, grinning from ear to ear.

"You have no idea what we're ready for tonight," Niki answered, with Jean smiling at her through the rearview mirror.

Before they were out of Central Park, Sizemore popped a beer and guzzled it down.

"Geez, I'm impressed! Where did you learn to drink like that?" Niki remarked, feigning admiration as she too opened a beer but sipped at it delicately.

"That's what I'm here for, to impress you ladies, and believe me, you won't be disappointed," Sizemore assured the girls, and then he howled again as he popped a second beer.

At the sound of the second beer exploding open, Jean reached back with three tranquilizers and handed them to Sizemore.

"What are these, babe?" Sizemore asked.

"Just a couple of uppers," Jean responded. "You are going to need lots of energy tonight."

"No thanks, babe. The only drugs I do are steroids. I'm an athlete you know, got to keep my body clean. Besides, believe me when I tell you, I've got great stamina. I won't be needing nothing except the sight of some naked female ass to keep me up tonight."

Niki caught sight of Jean's eyes in the rearview mirror and shot her a worried look. "Are you sure, honey?" Niki asked. "I mean I'll bet you've never been with two women before. You don't want to risk disappointing us, do you? It wouldn't be good for your reputation in school if it turned out that you couldn't handle it and word got around."

"No problem, babe. I can handle it. You girls will not be disappointed," Sizemore insisted.

"Fine, I mean, if you're chicken to take them," Jean said, flipping three of the look-alike vitamins into her mouth, and passing three more back to Niki who swallowed them with a chug of beer.

"Chicken? Nobody calls Peter Sizemore chicken, babe," Sizemore replied, swallowing the tranquilizers while guzzling the remainder of his second beer and then opening a third.

As the three traveled through midtown, the tranquilizers hit him. Sizemore looked around at the neon lights on all sides of him that suddenly seemed to be swirling together in an ever changing geometric pattern, as if he were in a massive kaleidoscope.

"Far fucking out!" Sizemore exclaimed, just before he blacked out and his head hit the seat next to Niki's lap.

"Whew!" Niki gasped, waving her right hand across her forehead, wiping away imaginary sweat. "*That* was a scary moment."

The girls left Manhattan through the Lincoln Tunnel and traveled down the New Jersey Turnpike to Exit 12, where they left the turnpike and traveled over the Goethals Bridge into Staten Island. They worked their way immediately down to the waterfront and traveled the shoreline of the island in eyesight of the Kill Van Kull, which was blackened by the night sky. Niki eventually directed Jean to turn into a darkened, debris-scattered lot in which a lone red brick building sat only a few yards from the bulkhead and the water. It was a single story warehouse-type building. A large, metal bay door sat in the center of the building, perpendicular to the street, with a smaller, metal door to the right of the larger door. Even in the dark, Jean could see where several windows had been recently bricked in with slightly less weathered brick in order to keep the place more secure.

Jean turned off the car lights the instant she turned into the lot. She pulled the car around to the waterside of the building, so that it could not be seen from the street. When Jean turned the car off, Niki got out and stuck her head around to the front of the building. There was no one in sight and no way anyone could possibly have seen them pull in. By the time Niki got back to the car, Sizemore had rolled over and was facing upward, snoring loudly.

"Let's drag him inside first before we tie him up," Jean suggested.

Niki went back to the front of the building and opened the smaller door, then raced back to the car. Jean was already trying to pull Sizemore's deadweight out of the backseat, with little success. With Niki's help, they were finally able to get Sizemore out of the car, but his weight was too much for them to carry. Jean, who had the upper part of his body, dropped him, and Sizemore's head hit the ground with a thud. He moaned.

"Sorry," Jean blurted out.

"Who are you apologizing to, him or me?" Niki wondered with a laugh.

"You," Jean smiled. "That asshole didn't feel a fucking thing. Even if he were awake, his head is as hard a rock."

Since they couldn't lift him, the girls decided to drag Sizemore's body into the building. They each took a leg and pulled. Sizemore's head bounced along the stones and other debris that littered the lot as they worked their way to the front of the building and through the door. Once they had him inside the building, they looked around trying to decide what to tie him to. The warehouse was one big room with a high ceiling held up by four pillars that formed a square in the center of the building, matching the corners of the walls. There were a number of garment racks on wheels scattered around the room, several of which had fur coats hanging from them. The only furniture in the warehouse was an old wooden desk which sat toward the far end of the building with a beat up leather office chair under it.

The girls decided to prop Sizemore up and tie him to the post nearest the desk. After dragging his unconscious body back to the post which they had chosen, Jean excitedly ran back to the car for the electrical tape, cord, flashlights, and her bag in which she had the scalpels. She set the flashlights on the desk so that they could better see what they were doing. Niki sat Sizemore's body up against the post and attempted to lift him into a standing position.

"I think we should undress him first," Jean noted.

"Undress him? Why would we undress him?" Niki wondered in an astonished tone. "It's not as if we're going to rape him or anything."

"I just thought it would be further humiliation for him. You know, make him feel more vulnerable, let him know who's in charge."

"If you really want to," Niki replied. "I mean, whatever turns you on."

Jean took off Sizemore's shoes and unbuckled his pants with Niki standing above her watching. As Jean started to pull Sizemore's pants off, she stopped for a moment and looked up at Niki. "The truth is, I've never seen a real one before, at least not that I remember."

"You've never seen a real what?" Niki asked, a puzzled look on her face.

"A naked man. You know, a penis. I mean, I've seen lots of pictures and stuff, but I've never seen a real one. It's not as if I have brothers or anything, and I never accidentally walked in on my father when he was around, at least not when I was old enough to remember. I'm curious, I want to see how it looks in real life, up close. I want to touch it." a somewhat embarrassed Jean explained.

"Fine! Just don't be too disappointed if it's not everything you expect. Especially given that it's not going to be excited. When they're flaccid, they kind of look like turkey necks, waddle and all."

They both laughed out loud as Jean went back to stripping Sizemore. She took off all of his clothes except for his Jockey underpants, saving them for a sort of final unveiling. They were both very impressed with Sizemore's athletic body. Peter Sizemore did not have an ounce of fat on him, and the muscles on his legs, abdomen, chest, and biceps were chiseled like the muscles on a Greek god.

"I had no idea steroids could have this much effect," Niki chuckled. "They should make them mandatory for every young man. Who cares whether it takes a few years off their lives."

Jean then nervously lowered Sizemore's shorts, leaning back as if she was afraid that something might jump out at her. Once his shorts were off and his manhood was out in the open, both girls stared in awe. It was way more than either expected. Even in a limp state, Sizemore was bigger than your average male. Jean was not disappointed. She immediately reached down and cupped Sizemore's testicles in her right hand, rolling them lightly in her palm at first and then squishing them together hard as if to see if they might burst. Sizemore grimaced as if he were having a bad dream.

Jean let go of Sizemore's jewels and wrapped her hand around his organ, holding it firmly but lightly, as if she had a baby bird in her hand that she did not want to escape but did not want to crush either. To the surprise of both girls, Sizemore's member grew firmer and longer in Jean's hand. Both girls felt heat rushing through their loins.

Niki broke the moment. "Let's not forget what we came to do. We don't have all night, and I want to make sure we have him secured before he wakes up. The way you're holding that thing, you could rouse a dead man."

Jean dropped Sizemore's erection from her hand but grew even more excited at the thought of slicing into it with a scalpel and watching the blood flow from it as Sizemore begged for mercy. She felt a hot wetness building in her groin at the thought.

They raised Sizemore into a standing position, leaning him against the post. Then Niki held him upright as Jean wrapped the electrical tape tightly around his mid-section, simultaneously securing his arms to his body and his body to the pole. When they were sure he wouldn't fall, Niki let go, and Jean lowered herself and wrapped tape around Sizemore's thighs and calves, staring at his package each time she passed it at eye level.

"Now, how do we wake him?" Niki asked.

"I'll get the cooler. A cold can of beer and some ice on his head and chest should snap him out of it," Jean replied, racing outside to the car.

Jean returned seconds later carrying the cooler in both hands. Niki took an iced-cold can of beer out of the cooler and began rolling it across Sizemore's forehead and then his chest, but with little success. Other than a slight flickering of his eyelids and a barely audible moan, Sizemore did not respond.

Jean had the same idea, but she took a handful of ice and rubbed Sizemore's testicles with it. He moaned louder this time but still did not wake up. Finally, Niki took another ice cold beer out of the cooler, popped it and poured it over Sizemore's head. It jolted him awake as the ice cold beer made its way over his face and down his neck and chest.

"What the fuck!" Sizemore hollered, shaking his head like a wet dog. At first, Sizemore had no idea where he was, then he tried to pull himself free from his bindings and realized that he could not budge. As the grogginess in his head cleared somewhat, Sizemore realized that he was buck-naked, other than the tape that was wrapped around his body. Then he saw Niki and Jean standing in front of him smiling victoriously. "Very funny bitches," Sizemore snarled. "Now cut me the fuck loose."

"Peter, I think you should change your attitude. Perhaps you haven't noticed, but you are completely naked and secured to a pole, and we are totally clothed and free. Not to mention that we are armed," Jean pointed out, waving her scalpel at him. "How about a little contriteness on your part? It might help you to keep that handsome little penis of yours," Jean continued, lightly jabbing Sizemore's scrotum with the scalpel.

At the pinch of the scalpel, Sizemore jumped as best he could, given the way that he was secured to the pillar. "Look, I don't know what this is all about, but I'm guessing that the seniors on the basketball team put you up to this. Either they're going to jump out from somewhere or maybe you're filming it for them. Either way, you're not scaring me, and I'm not begging you for anything. Okay? Furthermore, somebody is going to suffer a serious ass-whuppin as a result of what you've done. Now, the joke is over. Cut me free and tell me who put you up to this and maybe I'll go easy on you two," Sizemore gnashed.

"How can we make you understand, Peter? This is not a joke. If you don't start begging and begging good, this is going to be the last night of your young life," Niki threatened, waving her scalpel at him.

"Fuck you, *cunt*! Peter Sizemore doesn't beg anyone for anything," Sizemore shouted back defiantly.

At the sound of the word *cunt*, a word that Jean truly despised, she spun and slashed the scalpel across Sizemore's chest. Because of the fineness of the blade and the remnants of the tranquilizers, there was very little pain at first, but soon the laceration started to sting like a long paper cut. Sizemore looked down as the stinging spread across his chest. A thin red line of blood appeared. As he watched, the blood oozed from the laceration and dripped slowly in lines down his chest and belly. For the first time, Peter Sizemore realized that this was no practical joke.

"What the heck! Are you girls crazy or something? What did I ever do to you two?" Sizemore asked contritely, the anger in his voice replaced by fear.

"It's not specifically you, Peter. It's much bigger than just you. It's your entire gender. You're just a symbol, a representative on whom we have decided to exact a little vengeance on behalf of every woman who has ever suffered one form of disrespect or another at the hands of a man, since the beginning of time," Jean explained as if she were answering a question in History class.

"Okay, okay, you win. I'm sorry. I'm really, sincerely sorry, not just for any disrespect that I have shown to women, but for any disrespect that any man since the beginning of time has shown to any woman. All right? Now cut me loose, and I swear I'll forget that this ever happened. I'd be too embarrassed to report it anyway. I won't report you to anyone. I won't say a word to anyone. Just please cut me loose and let me go," Sizemore pleaded.

"I'm afraid it's too late for that now, Peter. There's no way that we could let you go now, not that we ever intended to anyway. I just wanted to hear you beg a little," Jean smiled evilly as she knelt in front of Sizemore and pierced his scrotum with her scalpel.

Sizemore screamed, more at the thought of where Jean was cutting than at the pain of the incision. Then he grew angry all over again. "Look, now this is enough. Cut this fucking tape right now or I swear when I get loose, and I will get loose eventually, I am going to bash both of your fucking faces."

Niki felt a rage run through her at the thought of Sizemore punching her in the face. An image of her father punching her mother in the face raced through Niki's mind, and she snapped. Niki decided that the time had come to shut Peter Sizemore up forever. She reached her right hand with the scalpel in it around the pillar and ran the scalpel meticulously across Sizemore's throat, as if trying to draw a straight line without using a ruler.

At first Sizemore screamed, "No, please God, no." But as the life began seeping out of him with the blood that was flowing from his throat, Sizemore murmured, "Help me Mommy, please help me."

As the blade of the scalpel cut through Sizemore's jugular vein, a momentary gush of blood spewed out of his throat as if it was coming out of a hose. The blood sprayed Jean who was kneeling before Sizemore with her scalpel still working at his genitals. Other than to wipe some blood from her eyes with the back of her free hand, Jean ignored the blood and sliced a clean incision right down the center of Sizemore's ball sac. She had hoped to do it while Sizemore was still alive, but it was too late for that.

Niki rounded the pillar and saw Jean neatly separating flaps that she had created in Sizemore's scrotum. With Niki watching, Jean reached in, pulled Sizemore's right testicle out, and sliced it free from its attachments. Jean placed the testicle on the floor next to her and then methodically reached in and severed the left testicle.

"He's already dead. What are you doing?" Niki asked, astounded by what she was watching.

"You'll see," Jean responded, looking up and smiling deviously at Niki.

"Look, I know that people who commit these kinds of crimes frequently take a trophy. But that usually winds up being the evidence that gets them convicted. This is supposed to be the perfect murder. Let's not make the same mistake that other people have made," Niki reasoned.

"Don't worry, I promise you no one is ever going to find these," Jean assured Niki as she took a plastic sandwich bag out of her purse, opened it, placed the testicles inside and secured it shut. Then she put the sandwich bag into the cooler of ice.

When Jean was done with her mock surgery, she ran the cooler out to the car while Niki cut Sizemore's limp body from the pillar and watched it crumple to the floor. Jean returned with two of the cinder blocks, and Niki wrapped the cord around Sizemore's body, running it through the cinder blocks as she did so. Jean went back to the car for the other blocks, and when she returned, Niki secured those blocks to Sizemore's body in the same way. Then, with great difficulty, they hoisted Sizemore's body onto the flat bottom of one of the wheeled garment racks, rolled him out to the bulkhead and dumped his lifeless body into the murky waters of the Kill Van Kull.

With Sizemore's body disposed of, the two got the cleaning stuff from the trunk of the car and thoroughly scrubbed the blood from the inside of the building, after which they put the mops and sponges into a heavy duty plastic garbage bag with all of Sizemore's possessions. Then they removed all of their own bloody clothing so that they were totally naked. They examined each other's body carefully, each surprised at how much blood had stained their bodies and caked on them. They removed what blood they could and decided to wait until they got home to thoroughly shower the rest off. Then they threw their own bloody clothes into the garbage bag, put on fresh clothes and drove from the scene.

On the way home, the girls stopped at an industrial sight garbage dumpster and threw the plastic garbage bags with their bloody clothes, the bloody mops and sponges and all of Sizemore's possessions into the dumpster. The two girls drove home exhilarated, satisfied that no one had seen them and no one would ever link them to the disappearance of Peter Sizemore. They were intoxicated by the thought of having just committed the perfect murder.

♥ ☿ ♣

"That was fucking righteous!" Jean exclaimed, unlocking the door to her apartment.

As usual, Jean's mom was staying out for the night, and Niki had told her mom that she would be spending the night at Jean's apartment. They entered the apartment with Niki carrying the cooler.

"I still think that taking his nads as trophies was a bad idea. What in the world were you thinking? Lets just flush them down the toilet now," Niki urged.

"No way! They are the most important part of the whole evening. I told you, I've fantasized about this lots of times. This is all part of my fantasy. Go get undressed and take your shower. Stay in there until I come in, and I'll check you to make sure that you got all of the blood off of you," Jean instructed Niki.

Niki went into the bathroom and ran the water as hot as she could stand it, jumped in and scrubbed herself as clean as possible. After several minutes, Jean entered the steamy bathroom already nude. She pulled back the shower curtain and stood admiring Niki's long, lean body as Niki stood with her head back and her eyes closed, enjoying the warmth of the water.

"I see some spots you missed," Jean muttered, when Niki finally opened her eyes and caught Jean staring at her.

Jean stepped into the shower, and the two took turns carefully inspecting and then sponging each other's body. While Niki washed the last specks of blood from Jean's backside, Jean wondered out loud, "Do you think I'm too fat?"

"I don't think you're fat at all. I think you have a great body."

When they were finished cleaning each other, they stepped out of the shower stall and took turns patting each other dry with fluffy towels, still inspecting each other's body to see whether they had missed any blood. Once both were dry, Niki began to step into a pair of panties but stopped at the sound of Jean's voice.

"No, don't. Your body is so beautiful, and I love looking at it. You certainly don't have anything to be ashamed of, and there's no one here except for you and me. Lets just stay the way we are."

The idea sounded strange but somehow exciting to Niki. "Sure, I guess . . . I mean . . . why not?"

The two exited the bathroom nude and were headed through the kitchen on their way to the living room when Niki's nostrils were hit with an incredible aroma. "What have you got cooking? It smells delicious."

"I thought you might be hungry, so I've started making something for us eat. The smell is a Bordeaux sauce I'm simmering. It's just a little red wine, a little butter, a little garlic, a little extra virgin olive oil. Nothing too fancy."

"Well, it smells great. I can't wait to taste it."

Jean made her way to the stove and lifted the lid of the pan with the sauce in it. Niki rushed over to inhale the aroma as the lid came off and steam billowed out. Inside, simmering away in a bubbling Bordeaux sauce were the last remains of Peter Sizemore.

At the sight of what was cooking in the saucepan, Niki jumped back from the stove. "Have you lost your fucking mind? I am not eating those. I am not fucking Hannibal Lechter," Niki shrieked.

"No, you are not Hannibal Lechter and neither am I. He got caught. We are not going to get caught. But we do have the same thing that made Hannibal Lechter special. We have brains," Jean responded calmly.

"Forget about it! I am not eating Peter Sizemore's balls," Niki repeated firmly.

"It's not just Peter Sizemore's testicles that we're going to eat, any more than it was just Peter Sizemore that we killed tonight. What we did was symbolic. Tonight we killed any power that any man has ever had or ever will have over either of us. We are now going to symbolically consume that power and make it our own. Like black widow spiders, we have established our superiority over the male, used him for our own pleasure, and now we are going to further assert our superiority by consuming the most essential part of the male species, his driving force, his only legitimate reason for existing," Jean explained

Niki laughed when she finally acquiesced and turned to see a bottle of Chianti sitting on the dining room table. "You're taking this Hannibal Lechter stuff seriously aren't you?"

When they were finished eating, they went to bed together and lay entwined in each other's naked bodies. "It really wasn't bad once you got past the idea, tasted kind of like liver," Niki chuckled. "But I don't think I could have gotten mine down without the sauce and the wine."

"I want to do it again," Jean said softly, ignoring Niki's comment.

Niki paused for a moment before responding. "Fine, but not right away. That's the problem with serial killers. They just keep going until they make a mistake and give themselves away. It's almost as if they want to get caught."

"I agree. Believe me, I don't want to get caught, but I do want to do it again. Promise me we can do it again," Jean pleaded. "Not right away, but some time."

"Well, we can't do it before the summer is over, that would be too soon, and once the summer is over you'll be up at Harvard and I'll be in New Haven. Next year, when school is out, we'll celebrate our first anniversary by doing it again. Then every year after that we'll pick someone randomly, and we'll do it again and again for as long as you like. No one will ever link us to the disappearances. Even if the bodies start showing up, the killings will be too far apart for the police to link them. We'll never get caught," Niki boasted confidently.

"I love you, Niki. I always have," Jean whispered.

"I know," Niki answered softly. "I love you too."

CHAPTER 3

A HAUNTING EXPERIENCE
JUNE 2003

Penelope Albright hitched a ride home from her Aunt Mags's funeral on Long Island in Sol Hirsh's yellow taxi. Penny and Sol stood outside of the brownstone at 180 East 80th Street looking up admiringly at the old structure. Penny had always loved the old brownstone, even when she was just a little girl, but never in her wildest dreams did she imagine that someday it would belong to her.

"They just don't make them like they used to," Sol remarked.

"It's beautiful," Penny responded. "Aunt Mags loved it like it was a part of her family."

"Your Aunt Mags was some kind of a lady. She was a bit nutty for sure, but quite a lady nevertheless," Sol reminisced. "She was in no hurry to go mind you, but once she knew that it was inevitable, it didn't seem to bother her at all. It was as if she knew that there was something out there on the other side waiting for her. Toward the end, all she was concerned about was making sure that you got the brownstone when she was gone. She used to tell me that her only regret was that she wouldn't be here at this moment to see you looking up knowing that the brownstone was yours."

"The O'Malley sisters all have their eccentricities, Sol, but they're all great ladies, and she was the best of the bunch. Don't ever tell any of the others, but she was always my favorite. I loved them all, but I loved her the most. It's too late now, but I really regret not coming back and spending more time with her before she died. Letters and telephone calls are nice, but it's not like being there in her presence, spending time with her. Of course, she never let on to anyone that she knew her time was near, not me, not any of the sisters, but that was just her way. Had I known, I would have been here when she passed, and I'd be willing to bet that each of the sisters would have been here too."

Penny Albright was the sole offspring of the seven O'Malley sisters. She had been born to the youngest of the sisters, Jen O'Malley, in 1977. Ironically, given that Jen was the youngest of the O'Malley sisters and the only one of the sisters to marry and have a child, she died before the rest. Jen and Penny's dad died in a tragic automobile accident in 1990, when Penny was only thirteen years old. Penny was in the car but survived the accident unscathed.

The remaining six O'Malley sisters took it upon themselves to raise Penny, each taking her for two months of the year, until Penny was eighteen years old and started college at New Mexico State University. It wasn't that none of the sisters wanted Penny that resulted in her being shipped around. To the contrary, any one of them would have raised Penny full-time. Penny wound up being shipped from state to state, one sister to the next every two months because they all loved her and wanted their share of her and that love.

Mother O'Malley was quite a woman herself. When she was only eighteen years old she gave birth to her first child, Maggie, or Mags as everyone knew her, in 1929 in New York City. Every four years thereafter for the next twenty-four years, Mother O'Malley had another child, each time a girl. Most believed that she would have continued having children despite her age had Mr. O'Malley not died in 1956, three years after the birth of Penny's mom.

The sisters, each a bit quirky in their own way, were great friends growing up. Unlike most siblings they rarely fought. But given the four year differences in their ages, as they grew older, one-by-one they drifted away from each other, each settling in a different part of the country. Mags was the only O'Malley sister to remain in New York with Mother O'Malley until mom died at the age of seventy in 1981. Together, Mags and Mother O'Malley ran *O'Malley's Pub*, which at Mags's suggestion later became the very successful *O'Malley's Fish & Chips Restaurant*. Shortly after Mother O'Malley's death, Mags franchised the operation, and within three years was a multimillionaire.

Then Mags sold the whole operation, bought the brownstone at 180 East 80th Street and turned the basement level into a bookstore. Mags loved to read, especially "whodunits" and ghost stories. She named the bookstore *Ghosts and Gumshoes* and stocked it exclusively with ghost stories and mysteries, preferably those in which the reader had to figure out who committed the crime. Some people quoted William Shakespeare, Charles Dickens, or maybe Mark Twain; Mags O'Malley quoted Agatha Christie, Raymond Chandler, and Edgar Allen Poe.

When people talked about Mags being a little nutty, they were referring to the fact that in her later life she fancied herself a bit of a clairvoyant and medium. She held séances and even claimed to have a conduit to the afterlife. She called him, her *Englishman*.

"You know Sol, I often wondered why you two never hooked up,"

Penny commented. "I mean you seemed to have enough in common, each a retired, self-made millionaire, each living alone in a New York City brownstone right next door to each other. You certainly seemed to be fond of each other. It always seemed to me that you two were a perfect match."

"I'd be lying if I said it never crossed my mind," Sol replied. "But Mags had her dream-man, even if he existed only in her mind. You know when a woman conjures up an image of man, it's kind of hard for a real man to compete. In Mags's mind, her *Englishman* was always charming and witty. He was always attentive, gallant, and well mannered. He was always impeccably dressed, and he was forever young and handsome. How could an old shlub like me, or for that matter any flesh and blood man, compete with that?"

Sol Hirsch was more than a bit unusual himself, by most people's standards. A short, barrel chested, seventy-two-year-old who still had a thick shock of white hair and eyebrows that matched, Sol was a self-made man who left the business world behind at the peak of his accomplishments, bought the brownstone next door to Mags and a yellow cab, and spent his substantial free time driving around the city picking up fares. Not that he needed the money, Sol had substantial savings and investments from the sale of his businesses, and he never had to work another day in his life if he chose not to.

Sol had started by opening a storefront insurance agency in lower Manhattan in the early fifties, primarily producing insurance for taxis. By the late fifties, he had cornered the insurance production market for cabs in the city, raking in huge commissions. In the early sixties, Sol started to have problems finding insurance carriers to underwrite the risky business, so he started his own insurance company, paying his agency huge commissions for producing the business and getting to invest the premiums as well.

Sol still wasn't happy because he had to pay an adjusting company heavy service fees to adjust his claims, and he had to pay astronomical fees to outside attorneys to handle the cases that went to court. He solved the problem of the adjusting expenses by opening his own adjusting company and having his insurance company pay his adjusting company the service fees. He solved the attorney's fees problem by hiring staff attorneys at nominal salaries to handle his cases.

By the end of the eighties, Sol was the owner of a small insurance empire, but he was not a happy man. He sold the whole works, bought the brownstone next to Mags and a yellow cab and found happiness riding around Manhattan picking up fares. No, it wasn't for the money that Sol Hirsh drove a taxicab. It was because he loved people, especially the kind of characters that one can only meet on the streets of New York City.

"In all of the time that I spent here, she never introduced me to her *Englishman*, she never even mentioned him to me," Penny noted. "But I can remember listening at the door of her sun parlor from time to time and hearing her talking to herself, which was not that unusual. I guess we all do that sometimes. But what used to scare me about Mags when I was little was that when she answered herself it was not in her own voice. She used to answer herself in a perfect Cary Grant imitation.

"I've never told anybody this before, Sol, not even Mags, but on my last stay here, when I was eighteen years old, I had the most incredible dream I've ever had. I dreamed that I woke up and there was this gorgeous man standing at the base of my bed smiling down at me. In this slight English accent, he told me he was sorry, that he didn't mean to scare me, but that I reminded him of a younger version of a woman he once knew. I even remember her name, Sol. He said her name was Helen Rose, and she taught him how to be a man. We talked until early morning when he insisted that I go back to sleep. He was the sweetest man, Sol. I would have sworn that he was real except for one thing. The guy in my dream was a dead-ringer for a young Cary Grant, looked just like him, sounded just like him, even dressed just like him."

Penny Albright was, in fact, a Helen Rose look alike. She had a stunning face with delicate, feminine features surrounded by long, natural blonde hair. A bit of a physical fitness buff, Penny had a perfect body, accentuated by an outstanding pair of runners' legs. Despite her incredible good looks, however, Penny had almost no experience with the opposite sex. In fact, after two horrifying sexual encounters when she was younger, Penny declared herself *chaste for life* and seemed to have no sexual drive whatsoever.

Penny's first experience with the male gender occurred when she was only thirteen years old. She was staying with Aunt May in Denver, Colorado at the time. Aunt May was the third youngest of the O'Malley sisters. Her eccentricity was that she liked men, lots of men, to the point that she kept a scorecard of the men that she had been with in her life, complete with the name of the man, date of the encounter, the type of sex engaged in, and a grade from one to ten. May was probably Penny's least favorite of her aunts because of her looseness. But like the rest of the sisters, May loved Penny and was always good to her, and Penny loved May back, though perhaps a smidgeon less than she did her other aunts.

On her first stay with May, not long after the death of Penny's parents, May made the mistake of leaving a boyfriend home alone with Penny early one morning while May ran out to get some groceries. Penny made the mistake of taking her morning shower while May was out. As Penny stepped out of the shower, the naked boyfriend forced his way into the bathroom and tried to force his way onto a terrified Penny. Though only thirteen, Penny knew a man's vulnerable spot. She kneed the boyfriend in his privates with all of her might and watched him drop to the floor with his hands covering his jewels and his legs squeezed tight together at the thighs. He was howling like a whipped puppy.

Penny grabbed a towel and raced from the bathroom, dripping water and trying to get the towel wrapped around her as she ran. She was prepared to run into the street in the frigid Denver air in just the towel if it was the only way to escape the boyfriend. As it turned out, she didn't need to. When Penny reached for the doorknob, the door swung open and Aunt May was standing on the other side of the doorframe holding a bag of groceries in her left arm. Penny didn't need to say a word. May knew exactly what had happened.

As a frightened Penny looked on, May dropped the groceries on her porch and headed straight for the kitchen and her carving knives. Just as May was about to pull the knife drawer open, the boyfriend burst into the kitchen, still totally naked and with a huge grin on his face. "So you like to play rough," the boyfriend shouted.

The grin vanished when the boyfriend saw that it was May in the kitchen and not Penny. May reached for the first thing that she could lay her hands on and wound up with her fist wrapped around the handle of a cast iron frying pan that was sitting atop the stove. She swung the frying pan at the boyfriend like it was a tennis racket and his head was the ball. The frying pan came down on the front of the stunned guy's head just below the hairline, and he hit the floor with a bang, out like a light. The skin across his forehead separated in a jagged line, and blood poured from the laceration onto the white linoleum floor of the kitchen.

Without missing a beat, May had the boyfriend's feet tucked under her arms and dragged him through the living room, leaving a trail of blood behind her. "Get the door for me, honey," May hollered to Penny. "I've got to bring the garbage out."

Penny opened the door and watched May drag the unclad boyfriend out of the house, down the stairs, up the walkway, and deposit him in the gutter. She came back into the house, retrieved the boyfriend's clothes and wrote a note that said only "Short Eyes," the prison term for child molesters. Then May went back outside, shoved the note into the boyfriend's mouth and dropped his clothes alongside of him.

Twenty minutes later, after a crowd of onlookers had gathered, a Denver patrol car pulled up to the curb outside of May's house. Penny was scared to death that they were going take her Aunt May away as May stepped out of the house onto the porch. The officer took the note out of the boyfriend's mouth, read it, and looked up at May on the porch. "Morning May," the officer hollered.

"Morning Pete. Cold out here this morning, ain't it?"

"This guy bothering you, May?" the officer asked.

"Not anymore he's not," May replied.

The officer picked up the boyfriend, put him into the patrol car and drove away. *Too bad he was scum*, May thought to herself as the police car drove off. She had given him a ten the night before.

May never saw the guy again, and though the incident did not convince her to change her ways, she never again brought a boyfriend home while Penny was staying with her. But so far as Penny's psyche was concerned, the damage had been done. Despite the fact that May assured Penny over and over again that she had done nothing wrong and had nothing of which to be ashamed, Penny carried with her a sense that somehow it was all her fault, that she must have done something to provoke the boyfriend or the incident never would have happened.

Penny's next and last experience of a sexual nature came when she was a freshman at New Mexico State. Some girlfriends convinced her to go to a local pickup bar with them. "Just some drinks and some fun," they assured her. Penny still would not have gone, save for the fact that she was the only one in the group who owned a car.

Once they got to the place, it wasn't long before the girlfriends had each made a score and left with one guy or another. Penny found herself sitting alone at the bar and was about to leave when she was approached by what appeared to her to be the most harmless little nerd she had ever seen.

"I hate these places," the little nerd said as he sat down next to Penny. "They're more like meat-markets than clubs. I couldn't help but notice that your friends had all left. So have mine, but I'm kind of used to that by now. I'm on my way back to my frat house, but I'd be happy to buy you a drink before I leave. Not that I'm looking to pick you up or anything. Even if I were into that kind of thing, I recognize that you're way out of my league. I just thought maybe you'd like a quick drink before you get going," the nerd offered.

Penny did not want another drink. She had already had more than she was used to, but she felt sorry for the little guy. "Don't be silly. I'd love to have a drink with you, but just one, then I've got to get going. It's getting late, at least, for me."

Penny ordered a cranberry and vodka and the nerd ordered a beer. The only other thing that Penny could remember about her time at the bar that evening was the nerd pointing out a couple on the dance floor. When she turned her attention back from the dance floor, Penny noticed that her drink had a considerable fizz to it, but she thought nothing of it.

The next thing Penny knew she felt as if she were waking up with a hangover. Still in a dreamlike state, Penny found herself lying on a couch somewhere with her skirt pulled up to her neck and her panties wrapped around her left ankle. The nerd was between her legs leaning over her, looking like a maniacal gremlin and humping like a wild man. Penny tried to resist but felt as if she had no strength in her body. She tried to scream, but when she did the nerd forced a little white pill down her throat. In a matter of seconds, Penny was out again. When she woke up, it was morning and Penny was in her car parked in the lot of the club.

Later, Penny regretted never having told a soul about her encounter with the nerd, but at the time she was just too embarrassed. She carried the shame of the incident with her silently, again feeling as if she must have done something to provoke the incident. That morning on her drive home from the bar, Penny swore off sex and men *forever*.

Sol handed Penny a piece of paper. "It's my cell phone number. My deal with Mags was simple. Any time she needed a ride, all she had to do was call me, and I would come as soon as I dropped off the fare I had in my cab. No charge, you know I'm not in this for the money. I do it for the company, and Mags was great company. Of course, Mags had to feel as if there was a *quid pro quo*, so what I got in return for the free rides was the right to use the bookstore as if it were a public library. If you'd like, I'd be honored to keep the deal in place with you. It's illegal for a yellow cab to be on call in this city, but we won't tell anyone."

"The honor would be all mine. You are too kind, Sol Hirsh."

Sol beamed at the compliment, but as Penny smiled back, she saw the smile slowly disappear from Sol's face. She realized that Sol was looking past her. Penny followed his eyes to a black stretch-limousine double-parked in front of the brownstone to the left of Penny's. Out stepped a familiar face, Joie Miller, a/k/a Mistress Joie, or as she preferred to be called, Maitresse Joie. Joie Miller was the last in the row of three self-made millionaires who lived side-by-side in the brownstones on East 80th Street.

"Ugh, it's that horrid woman," Sol groaned as Joie made her way to the curb smiling at Penny.

Like Penny and Sol, Joie was just arriving home from Aunt Mags's funeral. She was dressed in black from head to toe, including a form fitting black silk dress that ran down to her black leather high-heeled boots. But the color of Joie's garb had nothing to do with her mourning for Mags. Black was Maitresse Joie's color of choice. She never wore anything but black, and it was usually tight fitting black leather. She could pull it off though. Joie was fifty-two-years old, but she had the body of a healthy forty-year-old. Meaty but tight, Joie had full breasts and an ample posterior, the kind of behind that men like more the older they get. Her face didn't give away her age either. Naturally attractive, Joie had just enough work done on her face to keep it looking young without anyone being able to tell that she had paid for some of it.

"Hey, sweetie! How are you holding up?" Joie hollered as she reached the curb, but she made no attempt to approach Penny and Sol.

Penny was not in any way insulted. She knew that if Sol had not been there, Joie would have rushed over with a big hug to go with her greeting. But Sol and Joie did not get along, not even a little. When they were together they generally fought like a snake and a mongoose, frequently with Mags between them acting as the referee. Mags loved them both but preferred them separately.

"Hanging in there, Jo," Penny shouted back.

"I'm looking forward to having you as a next door neighbor, sweetie. As soon as you're settled in, come on over and we'll do tea," Joie offered, without ever acknowledging Sol's presence.

"It won't take me long. I'll stop by tomorrow afternoon if it's good for you," Penny replied. Penny liked Joie a lot. Mags always got a kick out of Joie, and Joie was great with Penny when she was little, though Penny was strictly forbidden from going into Joie's brownstone. Penny didn't find out why she was banned from Joie's home until Penny's last visit with Mags when Mags finally felt that Penny was old enough to hear how Joie had made her millions.

Josephine Miller was born in Columbus, Ohio to a working class father and mother. She moved to New York City directly out of high school in 1969 at the age of eighteen to pursue her dream of being a dancer on the New York stage. The only problem was that Josephine Miller was not that talented a dancer. The only stages she danced on after she got to New York City were those that were above a bunch of guys with drinks in one hand and dollar bills in the other. Though she found it degrading being almost naked and pawed at by a bunch of horny drunks, it paid the bills for her first couple of years trying to make it in Manhattan.

Then Josephine got to talking to a fellow dancer who was familiar with the underground S&M scene in lower Manhattan. When Josephine found out that she could make a whole lot more money degrading men than being degraded by them, she figured, *What the heck*? Josephine met with an experienced Mistress who ran a club in Greenwich Village specializing in satisfying fetishes involving females sexually dominating men. Once she was convinced that domination was not legally considered prostitution and that she would not have to engage in any form of actual sex, that is, that there would not be any penetration of either party, Josephine became Domina Joie.

Almost immediately, Domina Joie took to her new profession with great enthusiasm. Soon it was not just the money that was attracting her to the domination scene. Domina Joie had found a lifestyle that agreed with her in every way. She quickly became a 24/7 female dominant, or femdom for short, who lived the lifestyle inside and outside of her club. If you wanted to date Joie Miller, she let you know up front that you were to follow her every command, sexual or otherwise.

Because of her considerable good looks, dancer's body and sincere love for dominating and humiliating men, Domina Joie quickly became the most requested Mistress at her club. When a submissive male was with Domina Joie, he knew that he was with the real deal and not some coed faking it in order to make enough money to pay her way through college. After honing her skills, including an expertise with a bullwhip, and saving her money for several years, Domina Joie became Maitresse Joie and opened her own club. With a laundry list of regulars who had visited her and only her on a weekly basis, including several of New York's rich and famous, Maitresse Joie had a client base in place that assured her a thriving business from the day she opened the doors of her private house of domination on the Upper East Side of Manhattan.

But as much money as Maitresse Joie made with her house of

domination, it was not the club that made Maitresse Joie a millionaire; it was her business savvy and love for computers. In the mid-eighties, Maitresse Joie was one of the first business people to recognize the potential marketing power of the Internet. She had a domination web site set up before most legitimate business people even knew what the Internet was. When the Internet exploded, Maitresse Joie became known worldwide, and male slaves from England to Australia where paying $19.95 a month to visit Maitresse Joie's web site to see pictures of her abusing her actual male submissives, none of whom were allowed to share in the wealth. Soon Maitresse Joie was using her web site to market everything from pictures of herself in full Mistress regalia, to S&M toys, to worn hosiery and undies.

By the mid-nineties, Maitresse Joie was a multimillionaire. Once set for life money-wise, Joie decided that the web site and mail order business had become too time-consuming, and she sold them to another Mistress for a small fortune. By the 21st century, Maitresse Joie was seeing only two of her favorite, and most generous, male slaves on a regular basis and only a handful of others on rare occasions. Like Mags and Sol, Maitresse Joie had taken to a life of relative leisure.

As she made her way up the steps of her brownstone, Joie turned back to Penny. "It's a date, sweetie. I'll see you tomorrow afternoon." Then she finally acknowledged Sol. "By the way, Sol, thanks for the offer of a ride to the funeral. Now, when you finally admit that you really want me to take you over my knee and paddle your bare behind with a hairbrush, I may just have to say *no,* that is, unless you get on your hands and knees and beg me just right," Joie finished with a smile before heading back up the stairs.

"That'll be the day, witch," Sol shouted, his face turning red from anger and embarrassment. "As if she would have ever lowered herself enough to ride in a taxi cab," Sol groused, turning momentarily toward Penny and then staring back up at Joie. "She orders a limo to take her to the supermarket for crying out loud."

Penny could not help laughing, not just at what Joie had said, but at the fact that Sol's eyes were now following Joie's substantial rump up the stairs as it switched from side-to-side with each step she took.

"Man, I hate that woman," Sol grunted, after Joie closed the door to her brownstone behind her.

"You know Sol, they say that there's a thin line between love and hate," Penny teased.

"Got to run, honey," Sol blurted, ignoring the comment. "If you need anything, and I mean anything, you have my number. Don't hesitate to call."

"Thanks," Penny responded as she took the first step up toward the brownstone entrance, looking up admiringly at what now belonged to her. Then she stopped abruptly. Penny thought that she saw a face within a glow behind the curtain in the second floor window to her right. If it was a face, it was too far back in the shadows for Penny to make out features, but for a second it sure looked like a person. When she looked up again, it was gone.

"Sol," Penny hollered, catching Sol as he began making his way up the stairs to his own brownstone. "Is anyone supposed to be in the house? Maybe cleaning people or anyone like that?"

"Not that I'm aware of. Mags always did her own cleaning, right up to the end. Why? Any problem?"

Penny looked back up to the window to make sure that the face was gone. "No . . . No problem, I just thought I saw something that I guess I didn't."

Once inside the brownstone, Penny found herself looking down the familiar corridor toward the kitchen at the other end. A flight of stairs that led up to the second floor stood on the right side of the corridor. On the backside of the stairs was a second flight of stairs that ran down to the bookstore. Directly to Penny's right was Mags's favorite room, which she called her sun parlor. Like the rest of the house, it was furnished entirely with English antiques of a rococo style, complete with lion paws at the base of each chair and table leg. To Penny's left was a large dining room dominated by a long, ornate, cherry dining table and matching chairs, also English rococo style antiques.

Desperately in need of a cup of coffee, Penny headed for the kitchen. On her way down the corridor, she stopped at the stairway and kicked off her black, leather pumps, aiming them haphazardly at the bottom of the stairs. She unbuttoned her black, cashmere sweater, took it off and threw it over the carved railing that ran up the stairs. As she continued toward the kitchen, out of the corner of her right eye Penny caught sight of the smooth cashmere sweater slipping from the railing and landing on the oriental runner that ran the length of the hallway. She decided that it could wait; she'd get it later when she went up to bed.

In the kitchen, Penny made herself a cup of coffee and sat quietly for a while, reminiscing to herself about the times that she had spent in the brownstone with Aunt Mags. By the time she finished her coffee it was late afternoon. She washed her cup and the coffee pot, leaving them both to dry in the drainer on the sink.

Penny decided that she would go through the house the next day. The remaining O'Malley sisters had spent the previous two days and nights going through the brownstone, with the understanding that anything they found that had any value to them, sentimental or otherwise, was theirs for the taking. Each left with an armful, and Penny did not think there would be much of interest left among Mags's remaining things. She chose instead to check out the bookstore, which the O'Malley sisters had left untouched.

Penny headed down the stairs and spent the rest of the afternoon and a good part of the evening cleaning up, re-shelving books, and going through business records. The bookstore was not a moneymaker. In fact, Penny found to her surprise that the bookstore was deeply in the red. Mags, it seemed, did not always treat the bookstore like a business. Rather, to Mags the bookstore seemed to be more of a gathering place for friends and neighbors.

Penny, on the other hand, thought that the bookstore had the potential to be a thriving business. She had dreams of devoting part of the bookstore to rare and collectable books. Penny also knew that unless she wanted to join the Manhattan workforce, she was going to have to make the bookstore an income producer. Mags had left Penny the brownstone, but the rest of the estate was split up equally among the sisters. For the time being, Penny had only her own small savings on which to live.

♥ ♋ ♟

By the time Penny was done, it was dark and the coffee had worn off, she was exhausted and ready to lay her head on a pillow. She looked for a book to take with her, deciding on *The Ghost and Mrs. Muir* by R.A. Dick, which Penny knew to be a pseudonym for the real author, Josephine Aimee Leslie. Penny made her way up the stairs to the first floor, around the bend and toward the stairs to the bedrooms on the second floor. At the base of the stairway leading up to the second floor, Penny remembered her cashmere sweater and bent to pick it up, but to her amazement it was gone. She looked around, confused at the sweater's disappearance, and found it folded neatly over the railing where she had initially thrown it. The shoes, which she had haphazardly kicked off, sat upright, side by side, against the wall at the base of the stairs.

A chill swept up Penny's spine, and she could feel the fine hairs on her arms and the back of her neck standing up straight. Penny could not recall coming back to the stairs and straightening things up, but it had been a long and emotional day. She finally convinced herself that it was certainly possible that she had stopped at the stairs on her way down to the bookstore and simply forgotten about it. *After all, what other rational explanation could there be?* she thought.

Penny raced up the stairs to the master bedroom directly above the sun parlor, changed into an oversized cotton pajama top and cotton panties, folded down the comforter on the bed, and began to crawl in. But as she turned, something caught her eye. Sitting on an antique writing desk at the window that faced down onto East 80th Street was a Ouija Board and a single lit candle.

Though this was Penny's first night sleeping in the brownstone, she had been in the house with one or another of the O'Malley sisters on several occasions on the days leading up to the funeral. Penny had no recollection of ever having seen the Ouija Board, or the candle for that matter, on the writing desk or anywhere else in the house. Puzzled, Penny opened the drawer to the desk, placed the Ouija Board in it and firmly closed the drawer shut. She blew out the candle and headed back for the bed.

Penny was not surprised that Aunt Mags owned an Ouija Board, given her fascination with the occult. Penny was just surprised that she hadn't seen the thing in the days leading up to the funeral. *One of the sisters must have taken it out and left it on the desk today*, Penny assured herself as she crawled under the comforter, turned on a reading light and opened her book. *But why would anyone have lit the candle? It barely looked burned,* she thought.

It wasn't long before Penny's eyes grew heavy from reading, and she drifted off to sleep. She slept soundly until about three o'clock in the morning when she was roused by the feeling of something lightly brushing her hair off of her face. Without opening her eyes, Penny rolled over and pushed her hair back with her right hand. Then she sat bolt upright when she realized through her closed eyelids, that there was a light flickering in the room.

Upon opening her eyes, Penny saw that the candle sitting on the writing desk was again lit, and the glow of the flickering flame was dancing about the walls of the room as a light breeze blew through a crack where the window had been left slightly ajar. The Ouija Board was again sitting on top of the writing desk next to the candle. Again Penny felt the fine hairs on her arms and neck stand up. This time there was no doubt in her mind. When she got into the bed the candle was out and the Ouija Board was in the drawer. Something or somebody, perhaps Aunt Mags's spirit, wanted Penny at the Ouija Board.

Penny made her way nervously to the writing desk and sat down. She lightly touched the tips of her index finger on each hand to a finely carved, arrow-shaped, piece of maple wood that sat on four tiny legs on top of the Ouija Board.

"Aunt Mags, is that you?" Penny asked softly.

The arrow rocked lightly at first and then started to glide slowly across the board. Penny raised her fingers so that they were barely touching the arrow-shaped piece of wood, to ensure herself that she was not subconsciously directing it in any way. Instead of stopping, the arrow picked up speed. It moved to the upper right-hand corner of the board to the word "NO" which sat next to a black quarter moon. Then the arrow moved back to the center of the board.

"Are you Mags's *Englishman?*" Penny asked, not knowing who else it might be.

The arrow moved to the upper left-hand corner of the board to the word "YES," sitting next to a darkened circle, which Penny assumed was intended to represent either a full moon or the sun. Then, again the arrow moved back to the center of the board, as it would continue to do after it finished answering each question that Penny asked.

"Do you have a name?"

The arrow moved to the word "YES" and then down to a series of letters that arced in two rows in the center of the board, forming the complete alphabet in order. The arrow moved to the letter K, and Penny took her right index finger off the arrow entirely. When she was certain that the arrow was continuing to move, though she had only one finger on it, Penny reached for a pencil and a piece of paper with her free hand, and began to write down the letters as the arrow glided around the arced letters of the alphabet, halting briefly at certain letters. When the arrow returned to the center of the board and stopped, Penny looked down at the paper and saw that she had written the name "KERBY."

"Is that your first name? Do you have a last name?"

This time when the arrow finished moving, Penny realized that beneath the name "KERBY" she had written the name "BREWSTER."

"Is Mags there with you, Mr. Brewster?" Penny wondered.

"NO" the board answered.

"Where is Mags?"

The arrow started moving around the alphabet again, and Penny reached for a new piece of paper. When the arrow returned to the center of the board and stopped, Penny had written the word "HEAVEN."

"Why aren't you in Heaven, Mr. Brewster?" Penny asked.

When the arrow stopped, the letters read, "NOT SURE MAYBE BECAUSE IM NOT BURIED IN HALLOWED GROUND."

"Where are you buried, Mr. Brewster?"

When the arrow stopped this time, the letters read, "BENEATH THE BROWNSTONE."

"Why, Mr. Brewster? How did you die?"

The letters that Penny wrote spelled out the word, "MURDER," sending a cold chill up her spine.

"Could Mags talk to you without the board?" Penny asked.

The arrow moved to the upper right-hand corner and the word "YES."

"Could Mags see you?"

Again the arrow went to the word "YES" and then spelled out "WHEN SHE WANTED TO AND I WANTED HER TO."

"How is it that Mags was able to see you, Mr. Brewster?"

"MAGS HAD THE GIFT" the letters read.

"Are you saying that I don't have the gift, Mr. Brewster?"

The letters spelled out, "YOU HAVE SEEN ME."

"Where have I seen you, Mr. Brewster?" Penny wondered.

"HELEN ROSE," Penny wrote, and she immediately thought back to her lucid dream.

"Why can't I see you now, Mr. Brewster?"

"MAGS IS GONE" the letters read.

"What do I need to do to be able to see you again, Mr. Brewster?" Penny asked.

This time when she finished writing, Penny had written the word "SÉANCE."

Before Penny could ask another question, the arrow spelled out "SLEEP NOW."

"But I have lots more questions, Mr. Brewster," Penny said urgently.

The arrow spelled out "WE HAVE LOTS MORE TIME." Then it moved to the bottom of the board where the words "GOOD BYE" were written.

"Please, Mr. Brewster, I have more I want to ask you tonight," Penny persisted.

The arrow did not move again, but the candle on the desk blew out as if hit by a sudden gust of wind.

CHAPTER 4

GIRLS WILL BE GIRLS
JUNE 2000

Jeannie McCloone waited in the hallway outside of the door to her apartment, her foot wedged between the door and the frame to prevent the door from closing behind her. She stared anxiously at the elevator down the hall, watching the arrow above the elevator door as it worked its way first up to the floor above hers and then started down again. Like a child about to open a birthday gift, Jean's excitement grew as she waited for the elevator door to open and Niki Bach to step off.

It had been almost eight months since Jean had left for Harvard and Niki had headed for Yale, and despite the close proximity, the two girls had not been in each other's presence during that time. There had been lots of emails and telephone calls, lots of plans to get together, but the demands of Ivy League schools and new interests always managed to put a damper on those plans.

So much about Jean had changed in the time they had been apart, she wondered, worried really, whether Niki would like the new Jean. The baby fat was gone, replaced by well-defined little muscles, thanks to an extreme version of the Atkins diet. For two months Jean had gone without a single carbohydrate, putting her body into a serious state of ketosis, forcing it to live off of its stored fat until there was no visible fat left. Afterward, she stuck to a low carbohydrate diet and took to lifting weights with a passion. Using very light weights and lots and lots of repetitions, Jean's body was suddenly rippled with small but well defined muscles from her neck down.

Also gone were the mousy, brown, flyaway hair and the glasses. Jean had dyed her hair jet black and cut it short, slicking it back, with a single curl sweeping down onto her forehead. Hair-wise Jean had the appearance of a fifty's male greaser. Her glasses were replaced by soft contact lenses.

Jean's manner of dress had changed too. Gone was the straight-laced, collegiate style of her high school days, replaced by anything that might help to show off her new curves, with sleeveless blouses, miniskirts, and high heels being her new clothing of choice. Jean loved her new self, but she worried that Niki might find her new appearance too severe, the short hair and muscles too masculine. Despite wearing a miniskirt and high heels, Jean was concerned that Niki might find her too . . . *butch* was the word that came to her mind.

To Jean it seemed an eternity before the door to the elevator finally opened and Niki stepped out. Niki stopped short as she exited the elevator, and with her mouth agape she stared down the hallway at Jean. After several seconds, Niki let out an exaggerated scream. "Ahhhhhh! Look at you! I can't believe it's you! I love it!"

Jean held out her arms like a small child looking for a hug. "Don't just stand there. Hurry down here. I can't let the door close behind me or it will lock."

As Niki started toward her, Jean realized that she was not the only one whose style seemed to have changed. Niki was not wearing one of the fitted designer suits that she had been famous for in high school. To the contrary, she was dressed in an oversized gray sweat suit that made her appear to have gained twenty pounds. Her always coifed hair was tucked up into a Yankee baseball cap with only a ponytail sticking out of the rear. Instead of heels, Niki's feet were shod with red, high-top Converse sneakers.

Though there was still no mistaking Niki's God-given beauty, there was no makeup on her face enhancing her natural good looks. Jean could not recall the last time that she had seen Niki without makeup. Jean thought that Niki looked like one of those super models who are so naturally beautiful that they purposely dress down and go without makeup in order to let the world know that they don't have to work at it to be gorgeous.

Jean was relieved when the two finally came together and wrapped their arms around each other. She realized that the added weight Niki seemed to be carrying was just an illusion, created by the baggy sweat suit. Underneath the sweat suit was the same, tight, borderline skinny, body that Jean had known before.

"Do you really like it? You don't think the change is too drastic, do you?" Jean whispered into Niki's ear as they began to separate.

"Honey, I don't just like it, I love it. I don't know how you managed it. If I were you, I'd try to get a patent on the process," Niki gushed as she stepped back and lightly squeezed Jean's right bicep muscle.

Jean took Niki's hand and led her into the apartment. "You don't know how relieved that makes me feel. I was afraid that you might think I was too . . . you know, dikey looking, with the short hair and muscles and all."

"Sexy is the word that came to my mind when I first saw you," Niki replied.

"Good, that's exactly what I was hoping you would say," Jean blushed.

"Don't get me wrong. You know, guys still excite me sexually, but that doesn't mean I can't be sexually attracted to a woman. I mean, men do serve a purpose. I don't think I could be with a woman exclusively, but on the other hand, after our experience, I don't think I could ever be without a woman in my life either, sexually speaking that is," Niki explained.

"Believe it or not, those are my exact feelings. I was just afraid you might think that I had gone all the way the other way and it might scare you. In the past eight months I've really come to learn a great deal about myself sexually. More important, I've come to accept myself for what I feel sexually. I no longer feel ashamed of my sexual desires and fantasies, and I'm not ashamed to live them out either, and *yes* those fantasies do include men."

"Are you trying to tell me that you have a boyfriend?" Niki asked with feigned surprise.

"Not exactly," Jean said coyly. "For now, to use your words, let's just say that men *do serve a purpose* in my world, *sexually speaking that is*."

"I'm intrigued. Tell me more," Niki pleaded.

"In time. First let me look at you. I missed you so much. It has been so long. I can't believe that we were so near to each other and we weren't able to find time to get together."

"Freshman year of college at an Ivy League school will do that, but that won't be a problem next year," Niki noted.

"You don't think you're going to be just as busy next year as you were this year?" Jean wondered.

"I'm not going back next year. I haven't figured out how I'm going to tell mom yet. It's really going to bother her, but an opportunity has come up, and I am not going to let it slip by. It's my life and it's what I want that counts."

"It must be some special kind of opportunity if it's causing you to drop out of Yale. I thought you wanted to go to law school."

"I realized that was more what mom wanted than what I wanted. You see, I met this modeling agent up in New Haven. He was there at a fashion show on campus, and he approached me and asked if I would be interested in doing some test shots. At first, I thought he was just some nut, then I did some checking on the Internet and found out that he was the real-deal. He's with one of the most well respected modeling agencies in Manhattan. I did the test shoot, and the agency offered me a very substantial first contract. I have a lawyer going over the papers as we speak."

"Sounds glamorous! Lots of traveling, I bet," Jean said.

"Some, I'm sure," Niki replied. "In time anyway, but for the time being I'll be mostly here in New York City getting my feet wet. Some runway shows, some local advertising shoots, that kind of stuff."

"Great, then we'll be full-time neighbors again," Jean announced, with a glimmer in her eye.

Niki shot Jean a look of surprise. "*Full-time* neighbors? How's that?"

"I'm not going back to Harvard either. I've transferred down to Columbia for next semester."

"But why? Harvard was your dream school."

"Well, you're not the only one with fantasies that go beyond academics. For now, let's just say that I've developed a very lucrative hobby that promises to be that much more lucrative here in New York City than it would be in Cambridge. Anyway, it's not as if I'm giving up on my dream of medical school. Columbia is a great school, you know."

"You're being awfully secretive with your secret hobbies and secret sexual fantasies. What's a girlfriend for if you're not going to share your secrets with her?" Niki chided.

"Oh, in time I'm going to share my secrets with you. I'm just concerned that they might freak you out a little. I don't want you to judge me by my fantasies."

"Freak me out, after what we did together, do you really think there is anything that you might say or do that could freak me out?"

"That brings us to a whole different topic that is far more interesting and important than any fantasies or hobbies that I might have," Jean said. "You know, our anniversary is fast approaching and you did promise. I've been waiting patiently. I hope that you're not going to disappoint me."

"You know I could never disappoint you. In fact, I've been anticipating this as much as you have. I already have our next victim picked out," Niki announced, a wicked look in her eye.

"You do? Who is it? Do I know him?" Jean asked excitedly.

"Oh, you know him all right," Niki laughed. "In fact, if it weren't for him, we wouldn't be having this discussion."

"Danny O'Brien? Isn't that a little risky, two boys from the same high school going missing on the same date, exactly one year apart? It's a little close to home, isn't it? Don't you think the police might link the two? I thought we would go for a complete stranger this time."

"Don't be silly! It's perfect. Think about how exciting it will be doing him, knowing that he is the one who set the whole thing in motion. Even if the police do put the two together, there would be no reason for them to link us to the disappearances. They don't even know for certain whether Peter Sizemore is dead or alive. Even if they assume both of them to be dead, they would never suspect females. Women don't commit serial murders. You know how these macho cops are. They'd probably think some sex crazed gay maniac is roaming the streets kidnapping high school boys.

"Even if they do start investigating around here, it will just make it that much more exciting. It's like you've always said, we're much smarter than they are. It might even be fun talking to them if they decide to start questioning old high school friends looking for a lead, and the papers will eat it up. Think about how much fun it will be reading about it, knowing that we are the only ones who know what really happened. As long as we keep our mouths shut, as long as we don't tell another soul about our involvement, no one will ever suspect us. Why would they?" Niki noted.

"Okay, let's say I go along with Danny O'Brien as our next victim, how do we get him? The last I heard, he was on his way to some small college out in California on a baseball scholarship or something. How do we find him and set it up in time for the anniversary?" Jean wondered.

"That's easy, I know exactly where he is at this very moment," Niki replied as she made her way to a living room window overlooking Central Park. "Come here; I'll show you."

Jean looked puzzled as she made her way to the window and stared out at the lush green of the park. "He's somewhere in Central Park?" Jean asked, a bewildered look on her face.

"No, he's right there," Niki said, pointing to the skyline on the far side of the park.

Jean followed Niki's finger to the opposite side of the park and knew immediately at what she was pointing. Sitting within the center of the mass of standard shaped, quadrangular buildings was an eruption of conic form, an expanding spiral that rose into the sky bearing a mere abstract relationship to the city block on which it sat. Glistening white in the afternoon sun, the building reminded Jean of an upside down wedding cake.

"He's in the Guggenheim Museum?" Jean asked incredulously.

"You know his mother is big in the art scene in the city. Well, my mom was playing at a recital the other night and happened to run into his mother. It seems that he went to school in California because Miss Big Tits got accepted into the drama program at UCLA. His mother hates her by the way. Miss Boobies is staying in Los Angeles for the summer. She got a bit part in some summer theater festival or something. Danny begged his mother to let him stay in Los Angeles for the summer too, so he could be near her, but he couldn't find a job, so his mother insisted that he come home. She used her connections in the art scene to get him a summer job at the Guggenheim. He's in there right now."

"How do you know that?"

"This morning when the museum opened I was outside of the park, across the street from the museum. I watched him go in."

"Weren't you afraid he might recognize you?"

"In this get up, with sunglasses on, how could he, and so what if he did? I was out for a walk in the park. I'm allowed."

Jean made her way from the window and collapsed backward onto the couch. "Okay, then he's our next victim. He's certainly earned it. But he has to be the last one from around here. Now, how do we lure him in?"

Niki made her way to the couch and stood over Jean. "The same way that we lured Peter in silly. Look, he may pretend to be smitten by Miss Big Boobies, but he's still nothing more than a randy dog. The girlfriend's on the other side of the country. You know he's going to be on the prowl, looking for something with which to replace his hand. When I finish telling him how I still think about him when I'm with other men and offer up the possibility of a *ménage a trios*, his head may explode right there in the museum, especially when he gets an eyeful of your new look."

Niki eased herself down on top of Jean so that they were nose to nose. Jean could feel the warmth and smell the sweetness of Niki's breath on her face. "In the museum? We're going to the museum?"

"Tonight," Niki announced. "At first, I'll tell him that my running into him there was just a coincidence. I love the Guggenheim. I go there all the time. Then I'll confess that I knew he was working there for the summer and that I was hoping to run into him. I'll even tell him that I know his girlfriend is in California, and I thought he might be looking for some female companionship, no commitments of course. I'll be resigned to the fact that he belongs to Miss Big Tits. I'm just looking for him to satisfy my urge. Then I'll spring you on him, and I guarantee you that the trap will slam shut."

Jean felt the pressure of Niki's body on top of her, Niki's groin pressing hard into her own. "If we're going to the museum this evening, we don't have a lot of time. They close early, even on Friday nights, and I need a shower."

"Are you expecting your mom any time soon?" Niki wondered.

"She just left for some island in Maine with the girlfriend. She won't be back for two weeks."

"Good!" Niki responded as she sat up, wrapping her legs around either side of Jean's waist. "I need a shower too. We can kill a bunch of birds with one stone," she continued, as she started to lift Jean's shirt exposing the ripples in her stomach. Niki stopped when she saw the top of a tattoo sticking out of Jean's skirt just beneath her belly button. "Cool, you got a tattoo. Let's have a look," Niki said, lowering the zipper on Jean's skirt and starting to force the top of the skirt down.

Expecting to see a flower or perhaps a butterfly, Niki was surprised to see three Greek letters. The first looked like a fancy X, the second a drunken B, and the third an oddly shaped T. "A sorority? I didn't figure you for a sorority girl."

"Not exactly a sorority, but it does represent an exclusive club of sorts," Jean responded.

"Again with cryptic answers. Fine, let's see if I can figure it out. The X in the Greek alphabet is Chi, kind of a hard C, like in my name, Bach. The B and T are easy. B is Beta and stands for B, and the T is Theta and stands for T. Chi, Beta, Theta, CBT, I don't get it."

"I'll give you a hint. It has to do with my new hobby/business," Jean said.

"Enough, I give up," Niki replied, feigning exasperation. "I can't stand the suspense."

"Okay, but you have to promise not to laugh or think I'm weird or anything," Jean demanded as she eased herself out from under Niki and headed for the bathroom, as if she did not want to be looking Niki in the eyes as she told her story.

Jean finished undressing as she made her way across the living room to the hallway in which the bathroom was located. "I guess you know by now that I have this bizarre fascination with the male genitalia, kind of a love/hate relationship. Well, one night I was alone in the dorm on the Internet, and I punched in the words cock and balls, you know, looking for pictures of naked guys. What popped up was a bunch of web sites with the letters, CBT, in them. I followed one of the paths and could not believe my eyes. You probably won't believe this, but CBT stands for Cock and Ball Torture. It turns out it's a fetish, and there are literally thousands of guys out there who get off on having a woman strip them nude and abuse their genitals in one way or another. Really, otherwise ordinary guys who get sexually turned on by a woman abusing their genitals," Jean explained, finally looking Niki in the eyes and waiting for a reaction.

"You're kidding? What do you mean abusing their genitals?" Niki asked as she started toward the bathroom, shedding her own clothes onto the floor as she made her way.

"That's the really strange part. It seems that there are no limitations in so far as the male imagination is concerned when it comes to having their penises and testicles tortured. They all have their own thing when it comes to punishing their genitals. Some like having their penises or testicles punched, or slapped, or squeezed, or twisted. There's a group of women here in New York City who call themselves the *Satin Kick*. They do a little bit of all of the above, but they specialize in stripping a man naked, making him spread his legs apart, kicking him as hard as they can right in the balls, and watching him crumple to the floor and writhe around in agony. The amazing thing is that there are guys lining up willing to pay big dollars to have this stuff done, and there's absolutely no sexual obligation on the part of the woman. The woman doesn't even have to take her clothes off. At worst, some of these guys ask to wank-off in front of the woman after she finishes abusing them."

"That is bizarre, but what does all this have to do with you?" Niki wondered with a smile. "Don't tell me that your new hobby includes getting paid for kicking freaky guys in the gonads."

"Niki, I'm telling you that when I saw the pictures of this stuff on the Internet, it made me crazy. I mean it made me hot like you would not believe. I got addicted to it. I couldn't get enough of it. My whole life I've fantasized about doing some of the same things that I've just described, and worse, much worse. I thought I was the only one. I thought I was some kind of a nut or something. Then it turns out that there are thousands of people out there, men and women, who have been having the same fantasies, except they have been living out those fantasies. So I decided to start doing the same thing."

"Go ahead," Niki jumped in. "You can't stop there. It's just getting interesting."

"First, I put an ad in the campus newspaper. It just said CBT with my email address. I had six emails by the end of the week, including two from professors. It turned out to be mostly mild stuff, like punching and kicking. One guy had me tie his penis with a cord and yank him around the room, another had me clamp clothespins on his testicles and organ. I loved it. Their suffering was exquisite, and they all paid for my pleasure. So I expanded. I put an ad in a local newspaper and got lots more business. Then I opened up a web site and advertised through it. You'll never believe this, but I got requests from everywhere from the Netherlands to Japan. This stuff is huge in Japan."

"So you're telling me that you have started a cottage industry slapping guys in the balls and you're going to get rich doing it?" Niki laughed.

"It gets stranger and stranger. You see, there are loads of female dominants out there that do the milder forms of CBT, the slapping and kicking stuff. That means lots of competition, but the desires of lots of these guys go way beyond kicking and hitting. That's what I mean when I say there are no limitations to the imagination of some of these guys. Some of them get off by having their penises or scrotums pierced. Some want their scrotums inflated with saline until it's the size of a baby's head. Some want their testicles electrocuted with short bursts of electricity. Some want their penises tied at the base so tight that the blood stops flowing and their members swell and turn purple. Believe it or not, some want to be catheterized with everything from drinking straws to ballpoint pens. It's hardcore. The guy I told you about from the Netherlands, he wants me to castrate him.

"Anyway, a lot of the invasive stuff is more than what most Mistresses are willing to do, but that's the stuff that really turns me on. So I started going through the medical books, learning about catheters and injections, proper sterilization procedures, even some surgical techniques involving the male genitalia. If you know anybody who's interested, I'm sure I could do a vasectomy," Jean laughed.

"The bottom line is, I've developed this kind of specialty that I love, and at the same time I'm kind of filling a void. You know, I'm answering a need in the industry, which is why I've decided to move back to Manhattan. It seems that in so far as the hardcore stuff is concerned, other than Amsterdam, New York is the place to be," Jean finished as she spun around and bent over to turn on the shower.

Niki thrust her *mons pubis* into Jean's behind. "Well! Are you going to do it?"

"Do what?" Jean asked in a puzzled fashion.

"Castrate him?"

"We're trying to work out a price," Jean said with a nasty laugh, and then she sighed as she nuzzled her ass back into Niki's pubic area.

♥✄♟

The girls decided to take a taxi through the park to the Guggenheim. It wasn't that the walk would have been too far. To the contrary, the museum was just on the other side of the park, and the early evening weather was warm with a gentle breeze. They agreed that a walk through Central Park would be delightful. Unfortunately, the shoes that each had chosen to wear were not made for walking any distance.

Niki wore strapless heeled sandals to go with a floral print, cotton sundress that hung loosely and hit her about mid-thighs. A strong gust would have left little to the imagination, not that there was that much to be imagined anyway. With the sun behind her, the silhouette of Niki's supple body, including the outline of her thong bikini, was clearly visible for all to see.

Jean opted for pink pointy-toed mules, also with a sizable heel, all the better to show off her new calf muscles and push her firm glutes out a little further. She wore a tight, pink miniskirt and a white silk, sleeveless top to accentuate her perfectly rounded shoulders and biceps.

Inside of the windowless museum, the girls stood in the center of the circular court of the larger tower and stared up at the immense skylight above them. They marveled at the tilting, twisting ramp that surrounded them, spiraling upward and outward for six floors. The sight was dizzying. The building seemed almost to demand reverence. "A light flooded cathedral with a roadway to Heaven winding round its walls," was the way one architecture historian had described the space.

Niki was spinning her body in a circle with her head tilted back, following the expanding coil of the ramp upward when she stopped suddenly as her gaze hit the top level. Then she blurted excitedly, "There he is!"

Jean followed Niki's eyes up to the sixth floor of the building, but all she saw was the back of the head of someone who was leaning backward against the chest-high railing of the uppermost floor of the museum. Long blonde curls hung down from the back of the individual's head, touching the collar of his blue blazer. His elbows jutted out backward over the railing.

"How can you be so sure that's him?" Jean wondered. "I remember his hair being much darker."

"Oh, that's him all right," Niki assured Jean. "I saw him this morning from top to bottom. His hair is lighter, but don't forget he's been in the California sunshine for almost a year. He looks like a typical California surfer-boy now, with blonde hair to go with his bright blue eyes. You don't think he's been sitting in a dorm room studying, do you? I'll bet you that the only time he's cracked open a book has been while he was sitting on the beach."

The two took the elevator to the sixth floor. They agreed that Jean would exit the elevator first and make a point of walking directly in front of Danny. Niki stayed back, trying to be as inconspicuous as possible. She watched Danny from a distance, certain that he would not recognize Jean as she made her way by him without looking in his direction. Niki giggled to herself as Danny's eyes followed Jean's ass as she went by. *He's following the bait,* Niki thought. *Now let's get him into the trap.*

Danny's head was still turned, his eyes admiring Jean's rear view when Niki crept up behind him. "I'm looking for *The Kiss,*" Niki said seductively, startling Danny slightly.

Danny spun his head, following the very familiar sounding feminine voice. "What did you say you were looking for?" Danny asked, before realizing to whom he was speaking.

"*The Kiss,*" Niki repeated with a soft smile, after seeing recognition in Danny's eyes. "You know, the Max Ernst painting, *The Kiss.*"

"Hey, what are you doing here?" Danny asked in a surprise tone.

"This is the Guggenheim Museum, you know. People come from all over the world to visit this place. Personally, I love it here. I come here all the time," Niki lied.

"Well, I hope the fact that you've run into me won't cause you to stay away now. I mean, I hope you're not still mad at me. I wouldn't want to be the cause of you missing out on all of these great works of art," Danny laughed.

"Mad at you? Don't be silly! Life is far too short to carry grudges. Anyway, how could I be mad at the man who introduced me to the joys of womanhood? If it weren't for you, I might still be missing out on life's greatest pleasure. Instead, because of your great introduction, I've gone out of my way to seek out that pleasure in as many different varieties as possible. But the truth is that in all of my experiences, I still haven't found anything to compare with that first time."

"They say you never forget your first time," Danny replied modestly.

"I don't want to swell your head or anything, but try as I might, and believe me I've been trying, I just haven't been able to find anyone to touch me the way that you did," Niki gushed.

"That's very flattering, but it has only been, what nine or ten months? I mean, how much experimenting could you have possibly done in that time?"

"You'd be surprised. It's like I said, life is short. You have to live it to its fullest while you're still young enough to enjoy it. When you find something that you really enjoy, why not go after it?"

"Are you saying what I think you're saying, Niki?" Danny asked incredulously.

"Look, you don't think that I really spend my free time roaming around art museums by myself, do you? My mom ran into your mother the other night, and your mother told my mom that you were working here for the summer. I was hoping that I would run into you. You see, I also know that your girlfriend is still on the other side of the country in Los Angeles. I was guessing you might be lonely, looking for some female companionship. Don't get me wrong. I know you're spoken-for. I'm not looking to get in the middle of *that*. I'm just trying to return a favor."

"Return a favor? How's that?" Danny wondered.

"Well, you introduced me to something special; now I'd like to do the same for you, treat you to something you've never experienced before," Niki answered cryptically.

"I'm not the type to look a gift-horse in the mouth, but I don't get it. It's not as if I'm a virgin. How do you plan to go about introducing me to something I've never experienced? I'm not bragging or anything, but I have a girlfriend, and we've kind of done it all," Danny boasted proudly.

"Really? Well tell me, how many times has the girlfriend brought another girl into bed with you two? I'm betting never," Niki said, with a devious smile.

"You're kidding right? Are you telling me that you want to sleep with me so badly that you're prepared to try to entice me with a threesome before I even say no to you alone?"

"I told you, I'm always looking for new experiences. This is something I've only tried once so far myself, and, like I said, I feel as if I owe you one."

"Okay, you've got my interest piqued. I assume that you already have the other girl picked out and she has agreed to it. Who might she be?" Danny wondered.

"You remember Jeannie McCloone, don't you?" Niki answered.

"Jeannie McCloone?" Danny responded, as if completely surprised by Niki's choice for the third person for the threesome. "You've got to be kidding me, right? What you just did is like ruining a wet dream. I'd rather you and I just go at it alone than include her. I'm not that picky when it comes to sex, but she's just not my type. She might make me lose my hard-on."

"Really? I would never have guessed that by the way you ogled her when she just strolled by you," Niki remarked, again smiling.

"I think you're mistaken. I haven't seen Jean since graduation. I mean, it's not as if I knew her that well. I wasn't in any of her egghead classes or anything, but I'm sure I'd know her if she walked by me."

Niki looked around the sixth floor of the museum in an effort to show Jean's new body off to Danny, but Jean was nowhere to be found. Niki leaned over the railing scanning the floors below. The construction of the museum, with the ramp and rotunda, was intentionally designed so that viewers could observe each other, as well as the exhibits, from an unprecedented number of perspectives.

Niki finally spied Jean a floor below, standing before Alberto Giacometti's *Nose,* a surrealistic work in bronze of a male head within a steel cage, suspended by a rope from a cross bar. The work caught Jean's attention not just because of the head's enormous proboscis, but because the wide-open mouth of the bronze gave a vague suggestion of a scream, and the cage and cord from which the head hung evoked an image of the gallows. *One last scream of anguish from a man in the throes of death,* Jean thought to herself as she stared at the artwork.

"There! There she is! There's the new and improved Jeannie McCloone," Niki announced, pointing a satisfied finger down at Jean while looking over at Danny for a reaction. "Now tell me again how you think she might cause you to lose your erection."

Danny immediately recalled admiring the woman that Niki was pointing at as she had sauntered past him earlier. "You're telling me *that's* Jeannie McCloone? That's the woman you and I are going to be sharing a bed with?"

Niki did not say a word, she simply smiled at Danny and nodded her head. The trap had just slammed shut on Danny O'Brien, and he had no hope of getting out of it alive.

"It could not have gone better," Niki told Jean, as the two girls worked their way down the ramp toward the museum exit. "It's as if Nemesis, the goddess of destiny, is on our side. The only day that the museum is closed is Thursday, so we're going to pick him up on Wednesday night after work. Wednesday just happens to be June 24th, our anniversary. He thinks we're going to my aunt's summer house down at the Jersey Shore, a night of sex, a day at the beach to recuperate."

"Where are we going to pick him up? It has to be somewhere out of the way, somewhere no one will see him getting into our car," Jean noted.

"No problem. Get this, he is more concerned about someone seeing us together than we are. He's terrified that Miss Big Tits might find out about this. I had to swear that we would never discuss this with anyone. He actually came up with the idea that we pick him up in the parking facility under the Metropolitan Museum of Art. He's going to duck down when we exit just to be on the safe side. My concern is, what if he refuses the sedatives, like Peter did. For me, that was the scariest moment of the whole episode last time."

"Not to worry," Jean assured her. "I have no intention of risking that again. I've got something he won't be able to refuse. I've taken a bottle of chloroform from my mother's office. You drive this time. I'll sit behind him and wrap a rag with the chloroform on it over his face from behind. By the time he realizes what's happening, he'll be out like a light. Are you sure that we can get into the warehouse again? I have some special plans for Mr. O'Brien, but they're going to take time. We need a quiet place where we can feel secure."

"We can use the warehouse this time, but next year we'll have to find somewhere else to plan our party. It seems my mom is talking to a divorce lawyer. She told me that she's been planning it for a long time, but she refrained from filing until I reached the age of emancipation. She said that she was afraid that if she filed while I was still a minor, my father might have smuggled me out of the country to Russia, and she might never have seen me again. It kind of makes me feel guilty. She endured all those years of abuse to protect me. Anyway, she should be on her way to freedom around this time next year. I expect that my father's assets, including the warehouse, will be the subject of a division in the divorce proceedings soon. I wouldn't include the warehouse in any of our future plans."

"No sweat," Jean replied. "If we stick to our time schedule, we'll have a whole year to figure out where to take care of the next one. As long as we have a place to spend some quiet time with Danny O'Brien."

"He loves your new look by the way," Niki remarked. "He said he could hardly wait to see those muscles without any clothes on them."

"Did he really? How sweet! Maybe he's not so bad after all. I'll feel terrible disappointing him, but I'm afraid he's the one who's going to be providing the nude entertainment."

♥ ⚰ ♟

Niki and Jean sat in the dimly lit parking garage below the Metropolitan Museum of Art waiting for Danny to appear. Niki sat in the driver's seat with Jean in the backseat on the passenger side. They were surprised that when Danny showed up he came from inside the museum as opposed to just walking in through the garage entrance. They watched as Danny, with an overnight bag in hand, made his way to the rear of the car and looked around as if he was casing the vehicle for a robbery.

"Geez, he really is worried about that girlfriend finding out about this, isn't he? What does he think, that she has a private investigator following him around twenty-four hours a day?" Niki wondered.

"You'd think he was the one about to commit a murder," Jean responded with a giggle.

When Danny was satisfied that no one was around, he made a dash for the car door. He tried to get into the backseat, but Jean pointed him toward the front. He looked almost upset at the fact that the rear door was locked when he tried to open it.

When he finally got into the front seat, Danny explained, "I thought I'd get in the back, so it would be easier for me to duck down when we exit this place."

"Relax, the windows are tinted. No one is going to see you," Niki assured him.

"You can't be too careful," Danny noted, lowering his head as Niki started to drive out of the garage. "She lives right up the street, you know. Her mom or one of her girlfriends might just be walking by."

Danny stayed slumped in his seat until they hit Ninth Avenue and started to head south toward the Lincoln Tunnel. "You'll never see anyone she knows in this neighborhood," Danny remarked, a smile of relief on his face as he sat up.

Danny eyed Niki up and down, spending a little extra time checking out her long legs, most of which were exposed. Niki was wearing the shortest shorts Danny had ever seen. "Did I remember to tell you how good you're looking," Danny commented, finally looking up at Niki's face.

Before Niki could respond, Danny turned his attention to Jean in the backseat. "And look at you. Who would have thought that body was hiding underneath that layer of fat you carried around in high school. What did you do, make a deal with the devil or something?"

"Thanks," Jean replied. "I'm glad you like the change."

"There's plenty there to like. All you need now is a set of breast implants and you'd make any man happy."

Jean felt like she could scream, but before she could open her mouth to say anything Niki came to her defense. "What are you talking about? She has gorgeous breasts."

"Hey, don't get me wrong, I'm sure they're nice and all. It's just that they would be even nicer if there were a little bit more of them there to love. There's nothing wrong with breast implants, you know. Nowadays they can make them look and feel just like the real thing. Hey, if you had gotten breast implants in high school, we'd probably still be a couple," Danny remarked.

This time it was Niki who felt like screaming, but Jean attempted to calm the situation. "So you're a breast man?"

"Look, I appreciate the whole package. There's nothing wrong with a great set of legs and a shapely ass, but if you want to have the whole package, you've got to have a great set of boobs included, and where that's concerned, the bigger the better," Danny opined.

Jean was seething inside, but decided to bite her tongue. *I'll be putting him to sleep soon enough,* Jean thought to herself. "We should discuss this more later. I'm always interested in hearing about what it is that really turns a man on."

It was after they had paid the toll to get onto the New Jersey Turnpike that Jean decided it was time for Danny's nap. She reached into her pocketbook and pulled out a tightly sealed plastic sandwich bag, inside of which was a small rag soaked with chloroform. Jean opened the bag slowly and reached her hand in for the rag. As she did so, she heard Danny sniffing like a dog at a barbecue, his head swiveling from side to side with his nose in the air.

"What the hell is that smell? It smells like a freaking hospital in here."

Niki turned her head toward Danny, but looked at Jean out of the corner of her eye and saw that Jean was about to make her move. "This *is* the New Jersey Turnpike. You're liable to smell anything out here," Niki remarked, trying to get Danny to look her way.

Jean leaned forward and started to wrap her right arm around Danny's head, but Danny followed the scent behind him, and with a quizzical look started to turn his neck further to the left toward Jean in the backseat. When his neck was almost fully turned, Danny was surprised that he still could not see Jean. Jean had been forced to lean forward further and further in order to wrap her arm far enough around to reach Danny's face as it continued to turn toward the backseat. The further Jean reached, the further Danny's neck and body turned to try to find Jean.

Finally, Jean was able to get her hand and the rag over Danny's nose and mouth. As she did so, she pulled hard, snapping Danny's head forward again. Then she felt Danny's hands fly up against her arm trying to force her hand off of his face. Jean squeezed harder, pulling Danny's head tightly into her shoulder.

At the sight of Danny struggling to free himself from Jean's grip, Niki reached with her right hand and tried to pull Danny's hands down off Jean's arm. Niki lost control of the car momentarily, causing it to swerve across three lanes, narrowly missing several cars in the process. Eventually, they both felt the fight slipping out of Danny O'Brien. His arms fell to his sides, his neck slumped to the right and his body went limp. Jean let loose her grip, and Danny's head thumped against the passenger side window.

"Thanks for the help, but there is no way I was going to let go of his head once I got hold of it. I haven't been lifting all of those weights just to look good, you know," Jean crowed as she flung her left forearm upward and flexed her biceps.

Darkness was setting in as the girls exited the turnpike and started across the Geothals Bridge into Staten Island. When they stopped to pay the toll on the Staten Island side of the bridge, the female toll collector noticed Danny slumped against the passenger side window. She stooped to get a better look.

"Men!" Niki exclaimed when she saw the toll collector eyeing

Danny suspiciously. "They can sleep anywhere. You'd think he just had sex or something."

The toll collector blurted out a laugh as she handed Niki her change.

At the warehouse, the two discussed the difficulties that they had dragging Peter Sizemore's body into the building the last time, and they opted instead to get the old wheeled office chair from inside the building to roll Danny's limp body in on. They pulled Danny's body out of the car and propped him up in the chair, his head hanging backward and his arms dangling off either side. His heels bounced along the ground as they quickly but cautiously pulled the chair to the door of the warehouse.

Once inside the building, Niki aimed the chair toward the same column to which they had tied Peter Sizemore exactly one year earlier, but Jean tugged the chair toward the old desk that sat just opposite the pillar. "This way. I told you, I have something special planned."

With Jean leading the way, the girls hoisted Danny's body onto the desk, with his head at one end and his legs hanging off of the other. Danny's arms were splayed, hanging off either side of the desk down toward the floor. Once she was certain that Danny's body was resting securely on top of the desk, Jean went to work hurriedly removing his clothes, like a hungry child unwrapping a candy bar.

When she finally pulled his shorts off, Jean seemed somewhat disappointed. "He's not exactly a big man. I mean it's average . . . I guess . . . at least, from my experience, but for someone so obsessed with breast size, I thought he was going to be huge."

"The size is only average," Niki agreed. "But personally I kind of like it. It's nicely cut. The obstetrician that did the circumcision did a nice job."

"I guess you do like it. You did let him put it in your mouth as I recall," Jean chuckled.

"Yeah, but he's not the last one to have done that, and I haven't liked them all as much as I like his. I guess it's like he said, your first one is always a little special."

After they finished inspecting and discussing Danny's physical attributes, good and bad, Jean went to work tying him to the table. First, she secured his ankles to the legs of the desk on one end, then she tied his wrists to the legs on either side of the other end of the desk. Then Jean took another much longer piece of the same cord and started running it over the top of Danny's naked body, down the side of the desk, under the desk, up the other side and over the body again and again, taking a different angle each time. When she was done, Danny looked like a fly trapped in a spider's web.

Niki watched, amused by the seriousness with which Jean went about her work, wondering where all of the preparation was leading. Niki couldn't help but ponder what else Jean had in store for the unfortunate male creature who remained out cold, so far oblivious to what was happening to him. Niki's curiosity only grew when Jean raced out to the car and came back loaded down with an armful of accessories, including something that looked like an automobile battery, except with knobs on it. Jean also had a long electrical cable that was split at either end and looked somewhat like a battery jumper cable. Hanging around Jean's neck was a large, black, strap-on dildo.

"Can we wake him now?" Niki asked impatiently.

"Yeah, but first step into this," Jean instructed Niki as she spread open the harness to which the rubber manhood was attached.

"What in the world do you plan on me doing with this thing?" Niki wondered as she pulled the harness up and Jean tightened it around Niki's waist.

"You'll see soon enough, but don't tell me that you don't already feel empowered just by putting it on," Jean teased, smiling admiringly down at the enormous artificial organ.

Niki thrust her hips to the right and then back to the left, watching the dildo bounce back and forth with each twist of her hips. "It does kind of make me feel more threatening."

Jean reached into her bag and came out with several small, white tabs. She placed one under Danny's nose and cracked it open. A strong smell of ammonia filled the immediate area. A second later, Danny's head started to rock from side to side and then his eyes popped opened and immediately filled with a look of alarm.

"What happened? Did we have an accident or something?" a dumfounded Danny asked as he tried to make sense of the predicament in which he found himself.

"Nothing that has happened so far has been an accident," Jean said sarcastically. "Are you still feeling groggy, honey?"

"Yeah, a little," Danny responded, still trying to make sense of what was going on.

"We can't have that now," Jean commented as she cracked a second ammonia tab under Danny's nose, causing him to whip his head back as far as he could under the circumstances.

Finally, Danny realized the full seriousness of the situation, looking down to see that he was naked as the day he was born and his entire body, other than his groin area, was entwined with nylon cord. He attempted to move his arms first and then his legs but found that he was totally immobilized. "What the hell is this Niki, some kind of sick joke or something? Is this some kind of bizarre way of getting even because I dumped you? Get over it for crap's sake. Knock it off and cut me loose."

"It's like I told you, I felt as if I owed you a new experience. I'll bet you've never done anything like this before. Aren't you having fun yet, baby?" Niki taunted.

"Okay, I guess I don't have much choice but to go along with your twisted little game. Let's get on with it. The sooner we can get it over with, the sooner I can get the hell out of here, go home, and get you out of my life again," Danny snarled, looking down and for the first time seeing the strap-on hanging between Niki's legs.

"I'm afraid that you are not going home from here, Danny. You *will*, however, be going to visit with a friend of yours," Jean noted cryptically as she worked her way between Danny's legs, uncoiling a length of electrical cable as she made her way.

"What is your *sicko* friend talking about, Niki?" Danny asked, imagining what the cable might be for and beginning to worry as possibilities came to mind.

"Didn't you ever wonder where Pete Sizemore disappeared to, Danny?" Niki asked. "I'm sure you must have. After all, it was the talk of the whole school last year during graduation. Well, my *sicko* friend and I know exactly where Peter is, and very soon you are going to be joining him there. You see, Danny, this time I'm going to use you for my pleasure, and when I'm through I'm going to be the one doing the dumping. Only when I dump you, it's not going be just figuratively speaking. I'm going to literally dump your dead ass into the river."

Danny turned pale and began to sweat. He felt dizzy and nauseated, as if he were about to faint. He knew that if Niki and Jean were responsible for Peter Sizemore's disappearance and they had shared that information with him, there was no way that they were going to let him out of his binds alive. He tried desperately to pull his arms and legs free but could not budge any of them. He wriggled his body in every direction, hoping to loosen the cords around his mid-section, but he was unable to do so. Danny O'Brien finally resigned himself to his inevitable fate, knowing full well that at that point neither reasoning nor begging for mercy was going to do him any good.

"Straddle his neck," Jean instructed Niki, after they had finished watching with amusement Danny's futile attempt to set himself free. "Let's see how good he sucks a cock."

Niki followed Jean's order and climbed onto the desk. She sat on Danny's neck and pointed the strap-on at Danny's mouth. "Suck it, baby. Suck it good. Isn't that the way you said it to me, honey?"

Danny, however, was suddenly defiant. "Yeah, that's the way I said it. The difference is, unlike you, I'm no cock sucker. You're not putting that thing in my mouth the way I put mine in yours. You see, if you're going to kill me anyway, what incentive do I have to cooperate. You're not having any more fun at my expense, so you might as well just get it over with."

"Did he say that he needed some incentive to cooperate?" Jean asked through a laugh. "Let's see if I can think of a proper incentive." Then she took the electrical cable and attached it to the battery-like object that now sat below her, between Danny's feet. The other end of the cable was split into three separate wires, and at the end of each wire was a large alligator clip.

Jean took one of the clips and attached it to the head of Danny's penis. Danny squirmed and screamed at first, but the longer the clip remained on his organ the less it seemed to hurt. After several seconds, Jean took each of the other clips and secured them to each of Danny's testicles. The pain was severe, and Danny screamed in agony. The pain in his testicles did not lessen with time, and Danny's screaming did not lessen either.

"You sick fucks! You fucking whores!" Danny wailed.

"Still not cooperating I see. Let's try to give you a little more incentive," Jean taunted as she bent down and turned one of the knobs on the piece of equipment beneath her.

Niki looked down in amazement as the stream of electricity pulsed into Danny's genitalia. She could even feel a slight current of electricity entering into her own body through Danny. His body shook uncontrollably beneath her, causing her to have to hold on to Danny's shoulders in order to avoid falling off him. She rode him like a cowboy on a bucking bronco. The pupils in Danny's eyes rolled up into the top of his head, so that only the whites were showing. Danny's face turned a deep red, almost purple. The veins in his neck and temples swelled as if about to burst. His mouth clamped shut, and his face contorted into a bizarre grimace. He no longer looked like Danny O'Brien. He no longer even looked like a human being.

After several seconds, Jean reached down and cut off the flow of electricity. She made her way up alongside of Danny just as his body started to relax back into a somewhat normal state. With a satisfied expression, Jean looked down into Danny's eyes just as his pupils rolled back downward. "Now, how is it you like it said? Suck it, baby. Suck it good."

Danny felt life coming back into his body, but the pain in his testicles was still severe. He also had a severe burning sensation in his tongue, and he could taste his own blood as it began to fill his mouth. Danny realized that he had bitten the end of his tongue off when his mouth clamped shut. Despite the pain, a sense of fury raced through him. He looked up at Jean who was standing over him looking down into his eyes. Danny took all of his remaining strength and spit a mouthful of blood upward into Jean's face. The tip of Danny's tongue stuck on Jean's cheek momentarily before she wiped it off nonchalantly.

When Jean headed back to the power source, Danny realized the bad judgment in what he had chosen to do. "No, please no, I'm sorry. Really, please, not again. I'll suck it. Look, I'm sucking it," Danny pleaded as best he could with the tip of his tongue gone as he grabbed the end of the dildo into his mouth.

But Jean was not appeased. She let loose with another longer burst of electricity, causing Danny to go through the same gyrations with his body and contortions with his face. The only difference this time was that instead of biting off any more of his tongue, Danny's teeth clamped down into the thick rubber sex toy, putting the impression of his teeth around the entire thing.

Jean finally cut the power, and after several seconds Danny's body relaxed again. When his senses returned to him, he willingly sucked on the strap-on rather than risk another jolt of electricity. Niki grabbed a clump of Danny's hair in order to keep his head in place.

"Let me know if he stops cooperating. There's plenty more incentive down here if he needs it," Jean mocked, easing herself down between Danny's legs.

In time, Danny seemed to lose pretty much all sensation in his genitals. He was not certain, but he thought that he felt Jean removing the clips from his penis and gonads. Afterward, he felt a slight pinch in one testicle and then the other, but after what he had been through and given the numbness that had set in, the pinches did not faze him.

After a brief period, Jean emerged from between Danny's legs. He still had the strap-on in his mouth when she approached him smiling, her hands behind her back. "Let's see if you can guess what these are," Jean razzed as she took her hands out from behind her back and raised them in the air.

Between the index finger and thumb of each hand Jean held what Danny thought looked like little pink pigeon eggs. Still shaken from his ordeal, it took Danny several seconds to understand at what he was looking. When it finally hit him, his eyes rolled back up into his head, and he blacked out without saying a word.

"He's gone into shock," Jean noted. "I'll get some more ammonia tabs."

Niki reached down and placed the index and middle fingers of her right hand against the side of Danny's neck. "He's not in shock. He's dead. He doesn't have a pulse."

"Removing his testicles shouldn't have killed him," Jean offered as they cut Danny free and began securing the cinder blocks to his body.

"I guess with the electrical shock and all the excitement it was just too much for his heart," Niki surmised.

They loaded Danny's body onto the base of one of the garment racks and after checking the area, rolled him out to the river. As they plopped him onto the edge of the bulkhead, Danny's head came down hard on a metal spike. He let out a low moan.

"He's not dead!" Niki exclaimed.

"Well, he will be soon enough. Say hello to Peter for us," Jean taunted as she shoved Danny's body off the bulkhead and into the inky water.

"Just as well, I'm about ready to try this thing out on you," Niki remarked, thrusting her hips and watching the dildo still attached to her groin flop back and forth between her legs.

"Right after we shower and eat," Jean responded. "I'm starving, and I have a great new sauce for you to try."

CHAPTER 5

BEAUTY AND THE GHOST
JUNE 16, 2003

Penny's left eye struggled open first. The right eye remained glued shut, still smooshed into one of her king-sized pillows. Her body was curled in a fetal position, her other pillow squeezed tight between her knees with her arms wrapped around the top of it, pulling it to her breasts and belly. She was face to face with the digital radio clock that sat on the end table next to her bed. When her vision cleared and Penny focused in on the numbers on the clock, she bolted upright.

"Nine o'clock? It can't be nine o'clock," Penny said out loud as she attempted to shake the sleep from her head.

Penny Albright had not slept beyond six o'clock in the morning in more than twelve years. Rising early was one of several habits Penny had picked up from her stays with Aunt Brit. Aunt Brit was the second youngest of the O'Malley sisters, the closest in age to Penny's mom. A sun-worshiper, Brit took a vacation to Key West, Florida when she was in her in mid-twenties. She loved the area so much that she returned to New York only long enough to pack her things into her aging Volkswagen Beetle before she headed south again. Brit got a job tending bar and eventually managing a waterfront bar and grill, frequented primarily by Jimmy Buffet disciples. Later she bought a small house that was walking distance to both the bar and the beach.

For Penny, stays with Aunt Brit were like extended vacations, except for the fact that there was no sleeping late permitted in Aunt Brit's house. "Early to rise, early to shine." "The early bird catches the worm." If there was a trite saying having anything to do with the benefits of getting out of bed early, Aunt Brit knew it and repeated it often. After a while, Penny did not need any help from Aunt Brit in getting up early. Penny learned to love the quiet time of the early morning hours while most of the world was still in bed, stress free moments during which she could exercise and contemplate the world and her place in it, free from interruption.

After a few seconds of dazed thought, it hit Penny why it was that she had slept so late. The events of the night before rushed back into her mind, and she immediately spun her head and body in the direction of East 80th Street and the antique writing desk that sat at the window. When she did so, the confusion set back in. The Ouija Board that Penny was certain she had left on the desk the night before was gone.

Penny jumped out of bed and rushed to the desk, desperately searching for the notes that she was certain she had made in the early morning hours before she went back to sleep. They were not there. Penny pulled the drawer in the desk open and found the Ouija Board neatly put away. The pad that she had used for her notes was sitting in the same corner of the desk drawer from where Penny had taken it the night before, but the pieces of paper with Penny's notes on them were gone. She frantically rummaged through the rest of the room, looked around and under the desk, through the garbage pail that sat alongside of the desk and even under the bed, but the notes were not there.

Penny immediately headed into the bathroom that abutted the master bedroom. She splashed water on her face and looked at herself in the mirror that sat above the bathroom sink. "You're losing your mind, kid. You actually thought you had a conversation with a ghost for crying out loud," Penny said to her reflection. "Now get a hold of yourself. It was just a dream. A vivid dream, but it's not the first lucid dream that you've had in this house. Go back into the bedroom, do your yoga and calm yourself down."

Yoga every morning upon rising was another of the habits that Penny had picked up from Aunt Brit. Aunt Brit was a fitness fanatic with a sun-bronzed body that was as tight as a drum to show for it. She did an hour of yoga, actually a sweaty aerobic form of Ashtanga Yoga that Brit referred to as Power Yoga, every morning. She did a five-mile jog early every evening. Even as a young girl, Penny envied Aunt Brit's discipline and healthy attitude toward her body and mind. By the time she was fifteen, Penny started mimicking Brit's fitness routine. As she aged, Penny grew to appreciate both the yoga and long distance running more for the meditative opportunities that each offered than for their physical benefits. It wasn't long before Penny was as religious about her exercise pattern as was Aunt Brit.

Penny dried her face and made her way back into the bedroom where she pulled an exercise mat out from under her bed. She slipped off her cotton pajama top and stepped out of her panties before she started stretching. Penny always did her yoga sans cloths, something else that she had picked up from Aunt Brit. Aunt Brit was a devout nudist, a naturist is actually what she called herself, but Penny never really understood the difference. What Penny did understand was that

Aunt Brit felt no shame in her often naked body. Aunt Brit frequented a local nude beach whenever time permitted, loved to swim and sunbathe nude in and around her own mostly hidden backyard pool, and she almost never wore clothes around the house.

It took Penny some time, but before long she found herself growing more and more comfortable, not only with Aunt Brit's nudity, but with her own nakedness. Penny never went to the nude beach with Aunt Brit, but like Aunt Brit, Penny preferred her yoga in the morning without cloths. She frequently skinny-dipped in the backyard pool, finding it uniquely refreshing. Occasionally, Penny even spent time roaming around the house in nothing but her birthday suit, finding it incredibly liberating. Where she parted ways with Aunt Brit was, when the doorbell rang Penny headed for cover. In contrast, Aunt Brit thought nothing of answering the door stark naked, regardless of who was or might be on the other side. Friday night was pizza night at the O'Malley house, and the rumor was that the two delivery boys from the local pizzeria regularly had fistfights to see which one would get the O'Malley delivery.

When she finished her workout, Penny toweled her naked body dry and slipped on her pajama top before starting for the stairs to the kitchen. She reminisced about how in times gone by when she finished her exercise and headed downstairs Aunt Mags would always have a frosty cold glass of water waiting for her, followed by a steaming cup of fresh brewed coffee and toasted cinnamon bread slathered with butter. Like Mags, Penny loved her morning coffee with cinnamon bread, toasted until it was almost burnt and then saturated in butter. The butter, she felt, was a reward for the hard work that preceded it.

At the top of the stairs, Penny imagined that she could actually smell the coffee brewing and the cinnamon bread toasting in the toaster. By the middle of the stairs, Penny realized that her mind was not playing tricks on her. The smell of freshly brewed coffee and cinnamon bread toasting was, in fact, wafting up the stairs from the kitchen below.

Sol? Penny thought to herself as she reached the bottom of the stairs. *But how in the world could he have gotten in?*

At the bottom of the stairs, instead of turning for the kitchen, Penny made her way to the front entrance and attempted to turn the doorknob, but it was still locked and would not budge. She looked up and saw that the bolt locks and chain were still securely in place.

"Sol, is that you?" Penny called out, as she inched her way down the hallway toward the kitchen door.

For a second, Penny wished that she had bothered to put her panties on before coming downstairs. At the entranceway to the kitchen, Penny called out Sol's name again before she leaned her upper body through the doorway into the kitchen and peered to her right, seeing no one. She then turned her head to the left, still without putting her whole body through the doorway. Again, there was no one there, but when Penny looked toward the stove, she saw that the coffee pot she had left in the drainer next to the sink the day before now sat atop of a lit burner on the stove. Coffee was percolating up into the clear glass bubble that sat atop the pot. The cup that Penny had used the preceding afternoon and left in the drainer along with the coffee pot, sat in the middle of the stove between two sets of burners.

Penny hesitated before making her way into the kitchen. After she assured herself that burglars don't break into homes in order to have coffee and cinnamon bread toast, Penny entered the kitchen and made her way cautiously to the stove. *Each of the O'Malley sisters have keys,* Penny remembered. *One of them must have gotten in and locked the door behind them. Maybe she's downstairs in the bookstore,* Penny supposed as she started to pour herself a cup of coffee.

Reaching for the cup, Penny realized that beneath it was a small piece of white paper, the same shape and size as the paper she had written her notes on the night before. Penny lifted the cup and immediately recognized her own printing. The name KERBY was printed above the name BREWSTER in the center of the paper.

A shudder was still in the process of running up Penny's back and into her neck when a loud metallic sound rang out from behind her. Frightened by the noise, Penny jumped and twirled her body around just in time to see two darkly toasted pieces of cinnamon bread explode upward out of Aunt Mags's old metal toaster and then drop back down into their slots.

Penny moved directly toward the toaster and on her way saw that a butter plate with a bright yellow stick of butter sitting on it was resting next to the toaster, as if it had been waiting for the toast to pop. When Penny reached the counter on which the toaster and butter plate were sitting, she saw that beneath the butter plate was a second piece of white paper. She lifted the plate and was again confronted by her own printing. In the center of the paper the word SÉANCE was printed.

Penny found herself backing away from the counter and the paper, not wanting to believe what she had just seen. Before she could stop herself, Penny backed into the kitchen table. Without looking, she reached behind her for a chair, turned her body around, and plopped herself down into it. Penny felt faint as she rested her head in her hands. She decided that she needed something drink. When she brought her head up from her hands, Penny saw that sitting in the middle of the table was a tall glass of ice water, just like Mags used to greet her with.

After gulping the water down and settling her nerves, Penny finished pouring herself a cup of coffee and nibbled at a piece of buttered cinnamon toast. *If Kerby Brewster was murdered and buried under the brownstone, it had to have been done before the house was built,* Penny reasoned. *But when was the brownstone built?* Penny had no idea, but she knew that the deed to the property would have all of the information that she needed, and she also knew that Mags kept all of her important papers in an old chest in the attic.

Penny decided to take a shower before starting her search for the deed. She concluded that if she found the deed and could put an approximate sate on Kerby Brewster's death, she would spend the afternoon in the New York Public Library searching old newspapers to see whether Kerby Brewster's disappearance had made the press.

With her game plan set in her mind, Penny eagerly darted up the stairs, taking them two at time, and then raced through the bedroom, flinging her pajama top off as she made her way into the bathroom. Penny's fear had turned to fascination as she opened the clear glass door to the shower stall and turned on the water. After getting the temperature just perfect, Penny stepped under the flow of hot water, thoroughly enjoying its warmth on her naked body as she considered the possibilities. She stepped out from under the water and lathered her entire body thoroughly before stepping back under the water and rinsing the soap off. Once out of the shower, Penny toweled herself dry in front of the bathroom's full length mirror, admiring the results of her years of rigid exercise. Finally, she wrapped the towel around her body and put her hair up in a second towel as she headed toward the bedroom.

As she made her way by the makeup counter into which the bathroom sink was set, Penny felt a draft of chilled air sweep over her body. She had a sudden sense of being watched. Penny stepped back from the counter, and the cool air seemed to gradually warm again. She stepped toward the counter again, and it again felt as if someone had opened a refrigerator door with Penny standing in front of it. Penny stuck out her arm and ran it through the area above the counter where the air seemed to be the coolest. She did not know it, but Penny Albright had just waved her hand right through the mid-section of Kerby Brewster, who had been sitting on the counter admiring the beauty of Penny's naked body throughout the time that she had been in the shower.

Penny started to exit the bathroom, but stopped suddenly and turned toward the cool spot sitting on top of the counter. "Mr. Brewster!" Penny exclaimed. "You should be ashamed of yourself."

In the bedroom, Penny thought back to the contortions that she had put her nude body through earlier that morning during her yoga session. *Oh, my goodness! Could he have been in here while I was doing my yoga?* Penny wondered. She tried to recall whether there had been any cold spots in the room that morning, but there had been none. Kerby Brewster had been downstairs throughout the workout preparing breakfast. *Note to self,* Penny thought, *buy a leotard.*

After checking her bedroom for cold spots, Penny dressed and headed up to the attic. She found Mags's old chest and worked through it until she found a folder marked "Brownstone." Penny began looking for the deed, but as she did so something else caught her eye. Apparently, in the eighties, Mags had filed papers with the city seeking permission to do some major renovations on the brownstone. The renovations primarily involved replacing the right front cornerstone of the building. Then, in 2002, right around the time that Mags would have found out about her cancer, she apparently sought permission from the city to demolish the brownstone entirely. *What in the world was she thinking?* Penny asked herself. *Mags loved this old house more than anything in the world. Why would she have wanted to tear it down?*

Finally, Penny found a copy of the deed for the brownstone. The original was with Mags's attorney who had arranged for the deed to be transferred to Penny's name before Mags's death. The copy of the deed that Penny found in the attic showed that construction of the building had been started on November 24, 1933 and completed on December 28, 1933. The original owner of the building was the construction company that built it, *D'arcy Construction.*

Initially, Penny decided that she would call Joie Miller and cancel their afternoon tea, but she ultimately concluded that a quick chat with Joie before heading down to the library might be helpful. Perhaps Joie could shed some light on Mags's efforts to renovate and later demolish the building. At the very least, Joie might be able to explain what happened with those plans. Nothing in the "Brownstone" folder indicated why the renovation and/or demolition were not carried out.

Penny called before heading over to Joie's place but got the answering machine. She left a message that she was following up on their tea date. Penny said that she would drop by in a few, and if Joie was not there or too busy for tea, Penny would catch up with her later. Walking out the front door, Penny heard her own phone ring, but she decided that, like everyone else in the world, she would let the answering machine get it. Penny stood at her front door and listened for the message. She heard Joie Miller's voice.

"I could never be too busy for your company, sweetie. *Mi casa es su casa.* The door is open, so let yourself in. Just don't be surprised by anything you might see in here. Mine is not your typical household, you know."

♥ ☒ ♣

Penny made her way over to Joie's house, and following Joie's instructions let herself in. Despite the many years that she had visited Mags, Penny had never been in Joie's home, and she was terribly curious to see what it looked like inside. An image of a dungeon, complete with all kinds of torture machines, swept through Penny's mind as she tentatively stepped through the entrance. Once inside, Penny was taken by surprise. There was no torture rack or Iron Lady in sight, but what really surprised Penny was that, though Mags's brownstone and Joie's brownstone were almost identical from the outside, they were totally different inside.

Joie's brownstone opened into a semicircular foyer with a winding stairway running up the left side of the hallway. There was a room to the left, another to the right and a third larger room straight ahead sitting beneath the winding staircase. Penny could see that the larger room was a library. At the far end of the library, Joie sat behind an enormous mahogany desk with a phone to her ear, looking much more like an executive than a dominatrix, despite the fact that she wore a tight-fitting, black leather dress.

Joie continued to talk on the telephone as she motioned for Penny to come into the library. Penny picked up her pace as she went through the library door, almost relieved to find that the home was far more conventional than she had expected, or rather feared. As she entered the library and started for a chair that sat in front of Joie's desk, the peripheral vision in Penny's right eye caught sight of something strange. She turned her head to try to make sense of what she saw.

Standing in the corner of the room facing the bookshelves was what at first appeared to Penny to be an extremely tall woman dressed in a French maid's outfit. As Penny scanned the individual's body further, she realized that the skimpy skirt to the outfit reached down only to about mid-behind. Penny saw that sticking out from under the bottom of the skirt was a very hairy, clearly masculine, ass. Looking down further, Penny saw two heavily muscled, also hairy, man legs clad in fishnet stockings. They were wobbling somewhat on a pair of stiletto heels.

Penny stopped in her tracks. "Uh . . . it looks as if you're awfully busy, Jo. I'll stop back later," Penny stammered as she started to back out of the library, trying not to look to her right again.

"Don't be silly, sweetie," Joie laughed, hanging up the telephone. "Don't worry about her," Joie continued, using a feminine pronoun to refer to the obviously masculine person in the corner. "She's totally harmless. She's been a naughty girl, and she's being punished. When she's done with her punishment, she's going to be serving us our tea. Aren't you, Sissy Maid?" Joie finished, her tone suddenly becoming harsher.

"Yes, Mistress," the guy in the corner said, nodding his head in agreement, his long blonde wig almost falling off his dome in the process.

"Look, sweetie, you're a big girl now. This shouldn't upset you. I want you to feel free to come and go here as you please. Like I said, *mi casa es su casa*. But this is the way I live my life, so you are going to have to get used to it. It took Mags a while, but I think it kind of grew on her."

"It's not *my* embarrassment I'm worried about," Penny said, in a hushed tone. "What about him? Isn't he going to be a little upset at the fact that you're sharing his most secret fantasies with the world?"

"Sweetie, when he enters my home, he sacrifices any rights he may have in the outside world. In here, he becomes my slave, my property, and he follows my every command. Anyway, what do you think this is all about? Do you think he gets off on just wearing women's clothes? If that was all there was to it, he could dress up in his own home and save several thousand dollars a month. He comes here because he longs to be humiliated. Your being here just adds to that humiliation. I may actually charge him double for this session because he's going to get to serve two Mistresses and suffer twice the humiliation," Joie laughed, acting as if her slave was not in the room, though he was clearly within earshot.

Joie then broke into a softer tone so that the submissive in the corner could not hear her. "By the way, I do respect his desire for anonymity. Look!" Joie said as she rang a small bell that was sitting on the corner of her desk.

Sissy Maid turned and started to wobble over to the desk on his too high heels. Penny saw for the first time that the submissive was wearing a mask that covered his face from the mouth up. Colored feathers decorated the top of the mask. Penny also noticed that the skimpy skirt did not cover any more in the front than it did in the rear. As Sissy Maid wobbled toward them, the lower end of his manhood swung back and forth like a fulcrum. When Penny realized what she was looking at, she immediately turned her gaze forward and stared Joie directly in the eyes, as if afraid that looking back might cause her to turn to stone.

Joie chuckled at Penny's embarrassment and then reached into a small wooden box that sat in the center of the desk. She took out a Lonsdale, a long thin desert cigar. "You mustn't be intimidated by that little thing," Joie whispered. "At least, don't let *her* know that you are," she continued, placing the tip of the Lonsdale into a silver cigar cutter and snipping off the end with a twitch of her index finger. Joie stared into Sissy Maid's eyes menacingly the entire time that she was decapitating the cigar.

At the desk, Sissy Maid immediately dropped to his knees in front of Joie without Joie saying a word. After several puffs on the cigar to get it going, Joie extended her hand with the cigar in it in Sissy Maid's direction. Again without a word from Joie, Sissy Maid stuck out his tongue and Joie flicked cigar ash onto it. Sissy Maid swallowed the ash.

"Thank you, Sissy Maid," Joie said sarcastically. "Now run and get our tea."

"I have to be honest, Jo, this is all interesting and everything, but it's making me a little uncomfortable, to say the least. Would it be all right if you excused him for a while after he serves the tea, so that we can talk without the distraction?"

"Sure, sweetie, like I said, it takes some getting used to, but once you stop judging him, and me for that matter, for enjoying something that doesn't fall into the world's view of what is normal, it really will start to grow on you. I mean, as long as it's two consenting adults involved, who is to say what is or is not normal. In the real world, the man behind that mask is the CEO of one of the largest publishing houses in the country. He has nearly a hundred people working under him, and he spends most days ordering those people around and making one stressful decision after another. When he enters my home, all of that stress is taken off him. He is not allowed to make a decision on his own here, and he certainly does not boss anyone around. I give the orders in my domain. He just obeys them without question."

After tea was served and Sissy Maid was excused from the room, Penny got down to business. "Jo, did you ever attend any of Mags's séances?"

"Certainly, sweetie, lots of times. They were fun, but Mags got upset if you called them séances. Over the years, with the discovery of all the frauds and everything, the term séance fell into disrepute, so Mags insisted that we call them *sittings,*" Joie recalled.

"Did anything strange ever happen? Did you ever see any apparitions or anything?" Penny wondered.

"Well, no and yes. No, I never saw any apparitions. Yes, lots of strange things happened. I mean, if strange things don't happen at a séance what's the point in having them. I wouldn't have kept going back for more if nothing unusual ever happened. I never did figure out how Mags did the things that she did, but she could make all kinds of eerie things happen, books flying off shelves, strange noises, odd smells, that kind of stuff. She even levitated a table once, and she had this way of making the room suddenly go chilly as if somebody switched on an air conditioner all of a sudden."

"How did Mags explain it?" Penny asked.

"Mags always kept a straight face. Like a good magician, she never gave up her secrets. Mags would just say it was her conduit to the afterlife, you know, her *Englishman.*"

"Did she ever give her *Englishman* a name or explain how she first came in contact with him?" Penny wondered.

"Mags never told me his name or why he supposedly chose her, but she swore that the first time she actually *saw* him was the first time she did a séance, I mean, a sitting, in the bookstore. He supposedly stayed with her from that point on."

"Did Mags ever say anything to you about doing any major renovations to the brownstone, or maybe even tearing it down?" Penny asked, changing the subject.

"Sol's the person you want to talk to about that, sweetie. I know that some time ago Mags wanted to rip up the right front cornerstone of her building, the one that abuts Sol's house. Sol had an architect come in, and the guy said that if they took out the cornerstone, it might cause the wall of Sol's brownstone to collapse. Sol was apparently ready to fight Mags tooth-and-nail to stop her, you know, take her to court if he needed to. It was the only time I ever saw them angry at each other. Before the fight heated up, Mags dropped the idea just as suddenly as she had come up with it. Then a little over a year ago, when Mags first found out about her cancer, I heard that she was thinking about trying to get permission from the city to tear the whole building down. She dropped that idea pretty quickly too, but I couldn't tell you why. After that, all she talked about was making sure that you got the brownstone," Joie recalled.

"Jo, would you think I was crazy if I told you I was going to have a séance? I mean would you come?"

"Well, sweetie, yes and yes. Yes, I would think you were crazy, you know, in good way, like Mags, and yes I would come. In fact, I wouldn't miss it for anything. It would be like old times."

♥ 💤 🕵

Penny called Sol on her cell phone from the steps of Joie's brownstone. Sol said he was in Harlem dropping off a fare and would be down in about ten minutes. Exactly ten minutes later, Sol pulled up in front of Penny's house. Penny was sitting on her steps waiting.

"You'll never guess who I just dropped off at Sylvia's Restaurant up in Harlem. Danny Glover," Sol said excitedly, without waiting for Penny to offer a guess. "You know, the black guy from the *Lethal Weapon* movies with Mel Gibson." Penny knew Danny Glover as Oprah Winfrey's mean husband in *The Color Purple.*

"A nice guy, really down to earth," Sol continued, before Penny could utter a word. "He's even bigger in real life than he looks in the movies. The only problem is, the guy kept complaining about cab drivers. He says we don't stop for black people, we won't go up Harlem. I told him I've been picking up black people and driving up to Harlem every day for as long as I've been in this business, never had a problem. When I owned my agency, we had a satellite office right in the middle of Harlem. I used to be up there all the time, never had a problem. So I gave him my cell phone number, and I said to him look, the next time you're in town and you know you're going to be needing a taxi, call me a little in advance, and I'll take you anywhere you want to go, no extra charge or anything like that. He said it's a deal, and he wrote my number down."

"Good afternoon, Sol," Penny interjected, when Sol finally stopped to take a breath.

"I'm sorry. Was I rambling?" Sol asked apologetically. "It's just that even in Manhattan it's kind of rare to get a famous actor in your cab, and usually when you do, they're all uppity and stuff. So when you get somebody famous, and he's like a real person and he treats you like you're a real person too, it's kind of exciting."

"Don't be silly. It was a great story," Penny said.

"Okay, so tell me where I can take you and then tell me about your day so far,"

"Well, I'd like to go to the New York Public Library. As far as my day, I had a nice, though somewhat bizarre, tea with Joie Miller."

"Get used to it, honey. Everything that has anything to do with Joie Miller is bizarre," Sol grumbled. "Now, I assume that when you say you want to go to the New York Public Library, you're talking about the big one, the Humanities and Social Sciences Library down in midtown, but why does someone who owns a bookstore want to be taken to a library?"

"I just need to do some research," Penny responded, before changing the subject. "Sol, Jo tells me that a while back you and Mags had somewhat of legal a battle about some renovations she wanted to have done to her brownstone. What was that all about?"

"That Joie Miller has one big mouth. It was nothing really, only lasted a couple of weeks or so. Mags came to see me one day and told me that she had filed some papers to get a permit to have the cornerstone on her house removed and the foundation underneath it dug up. I said no problem, but then I had an architect come in and look at the buildings. You know, my building's left wall abuts your building's right wall. The architect had some serious concerns. He said if the cornerstone of your building was removed and it wasn't done just perfectly, it would cause the wall of my building to settle, you know, sink, resulting in major structural damage and maybe even a total collapse. Well, you know how much I love that old building, so I told Mags that if she couldn't give me a damned good reason for what she wanted to do, I intended to hire a lawyer to stop her.

"Mags came back to me with this nutty, metaphysical response. She told me that all she could reveal was that she was trying to help a dear friend get to Heaven, and that this was the only way to do it. She wouldn't tell me what the heck she was talking about or who this friend was or anything like that, so I said, 'I guess I'll see you in court.'

"Mags didn't speak to me for two weeks, and then she came over to tell me that she'd withdrawn her papers. She said that she had gone over it again and again with this dear friend whom she was trying to get to Heaven, and he said that he'd rather stay in limbo than damage our relationship. To this day, I still don't know what the heck it was really all about, but thankfully it didn't hurt my relationship with Mags at all. In fact, neither of us ever mentioned it again, and it probably would never have been mentioned again if it wasn't for Joie Miller's big mouth."

"Actually, I was going through some of Mags's old papers and found out about it myself," Penny replied. "I was the one who mentioned it to Joie first. Did you know that shortly before her death Mags considered demolishing the whole building?"

"Sure I did, but before I could investigate, the city apparently told Mags that all of these brownstones are in a historic district. She couldn't have taken hers down even if there were no objections. As soon as she found out there was no way she would be allowed to knock the building down, getting the building to you became the most important thing in the world to her, even more important it seemed than fighting her cancer."

"Would you think I was crazy if I asked you to attend a séance with me?" Penny asked.

"I'm not sure. Have you invited the shrew next door?"

"Of course! It's not as if I know that many people in the neighborhood, at least, not people I would invite to a séance anyway."

"I guess, as a favor to you, I'd come," Sol said, acting as if he were reluctant only because Joie Miller was going to be there, but Penny felt like there was more to it. She thought that maybe, just maybe, the fact that Joie was going to be there was really the motivating factor for Sol's acceptance of the invitation.

Sol pulled his cab up to the main entrance to the library on Fifth Avenue. "I'm not certain how long this is going to take," Penny noted. "I don't want to inconvenience you any more than I already have. I'll take the subway home."

"Not on your life," Sol responded quickly. "I'll pull the cab around the corner and find somewhere to sit. I'm in the middle of Raymond Chandler's *The Big Sleep*. You know, one of his novels with Private Eye Phillip Marlowe as the main character. I'll read a couple of chapters while I'm waiting. Just ring me when you're almost done."

Penny jumped out of the cab and started up the steps between the two massive stone lions that flank the stairway leading into the library. She ran directly between two Con Edison workers in yellow hardhats who sat on the stairs munching on sandwiches and drinking beer out of cans hidden in brown paper bags. Their heads turned in unison as Penny ran between them.

"You're bouncing pretty good there, honey," one remarked, eyeing Penny's breasts heaving up and down with each step.

"You got some legs there, girly," the other commented, never looking up higher than Penny's bare thighs.

Penny ignored them both and continued up the steps and into the library. Inside the building, Penny waited in line to go through the metal detector. As she was clearing the metal detector, Penny asked the guard at the entrance if there was a computer room in which she might be able to research information in old newspapers.

"I don't think we're quite that advanced yet, lady," the guard responded. "Try Microfiche Room 100. They might be able to help you," he continued, directing Penny down a cavernous corridor at the end of which was the microfiche room.

Once inside the room, Penny found not computers, but rows of file cabinets and old fashion projectors that needed to be turned by hand. She made her way down one of the rows of file cabinets and saw that each of the cabinets had a small sign sitting atop it identifying the newspapers that were in that cabinet. Each of the long thin drawers in the cabinets had dates on them indicating the dates for the newspapers within them. Penny chose the cabinet marked *New York Times* and the drawer for the year 1933. Inside of the drawer, Penny found several reels of microfiche, each labeled by date. She took the reel covering the period from September 1933 through December 1933 and made her way to one of the canopied projectors.

Penny placed the reel onto the spool and started to spin the reel by hand. She looked carefully through the true news sections and spun quickly through the other sections, including the sports and entertainment sections, that is, until she caught a glimpse of something in the entertainment section of one of the papers that demanded her attention. Penny reeled slowly backward until she reached the page that had caught her eye. She sat in awed silence staring at the paper. It wasn't anything directly related to Kerby Brewster that caught Penny's eye. Rather, Penny found herself staring directly into the face of a woman who looked exactly like a slightly older version of herself. The lady had the same eyes, same hair, same smile, even the identical body type.

When she looked down at the caption beneath the photograph, Penny was staggered. The caption identified the woman as actress Helen Rose. It indicated that Helen Rose would be returning to the

New York stage for the first time in years to play the lead in a stage version of *Diamond Lil,* the play originally made famous by Mae West before she became a movie star. Penny asked the librarian at the desk for instructions on how to copy the photograph and caption before she renewed her search for information on the disappearance of Kerby Brewster.

After almost an hour of spinning the reels and reading some portion of every article that had anything to do with a missing person, Penny found the article she had been searching for. When she finished reading the article, Penny was almost sorry that she had found it. The headline read, "Local Private Eye Attacks Famed Builder and Wife, Disappears with Fortune."

The article indicated that according to respected construction magnate, Patrick D'arcy, he had his wife approach Brewster with a request that Brewster hand deliver $200,000 in cash to a business associate of D'arcy's in Miami, Florida. According to the article, Brewster initially accepted the offer to act as courier, but later that evening when he met with D'arcy and his wife to pick up the cash, Brewster apparently decided that the fee offered for transporting the money was not nearly as attractive as the money in hand. Brewster allegedly attacked D'arcy and his wife, causing severe injuries to both. To add insult to injury, after knocking Patrick D'arcy unconscious, Brewster allegedly sexually assaulted Mrs. D'arcy before she finally fought him off. Police photographs of Patrick and Renata D'arcy confirmed the severity of the beatings, and a medical examination confirmed the sexual assault. Despite an intense manhunt, neither Brewster nor the money had been found. The article further indicated that D'arcy had offered a $20,000 reward for any information regarding the whereabouts of Kerby Brewster or the missing $200,000.

A flood of emotions ran through Penny as she read the article. At first, she just felt a major sense of disappointment. Penny was really looking forward to the séance and being face to face with a real ghost, at least, when she thought that the ghost was going to be a charming and witty gentleman. Based on the article, however, this ghost was none of that. This ghost was a violent thief, and worse, a rapist. When those words ran through Penny's mind, the disappointment turned to fear. If Kerby Brewster was everything that the newspaper portrayed him as being, Penny was living in a house haunted by a violent rapist. What she needed, she thought, was not a séance but rather an exorcism.

Penny's fear turned to confusion when she started to think about how much Mags cared for this ghost, how she told everyone that he was charming and sweet, how she was prepared to destroy her beloved brownstone because she apparently thought it might be a way to release Kerby Brewster's soul to Heaven. *Sure, Mags could have been conned,* Penny thought. *But why would a ghost feel the need to con anyone?* More important, though Penny had only been in the presence of the spirit of Kerby Brewster for a short period of time, she felt certain that the person she had met when she was only eighteen years old was not capable of doing the things that the newspaper alleged.

Penny had the article copied and spent another hour looking for any follow-ups, but she found no further mention of the disappearance of Kerby Brewster. As she stood on the steps of the library dialing Sol's cell phone number, Penny made up her mind. She would have her séance, or sitting, or whatever the proper word was, and she would confront this ghost with the allegations against him. After all, what alternative was there? It was not as if she could just ignore him, even if she wanted to. Penny hoped that Kerby Brewster would have the right answers to her questions.

"Sol, did Mags ever mention someone by the name of Kerby Brewster to you?" Penny asked, after she had settled herself into her seat in the cab.

"Nope," Sol answered.

"Have you ever heard of a guy named Pat D'arcy? He was apparently a mogul in the construction business in the city back in the twenties and thirties."

"Sure, Irish Pat D'arcy built the brownstone you're living in, mine and Joie's too. But construction wasn't what got Irish Pat D'arcy his reputation. Irish Pat was a big-time mobster in his day. He made a ton of money as a bootlegger before prohibition. He died sometime in the mid-thirties, a gruesome death as I recall. He apparently asked his wife for a divorce, and she woke him up the following morning with a pot of boiling hot olive oil right in the face. He never made it to the hospital. She did though, the court found her innocent by reason of insanity. She spent the rest of her life in an upstate hospital for the criminally insane."

Of course, the lease showed "D'arcy Construction" as the builder and first owner of the brownstone, Penny remembered. *But if Kerby Brewster disappeared with Pat D'arcy's money on November 23, 1933, how did he wind up under a D'arcy Construction project that was started on November 24, 1933?* Penny wondered.

♥ ☒ ♣

Penny scheduled the séance for ten o'clock Friday night. She was not certain how long the séance would take, and she did not want to risk keeping anyone up late during the workweek. Penny invited Carmella Garcia to be the fourth person in the séance, only because Penny's understanding was that everyone had to be holding hands, and she didn't think that three people would be able to stretch their arms around any of the reading tables in the library.

Penny knew Carmella because she had worked for Mags in the bookstore off and on for several years while Penny was growing up. In fact, Penny's real reason for calling Carmella was to see whether she might be interested in working in the bookstore again. It was only after Carmella had accepted the job offer that Penny extended the invitation to the séance. Carmella was not crazy about the thought of trying to contact the spirit world and probably would not have accepted the invitation had she not felt indebted to Penny for the job.

As if provided by the special effects people on a horror movie set, an intense thunderstorm, complete with a torrential downpour and frequent lightning strikes, hit the metropolitan area just in time for the séance. Sol, Penny, and Carmella were already sitting at one of the reading tables in the library when Joie walked in, fashionably late, wearing a black latex raincoat and matching hat.

"I'm soaked," Joie complained, ripping off her hat and shaking out her hair.

"How wet could you have gotten?" Sol asked sarcastically. "You came from six feet away."

"Wet enough dear," Joie replied. "Would you like to run and get me a towel? I'll let you dry my feet for me."

"Feet? I thought your kind had hooves," Sol countered.

"Now that you two have said your hellos, perhaps we should get started with this thing," Penny interrupted, turning out the lights and lighting candles in the center of the table that she had chosen for the sitting. With the lights out, the regular flashes of lightning became that much more intense, lighting up the room with each strike. As the group quieted to set the mood for the séance, the sound of the sheets of rain pounding down onto the pavement outside of the bookstore seemed that much louder.

"Now, my understanding is that we have to sit around the table and hold hands," Penny started. "But if Mags went about this in a different way, let me know."

"Sounds right to me," Sol recalled as he sat down and extended his hand toward Joie. "Oops, I think I'd rather be on the other side" he said, when he realized whom he had sat next to.

"It's all right, honey. It's what they call a Freudian slip. You're really right where you want to be. I won't bite you, at least not too hard anyway," Joie teased.

"No thanks. I don't want to catch anything, and I didn't bring my rubber gloves with me," Sol replied, while making his way to a spot between Penny and Carmella.

"Rubber? Is that what turns you on, dear? If I had known that I would have left my raincoat on for you," Joie laughed.

"If you two wouldn't mind calling a truce for a few minutes, we can get started," Penny interrupted the exchange, extending her right hand to Joie on one side and her left hand to Sol on the other.

"You know sunthin, Miss Albright? On second thought, I dun thin this is such a good idea," Carmella said in a heavy Hispanic accent. "Suntines the spirits, they don't want to be deesturbed and you wind up makin them mad. Suntines, you dun get the good spirit you looking for. You get an evil spirit instead. I read a book on this once, and the people who had the séance accidentally opened a hole to the other side, and a demon spirit cane through. She started possessing people and doing all kinds of evil thins."

"Sounds like somebody I know," Sol remarked. "But you don't have to worry about that here, Carmella. No evil spirit is going to enter into this room. It would have too much competition."

Penny just ignored everything that was being said and tried to proceed with the séance before Joie got off a rejoinder. "If everybody would just close their eyes and remain silent, we'll see if we can make a contact."

"Mission Control, we are ready for blast off," Joie said playfully as she closed her eyes and quieted herself.

"We are here tonight in an effort to reach the spirit of the dearly departed, Mr. Kerby Brewster," Penny began.

"Kerby Brewster? Who the heck is Kerby Brewster? I thought we were going to try to reach Mags and see how her passing went," Joie interrupted.

"Shhh! You need a conduit to the other side. Hopefully, Kerby Brewster will be our conduit," Penny explained. "Mr. Brewster, if you can hear me, please give us some kind of a sign."

Penny couldn't see him yet, but the spirit of Kerby Brewster was standing right behind her. He leaned over Penny's left shoulder and whispered into her ear. "Exactly what kind of a sign would you like, kiddo? I've got lots of them. Mags used to like the flying book, but that may be a little much for a first sign. How about we start it off with just a few raps on the table?"

Startled, Penny looked back over her shoulder before Kerby had finished his thought. She could still hear his very identifiable voice whispering in her ear as she turned. Though she couldn't quite make out a figure yet, Penny was certain that she saw sort of glow behind her. Then the room brightened up for a second with a flash of lightning, and the glow took on the form of a male figure. Penny's usually rosy complexion turned ashen.

"Are you okay, honey?" Sol asked, just before they heard the first rap on the table.

"That was awfully good, sweetie. Did Mags teach you that?" Joie asked, not believing for a second that the noise was a sign from beyond.

Then the first rap was followed by a second and a third. "*Madre mio!* This is not good," Carmella groaned.

Penny watched as the glow began to make its way around the table until it was hovering over Carmella. As the aura moved, Penny could see that it was gradually taking on more and more form. When he reached Carmella, Kerby bent down over her and wrapped his arms around her as if to hug her. To Penny it seemed as if Carmella was being enveloped in a thickening white fog.

"*Dios mio!*" Carmella bellowed. "Do you feel it? It feels like sunbody has covered me with a damp blanket."

"It's probably just Sol, deary. He's about as exciting as a wet blanket," Joie joked.

"It's just your mind playing tricks on you," Sol offered.

When Kerby released his hold on Carmella and raised his head, Penny watched in awe as the amorphous form that made up the head started to take on even more shape. Though Penny could still see clear through the figure, she also saw facial features, a nose and a mouth and eyes were gradually forming and becoming more distinct.

The head of the figure turned toward Penny. "Don't stop now, kiddo. I mean lots of women have seen through me in my lifetime, but not quite this way. We've got a little further to go yet."

"What should I do? It's not as if I've ever done this before. Where do I go from here?" Penny asked, looking at Kerby.

"Who are you talking to, honey?" Sol wondered.

"If you don't want them to think you've completely lost your mind, I suggest that you not talk directly to me while they're around. You see, they can't see me or hear me. Watch!" Kerby said as he ran his hand in front of Sol's face with no reaction from Sol. Then he leaned over so his mouth was right next to Joie's ear. "Boo!" Kerby shouted, but Joie did not flinch. "As far as what to do, just keep doing what you're doing, kiddo. It seems to be working pretty well so far."

"We have received your sign, Mr. Brewster." Penny continued. "I can feel your presence, but we need you to make your presence even stronger, so that we can use you to communicate with Mags in the afterlife."

"That's good. I liked that," Kerby smiled as he held his hand up to his face and saw it becoming increasingly solid in appearance. "It's working for me, kiddo. How about you?"

Penny stared in amazement as the spirit of Kerby Brewster seemed to take on more and more substance. Penny realized that though he still looked somewhat like a thick cloud of white smoke, the apparition was now so thick that she could no longer see through it. She could even make out the expressions on his handsome face. There seemed to be an ever present smile, a smile with warmth to it.

"While we're waiting for this to happen, I think we'd better keep them entertained. This one always goes over big," Kerby remarked as he crawled under the table, placed his back against it and lifted it slightly off the ground, keeping it up in midair for several seconds before letting it drop back hard to the floor.

"Now that was impressive," Joie offered. "In all the times that I did these with Mags, I only saw her do that trick once."

Penny was astounded when Kerby came back out from under the table. He looked almost like a real, live person. His face and even his clothes had taken on color.

"This dame has always been hard to impress," Kerby noted, staring at Joie and shaking his head. Joie had her head under the table as if trying to figure out how Penny had gotten it off the ground. "Well, she's not leaving here tonight without my sending a shiver up her spine," Kerby added, turning his attention back to Penny.

Penny watched in disbelief as Kerby made his way toward her and then stood directly behind her. "You just relax for a second, kiddo, and allow whatever happens to happen. Whatever you feel, don't try to fight it, just allow your body to go with the flow. This one is guaranteed to get the fine hairs standing at attention."

Before she realized what was happening, Penny felt as if she were going into a trance-like state. Then, through no effort of her own, Penny's mouth began to move, but it wasn't her voice that came out. It was Kerby Brewster's voice, slight English accent and all.

"Mags O'Malley says to send her love from the other side. She wants you all to know that while she enjoyed her time here with you in this world, she has found true peace where she is now. Mags says that she knows you all miss her, but she doesn't want you to feel sorry for her. She has never been happier than she is at this time," Kerby said through Penny, then he allowed Penny to take control of her own body again.

Carmella was praying quietly in Spanish. Sol suddenly looked more serious than Penny had ever seen him. But Joie Miller still had the smirk on her face.

"Now that was a good trick. I give you credit. I admit that I could never figure that one out, but you're still not convincing me that we're communicating with the spirit of some dead guy," Joie declared.

Penny looked back at Kerby and realized that to her, he now looked just as real and alive as anyone else in the room. She found it hard to comprehend how she could see him so clearly and the others could not see him at all.

Kerby looked into Penny's eyes and saw the confusion. "You look as if you just saw a ghost, kiddo. Can't figure the whole thing out, huh? Well, me neither. Just write it off to the fact that you have the *gift* and they don't. Now, as far as that one over there is concerned, it looks as if I'm going to have to pull out all the stops tonight."

"Are we done?" Carmella asked nervously. "Can I go hone now?"

"Not just yet," Penny answered.

Carmella, Sol, and Joie just stared at each other waiting for something else to happen. Penny was transfixed on Kerby as he made his way behind the counter on which the cash register sat, some distance from the reading table at which they were sitting. She wondered what he would do next. Behind the counter, Kerby reached up onto the wall and removed a set of bagpipes that Mags kept there, more as a decoration than anything else. Mags loved the pipes, so did Kerby. At Mags's funeral, a lone piper had stood on a distant hill playing her favorite pipes tune, *Danny Boy.*

The whole table jumped at the first squeal of the pipes as Kerby leaned down behind the counter and began to play. Then the unmistakable notes came together and the group sat in confounded silence as the melancholy *Danny Boy* wailed out from the pipes. Penny looked over at Joie and saw tears welling up in her eyes.

"Okay, sweetie, you win. I don't know whether I'd call that playing fair, but that one made a believer out of me," Joie conceded through her tears. This time there were no wise cracks from Sol Hirsh.

♥♋♟

After the others had left, Kerby sat at the reading table opposite Penny and said, "The bagpipes were a nice touch, don't you think?"

Penny did not respond. She was speechless. She just sat staring at Kerby on the other side of the table, trying to convince herself that she had not lost her mind. She was really sitting with a ghost, a ghost who to her looked as real and alive as any living, breathing human being she had ever met. To top it off, this was not your average ghost. This ghost bore an uncanny resemblance to Cary Grant, not only in his face and body, but also in his mannerisms, speech, and dress. Then Penny remembered something else, something that she did not want to believe was true about this ghost. In real life he may well have been a violent man, a thief, and a rapist.

"You look as if you've about had it for this evening, kiddo," Kerby noted. "I suggest that we put you to bed for the night and start fresh in the morning."

"Oh no, you don't. You're not dismissing me and sending me off to bed this time. I have way too many things I need to ask you," Penny responded firmly.

"That's my point exactly, kiddo. There are way too many things that we need to talk about to do it all in one night, especially given the lateness of the hour. We'll have plenty of time to go over all of the things you want to discuss. Now, you go up and get some sleep. No offense, but you look beat. In the morning, I'll have your breakfast ready and waiting for you, and we can spend the whole day together discussing whatever you like. You can lay out whatever ground rules you have for our . . . cohabitation. I think you'll find that I'm about the best roommate anyone could ask for. If you need someone to talk to, I'm here. If you get sick of seeing me, you snap your fingers and *poof* I'm gone, and I don't come back until you're ready to see me again. When we're done with the ground rules, I'll answer all of the questions that I'm sure you have about who I was, why I'm here, and what it's like being a spirit. Now, why don't you go up and hit the hay?"

"Because I don't plan on spending another night under the same roof as you unless you answer some questions to my satisfaction," Penny said in a serious tone.

"Sure, kiddo, sure thing" Kerby replied, looking confused. "Fire away."

"Let's start with you explaining this," Penny said, taking a folded up copy of the newspaper article she had taken from the library out of her pocket. Penny unfolded the article and tossed it across the table in front of Kerby. She did not realize it as she tossed the article, but the photocopy of the newspaper photograph of Helen Rose was folded under the article. As they flew across the table, the two pieces of paper separated and the photograph slid off the table. Kerby glanced for a second at the newspaper article, but then his eyes followed the photograph as it fluttered to the floor at his feet. He bent and picked it up, staring at it the entire time as if mesmerized by its contents.

"Where in the world did you find this?" Kerby asked, finally looking up from the photograph and making eye contact with Penny.

"I was looking for information about your disappearance in old newspapers down at the library, and I came upon the photograph by accident," Penny explained. Kerby was back to staring silently at the picture. "She must have been very special to you," Penny added.

"Let's just say that after her, every woman seemed that much more special to me," Kerby replied. Then he held the photograph up and looked back and forth from the photograph to Penny as if comparing the two. "I told you that you two looked amazingly alike. Didn't I? She looks as if she could be your big sister."

"Yeah, there is a little resemblance there, I guess. But it's not the photograph I wanted to discuss, it's the article," Penny said, nodding her head down to the piece of paper on the table in front of Kerby.

Kerby took his time reading through the article with a serious expression on his face, and then he smiled up at Penny. "That Pat D'arcy was a shrewd one. He really knew how to cover his tracks. By the way, I see your concerns, but I assure you that there is very little in this article that is true."

"Why don't you separate the fact from the fiction for me?" Penny insisted.

"Well, it's true that Pat D'arcy, better known at the time as Irish Pat, was a czar in the construction industry, but that wasn't his real business. He made his millions as a bootlegger, used his construction companies to launder his illegally gotten gains. Not quite the respectable businessman he's portrayed as here.

"It's also true that Renata D'arcy came to see me on the afternoon of November 23, 1933, to ask me to handle a job for her, but it had nothing to do with acting as a courier. Renata thought that Irish Pat was about to leave her for another woman. She wanted me to do surveillance on him. You know, get some dirt, incriminating pictures, that type of thing. Well, where Irish Pat was concerned that was risky business, and I was not inclined to accept the job offer. Renata tried to convince me to take the job by offering me $200,000, laid it right out in front of me on the table. So that part of the story is true, except the money was not given to me to be delivered to someone else. It was mine for the keeping, assuming that I got Renata D'arcy what she wanted."

"Do you expect me to believe that this woman paid you $200,000, which in today's currency would be about $2,000,000, just to get some incriminating pictures of her husband with another woman?" Penny asked disbelievingly.

"It was a different time, kiddo. There was no such thing as a "no fault" divorce back then. Proving adultery might have meant a great deal of money to Renata D'arcy. But that really was not the reason she offered me that kind of money. You see, if you were crossing Irish Pat D'arcy, the stakes were automatically astronomical. He was not somebody to mess with. Think about it, as it turned out, the deal was not worth the money. It cost me my life.

"Anyway, after negotiating a few extras, I took the job and the money. That same evening I ran into Irish Pat at one of his clubs. Unfortunately, he already knew about my arrangement with his wife. He had beaten the information out her, beaten her beautiful face to a bloody mess. The pictures that the police took were the result of what Irish Pat did to her. I never laid a finger on Renata D'arcy, or any other woman for that matter, not in anger anyway," Kerby assured Penny.

"That explains *her* injuries, but what about *his*? The article says that almost every bone in Pat D'arcy's face was broken. Do you expect me to believe that he did that to himself in order to make it look good?"

"Not at all, I take full responsibility, or rather full credit, for that. Once I saw what Irish Pat had done to Renata, I kind of flipped. By then it was a foregone conclusion that my life was over anyway, so I figured I had nothing to lose. Before Irish Pat's bodyguards got to me, I was able to do some damage. You might not believe it to look at me, but I was quite good at that kind of thing back then," Kerby bragged.

"So you were in a room with a mobster and his bodyguards and you were quick enough to break every bone in his face without him doing any damage to you?" Penny continued her interrogation.

"Without them doing any damage to me? Kiddo, you seem to forget, I'm dead."

"Yeah, but it looks like you died without a mark on you. I would have thought that a mobster who had just suffered a severe beating at your hands might have thought of a . . . lets say a more creative way of exacting his revenge. From the looks of you, it seems as if he didn't even manage to knock the crease out of your pants," Penny noted.

"How does an ice pick to the back of the head sound? Pretty creative I'd say," Kerby smiled. "Fortunately for me, it wasn't as painful as it sounds. Even better, it makes for a more attractive corpse, no obvious damage to the face or body. You see, when you get stuck in limbo, like I am, the way you look when you go is the way you stay until you finally cross over."

"So after he murdered you, he got rid of your body by burying you under the right front cornerstone of this brownstone, which his company just happened to be starting work on the next day," Penny presumed.

"I'm not sure from where you got your details, but that, kiddo, is exactly right. I've been in this house ever since. Now, if you feel safe enough, how about you go up to bed and get a good nights sleep, and we'll continue this conversation in the morning?" Kerby suggested again.

"Just so I'm clear before I go up to bed, you did not lay a finger on Renata D'arcy, I mean, there was no sexual contact. Is that right?" Penny asked.

"I never said *that*, kiddo. I said I never assaulted or raped Renata D'arcy," Kerby corrected her.

"I'm sorry I asked." Penny replied as she headed up the stairs with a yawn. "Oh yeah, just one ground rule before I go up. You're not allowed in my bedroom in the morning until I'm finished exercising. And from now on, stay out of my bathroom when I'm in there."

CHAPTER 6

FOOLS RUSH IN
JUNE 17, 2003

Penny only had a couple of hours sleep, but she was up with the sun, eager to find out more about Kerby Brewster and the world of spirits in general. Penny had never really believed in ghosts, but even before she met Kerby Brewster, she was generally open minded and prepared to accept the possibility that there might be spirits of the dead walking this world. After all, history showed that lots of apparently normal people claimed to have seen ghosts.

Penny walked around the bedroom nonchalantly checking for cold spots, trying not to be too obvious as to what she was doing. When she was sure that there were none, she slipped off her clothes and proceeded with her yoga routine, but she was unable to empty her mind as she usually did. It was occupied with the image of Kerby Brewster in his formal wear.

As Penny made her way down the stairs, the familiar aromas of fresh brewed coffee and cinnamon toast hit her. It was almost as if Mags was back taking care of her. Entering the kitchen, Penny saw her glass of ice water sitting on the table and spotted the coffee pot percolating on the stove, but she was disappointed when she looked around and Kerby was nowhere to be seen.

"Mr. Brewster? Are you here?" Penny called out, her eyes searching the room.

"Look, kiddo, you have to stop calling me Mr. Brewster. You're making me feel old," Kerby kidded. Penny looked to the stove again. This time Kerby was there pouring a cup of coffee. "After all, in one sense I'm only a couple of years older than you are."

"True, but in reality you're about seventy-five years older than I am. Nevertheless, if it makes you feel better about yourself, I'll be happy to call you Kerby, but you have to promise to stop calling me kiddo."

"Suits me, kiddo. How about if I call you Monkey Face? That's what Cary Grant called Joan Fontaine in *Suspicion*," Kerby offered.

"Never mind, kiddo will be fine," Penny replied. "I never much cared for Cary Grant's character in that movie. His character was a murderer, you know."

"Don't be silly, kiddo. The public never would have forgiven Hitchcock if Grant turned out to really be a murderer in that movie."

"I know, I know, that's why the studio made Hitchcock change the ending. But if you read the book on which the movie is based, *Before the Fact*, a copy of which just happens to be downstairs in the bookstore, you'll see that Grant's character really was a murderer, and the glass of milk he brought up to the Joan Fontaine character really did have poison in it," Penny explained.

"You know something, kiddo? I think life with you may wind up being even more interesting than it was with your Aunt Mags," Kerby smiled.

"By the way, where were you when I came into the kitchen. One minute you weren't there and the next minute you were," Penny asked.

"It's like I told you, the way it seems to work is that you can see me whenever you want to see me and I want you to see me. Take away one or the other, and it's like I'm not here. I mean, I'm still here, but you can't see or hear me."

"Well, that hardly seems fair, that you can be invisible to me whenever you want," Penny complained.

"It's one of the perks of being a ghost, but you have to learn to accept the good with the bad. If there were a way to trade places, I'd be happy to make the switch."

"I'm all ears, tell me about it," Penny replied. "Like why do some people become spirits and others move right on to the afterlife?"

"There's a lot about it I don't understand myself. It's not as if you get a seminar or an instruction booklet before you get here. Most of it you have to piece together on your own. It seems from what I've been able to learn that people wind up caught in limbo for different reasons. Some wind up here because they die before their time. It seems that many of the people in this condition died violent deaths. Almost none received a proper burial according to the dictates of their religion, whether it be a cremation or burial in hallowed ground. Others seem to be here almost by choice, though they don't seem to realize it in their own heads. It's like there was something they needed to do before they died but they never got a chance to complete. As best I can tell, in my case it seems to be a result of a combination of factors, the violent death, dying before my time, and, most of all, not being buried in sanctified ground."

"That's why Mags tried to dig up the cornerstone and later tear down the building, so she could dig you up and get you buried in a cemetery somewhere."

"Good old Mags, she loved this place more than anything on earth, but she was prepared to tear it down if it meant getting me the heck out of here. The first time, she was ready to go war with Sol. I had never seen her so riled up. You have no idea how hard I had to work on her to calm her down and get her to realize that her friendship with Sol was even more important than what she was trying to do for me. The second time, she could not be reasoned with. She knew she was going, and she was determined to see me go with her. Did you know that she even bought me a cemetery plot next to hers to make certain that I wouldn't be dumped into some Potter's Field? If it hadn't been for the position taken by the city, she would have gone ahead and torn the building down, no matter how hard I tried to convince her not to," Kerby recalled.

"By that point, why would you try to stop her? Why not just let her tear it down and free your spirit to move on?" Penny wondered.

"Because of you, kiddo. Mags knew you loved this house almost as much as she did. She wanted nothing more than for you to have it, but she was prepared to sacrifice that if it meant getting me out of here. I couldn't stand the thought of Mags being deprived the right to leave the house to you, or the thought of you being denied the house because of me. We argued about it endlessly, until the city came back and said forget about it. Even after that she started calling these fly-by-night demolition companies to see if she could get somebody to tear the building down without a permit. I got her to back off that by telling her about the first night you and I met. I had never mentioned it to her before. You should have seen her eyes light up when I told her. Once she realized that you had the *gift*, same as her, she backed off and went to work ensuring that the house would be yours upon her death."

"So let me see if I have this right, when you're not here, you're roaming around town visiting with other spirits and comparing notes? I mean how else could you know so much about how and why some people get stuck in limbo and others don't?"

"I hardly go roaming around town. I only wish that were the case. The fact is that I can't leave this house, at least not to enter into your world. One foot outside of the front door and I'm in . . . I guess what you would call purgatory. Not a very nice place, and you don't go there without some risk, but you're correct that it is where I get to share information with other spirits." Kerby said.

"You mean to tell me that other than the trips that you make to this purgatory, or wherever, you have not been out of this house in seventy years. No wonder Mags was so determined to set your spirit free. What's it like in this place you go to, and what do you mean when you say there are risks?" Penny asked.

"Basically, I guess you'd describe it as this vast wasteland, kind of like an enormous desert, not much there really. What there is there are spirits, lots and lots of lost souls. I call them lost souls because most are there, not only because they haven't been able to get to the other side, but also because they haven't been able to find their way back to their resting places here on earth either. It seems that each spirit has a portal to this wasteland. Mine is right outside that front door. The problem is, once you're through the hole, it closes right up behind you, looks just like the rest of the place. If you can't make your way back to the exact spot from which you left, you can't reenter this world. If you lose your portal, you're stuck in purgatory forever, or until somebody finds your body here on earth," Kerby explained.

"How did you know the first time that you went through the portal that you had to come back through the same spot?"

"You find that out pretty quickly, kiddo. The minute you go through, you realize that the doorway is gone. I was just fortunate that a Good Samaritan happened to be passing by on my first time through and educated me before I got too far away from my hole, otherwise I never would have gotten back here. Now, when I make my occasional visit in, I make sure that I don't move more than a foot or so away from where I entered. I only talk to those who venture near enough to my portal."

"That sounds horrible," Penny sympathized as she took a bite out of her cinnamon toast while Kerby buttered her a second slice. "Aren't you having coffee?" Penny asked, when she realized that Kerby had not poured a second cup for himself.

"I could, but it would be kind of pointless. No nerve endings in these or anywhere else," Kerby said, holding out his hands and wiggling his fingers in front of Penny. "No taste buds either."

"So you don't feel anything?" Penny asked incredulously.

"That depends on what you mean by feelings. I feel lots of things, just not with my nerve endings. I still feel things emotionally. I still have the memories of the things I loved, what they felt like, what they tasted like. I still have desires and cravings for those things, just like when I was alive. Unfortunately, acting on those desires and cravings is just not as fulfilling as it used to be."

"That's so sad. I can't even imagine what that must be like," Penny said.

"Well, imagine that you're not really hungry, but you walk into this kitchen and there's this luscious chocolate cake sitting on the table. You weren't hungry when you entered the room, but the cake suddenly presents an incentive object. You see it, and your mind tells you what it will taste like when you put it into your mouth. You imagine the taste, the flavor of the chocolate, the moist texture of the cake and the creamy texture of the icing mixing on your tongue. Suddenly, though you weren't the least bit hungry minutes earlier, there is nothing you want more than to get a bite of that cake into your mouth. So you slice a piece and bite into it, but there is none of what you were expecting. There's no taste, no texture, and with that goes all of your expectations, all of your desires. Not much point in taking a second bite, is there? That's kind of what it's like being a spirit. You never really get hungry, but when you see that incentive object, the memories flood in, the longings and desires return. The only problem is that when you follow up on those desires, the actual event is just not what you were hoping for," Kerby explained.

"This may sound silly, but can I feel you? I mean, you look solid to me, but if I touch you will I feel anything or will my hand go right through you?" Penny wondered.

"Why not let's give it a try, kiddo," Kerby suggested, reaching his hand across the table.

Penny stuck out her hand and reached nervously for Kerby's hand. She was not certain why, but she wanted desperately to feel something when she touched him. When their hands met, Penny pulled her hand back quickly. What she felt was more than just skin on skin. It was like a tiny electrical current had run into her fingers and even slightly up her arm before she withdrew her hand. It wasn't an unpleasant feeling, to the contrary, it was quite nice, but it did shock her slightly at first.

"That wasn't much of a touch, kiddo. You need to loosen up a little bit," Kerby commented.

"You . . . tingled me," Penny responded, reaching her hand back across the table toward Kerby's still outstretched palm.

"Not to be immodest, but women used to tell me that even before I died," Kerby boasted with a wry smile. "Seriously though, it takes a little getting used to," Kerby added as Penny's hand reached his and closed around it, the warm tingling sensation continuing as long as her hand was in his hand.

"Do you mean to tell me you don't feel that, you don't feel anything?" Penny asked.

"Not a thing," Kerby responded, but Kerby was lying. He felt it all right, maybe not on the outside, but in his heart and in his mind he felt it. The memories were flooding in and the longings and desires were returning. Kerby felt it all right, and he knew it.

"How about other people, people who don't have the *gift* as you call it. Is there any way for them to feel you?"

"It gets tricky there, kiddo. Once someone with the gift conjures me up by way of a séance, like you did, as long as I'm in that person's presence, other people can feel me if I want them to. I can touch them in the same way I can touch you. If I'm not in the presence of the person with the gift, I can touch inanimate objects, even move them about if I choose to, but no other person can feel me. All they get is a slight sense of coldness when I'm around. You may have noticed that you haven't felt that chill since you invoked my spirit, so feeling around for cold spots won't do you any good anymore. You'll just have to learn to trust me," Kerby teased.

"I have loads more questions," Penny said. "But I have to get going. I want to see if I can get tickets for the Shakespeare Festival tonight at the Delacorte Theater. Every year they do a different Shakespearean play in the park with big name actors and everything. The best thing is, it's free, but you have to get in line early in order to get your tickets in the afternoon for the performance that night. This year they're doing *Hamlet* and Toby McGuire is playing the lead. They're starting the performances earlier in the season than they usually do because it's the only time that McGuire was available."

Kerby followed Penny down the corridor as she made her way to the stairs. "Our first full evening together and you're going to ditch me for *Hamlet* and Spiderman."

"It's good to see you're up on your pop culture. Nobody likes a smug ghost, you know," Penny joked as she reached the top of the stairs. "But seriously, it's like you said last night. It seems that we are going to have all the time in the world to get to know each other, and I promised Sol I would get the tickets so he and I could go together."

Penny started to enter her bedroom but stopped and looked back down at Kerby who remained at the base of the stairway smiling. "Kerby?" Penny said, turning serious all of a sudden. "That first morning, when you watched me showering, was I that piece of chocolate cake?"

Kerby's smile vanished just before he did, with no answer to the question. But as he disappeared from sight, Kerby realized that Penny had fully grasped the concept that the chocolate cake example was intended to convey.

"I know you were in there, and I know you can hear me too," Penny chided as she closed the door behind her. Then she stuck her head back out. "I'm taking my shower now, so don't come up."

In her mind though, Penny confessed that the idea that the handsome Kerby Brewster was intrigued enough by her naked body to have sat and watched her shower excited her. Her whole life she had taken great care to keep her body healthy and attractive. Like Aunt Brit, Penny had come to learn that her nude body was not something of which to be ashamed. In fact, she was quite proud of it. *What harm was there in giving Kerby Brewster a thrill he probably hadn't experienced in seventy years or so,* Penny thought to herself. Then Penny admitted something else to herself. *Kerby Brewster was not the only one who might be thrilled if the situation presented itself again.*

♥ ⚔ ♟

With the sun just beginning to set, Penny headed for the door. Kerby was hot on her heels. "I don't have time to argue about this anymore," Penny snapped. "Sol is going to be waiting for me."

"Come on, kiddo, what fun can there be in going to see a Shakespeare play by yourself? Stay home with me, we'll pop in Mags's *North by Northwest* video and enjoy a movie. I'll even make you popcorn," Kerby pleaded.

"We can watch *The Man on Lincoln's Nose* any night. I did not wait in line for two hours for tickets to *Hamlet* to change my mind now just because Sol can't make the play," Penny insisted.

"The man on what?" Kerby asked. "And what's up with Sol anyway, backing out at the last minute is not like him. I don't like the idea of your going to this thing by yourself and having to come home alone that late at night."

"*The Man on Lincoln's Nose* was the working title for *North by Northwest* while it was being made. I'm surprised you didn't know that. As for Sol, he was set to come with me, but he got a call from Danny Glover. You know, the actor who played Oprah's mean husband in *The Color Purple.* Sol has a deal with Glover that whenever he's in town, all he has to do is call Sol and Sol will go and pick him up. Apparently, Glover has had some problems with racist cab drivers in the past, and Sol is trying to make amends on behalf of the profession. Well, Glover called Sol late this afternoon to tell him that he is going be flying out of Kennedy Airport tonight at ten, that would be right in the middle of the play, so Sol is going to have just enough time to drop me off at the Delacorte, pick Glover up and scoot over to Kennedy. Now, if you don't let me get out of here, he's not even going to have time to do that, so back off would you?" Penny snapped again as she opened the door.

Kerby knew he was not going to be able to follow much further. "No kidding, Sol is standing you up for Danny Glover? Doesn't say much for Sol's taste, but I guess I can understand. Nevertheless, you should not be doing this alone at night. Your Aunt Mags would never forgive me if I let you go and something happened to you."

"I'm a big girl now. I can take care of myself, and leave Mags out of it," Penny said sternly, taking her first step out the door.

"You know, when Mags and I were at an impasse on something important to each of us, we took each others' feelings into consideration, and we settled our differences like adults," Kerby recalled, in one final effort to get Penny to change her mind.

"Okay, let's hear it. I suppose you're going to tell me whether I want you to or not," Penny groaned. "How did you and Mags resolve these kinds of conflicts?"

"Did you ever play rock, paper, scissors?" Kerby asked, breaking into a huge grin.

"That's the adult way in which you and Mags resolved your differences? You played rock, paper, scissors?" Penny replied sarcastically.

"What's the matter, chicken, afraid the dead guy might beat you?" Kerby taunted.

"All right, I'm going to humor you this one time," an exasperated Penny replied. "Then when I finish beating you at your own game, I'm going to see *Hamlet* with Toby McGuire."

Kerby remained just inside the doorway with Penny outside, her back to the flight of stairs. "Ready, rock, paper, scissors, shoot," Kerby shouted, and then he stuck out a flat hand indicating his choice of paper. Penny threw out a rounded fist indicating her choice as rock.

"I won!" Kerby exclaimed. "Paper beats rock."

"Wait a minute, I haven't played this game since I was a kid. You have to explain to me how a piece of paper can possibly beat a rock," Penny demanded.

"Paper covers rock," Kerby remarked, reaching his hand through the doorway and wrapping it around Penny's still outstretched fist. Kerby's touch sent a light current into Penny's hand. "Now come on back in," Kerby insisted, gripping Penny's hand and tugging her back toward the doorway.

"Hold on there. That doesn't sound right," Penny argued as she pulled her hand back hard attempting to free it from Kerby's grip. Her hand popped free suddenly, and Penny went reeling backwards, off balance, toward the stairs. Penny had just about gotten her balance back when her right heel slipped off the top step and she felt herself beginning to fall.

At first, Kerby stood frozen in the doorway, believing that the minute he stepped through, he would disappear into the wasteland. But when he saw Penny about to topple head-over-heels down the stairs, Kerby sprung his body at her. To his surprise, he did not disappear upon exiting the doorway. He grabbed hold of Penny's blouse between her breasts just as she was about to start her backward tumble down the stairs. In one swift motion, Kerby pulled Penny back to him, nestled her against his body, and hugged her in his arms, a feeling of relief overcoming him.

Kerby looked down into Penny's stunned eyes. "That was a close one, kiddo," Kerby whispered. "I don't want to lose you already. I'm just starting to like you."

Penny could feel the warm tingling sensation rushing through her body wherever it came into contact with Kerby's arms or body. Aside from the tingling, Penny felt safe in Kerby's arms. She felt a security unlike anything she had felt since her parents died. Staring into Kerby's eyes, Penny also felt as if someone had tied her tongue in a knot. She didn't know what to say. When she finally spoke, all she could think to say was, "I thought you were supposed to disappear when you came out that door?"

"So did I, kiddo," Kerby responded, finally releasing his hold on Penny. "I don't get it. This has never happened before."

"Kerby," Penny said, a thought clearly having come to her mind. "When Mags was alive, did you ever try leaving the house with her, like holding her hand or just staying close to her?"

"No, it's not something that ever occurred to either us, but maybe you're onto something, kiddo. Let's give it a try," Kerby suggested, grabbing Penny's hand and heading down the stairs pulling her along with him.

When Penny turned to start down the stairs, she saw Sol standing at the bottom of the steps staring up with his mouth agape. It was apparent that Sol had just witnessed her as she appeared to defy gravity, then carried on a conversation with no one in particular. Now she was skipping down the steps, her left arm swinging like a child's might swing if the child were walking down the street holding a parent's hand.

"I'll be right with you, Sol," Penny said through a huge grin as she past a stunned and silent Sol Hirsh.

Halfway down the block, an amazed Kerby said, "I can't believe this. I've been stuck in that house for seventy years not knowing that all I had to do was take Mags's hand and I could have gone anywhere I wanted to."

"Maybe you don't even need to hold my hand, not that I don't like it, but maybe you just need to stay close to me?" Penny theorized. "I mean you weren't holding my hand when you first came through the door and you didn't disappear."

"Let's give it a try," Kerby suggested. "Just keep your hand close and clamp it shut if you see me start to disappear. Remember what happens if you lose me. There's no way that I could find my way back to my portal from here."

Kerby eased his grip on Penny's hand and she did likewise, keeping her hand close and ready to grab his hand again at the first sign of trouble, but there was none. As their hands parted, Kerby remained just as apparent as he had been. They walked back to the brownstone together, shoulder to shoulder.

"I don't want to push this too much until we can work out a plan to make sure you don't lose me if I get too far away and disappear. But I'd say that as long as you don't mind staying this close for the rest of the night, you've got yourself a date for the theater," Kerby announced.

"I'd be honored," Penny replied out of the side of her mouth as they reached a still bewildered Sol Hirsh. "Ready if you are Sol," Penny said, and the three headed for Sol's double parked cab.

♥ 👻 🕵

After Sol dropped them off at the Delacorte Theater, Kerby marveled at the structure. The Delacorte, Kerby realized, is an impressive outdoor amphitheater, done in the typical Greek style, with its audience seats arced around the stage, rising to a considerable height, each row of seats slightly higher than the row before it. But Kerby recognized that what makes the Delacorte so impressive is the scenery that surrounds it. Set in the Great Lawn area of Central Park, just beyond the theater the medieval-like Belvidere Castle rises above the natural splendor of Turtle Pond, offering an image reminiscent of Camelot, the entire vista clearly visible from areas inside the Delacorte.

Once in the theater, Penny and Kerby rushed ahead of the crowd to the top row, and Penny sat in the aisle seat, so that Kerby could sit on the stairs in the aisle to ensure that no one sat on top of him. Kerby stood at the top of the aisle alongside an usher, waiting for the seats in the row to fill up. Once everyone was seated, Kerby sat on the stairs in the aisle with the usher standing directly above him. A middle-aged man with a toupee that looked like a small dog sitting on his head sat alone on the other side of Penny.

"This is incredible. The last time I was in this area, what is now the Great Lawn was the Croton Reservoir. They were just starting to fill it in with the stones from the building of Rockefeller Center. I can't believe what they did up here. Much of this area looked like swampland when I was last here. Now they have free theater where the swamp used to be," Kerby noted, shaking his head as the lights in the amphitheater dimmed and the actors entered the stage.

"Shhh," Penny hushed, turning toward Kerby in the aisle.

"I haven't said a word, lady," the usher standing above Kerby whispered in response.

"Quiet," the guy with the toupee snapped at the usher.

Kerby smiled. "Now look at what you've gone and done," he kidded as he rose and stood next to the usher again.

"Would you please behave yourself?" Penny whispered up to Kerby.

"What are you talking about, lady? I haven't done a thing," the usher said indignantly.

"Would you leave this lady alone so that we can all watch the play?" the toupee hissed at the usher.

As the play started, Kerby stationed himself directly behind Penny, but he seemed more interested in scanning the area outside of the theater than he was in watching what was going on onstage.

"Would you be still?" Penny demanded looking behind her.

"Lady, I haven't moved a muscle," the usher responded, his tone growing somewhat harsher.

"Son, I intend to report you to the theater management if you don't cease harassing this young lady," the toupee threatened, his voice also rising.

On stage, Horatio and Marcellus had entered, followed by the ghost of King Fortinbras. "Peace, break thee off; look, where it comes again!" Marcellus said, referring to the appearance of the ghost onstage.

But Kerby was not the least bit interested in what was going on onstage. From where he stood, Kerby had a clear view of a section of Turtle Pond just below the Belvidere Castle. Something had caught his eye in the area of the pond.

"Look at that! There's a guy running around naked alongside Belvidere Lake. Is it legal to run around naked in the park now?" Kerby wondered.

"It's not Belvidere Lake anymore. It's called Turtle Pond now. Now please be quiet. There's one of your kind onstage. One would think you'd at least be interested in this part of the play," Penny whispered to Kerby. After a pause she turned to Kerby again and said, "No, it is not legal to expose yourself in Central Park."

"Has he exposed himself to you?" the toupee asked in a shocked tone, looking around Penny toward the usher. "Put that thing away right now or I'm going to find a cop. This is not an Iggy Pop concert," the indignant toupee snarled.

"Who the heck is Iggy Pop?" the young usher wondered, making his way down the stairs, finally having decided to find another place to stand.

Kerby stooped over Penny's shoulder. "Follow my finger and tell me that there's not a naked guy over there alongside the pond," Kerby said, pointing his finger in the direction of the pond below Belvidere Castle.

An exasperated Penny acquiesced. "All I see is a little mist rising from the pond, glowing in the moonlight."

Kerby stared harder. "Do you want to know why I see a naked man and you only see a glow?"

"Don't tell me you have better eyesight than I do. My vision is twenty-ten, better than normal," Penny whispered.

"It's not your eyesight. You're having trouble making the guy out because he's a ghost."

"A naked ghost in Central Park?" Penny asked sarcastically.

"That's right, and we're going over there right now to see what's going on with him," Kerby demanded.

"I'm not leaving this theater until this play is over," Penny insisted, her voice rising again.

"No offense, lady, but there are those of us who wish you would leave the theater now, so that we might enjoy the play," the toupee whined.

"I'm not leaving and you can't leave without me. Toby McGuire hasn't even been on stage yet," Penny growled back at Kerby.

"Come on," Kerby demanded, grabbing Penny's arm. "If you don't come right now, I'm going to snatch the squirrel off that guy's head and throw it up on the stage, and guess who he's going to blame for it. If you really feel a need to see Toby McGuire, we can rent *Cider House Rules* on the way home."

"Geez, you are an annoying ghost," Penny groaned, getting up from her seat and starting down the aisle.

♥ ⌀ ♣

"So, they call it Turtle Pond now," Kerby said as they got onto the trail near Belvidere Castle and began walking in the dark toward the pond. "I'll bet you didn't know that Cary Grant played the role of the Mock Turtle in the first talking version of *Alice in Wonderland*," Kerby said to the still annoyed Penny.

"No, I didn't know that," Penny growled.

"In 1933, Paramount decided to do the movie and insisted that all of the big name stars it had under contract play a role. Charlotte Henry played Alice, Cary Cooper played the White Knight, W.C. Fields played Humpty Dumpty, and Cary Grant played the Mock Turtle. The only problem was that the costume that Grant wore covered his face, so you really couldn't tell it was Grant in the role," Kerby explained as they left the trail and entered into a wooded area near the pond.

"Really," Penny grumbled as if she didn't care, but in her mind she admitted that this was all news to her. Penny thought she knew a great deal about old movies, but she had never even heard of this version of *Alice in Wonderland*, and she made the decision right there to seek out the video, if it were available.

As they made their way through the wooded area leading to a clearing near the shore of Turtle Pond, the amorphous glow grew gradually clearer to Penny. She now realized that it was, in fact, the figure of a man, a man who appeared to be entirely without clothes. Penny grew slightly nervous when she realized that the apparition seemed very much aware that they were approaching. He stared at them with as much surprise and interest in his eyes as Penny had in hers. When they reached the apparition, all three remained silent for several seconds, staring up and down at each other as if sizing each other up.

The apparition spoke first. "You're one of us, aren't you, Mister?

You're a ghost like me," the apparition remarked. "She's not though, but she's on to you, isn't she? I mean, she's aware of you like she would be aware of a live person. Now how can that be? I've been here for a while and seen lots of living people, but none of them have ever been aware of my presence, that is, unless I happened to be feeling mischievous. But even then there was no way for them to see me. Can she see me too, Mister?" the apparition asked, uncertain whether he should be embarrassed or perhaps attempt to over himself. "Can she hear me?"

Kerby looked to Penny for a response. "I can see him, just not clearly the way I see you. I can hear him too, but it sounds like he's in an echo chamber," Penny noted, talking to Kerby as if he had to translate for her.

"He's dead, not deaf," Kerby snickered. "He doesn't need me to interpret for him? You can speak to him directly if you want to."

"So what gives?" the apparition asked. "How is it that a ghost like you is hanging around with a cute live chick like her?"

"That's a long story," Kerby replied. "But at the moment, the more important thing is that we happened to spot you here and perhaps we can help you out."

"You mean tell somebody where my body is, so that they can recover it and give me a proper burial?" the ghost asked hopefully.

"That's what I mean. I assume your body is somewhere in the pond, but judging from the looks of you, I'm guessing yours was no accidental drowning. In fact, it looks as if you had a run in with some very nasty characters," Kerby noted, looking down at the apparition's severely mutilated genitalia.

"Nasty is not the word for these two, Mister. We're talking psychopaths, I mean no conscience bitches. And from what I overheard, I wasn't the first, and they weren't planning on me being the last either. Seems they do this once a year, every year, same time each year," the ghost said.

"Why don't you tell us about it?" Kerby suggested. "Maybe aside from getting you out of here, we might be able to stop your friends from doing this again."

"It was just about a year ago, June 24, 2002," the apparition began. "I know the date because a friend of mine was celebrating a birthday. We lived across the river in Union, New Jersey. 'Lets head over to the city and celebrate my birthday,' my friend says. 'We'll hit some clubs up on the Upper East Side, have a few drinks, pick up some chicks.' I figured, what the hell. I had a night out from my old lady because it's his birthday, let's go for it. It was the biggest mistake of my short life.

"We decided to stop at a place he knew up on Second Avenue near East 84th Street called *Dorrian's The Red Hand*. 'Lots of very young, very horny chicks,' my friend said. Sounded good to me, so that's where we started. Turns out he was not exaggerating. By eleven thirty, some cute little babe comes up to him and asks him if he's into Ecstasy, you know, the club drug. Well, it ain't my thing, but he says, 'Yeah' and a few minutes later they're on their way out the door. 'Don't bother waiting around. I know my way home,' he hollers to me on his way out.

"Almost as soon as he's out the door, I notice this tall, gorgeous blonde giving me the eye, I mean just staring at me. I recognized her right away. I seen her picture on magazine covers, and I'm kind a sure she's been in a couple of television commercials too. At first, I'm thinking, what's she staring at me for, maybe I got some food on my face or something? I go to the men's room, and when I come back, she's in the seat next to mine.

"Before she even tells me her name, she starts asking me all these questions about my sex life. Have I ever done this, have I ever done that, ever tried this position, ever tried that position? I hadn't done any of the things she's asking me about, but I'm like, 'Oh yeah, I done this and that, lots a times.' Then she pulls this string of beads out of her pocketbook. I'm not talking pearls here, I'm talking beads about the size of jawbreakers. She asks if I've ever had a woman stick a string of beads up my butt and pull them out one at a time while she's giving me oral. She says, 'You've got to leave a couple in there until the guy's about to climax and pull the last ones out just as he's letting loose.

"I'm thinking to myself, *Thank you lord. I don't know what I did to deserve this, but I must be doing something right*. Then just when I think life can't get any better, this chick really blows my mind. She says, 'Hey, there's my friend over there. She just came in.' Cute little brunette, all toned up with muscles popping out of her arms, you know, like Madonna is now. Not really my thing, but still cute, okay. The blonde asks me if I've ever had a threesome, and when I admit I haven't, she asks if I'd like to try one with her and her girlfriend. You hear that, Mister? She asks me out of the blue if I would like to have a fucking *manage a trios* with her and her cute little girlfriend. I thought I had died and gone to Heaven.

"I decide I'd better use the bathroom one more time before we go, and when I get back, the cute brunette is there, all smiles, and I got another drink waiting for me. The blonde, who still hasn't told me her name or introduced the girlfriend, says she bought me one for the road. I'm thinking, life don't get any better than this, now the broad is buying me drinks. She says, 'You finish your drink. We'll go get our car and pick you up outside.' For a second I thought I was on reality television or something. You know, I'm going to go outside and find out that it was all a practical joke. My buddy is going to be outside with a television crew laughing his ass off. But when I get outside, I hear a horn beeping and there they are parked down the block waiting for me.

"What happens for the next hour or so I really can't say for sure because I barely made it to the car before I was out cold. Turns out the blonde chick slipped me a fucking mickey in the drink she bought me. When I wake up, I'm tied to that tree over there, my package and everything else out in the open, and the string of beads is hanging out of my behind. Let me tell you, Mister, it ain't what it's cracked up to be. By the way, when I say I was tied up, I mean I was fucking tied up. One of these chicks knew how to tie a knot. I was tied so tight that the cord was cutting into my skin, my wrists were bleeding, and I could hardly breathe. I knew right away this was no kinky little sex game these girls were playing.

"The two broads are standing there smiling at each other like they're all kind a proud of their handiwork. I say, 'All right, what's going on?' My tone was not nasty or anything, given the position in which I had found myself. I mean, I wasn't looking to piss these girls off any more than they already were.

"The tall chick asks me if I ever heard of the "Central Park Jogger." I don't even know what the fuck she's talking about. I never jogged in my life. So she tells me a story about this woman who's out jogging in Central Park at night and gets attacked by this wolf pack of young guys. She says that these guys took turns raping this woman and then they bashed her head in with boulders. She asks me if I know where these guys are now. I say, 'I don't know, but I hope the bastards are rotting away on Rikers Island. They should cut their balls off.' They looked at each other and laugh heartily at that remark, as if it was a private joke or something. Then the tall one tells me 'No, these guys are all walking the streets today, free men.'

"Then the little one asks me if I ever heard of the "Preppie Murder Case," Jennifer Levin and Robert Chambers. Again, I got no idea who the hell she's talking about. She tells me maybe I need to read a newspaper once in a while. The tall one laughs and says, 'Too late for that now.' Then the little one says this Jennifer Levin was a sweet young girl, and Robert Chambers was this jerk off who lured her out of the same bar that we were just in, you know, the one I told you about, *Dorrian's The Red Hand*. She says this guy Chambers took this girl to Central Park, had sex with her and then strangled her to death. She asks if can guess where this guy Chambers is now. By this time I'm onto the game. I say, 'My guess is that he's walking the streets, a free man, or you wouldn't be asking me that question.' 'Good guess,' she says and then she laughs.

"'I suppose you're wondering what this has all got to do with you,' the tall one says. It's like she's reading my fucking mind because that's exactly what I'm thinking at that moment. Then she tells me that I have been chosen as the sacrificial lamb that is going to pay for the damage that was done to the "Central Park Jogger" and Jennifer Levin and every other woman who has ever been attacked or raped or abused in Central Park. It's like it's some kind of a religious ceremony or something with a sacrifice and all. Then she offers me this one way out. She says if I apologize for all those past wrongs and beg for forgiveness, maybe I might walk out of Central Park alive.

"Hey, I ain't that proud a guy, so I start coming clean and begging like a woman. I say, 'Listen, all that talk back there in the bar, that was all bullshit. I've never done none of that stuff.' Which, like I said, is the truth. You see, I was a young guy when this happened, but I was also a married man. Knocked my high school sweetheart up and did the right thing, married her before the baby came. I thought mentioning this might get me some brownie points, so I say, 'I'm really sorry for what happened to the two young ladies you mentioned and any other young ladies who may have been assaulted in this god-forsaken place, but I never did nothing like that.' I say, 'Look, I'm a married man, never even cheated on my wife before. I got a beautiful baby girl at home.'

"This apparently was the wrong thing to say to these two. 'Shut him up,' the tall one hollers, and the little one sticks a ball gag in my mouth, a fucking ball gag. Do you believe it, Mister? These chicks came prepared with a ball gag. Once it's in and I can't even hear myself scream, the tall one starts kicking me in the fucking nuts like she's the place kicker for the New York Giants. 'You scumbag! You have a wife and a baby girl at home and this is how you spend your evenings,' she's shouting with every kick. You're a guy, Mister; you can imagine what that must have felt like. I was in agony, felt like I was going to pass out, but as you can see, the worst was yet to come," the apparition said, looking down at his mangled genitals.

"You see, the tall one is mean, but the little one is pure evil. She reaches into her pocket and comes out with a forty-penny nail, you know, the long thick ones. She's got this little mallet, like the kind a doctor uses to test your reflexes, and she starts tapping the nail up into my urethra. It was the most painful thing I ever felt in my life. With each tap she looks up at me like she's getting off on the pain in my face. Then she smiles at me and tells me to stop being a baby, that there are men out there who pay her lots of money to do the same thing to them. I don't know if it's true or not, but if somebody is paying her for that, he's one sick puppy.

"By the time she gets the nail all the way up, so that only the head is sticking out of my package, I'm about to pass out. Before I lose consciousness, I look over at the tall one. She's just standing there like she's a nurse observing a doctor during surgery. The little one looks up and, lo and behold, the big one hands her a scalpel. At first, I thought I was dreaming, but I swear to you it was a scalpel. I look down and the little one has already cut right through my ball sac and is in the process of slicing my left nad free. I started to puke, but with the ball gag in my mouth there was nowhere for it to go. I wound up choking to death on my own vomit."

"And that's the last thing you remember?" Penny asked.

"You can tell you ain't no ghost, lady. They didn't know it, but after I died, I sat right there under the tree and watched the rest. It took me a few minutes to figure out that I was dead and this was my body they were fooling around with, but it sinks in after a while. You know how that is, don't you, Mister?

"Anyway, first they put my balls into a sandwich bag and put the bag into a little cooler full of ice. It looked like they were saving my gonads for a transplant or something. They cut me down from the tree and used the same cords to tie cinder blocks to my body. The whole time they're talking about the other guys that they did and how my murder compared to the others. It seems that they did two kids from their high school in back to back years. Killed both of them in a warehouse on the water in Staten Island and dumped their bodies right there in the water. The other guy was a year before me. They did him in a park somewhere along the Hudson River and dumped him into the Hudson.

"Now get this, after they get me all tied with the cinder blocks secured, they strip off all of their own clothes. I'm telling you they're out here in the park like two little nymphets, *au naturel*. Together they drag my body into Turtle Pond until the water is up to their breasts. Then they let me go, came out, pulled towels out of a bag, and took turns drying each other off like they're at the beach or something. Looked like they were really enjoying themselves while they were doing it too. While they're drying each other off, I noticed that the little one's got a big tattoo between her belly button and her crotch. It's three Greek letters, Chi, Beta, Theta; CBT. I know cause, you see, I'm Greek; the name is Nicholas Demopolous."

When Nick finished telling his story, Penny took out a small pad and pen and they had him go over his descriptions of the two girls and their car again, with Penny writing it all down this time. Penny also had Nick write the Greek letters for her, so that there would be no error in the transcription. Kerby also had Penny write down everything Nick could remember about the locations of the other murders the girls had discussed. Kerby seemed almost as intent on locating the other spirits as he did on tracking down the girls.

"So when do you think you might have somebody come and take me out of here?" Nick asked. "It's been a while, and I know my wife is wondering where the hell I've been. This is going to be hard on her with the baby and all, but, at least it will bring some closure. My kid won't grow up thinking I just deserted her."

"I'll make a call on my cell phone as soon as we're done here," Penny assured him.

"Oh no, you won't," Kerby objected. "Most calls to the police are automatically traced now. If they trace the tip to you, you're going to have a hard time explaining how you knew that there was a body out there in chest-deep water, especially if you plan on offering them any information as to the people who did this. We'll need to discuss how you're going to make the call and exactly what you're going to say before you do anything."

"In any event, we'll make the call by sometime tomorrow morning. We'll get somebody out here within the next day or so," Penny promised.

"Thanks, lady," Nick said. "You have no idea how difficult it is being this way, stuck in limbo. What about you, Mister? Why haven't you had your body properly buried so that you can pass over? From the way you're dressed, I'm guessing you been hanging around a lot longer than I have."

"It doesn't seem to be in the cards for me, Nick, complications beyond our control, but who knows, maybe someday. At least I'm not getting any older while I'm waiting. If you're going to wind up like this, I guess there's something to be said for the old axiom, "Live fast, die young, and leave a good-looking corpse," Kerby smiled.

"It looks like you managed that, Mister. Anybody ever tell you, you look just like Cary Grant?"

"I've heard that once or twice," Kerby replied with a smile.

As they headed away from Turtle Pond, Penny reached into her pocketbook and pulled out her cell phone. "Who are you calling at this hour?" Kerby wondered.

"I thought I'd call Sol and see if he could give us a ride home."

"Oh no, you don't," Kerby said. "This is my first night out in about seventy years. I don't want to end it in the back of a taxi. Let's take a nice leisurely stroll through the park. We can chat and just enjoy the moonlight and the night air. You don't know how much I've longed to do things just like this. It really is the simple things that you miss most when you can't have them, the things that you take for granted when they're at your disposal every day."

"I don't want to disappoint you, it's such a sweet thought and everything, but you obviously have not been keeping up with the times. Didn't you hear what Nick just said about the Central Park Jogger and women being attacked in the park? I don't know about in your day, but today it is not safe for a woman to walk alone in Central Park at night," Penny commented.

"Ahhhh, but you are not alone; you're with me. Who better to protect you than a ghost?" Kerby pointed out.

"I don't think this is a good idea. It's like an invitation to trouble, but if you insist and you're sure you can protect me, I guess it is a nice night for a walk. It might be kind of fun, kind of like taking the park back for the civilized people of New York."

Midway through the park as the pair rounded a bend in the road, Penny's worst fears were realized. Headed directly for them were three of the meanest looking thugs she had ever seen. The minute they saw Penny headed in their direction, they started laughing and giving each other all kinds of handshakes and high fives. Penny stopped abruptly and started backing up.

Kerby caught Penny by her arm. "Where do you think you're going? I thought we were going to take the park back for the civilized New Yorkers. Anyway, this looks like it might be fun. Don't go and ruin it for me now."

"This is not a good idea. I think we should run," Penny suggested.

"Well, you know what they say, kiddo, 'Sometimes angels rush in where fools dare not tread,'" Kerby replied as the trio neared them.

Two of the three blocked Penny's path while the third one circled behind her as if to cut off any avenue of escape. "Hey, baby, you looking for us?" one of the group taunted.

"We been here all night waiting for you. First we gonna have a look through your pocketbook, then we gonna go through the rest of your clothes, then we gonna go over in the grass and the party really starts," the smallest one in the group threatened, whipping out a switch blade and heading in Penny's direction. "Now, be a good girl, don't give me no trouble, and just hand me the pocketbook," he continued, reaching to stick the knife under Penny's throat.

Kerby stepped between the thug and Penny, grabbed the guy's wrist and hand and snapped it backwards hard. A loud cracking sound echoed through the woods, followed by the thug's howling.

"Kerby! Was that really necessary?" a shocked Penny shouted. "It sounded like you broke his wrist."

"A couple of weeks in a cast and he'll be fine. Anyway, it's not as if he didn't deserve it," Kerby said, easing the knife out of the thug's hand as he lowered him to his knees by bending his broken wrist back even further. Kerby took the knife by its blade and threw it hard to the ground. It landed right between the legs of the other thug who stood frozen in front of Penny watching the events unfold.

"Did you see that shit?" the awestruck guy blurted, looking down at the knife between his legs. "She must be some kind a voodoo bitch or something."

The guy working his way behind Penny missed everything that had gone on in front of her. "Damn, man, you let a pussy put down. Let's see if she got some voodoo that can deal with my shit," the guy behind her snarled as he started toward her, knife in hand.

When the guy made his move, Kerby reached for a large, grated garbage can that sat on the side of the pathway. The thug stopped short when he saw the garbage can rise up off the ground, seemingly by itself. As the thug watched in disbelief, his eyes seeming to open wider than they were meant to, Kerby lifted the can up over his head and brought it down hard so that the guy's head and upper torso were thrust inside of the can, garbage spraying down around him. The thug never moved an inch as the bottom of the can came crashing down viciously on top of his head, driving him to his knees, his upper body confined within the can. He remained still, looking like a caged animal. When

Kerby looked up, he saw the third guy beating a path through the woods in the opposite direction.

Penny grabbed Kerby by his arm. "That's enough of that. I think you overdid it a little there. Let's get out of here before the police come and we get into trouble."

"What? Did they do away with the self defense laws in this state?" Kerby wondered. "I thought I went quite easy on them, all things considered."

"Let's go," Penny demanded, pulling Kerby down the trail away from the scene.

Exiting Central Park, Penny stopped as if a thought had come to her. She turned to Kerby. "You got that wrong back there."

"Got what wrong, kiddo? I thought I did well," Kerby replied.

"No, I mean the saying. You got it backwards. You said, 'Sometimes angels rush in where fools fear to tread.' The saying is from Alexander Pope's *An Essay on Criticism*. It goes, 'Nay fly to altars; there they'll talk you dead; For fools rush in where angels fear to tread.'"

"I don't know anything about any Alexander Pope," Kerby responded. "The quote I used is from *The Bishop's Wife* with Cary Grant and Loretta Young. You know, the one where Grant plays an angel named Dudley. Anyway, given the situation, the way you said it wouldn't have made sense. Had I said it the way Pope did, you would have been the fool, which I guess would have made me the angel. I'm not quite there yet, kiddo," Kerby said with his characteristic smile.

CHAPTER 7

A BOOK STORE BY ANY OTHER NAME
JUNE 18, 2003

*A*s she headed downstairs for breakfast, it dawned on Penny that with all of the excitement of the preceding days she hadn't picked up her mail. Before starting toward the kitchen, Penny reached out of the front door and grabbed a stack of mail from the box next to the door. She leafed through the pile of mostly junk mail as she ambled down the corridor toward the kitchen. The only letter that caught her eye was one from the Law Firm of Mark Libby, marked "Urgent" on the envelope.

Libby was the lawyer handling Mags's estate. At first, Penny thought that the original of the deed for the brownstone might be in the envelope, but the envelope didn't feel thick enough to be holding a deed. When she tore the envelope open, what Penny found was a letter, also marked "Urgent" on the top. Penny read the letter as she entered the kitchen.

Kerby met Penny at the kitchen table with a cup of coffee. "You'd better drink this up, kiddo. I'd say we have a very busy day ahead of us. I have some ideas on following up on the leads that Nick gave us with regard to the murders and the whereabouts of the stranded spirits."

"It looks like that's going to have to wait until another time," Penny replied, looking up from the letter for the first time. "It seems that Mags's lawyer, Mark Libby, has taken the liberty of setting up an appointment to see me this morning. The letter says it's absolutely essential that we get together at the earliest convenient moment, and he has apparently decided that this morning is convenient for both of us. It appears that we are going to be spending the morning with Mr. Libby."

"Count me out, kiddo. Generally speaking, I don't care for lawyers, never have. I was only in the presence of this Libby guy once, when Mags was too sick to go to his office and he came here. He was not overly sympathetic to the fact that Mags was near death. He was all business, even complained about the fact that he was losing money while he was out of his office. The guy really made my skin crawl, or he would have if I had skin that was still capable of crawling. I'm afraid that if I go down there with you and he treats you with the same lack of respect, he may wind up with his head in a garbage can," Kerby laughed.

"I know what you mean. There's something about him that creeps me out too. Do you have any idea how Mags chose him to do her will and handle her estate?" Penny asked.

"He apparently handled some business transactions for Sol back in the day. Sol warned Mags that the guy didn't have much personality but said that when it came to the law this Libby knows his stuff. You know Mags, she thought she could charm anybody, and she was more concerned about getting things done right than about dealing with the right kind of character."

"Well, then it looks as if I'm going to be spending some time this morning alone with Mr. Personality. While I'm gone, why don't you lay out an agenda, and as soon as we can we'll see what we can do about preventing a murder and catching a couple of murderers, not to mention sending some spirits on their way skyward."

♥ 👗 ♟

Sol was next door when Penny called. He had the cab in front of the brownstone when Penny walked out her front door. They were on their way to midtown with Sol giving Penny some insight into the workings of Mark Libby's mind when Penny remembered that she had forgotten to tip the police off as to the whereabouts of Nick Demopolous's body. Remembering what Kerby had said about the police tracing phone calls, Penny had Sol pull over to the first payphone she spotted with a parking space anywhere near it.

Sol pulled up in front of an Asian grocery with a payphone only a few doors down. Pulling to the curb, Sol almost hit the grocer who was standing alongside the curb, hosing clean the area in front of his outdoor fruit and vegetable stand. The grocer was furious as Penny stepped out of the cab. "Don't worry about him," Sol noted. "I'll handle him; you just make your call."

The grocer stood only about five feet tall, but he was as angry as a wasp that had just had its nest disturbed. "You no park here," the red-faced grocer shouted at Sol as Penny headed for the payphone. "Look! Look at sign!" the grocer screamed, pointing up at a "No Parking Sign" directly in front of Sol's cab. "It say you no park here."

"I'm not parking," Sol explained. "I'm just stopping long enough for my ride to make a telephone call."

The little grocer was not satisfied. "You think I no read English. Sign say no stopping, no standing. I gonna take down your number and report you to police and Taxi Commission," the little guy hollered, taking out a pen and paper and writing down Sol's license plate number.

Sol wasn't the least bid concerned about being reported to the police or the Taxi Commission, but he knew that if a complaint were filed with the commission, it would mean paperwork that he would have to handle.

"Are those fresh peaches?" Sol asked, exiting his taxi. "I like my peaches like my women, ripe but nice and firm, a little sweet but a little tart too."

The grocer laughed hysterically at Sol's joke. "That funny! Everything fresh!" the grocer exclaimed, his voice calm now. "Peaches are fresh, nice and firm, just like you like. Cherries are fresh too. You like cherries?"

"I love cherries. Give me a pound of cherries and three peaches," Sol said, after squeezing one of the soft, overripe peaches.

"Sure, sure thing, right this way. I take care of you very fast before police come. I no want you get ticket, you know," the grocer chirped, checking down the street to make sure that Penny was still on the phone.

Penny finished her call just as the grocer finished giving Sol his change. She had kept the call as brief as she could. Penny tried limiting her information for the time being to the exact location of Nick's body, but the emergency operator pressed her for details. Penny gave her Nick's name and told the operator the exact date of his disappearance. When the operator pressed for a cause of death, Penny even gave her a brief description of the injuries Nick had suffered. When the operator asked Penny to hold on for a few minutes while she put the information into the computer, Penny panicked, hung up the phone and headed back for the cab.

"Come back soon. You park here any time," the grocer announced, smiling mightily at Penny and Sol as they got back into the taxi.

♥ ⚱ ♛

Mark Libby's office was not what Penny had anticipated. Given its location in an upscale neighborhood in midtown Manhattan, Penny envisioned a spacious, carpeted office with tasteful wallpaper and paintings on wood trimmed walls. She figured that she would be greeted in a separate area by a receptionist and then led into a room with perhaps a couple of secretaries sitting behind real wood desks and surrounded by real wood cabinets. Then she thought she'd be taken in to see Mark Libby, who she imagined sitting in his office in an oversized leather chair behind a real oak desk.

Instead, Penny entered into a tiny outer office that looked as if someone had had a food fight in it. The carpeting and wallpaper were covered with stains of some kind, though Penny didn't care to imagine what might have caused them. An overweight secretary sat behind a metal desk snapping gum in her mouth. She was surrounded by metal filing cabinets. But what struck Penny most about the office was the fact that, despite all of the metal filing cabinets, there were tens of legal red rope files scattered around the office, most of them bursting at their seams.

There were no niceties from the secretary either. "What can I do for you, doll?" she asked, looking down at a file on her desk.

"My name is Penny Albright. I have an appointment to see Mr. Libby this morning."

"Did you call to confirm?" the secretary asked, still without looking up.

"No, I just got the letter this morning. He chose the date and time."

The secretary finally made eye contact while blowing a bubble with her gum. Then she looked down at a desk calendar on the corner of her desk. Popping her bubble just before she spoke, she said, "He must have forgotten. It's not on his calendar."

"The letter was marked *urgent*. It said that he needed to see me as soon as possible," Penny explained.

"All of his letters say that. I'll see if he has the time to see you this morning," the secretary said, just before she stuck her head into an office behind her. "You're lucky, he can see you right away," the secretary announced when her head reappeared.

Mark Libby's office was as depressing as the outer office; same stained carpeting and wallpaper, same metal cabinets and red rope files scattered around. Libby sat in a frayed cloth chair behind a gray metal desk that was only slightly larger than the one the secretary sat behind.

"Come in and take a seat, Miss Albright," Libby instructed, pointing to a chair in front of his desk that was already occupied by a large red rope file.

Penny waited for a second, thinking Libby might actually get up and move the red rope. When she realized that he was oblivious to her expectations, Penny lifted the file to move it down to the floor next to the chair. As she did so, the red rope split at a seam and the papers in it scattered to the floor.

"Careful with that!" Libby hollered. "That's important stuff. Everything in there is in a particular order."

Penny reached for the papers, but stopped at the sound of Libby's rebuke. "Don't worry about it now. The damage is already done. I'll have to have my secretary straighten it out later."

"I'm afraid I have some tough news for you, Miss Albright," Libby continued as Penny eased herself into the chair.

"Is there something wrong with the execution of the deed?" Penny asked, a sound of serious concern in her voice.

"No, the deed was signed and the property transferred properly. The brownstone is yours; at least for now," Libby answered cryptically. "Your problems are related to financial circumstances surrounding the brownstone. You see, Miss O'Malley knew that you didn't have much in the way of assets. Her desire was to see that you took the brownstone free and clear. Unfortunately, she got extremely ill and then died before we got everything done."

"I'm not sure what you're saying. Does someone else have a legal interest in the brownstone?" Penny asked, now in a surprised tone.

"In a way, yes. Your aunt kept a somewhat substantial mortgage on the brownstone for income tax purposes. The interest on the mortgage is an income tax write-off. Miss O'Malley had intended to pay off the mortgage with her assets before she died, so that you could take the property free of any encumbrances, but she never got around to doing it before she passed on."

"How much is the mortgage?" Penny wondered.

"Given the overall value of the brownstone, which is in the millions, the mortgage is not much. It's only about $250,000, but you take the property with the obligation to make the monthly mortgage payments, which given your current lack of income may prove difficult."

"I'll work it out somehow," Penny assured him.

"If that was your only problem, you'd be okay, but it's not. You see your aunt was seriously delinquent in her real estate tax payments. According to my review of her records, she had used the wrong classification for the building in calculating her real estate taxes for almost as long as she owned the brownstone. New York City has four classifications for property located here. Shortly after your aunt bought the brownstone, those classifications were changed. I'm not sure who was advising her on her choice of classification for the building at the time, but she was two classes below what she should have been. She wound up paying far less than what she should have in real estate taxes over the years. My numbers indicate that at the time of her death, your aunt owed the city back taxes in excess of $175,000, not including interest," Libby explained.

"Did Mags know about this?"

"I informed Miss O'Malley of the shortfall, and again it was her intention to correct the deficiency before you took the brownstone, but again she died before any action was taken. Even though I knew of your aunt's intentions, she never took any formal or legally sufficient action to change her will. I was legally obligated to distribute the assets as the will provided, despite the fact that I knew Miss O'Malley intended otherwise. Under the circumstances, it seems that you are obligated to pay the penalty," Libby asserted.

"Is the city aware of all of this?"

"They will be as soon as I inform them, which as an officer of the court I am obliged to do. I could lose my license if I were to be involved in an ongoing scheme to defraud the city of taxes it is rightfully owed."

"What happens when they find out?" Penny asked.

"Either you pay the deficiency, or the city forecloses on the property; you know, takes the building. Now, the city is not generally interested in being in the real estate business. Frequently, they'll work with you, but given the nature of your property, i.e., a very valuable brownstone in a historic district on the Upper East Side, I tend to think that someone in city government will take notice and try to take advantage of the situation. They'll try to take the building quickly at substantially less than its true value and arrange to have it purchased by a friend at a scam auction," Libby predicted.

"Can they do that?" Penny asked, a sense of outrage in her voice.

"This is New York City, Miss Albright, anything can happen here. Just as an example, given the people that I know in the city bureaucracy and my understanding of the inner workings of the system, if I wanted to make a play for your building, I could have it by the end of the year," Libby boasted.

"Well, then can't you do something to hold them off or get me a payment schedule?"

"Like I said, under the right circumstances they'll work with you, but given your lack of assets and/or income at the moment, with what do you plan to pay them? I can't even figure out how you plan to make your monthly mortgage payments," Libby snorted.

Penny felt nauseated. "I need to think my options through," she groaned, getting up and heading for the door.

"At this point, I don't know that you have much in the way of options. However, I do have a proposition that you might be interested in before you leave. Like I said, your property is in an attractive location. It's a building that I must confess I would not mind owning myself. I would be willing to pay you market value for the building, to be determined by the average between what your appraiser says the building is worth and what my appraiser says the building is worth. Of course, I would have to purchase the property from you through a shell corporation. I couldn't transact business directly with you because I might be seen as having a conflict of interest."

"I have no intention of selling the brownstone, Mr. Libby," Penny declared adamantly as she stepped through the doorway into the outer office.

Libby caught Penny just as she reached the exit for the outer office. From his office door Libby hollered, "I'm trying to be fair with you, Miss Albright. I've offered you market value. Remember what I said about my friends in city government. If you choose not to cooperate with me, I'll still have the building by the end of the year, but you will have much less than you would have had if you dealt with me directly."

"Don't threaten me, Mr. Libby! I'm not selling the brownstone, not to you or your dummy corporation or anyone else. And I'm not letting the city take the building away from me either," Penny shouted defiantly.

"Nevertheless, I'm going to keep the offer on the table for the time being. Sleep on it a couple of nights. When you change your mind, you have my number," Libby grunted, ducking his head back into his office. Then his head popped back out. "By the way, we never had this conversation. I've got a witness who will swear that she was present for our entire meeting and this subject never came up," Libby added, looking at his secretary who snapped her gum again and smiled.

Just as well I didn't bring Kerby with me, Penny thought as she waited for the elevator. *That guy would have felt right at home with his head in a pile of garbage.*

♥ ♧ ♠

As Penny and Sol made their way back uptown on Park Avenue, they ran into gridlock traffic and were stopped for a substantial period of time opposite an outdoor café at the corner of 79th Street. Penny was deep in thought about how to avoid losing her new home and her new friend. Her eyes remained glued on the back of the seat in front of her. Had Penny looked to her left before traffic started to flow again, she would have seen two young women seated outside at the café, sipping frothy cappuccinos from little white cups. One of the women was a tall, beautiful, rail-thin blonde. The other woman was shorter with dark hair and a curl on her forehead, her right bicep muscle formed a perfectly round little ball each time she bent her elbow to lift her cup to her mouth.

"I want you to pick again this time," Jean insisted.

"I thought we were going to take turns. I picked last time," Niki responded.

"I know, but you're better at picking than I am. Taking the guy out of *Dorrian's* and doing him in Central Park was pure genius. I never would have thought of something like that. I'm not that creative. As you well know, the one guy I picked was a major disappointment for me. You pick who and where again this year."

"Actually, to tell you the truth, I'm glad to hear that you feel that way. I've already picked somebody out, and I was hoping you'd agree with me that he's a perfect candidate. I even know where I want to do him. I've planned something a little different this time," Niki noted with a devious smile.

"Tell me about him. Do I know him?" Jean asked excitedly.

"Well, you've never met him, but you've seen him lots of times. In fact, you've even seen him in his underwear. Do you want to guess, or should I just tell you who he is?" Niki teased.

"Just tell me, given that hint, I don't think I could possibly guess anyway."

"Why? You've seen so many men in their underpants lately," Niki laughed. "I want to do Damian Bradford," Niki added, her demeanor suddenly turning serious.

"You want to do Damian Bradford? The male-model? The guy who's got a poster of himself dressed in nothing but his tighty-whities in the middle of Times Square?" Jean asked incredulously.

"I told you you'd seen him in his underpants," Niki chuckled.

"It's kind of hard to miss seeing him in his underwear. The poster in Times Square is as big as a building, and it seems as if every magazine spread I've ever seen the guy in he winds up stripping down to his briefs. Not that I'm complaining. I mean, he's got a killer body."

"He's got a better build than Peter Sizemore had. His muscles are thicker, more mature looking. And believe me when I tell you, he's not stuffing anything into his shorts to make him look bigger in those ad campaigns. If only he had a brain to go with the body. The guy is a complete airhead. He would have made Danny O'Brien look like Einstein," Niki joked.

"The only thing that causes me concern about selecting him is that maybe your connection to him is a little too close, maybe you know him a little too well. Didn't you two go out for a while?"

"Not really, not publicly anyway. He never took me out anywhere or anything. We were just what you might call *fuck buddies*. If I had an itch, I called him and he came running. If he was in the mood, he called me, and I helped him out. The only problem was, he was always in the mood. My phone rang three times a week, and I know I wasn't the only girl with whom he was having that kind of a relationship. Not that I minded. He was never boring in bed, I can tell you that much. He's about as kinky as they come, always looking to try new stuff. One night he'd want to blindfold me and tie me to the bed, the next night he'd want me to blindfold him and tie him to the bed. A couple of times he even asked me to ride him from behind with a strap-on. I had to call him *my little whore* while I was doing it," Niki laughed.

"I don't blame him. You've gotten awfully good with that thing, but now I'm starting to feel jealous."

"There's nothing to feel jealous about, that was a rare thing with him. Believe it or not, what really turns him on is feet. The guy would spend hours rubbing and kissing my feet. He loved to suck on my big toes, and to tell the truth, I loved having him do it too. They say that it's the closest that a woman can get to experiencing what it feels like for a man when he's having oral sex performed on him. I don't know whether that's true or not, but it is a unique sensation."

"How did *he* get off from that?" Jean wondered.

"Sometimes he would handle himself while he was doing it. Sometimes when he was done, I would rub his member up and down with my feet in order to relieve him," Niki noted.

"Okay, but how did *you* get off from that?" Jean continued.

"Don't worry about me, I always got mine. Let's just say that when Damian Bradford sticks out his tongue, Mick Jagger and Gene Simmons put theirs away in shame," Niki laughed.

"It sounds as if you have it really good with this guy. Why would you want to get rid of him?"

"I *had* it really good with him, past tense. He's got a serious girlfriend now, another model. On top of it all, she's a rival for my jobs. I can't stand the arrogant bitch. He doesn't want to see me anymore because he's afraid that she might find out. Does that sound like somebody else we used to know?" Niki said with a smile.

"If he doesn't want to see you anymore, how do you plan to lure him in?"

"I told you, he's kinky. He might not be intrigued by a threesome though. I'm certain he's had them before. I'll have to think of something unusual, perhaps something involving our feet. Who knows? I'll tell him I just want him one last time for old times sake. If I can think of something sexually unique, he won't hesitate, but if he balks for even a second, I'll threaten to tell his new girlfriend about some of our nights together. It's not like I was his whore or anything. I don't have any obligation to keep any client confidences. He'll come around, one way or another," Niki assured her.

"Okay, so where do we take him?"

"You know I bought a boat, right? It's not too big or anything, but it has a nice spacious cabin with a queen size berth. I'm able to handle it by myself now, you know, get into and out of its mooring spaces. Once you're out in the river, it's easier than driving a car. We'll do him at night on the boat under the stars. I'll pull the boat down by the Statue of Liberty, and we'll do him with Lady Liberty looking down on us. We can dump his body right over the side when we're done with him."

"I love it!" Jean exclaimed. "I knew you'd come up with something creative. You have that kind of mind."

"I'm more interested in how creative you're going to be with your thing. Have you got any new ideas?" Niki wondered.

"In that regard, we haven't even scratched the surface yet. I'm thinking about using his genitals like a pincushion. I just got this new set of needles, really thin like acupuncture needles, except I don't use acupuncture points. You can slide them in one side of a penis and out the other without doing a whole lot of internal damage. Lots of pain without that much blood. Once his organ looks like a porcupine, I'll heat the needles like an acupuncturist might, except I'll let them get red hot," Jean explained, her eyes glazed over almost as if she were living the moment as she spoke.

"And you say you're not a creative thinker. I couldn't think up something like that if my life depended on it. You should see a shrink and try to determine from where in your mind these dark thoughts originate," Niki suggested, only half joking.

"It just so happens that is exactly what I'm doing. I told my mother what I was doing to make a living while I finish school. She wasn't the least bit upset, but like you, she thought it would be good idea to try to find out why it is that these acts excite me the way they do. So she set up an appointment for me with somebody recommended to her by one of her doctor friends."

"You haven't said anything to this doctor about what we've done, have you?" Niki asked, a look of concern on her face. "That's how the Menendez boys got caught after they killed their parents."

"Just because I'm seeing a psych it doesn't mean I've lost my mind. Of course I haven't said anything to her about us. I just talk about what I do in my profession and what my life was like growing up."

"Has she reached any conclusions about where these dark desires come from?" Niki asked, a look of relief on her face.

"She's giving me what she calls regression therapy, or hypnoanalysis, or something. She hypnotizes me and supposedly takes me back to my earliest childhood to see whether there were any psychological traumas that I may have suffered that I can't recall now with my conscious mind."

"And what has she found?" Niki wondered, seeming sincerely interested.

"According to my psych, my father abused me sexually from the time that I was three years old until the time that he left when I was ten. She says he forced me to fondle his penis and even take him in my mouth. She says that's where my love/hate relationship with the male genitalia started."

"What do you think? Is it true? I mean, wouldn't you remember if your father sexually abused when you were ten years old?"

"I would certainly think so. I've listened to the tape recordings of our hypnosis sessions, and it's true that I did describe those kinds of encounters with my father, but when I listen to her questions, it seems to me that she's leading me to say the things that she wants to hear, and under hypnosis I'm saying them to please her. When I told her that I was certain I would have a conscious recollection if my father had sexually assaulted me when I was ten years old, she said that the mind has a way of protecting itself by shoving traumatic experiences into the subconscious. Still, to tell you the truth, at this point I'm not buying it."

"Have you asked your mother about any of this? Do you think that perhaps it might have had something to do with your mother and father splitting up?" Niki wondered.

"Sure, I asked. My mom thinks my doctor is crazy. Don't get me wrong, she hates my father with a passion. If she thought she could find him and pin something like this on him, she'd be more than happy to do it. But mom said there is no way that what I've been describing under hypnosis could have ever really happened. She said that if anything like that had ever happened under her roof she would have known about right away. She said that if she even suspected that something like that had been going on, she would have cut my father's balls off. She actually said that, *she would have cut his balls off.* I didn't know whether to laugh or cry," Jean recalled.

"Has your mom offered an opinion on where these desires come from?"

"She says that when I was three or four she took me to some reptile show at the kids' section of the Central Park Zoo. According mom, the guy that was putting on the show stuck a large, harmless Garter Snake in my face. Well, apparently the thing struck me, bit my cheek and held on. You know, they have no teeth to speak of, but they can still pinch a hold of you. Mom says that before the guy could react, I panicked and grabbed the snake by its tail, pulled it from my cheek and started whacking its head on the ground like it was a bullwhip, until its head was mangled and covered with blood. Mom says that the zoo guy screamed at me for killing the snake, but afterwards a bunch of the mothers surrounded me and congratulated me, told me what a brave little girl I was. Mom even bought ice cream for me as a reward."

"So you think that's where it all started, with you being attacked by a Garter Snake at the Central Park Zoo at the ripe old age of three or four?" Niki giggled.

"It makes as much sense to me as what the psych concluded," Jean replied. "The bottom line is that I'm curious as to why I feel the way I do and do what I do, but regardless, I'm not going to stop doing it. I love it. I'm not ashamed of it, and I'm not looking to *modify my behavior* as the psych has suggested."

"Well, if it's worth anything to you, I love you just the way you are," Niki said.

"Good! That reminds me, another one of those Latex and Leather Galas is being planned for the end of this month, and the slave that I was going to bring with me is going to be out of town. I thought you might like to join me again. You seemed to have fun the last one we went to together," Jean recalled.

"Are you kidding me? The last one was a blast. I'll go home and get my black latex out of storage as soon as we leave here," Niki replied enthusiastically.

"Great! I'll call the Mistress who's throwing the gala this time and let her know that I'll be there with another dominant female as my guest. The only thing is, I'm still waiting to hear exactly where and when this one is going to be. It seems that there's been some problems with the location the Mistress normally uses."

"Wherever! If it's the same cast of misfits and the same sexual shenanigans as last time, I'll be there." Niki said.

♥ ♋ ♣

The distress on Penny's face was apparent when she came through the front door of the brownstone. "What is it, kiddo?" Kerby asked, before the door had even closed behind her.

Penny did not want to burden Kerby with the possibility that she might actually lose the brownstone, and worse yet, that before long Mark Libby might be its new owner. "Nothing important," Penny lied.

"A lawyer sends you a letter marked *urgent*, you meet with him and come home looking as if you just got news of another death in the family, and you expect me to believe that there's nothing important on your mind?" Kerby challenged. "You know when Mags was here-- " Kerby started a thought but was cut off by Penny before he could get it out.

"I wish you wouldn't do that," Penny snapped. "I asked you to leave Mags out of things. What were you going to tell me, how you and Mags worked out all of your problems with the *Magic Eight-Ball* or something. Some problems have to be dealt with seriously."

"Okay, now we're getting somewhere. So far, I know that there is a serious problem that has to be dealt with in a serious manner. Now, what I was going to say, if you'll let me finish this time, is that when Mags was here and she had a problem, we talked it out, put our heads together and made a decision on a course of action. One thing is certain, you can't just ignore serious problems. They don't go away by themselves. It was only when all else failed that Mags and I would get out the *Magic Eight-Ball*," Kerby said, breaking into a smile.

Penny smiled back, but she still could not bring herself to talk about the possibility of losing the brownstone. "I'm sorry I snapped at you. It's no big deal really. It's just that Mags had a mortgage on the house that she intended to pay off before she died, so that I could take the brownstone free and clear. Unfortunately, Mags got too sick to deal with it and died before the mortgage was paid off."

"That's not possible, kiddo. Mags and I talked about this often. She never gave me specifics, but she assured me that everything had been taken care of. She personally signed all of the paperwork and ensured that everything that needed to be filed got filed, or so she thought. She said that Libby had the originals of everything in his office," Kerby recalled.

"Well, Libby must have dropped the ball, intentionally or otherwise, because there is still an outstanding mortgage on the property. He showed it to me. It's not as if I can sue him for malpractice or anything, at least not with you as my only witness."

"What possible motive could that lowlife have for purposely not paying off the mortgage?" Kerby wondered.

Penny realized that she had slipped, but she still was not prepared to burden Kerby with the fact that Libby wanted the property for himself and might actually become Kerby's housemate before long. She had decided not to discuss the real estate tax problem with Kerby just yet. Penny felt that she needed time to give it more thought herself before she let Kerby know about it.

"I don't know what his motive might have been," Penny lied again. "The important thing now is that I figure out in a hurry how to develop an income stream sufficient enough so that I can meet my monthly mortgage obligations."

"That's not a problem, kiddo. For the time being, you can take out a loan somewhere, maybe even a second mortgage, use that money to keep your head above water until we turn the bookstore into a moneymaker. I have some ideas on that front too," Kerby noted.

"What bank is going to lend me money? I have no income to speak of now, and no credit record."

"Of course you do," Kerby retorted. "In this day and age everybody has a credit record. You must have credit cards?"

"Never owned one," Penny shot back.

"Well, you must have purchased something, a car maybe, that you paid off over time."

"Nope," Penny answered. "My feeling about buying things on credit is that if I can't afford to pay cash for something, I can't afford that something. If I can't afford that something, then I don't need that something. I don't believe in paying interest to someone in order to buy something that I can live without."

Penny's words on the subject of credit and interest came right out of the mouth of Aunt Flo O'Malley. Aunt Flo was the second oldest of the O'Malley sisters, right behind Mags. Aunt Flo's quirk, so to speak, was that she was a bit of a hoarder, though tightwad might be the better word to describe her. Mags used to say that her sister Flo had the first dime that she ever made, literally, not something that she kept to hang on her wall as a keepsake either. Aunt Flo lived just outside of Little Rock, Arkansas. She moved there when she was in her thirties after she read an article saying that Arkansas had the lowest cost of living index of any state in the country.

When she first got to Arkansas, Aunt Flo bought a flower shop. She loved flowers, especially arranging them in unique ways and color patterns. At first, she lived in the back room of her shop, so that she wouldn't have to pay rent to anybody. She slept on an old sofa and kept her food in the same coolers that she used for her flowers, so that she wouldn't have to spend money on a refrigerator.

Five years later, Aunt Flo bought a big old house up on a hill outside of Little Rock. At the closing, Aunt Flo showed up with the purchase price in cash and plopped the money down on the desk in front of the stunned seller and attorneys in the office. Aunt Flo never borrowed money for anything and never bought anything on credit. The first thing Penny could ever recall Aunt Flo saying to her was, "My feeling about buying things on credit is that if I can't afford to pay cash for something, I can't afford that something. If I can't afford that something, then I don't need that something. I don't believe in paying interest to someone in order to buy something that I can live without." It was like a mantra for Aunt Flo, and Penny heard it so often that she would occasionally repeat it verbatim without even realizing what she was saying.

Penny did not mind Aunt's Flo's miserly ways, maybe because she was the only person in the world on whom Aunt Flo would splurge indulgences. In doing so, however, Aunt Flo never failed to point out the importance of spending within one's means.

"Do you know why I'm buying you this, honey?" Aunt Flo would ask.

"Because you can afford to pay cash for it," was the answer Penny had been taught to give.

"That's right, dear, and if I couldn't afford to pay cash for it, you would not be getting it," was how Aunt Flo always responded, with a smile.

The fact was that by the time Penny started to visit Aunt Flo, Aunt Flo could have afforded to pay cash for anything either of them wanted Penny to have. By then, Aunt Flo had sold the flower shop, though she kept her love for flowers, having created the town's most impressive flower garden in and around her entire house. In the late eighties, Aunt Flo read an article in *Reader's Digest* about a new way of investing one's money called "day trading." Up until that time, Flo had never even considered placing her money in someone else's hands, not even a bank. Flo preferred to keep her substantial liquid assets in various hiding places around her house.

After educating herself on the process of day trading, Aunt Flo bought her first computer, with cash of course, and went to work day trading stocks. Later, she taught a bunch of her bridge club members the process. Together they bought several more computers and the group spent their afternoons at Flo's house trading stocks. They made a killing on tech stocks on the NASDAQ from the mid-nineties into early 2001 and bailed out just before the plunge. In 2002, the geriatric group was featured on the *Today Show* because, average-wise, they were out earning every one of the major brokerage houses. Penny loved watching Aunt Flo at work on her computer and listened to every word she uttered when it came to economics. For better or worse, Penny was a Flo O'Malley disciple when it came to money matters.

"You got that from your Aunt Flo, didn't you?" Kerby mocked. "I heard those exact words spoken by Flo O'Malley every time she ever came here for a visit."

"That's right, and I'm not embarrassed by that either," Penny responded. "Aunt Flo is a bit of genius when it comes to money, you know?"

"Your Aunt Flo is a bit of nut, just like all of the O'Malley sisters," Kerby commented. "Even Mags admitted that. Actually, Mags was kind of proud of it in a strange way. But the truth is that lunacy doesn't just run in your family, it practically gallops."

"Stop doing that too," Penny demanded.

"Stop doing what, kiddo?" Kerby asked.

"Using quotes from Cary Grant movies as if you just made them up yourself," Penny chided with a straight face that gradually broke into a grin.

"You're good, kiddo. I thought I'd be able to slip that one by you," Kerby noted.

"It's from *Arsenic and Old Lace*. Mortimer said it about his crazy aunts before he found out that they weren't really blood relatives," Penny remembered.

"Like I said, you're good, kiddo, but you have to admit that given that he said it about his nutty aunts, it kind of fits perfectly here, doesn't it?"

"Can we get back to business?" Penny said. "Let's forget about my getting a bank loan and move on from there."

"Okay, then how about a personal loan? There's Aunt Flo, you may be the only person in the world to whom she would lend money, but there's no question she would give it to you."

"Not a chance, I could never ask Aunt Flo, even though I know she would do it," Penny responded quickly.

"How about Sol or Joie or both of them? Between them they have more money than some small countries."

"They would give it to me too, but I could never ask them for the kind of money I need, at least not without some definite way to pay them back."

"Look, it's very clear, kiddo, that there is not going to be anyone that I might suggest from whom you would be comfortable borrowing money, so why don't we direct our attention to how you turn the bookstore into a moneymaking enterprise. Like I said, I have some ideas," Kerby repeated.

"I already have a plan for turning the bookstore around and making it profitable, but it's going to take time, and I'm going to need capital for that too," Penny pointed out. "My intention is to eventually devote a section of the store to rare and collectable books. One of my professors from college used to be in the business. He's getting on in age and is going to be looking to sell off his collection in the near future. He's promised me the first opportunity to purchase his collection at a very reasonable price. The problem is, he's not quite there yet, and like I said, it's going to take some substantial start up capital to get it off the ground."

"Sounds interesting, for down the road," Kerby remarked. "But what I have in mind is more of a quick-fix and shouldn't cost a whole lot of money."

"I'm listening," Penny replied.

"Think about it, kiddo, what's the only sure fire sell in this society? What do marketers use to sell everything from beer to high heel shoes?" Kerby asked. "Sex," he answered, without giving Penny the opportunity to offer an answer, which she did, in fact, know.

"I'm thinking you should change the name of the bookstore from *Ghosts and Gumshoes* to *Sex, Ghosts, and Gumshoes.* You have to admit that will catch people's eye, right? Then you devote a section, perhaps somewhere private in the back of the store, to books that deal exclusively with erotica and sexual subjects. We could order the books strictly from consignment sellers, so that there will be no substantial cash outlay on your part."

"Do you want to know what I think?" Penny asked sarcastically. "I think that there are enough porno shops in New York City without my adding to the problem."

"Wait! Wait! Wait!" Kerby exclaimed. "You've got a bad attitude on this subject. All sex is not pornography, you know? Even the old geezers on the United States Supreme Court recognized that. Sex is a beautiful and fun thing when engaged in the right way between consenting adults. You need to loosen up a little. Haven't you ever watched *Sex in the City?* Women today are supposed to be sexually liberated. If you keep your present mindset, you're going to miss out on life's greatest pleasure."

"Okay, Dr. Ruth, if you're not planning on porn magazines and peepholes, what are you planning to have in your little private sex section in the back of my bookstore?"

"I'm talking about sex in a fun and tasteful way, perhaps even geared mainly for the liberated woman. I'm talking about classic novels with sex as the primary subject or theme. I'm talking about erotica, not pornography. You know, authors like D.H Lawrence, John Cleland, Pauline Reage and Pierre Louys. I'm talking about novels like *Lady Chatterly's Lover*, *Memoirs of a Woman of Pleasure*, *Story of O,* and *The She Devils.* There are lots of novels of erotica that women throughout history have loved, many have even been written by women. You can go all the way back to *The Songs of Solomon* in the *Old Testament* or to the Greek poet, Sappho, who just happened to be a woman. You can be the one to turn the modern woman onto some of these classics. They'll love them," Kerby insisted.

"Okay, you've got my attention, I'm listening, keep going."

"Of course, you'd have to have a section for the more contemporary writers of sexy or erotic fiction as well, especially the female writers. You know, Candace Bushnell, Susie Bright, Marcy Sheiner, there's a slew of them out there. Have you ever read Anne Rampling's *Exit to Eden?* It's a fun, sexy read. Then there would have to be a "how to" section, which should include everything from the *Kama Sutra* to the *Joy of Sex.* You'd have to get a little kinky too, you know. You can't be judgmental on these things. If it's an adult game, between consenting adults, and nobody gets hurt, why should you care? So, I'm thinking perhaps a section on fetishes, whatever they might be, you know, like dressing up or dominance and submission, whatever.

"You could create a book club dealing solely with erotic novels, have regular meetings at the bookstore. You could bring in authors to discuss their books and do signings. You could even have seminars, schedule experts in different areas to discuss different sexual techniques and things. I bet your neighbor next door would be tickled pink to do a lecture on dominating the male animal, and the ladies in the area would get a kick out of it too. The more people you get coming through those doors, the more sales you'll make, and not just in your sex section," Kerby argued.

"I'm not saying, *no*. It actually sounds interesting. I'm willing to give it some thought," Penny conceded. "But you're scaring me. You seem to know too much about this stuff."

"Let's just say I had a good teacher, and I've had a lot of time to kill on the Internet. Ghosts don't need sleep, you know?" Kerby laughed.

"Well I do, and I want to spend some time in the bookstore going through the books and talking to Carmella before I go up to bed. I'm afraid we've lost a day. We're going to have to wait until tomorrow before we start tracking down our murderers. The important thing is that I informed the police of the whereabouts of Nick's body," Penny noted.

"You did what?" Kerby asked in an astonished tone. "I thought we were going to talk about that before you made the call."

"Don't worry! I was very careful. I called from a payphone a couple of blocks from here while I was out with Sol. There's no way anyone is going to trace the call to me," Penny insisted, heading for the stairs to the bookstore.

When Penny reached the stairs, she turned back to Kerby. "Did Mags really watch *Sex in the City* with you?"

"She loved it," Kerby recalled. "Of course, her favorites were *Murder She Wrote, Columbo,* and *Barnaby Jones,* in that order.*"

CHAPTER 8

JUST A LITTLE PATIENCE AND FORTITUDE
JUNE 19, 2003

When Penny hit the bottom of the stairs, she was surprised to hear Kerby's voice coming from the sun parlor instead of the kitchen. "That was another late night for you, kiddo. You were down in that bookstore until after midnight. You should try sleeping in once in awhile."

Penny entered the sun parlor and plopped herself down into Mags's favorite chair. Kerby stood at the center window holding the curtain opened slightly, as if there were someone outside whom he did not want to know that he was there.

"Getting up early is a habit I don't care to break. Sometimes I wish I was like you, so I wouldn't have to sleep at all," Penny commented. "Anyway, you'll be happy to know that I've decided to go with your idea. I talked to Carmella, and she's ordering the sign change this morning, then she's going to start cleaning out a section in the back of the store. That is, unless she spooks herself out of there first. She's still scared to death of the place. She insisted that I move the bagpipes upstairs or she wouldn't go behind the counter anymore. By the way, she's not at all happy about the change. She says that she doesn't think her husband is going to let her keep working in a *sex shop*.

"I spent the better part of the night going through booklists on the Internet and ordering the books that I thought met our criteria. It wasn't easy choosing either. There's a very fine line between pornography and what you call erotica."

"You should've asked for my help. You said yourself that I know more about this stuff than perhaps I should," Kerby said. "I was thinking that if you did like the idea, once we get everything set up, we could have a *Grand Opening*. Maybe you could ask the Maitresse next door to do a presentation. You know, nothing hardcore, just something light and fun to get people to stop in."

"Actually, I was planning to stop over there this afternoon sometime and fill Joie in on our plans, let her know that I was going to ask her to give a talk at some point. I'm sure she'll be up for it."

"Good! There's something else I'd like you to talk to her about, related to the Demopolous thing," Kerby said. "We need to start following up on his leads and see where they take us. If Nick is correct, the clock is ticking. Don't forget, these aren't just serial killers we're dealing with here, they're also women. They won't forget an anniversary. They've probably already planned their next kill."

"I'd like to know more about these clues that you say you picked up from what Nick told us and how you think we should follow up on them," Penny remarked. "But I'm not sure I see how Joie Miller fits into all of this."

"I'll get to what I think Joie brings to the table later. Let's go through things in order of priority. The first thing we need to do is head down to the public library. As I recall, you have some experience investigating missing persons using old newspaper articles. You remember that Nick said these girls kill somebody once a year, every year, the same time each year. He said he was killed last year on June 24th. He was sure of the date. If Nick is right, he was the fourth guy they killed, and if we don't stop them, this year's kill will be their fifth. The girls apparently said that they started their killing spree by offing two kids from their high school in back to back years.

"As a result of all that, we know the exact year, month, and day on which each of the high school kids went missing. Believe me, a high school kid, from what I expect will be a white middle-class high school, goes missing in New York City, it is going to make the papers, perhaps not right away, but within a week or so. Two kids from the same high school go missing on the same date in back-to-back years, it's a big story. The newspapers are going to be writing about it. I think that this morning we need to find out who these two kids were and hopefully what school they went to. These girls seem easily identifiable from the descriptions that Nick gave us. If we can get hold of a high school yearbook for the year that these kids would have graduated, we may be able to pick our murderers right out of the book."

"Sounds good. I'm ready, but where does Joie Miller fit in?" Penny wondered.

"You recall that Nick said that when the shorter girl was driving the nail into his privates, she made fun of him and said that she knew guys who would pay her a lot of money to do the same thing to them. She has to be a part of the S&M scene in New York City. In fact, if she's getting paid, she must be a professional dominatrix. I can't be sure, but I'm guessing that the femdom community in New York City is not that large and probably close knit. In this day and age, it wouldn't surprise me if they have an industry-wide association, with meetings and everything. I also doubt that there are many Mistresses in the city who are skilled at driving a nail into a guy's pride and joy. With Nick's description and the killer's apparently unique skills, not to mention her unusual tattoo, there's a possibility that Joie might be able to identify this girl for us."

"I'll go see Joie as soon we get back from the library. First I'll talk to her about our plans for the bookstore and ask her if she'd be interested in doing a presentation. I'll use that as a way to lead into my questions about who this girl might be. You got anything else?"

"Yeah, Nick said that the two kids were killed at a warehouse on the water in Staten Island, and the guy before him was killed in a park on the Hudson River. Finding the two kids' spirits might be difficult, given that Staten Island is obviously surrounded by water, but when I think of a park on the Hudson River in Manhattan, the one that immediately comes to mind is Riverside Park. I'm thinking that if you can find an excuse to get Sol to take you on a tour of Riverside Park, preferably at night when no one else is around, we may be able to find the spirit of another victim. Maybe he'll be able to offer something helpful, but even if he can't add anything, at least we can tip the police off to his whereabouts and send him on his way, like you did for Nick."

"Sol will be game, though I don't know what reason I might offer him for wanting to tour Riverside Park at night. On the other hand, it may not matter since I suspect that Sol is already starting to think I'm a bit looney. I mean, after the séance and then the other day on the steps, what else could he think?" Penny laughed. "Got anything else?"

"I think we need to stop at *Dorrian's The Red Hand* for a drink, also at night, in the hope that we can catch the same bartender on duty that was there last year when Nick went missing. I'm sure the police have already talked to the guy. Nick's buddy must have told the police where he and Nick started that evening, but it's still worth a shot. Since the girls walked out of the place before Nick, the bartender probably didn't even realize that they had actually left together. He may not have even mentioned the girls to the cops. Those girls may be regulars in the place. Even if they're not, Nick said that he had seen the one girl on magazine covers and maybe even on a couple of television commercials. The bartender might just know who she is and what magazines and commercials we need to be looking at."

"Is that it?" Penny asked.

"Yeah, except that I'm a little concerned about exactly what you said to the emergency operator when you made your 911 call," Kerby remarked.

"Why are you still so worried about that? I told you, I called from a payphone. There's no way that the call could have been traced to me," Penny reassured him.

"I'm worried because two cops have been sitting across the street in an unmarked car since the sun came up," Kerby replied, looking out of the slit in the curtain again.

"How do you know that they're cops?" Penny wondered.

"It takes one to know one. I was on the force for nine years. I know what a cop on surveillance looks like. Now, exactly what did you say on the phone?"

"I told the operator where the body was, who the deceased was, and what kind of injuries he had suffered," a red-faced Penny noted.

"Pen-ny, Pen-ny, Pen-ny," Kerby said in an exaggerated Cary Grant imitation, though he sounded a lot more like Grant when he spoke in his normal voice. "What are we going to tell these cops as to how you came to know all of these details about Nick Demopolous's murder? It would have been difficult enough to explain if you had just told them where the body was."

"He never said that," Penny grumbled, ignoring Kerby's question.

"Who never said what?"

"Cary Grant never said 'Ju-dy, Ju-dy, Ju-dy,'" Penny said, mimicking Kerby's Grant imitation.

"Of course he did. He must have. Every impersonator who has ever done a Cary Grant imitation has used that line. Grant had to have said it in one of his movies," Kerby insisted.

"Nobody knows quotes from Cary Grant movies better than you do. If he said it in one of his movies, tell me which one it was," Penny challenged.

"Don't try to change the subject," Kerby muttered, not having been able to come up with the name of a movie in which Grant might have uttered the famous line. "The more important thing is how are we going to explain your knowledge of Nick Demopolous's murder to the police."

"He said, 'Su-san, Su-san Su-san' to Katherine Hepburn in *Bringing Up Baby,* but he never said 'Ju-dy, Ju-dy, Ju-dy,'" Penny insisted. "As far as the two guys across the street are concerned, assuming that there really are two guys across the street, I don't even believe that they're cops. If they are, they certainly would have come over to question me by now."

"Trust me, they're cops," Kerby declared.
"Then I'll just tell them I'm psychic," Penny cracked.

♥ ⌇ ♟

"I still think we should have called Sol," Penny noted, as the duo hit the bottom of the steps and headed east toward Lexington Avenue. Then she glanced back over her shoulder in the direction of the car across the street from the house. The two guys in the car sat behind tinted windows that made it impossible to tell exactly what they looked like. Though it was clear they were eyeballing Penny as she made her way up the street, neither made a move to exit the vehicle or follow her.

"You can't deprive me of this, kiddo. Don't forget, I haven't been underground in more than seventy years. This is something I have really been looking forward to, a ride in a subway car," Kerby exclaimed, as they walked up to Lexington Avenue.

When they hit Lexington Avenue and turned left on their way to the 86th Street Station of the Lexington Avenue Subway Line, Penny looked back again. The two guys were still in their car.

"I told you they aren't cops. If they're cops, why aren't they following me?" Penny questioned.

"They're cops," Kerby assured her.

"By the way, I'm quite certain that the subway system is not what you remember it as being," Penny snickered.

At the bottom of the stairs in the station Kerby said, "You're wrong, kiddo. It looks pretty close to what I remember, a lot grimier maybe, but that's to be expected. The posters on the walls are a little racier, but that's to be expected too. Otherwise, there's really not that much difference."

"I wasn't just talking about the appearance of the place. I was talking about the attitude of the people who frequent it. If you think Central Park was dangerous, try coming down here at night by yourself," Penny commented, after which she stopped at the token booth and bought herself two tokens, so that she wouldn't have to stop again on the return trip. "There's a reason those people are behind bulletproof glass," Penny noted, when she finished paying for her tokens.

"You keep forgetting who you're with, kiddo," Kerby laughed as they went through the turnstile and headed for the downtown trains. "You know what Mohammed Ali used to say, 'You can't hit what you can't see.'"

"I remember who I'm with all right. I just don't care to hear the sound of human bone breaking again for a while," Penny groaned.

The only other person on the subway platform when they got there was a huge guy sitting on a bench wearing a muscle tee shirt and a Mets cap that he had on backwards. Even sitting down he was as tall as Penny. A local train on the Number 6 line pulled in almost immediately, and the guy jumped up. Despite the fact that the platform was empty, the guy stood directly next to Penny as she waited for the train to stop, and the door to open. When the door opened, the guy shoved his way past Penny and sat in the last open seat in the car, right next to the door.

Kerby stood in front of the door, next to the guy. Penny grabbed an overhead handrail in the center of the train directly opposite Kerby.

"That wasn't very polite," Kerby noted, glaring at the guy.

"Don't even think about," Penny whispered, easing her body in Kerby's direction and turning her head away from the big guy. "It's a short ride, and I don't want any trouble."

"No trouble at all," Kerby replied as the train pulled to a stop at the 77th Street Station.

When the door to the subway car opened, Kerby reached over, snatched the Mets cap from the big guy's head and flung it out of the door as if it were a Frisbee. The guy looked up at Penny like he wanted to blame her for it, but he couldn't figure out how she could have possibly done it. Just before the door closed, the big guy followed his cap out onto the platform. "Mutha fucka," was all he said as the door slammed shut, leaving him out on the platform staring at the departing train.

"There you go!" Kerby exclaimed. "I thought he might want to be a gentleman and give you that seat." Penny just shook her head and sat down for the remainder of the ride.

They exited the train at the Grand Central Station on 42nd Street and Lexington Avenue and made their way upstairs to Grand Central Terminal. "They built this place back in 1913, and even back then it cost $43 million to construct. They offset the cost by selling *air rights* over the building, and the big shot builders scrambled to purchase them too. They built a Waldorf Astoria Hotel up on Park Avenue, and do you know how they powered their elevators? They used the third rail electricity current provided by the New York Central Railroad. The inside of this place still looks almost the same as I remember it in 1933, except maybe a few more shops and a few more people," Kerby recalled.

Exiting Grand Central, Kerby and Penny headed west on 42nd Street until they got to Fifth Avenue, where they crossed the street, made a quick left, and found themselves standing at the base of the library steps looking up at the enormous marble lions that sit proudly on either side of the library entrance.

"I bet you didn't know that the lions have names, did you?" Kerby remarked.

"It never occurred to me," Penny replied.

"Originally, they named them John Jacob Astor and James Lenox after the library's founders. Then they changed their names to Lord Astor and Lady Lenox, even though as you can see from the manes they're both males. Then, sometime after the depression hit in 1929, Mayor Fiorello LaGuardia changed their names to Patience and Fortitude, for the qualities he felt New Yorkers would need to survive the depression. That's Patience on the south side of the library steps to your left, and Fortitude to your right on the north side."

As the pair looked toward Fortitude on their right, they saw a slightly overweight, middle-aged woman standing at the lion's feet smiling broadly. She was waiting patiently for her husband who stood on the ground below to snap her picture. As if feeling Kerby and Penny turning their gazes toward her, the lady's head turned in their direction and she lost her pose and her smile.

"Over here Harry!" the lady shouted excitedly as she made tracks in the direction of Kerby and Penny.

Her husband, dressed more like he was on a tropical island than in New York City, wearing a floppy fishing hat, floral shirt, sandals with white socks, and Bermuda shorts, took off after her with his camera dangling from his neck. "Where the heck are you going, Myrtle? I haven't gotten the picture yet," Harry hollered as he ran.

Kerby and Penny were each puzzled as the woman raced at them, not just at the fact that she was running toward them, but because her eyes were focused on Kerby and not on Penny. Kerby leaned toward Penny. "She's got the *gift*, kiddo. She can see me just as clearly as you can."

I thought you could avoid being seen if you wanted to."

"Too late for that now," Kerby replied as Myrtle approached them.

"I'm sorry!" Myrtle exclaimed, staring up at Kerby. "I don't mean to be a bother, but has anyone ever told you that you look just like Cary Grant?"

"Yeah, I've been told that," Kerby replied as Harry arrived on the scene.

"Myrtle, what in the world are you doing?" Harry asked.

"Look, Harry! Doesn't he look just like Cary Grant?" Myrtle said.

"Doesn't who look like Cary Grant, dear?" Harry responded, now looking at Penny with a bewildered look on his face. "Don't mind her," Harry whispered to Penny out of the corner of his mouth. "She gets this way sometimes. It doesn't happen often, just once in a blue moon. She imagines that she sees people who aren't there." Penny just nodded her head in response.

"The gentleman, Harry, doesn't he look just like a young Cary Grant?" Myrtle persisted.

"It's happening again, Myrtle. There's nobody there. Cary Grant is dead, dear."

Myrtle looked at Kerby and circled her left temple with her left index finger making the, *he's coo-coo* sign. "Don't mind him," Myrtle said under her breath as she leaned toward Kerby. "He's suffering from a little premature senility." Kerby nodded his understanding.

"I know Cary Grant is dead, dearest," Myrtle continued, out loud now. "I was his biggest fan. He died of a stroke in Davenport, Iowa on November 29, 1986, at the age of 82, though he looked much younger. I never said that this gentleman was Cary Grant. I said he looks just like Cary Grant. Doesn't he, cutie?" Myrtle asked, looking at Penny now.

"Just humor her," Harry mouthed to Penny while circling his right temple with his right index finger.

"He certainly does," Penny answered Myrtle with a smile.

"Would you mind taking a picture with me under the lion?" Myrtle asked Kerby.

Kerby looked at Penny and shrugged. "Sure, I don't see why not."

Kerby and Penny followed Myrtle up the steps to a point just below Fortitude. Penny stood as close as she could to Kerby without being in the picture. Harry went along with the whole thing, stood down below them on the ground and shot the picture. He didn't even flinch when Kerby bent down and offered Myrtle his cheek, which she eagerly smooched, though it appeared to Harry that she was kissing thin air.

"What an absolutely darling couple!" Myrtle exclaimed, waving her hand excitedly at Kerby and Penny as they headed for the library entrance.

"Yes Myrtle," Harry agreed, shaking his head. "You don't expect to meet couples like that in New York City."

"I'd like to be there to see her face when they develop that picture,"

Kery said as they entered the library. Once inside the library, Penny led Kerby to the room in which the old newspapers were kept on microfiche. She stopped at the file cabinets containing the 1999 and 2000 *New York Post* newspapers and took out the microfiche for June and July of each year. Once at the projector, it took no time at all before Penny had found an article dealing with the disappearance of Peter Sizemore. The article, which ran five days after Sizemore's disappearance, didn't offer much in the way of detail. It contained only the basic information, including Sizemore's age and physical description, the date of his disappearance, and a statement from his mother, in which she said that Sizemore had left the house on the night of his disappearance without telling anyone where he was going. The mother insisted that there had been no family problems and that her son was not the type of boy to run away from home.

Penny found several follow-up articles in the papers for the two weeks following the disappearance, but there was not much more in the way of details. They learned that at the time of his disappearance, Peter Sizemore was finishing up his sophomore year of high school. It was noted that Sizemore was an average student academically but an exceptional high school athlete. The name of the high school he attended was not included in any of the articles.

When she turned her attention to the 2000 murder, it took Penny even less time to find an article about the disappearance of Danny O'Brien. The disappearance of Danny O'Brien made headlines in the *New York Post* only two days after he went missing, before the police had even started a serious investigation. O'Brien's mother knew how to work the reporter. She didn't just report her son's disappearance, she made a point of letting the reporter know that her son had only recently graduated from the same high school as Peter Sizemore, the boy, she reminded the reporter, who had gone missing precisely one year earlier and who had never been found. She also made a point of informing the reporter that despite the similarities between the two cases, the police were not yet investigating her son's disappearance seriously enough to suit her. To top it off, mother O'Brien offered a $25,000 reward for any information leading to the whereabouts of her son.

This time, thanks to mom's persistence and connections, follow-up articles on the disappearances of both Sizemore and O'Brien ran for several weeks after O'Brien's disappearance. Later articles identified the high school that both boys had attended as the New York High School for Science and Technology. There were even interviews with teachers and previous students from the school. One of the previous students interviewed, whose face appeared in a photograph alongside of her interview, was a cute brunette with short cropped hair and a curl hanging down onto her forehead. She was identified as Jean McCloone, the valedictorian of the school the year that Danny O'Brien had graduated.

Jean was quoted in the article as saying that she had never met Peter Sizemore, but that she had seen him play on the football and basketball teams and was very impressed with his, "athletic form." She didn't say athletic ability or athletic talent. She specifically said "athletic form." Jean was quoted as saying that she knew Danny O'Brien through a close friend, and thought that he was "one of the sweetest, kindest, most considerate boys she had ever met."

"Bingo!" Penny whispered to Kerby when she finally saw the name of the high school. "Now all we have to do is find some yearbooks for the years that the two kids were in school and see if we can find a tall attractive blonde and a short muscular brunette."

"Then all we have to do is find enough evidence to convince the police that those girls committed the murders, and *you* didn't," Kerby replied.

"Are you still on that kick?" Penny groaned. "If I'm a suspect in a murder case, then please tell me where the police are?"

"Just look over your shoulder, kiddo," Kerby answered.

Penny looked over her shoulder toward the information desk and saw a rather gruff looking gray-haired man in a wrinkled suit and a loosely tied green tie. As Penny eyed him, the guy looked away from her and began conversing with the librarian.

"I think you're paranoid. What in the world makes you so certain that guy is a cop?" Penny wondered.

"It's the stains on his tie. Only a cop on surveillance could manage to get both coffee and raspberry jelly stains from a donut on his tie and not even bother to clean them off."

"I'll give you the coffee stains, but how do you know that the other stains are raspberry jelly from a donut?"

"He still has some of the powdered sugar on his mouth and lapel." Kerby noted.

"Even if you're right, that still doesn't make him a cop," Penny insisted, heading for the file cabinets to return the microfiche.

The crusty looking guy turned and headed for the exit as Penny started in his direction. When she turned down the aisle toward the microfiche cabinets, Penny heard the librarian's voice. "I'll put those away for you dear," the librarian shouted anxiously, louder than Penny had ever heard a librarian speak before.

"Penny stopped and looked at the librarian with a quizzical look and then at Kerby. "That's okay, I know where they go. I don't want to make any extra work for you."

"Oh, it's no problem," the librarian insisted, coming out from behind the counter and heading quickly for Penny. "It's my job," the librarian said, snatching the microfiche out of Penny's hands and turning back toward her desk.

"Okay, so he's a cop," Penny conceded as they exited the microfiche room.

"Really, what tipped you off?" Kerby said snidely.

"A city employee insisting on doing work she might be able to get out of, I don't think so. She wanted that microfiche to see what I was looking at. Okay, so you were right, he's a cop. Now what do I do?" Penny asked.

"I guess you just tell him you're psychic," Kerby answered, hiding a smile.

Outside the library they agreed that Penny should call Sol for a ride a home. She could use her extra token another time. When Penny called Sol, he was just dropping off a fare down in Greenwich Village and said he would be up in fifteen minutes. Kerby begged Penny to take a walk down to Times Square while they were waiting, so Penny called Sol back and asked him to pick her up on 42nd Street at Broadway.

♥ ♋ ♣

"Now this is different from what I remember," Kerby remarked as they reached Times Square. "Neon lights really weren't introduced into the United States until 1923, so there was a lot less neon around the last time that I was here. But I have *some* memories of this place.

"The first time I ever saw Cary Grant in person was right on this spot in 1922. Of course, at that time nobody knew who Cary Grant was. In fact, at that time, his name was still Archibald Leach. I found out later that Grant had been touring the United States working as an acrobat with an English group called the Pender Troupe. When the group ran out of money and headed back to England, Grant decided to stay in America. In order to pay the rent, he got a job in Times Square stilt walking with a sandwich board and megaphone, shouting to people about what was going on at various cinemas and theaters in the area. I looked up at him, and he looked down at me. I'm telling you, it was as if I were looking into a mirror. I know it was eerie for me. It must have been for him too, almost knocked him off of his stilts, but neither of us ever uttered a word to each other.

"Then, of course, I was on this very spot for the New Year's Eve celebrations almost every year from the year my family arrived in this country until 1932. I'll bet you don't even know how that tradition started. Do you, kiddo?" Kerby commented.

Penny was actually starting to enjoy the history lessons that Kerby had been giving. "Nope, I really don't. Why don't you tell me about it?"

"At the turn of the century, the *New York Times* was being run by a guy named Adolph Ochs. Ochs's main competition came from New York newspapers owned and operated by the one and only William Randolph Hearst. In an effort to establish the *Times* as New York's premier newspaper, Ochs built the *Times* headquarters right here on this spot. The building officially opened on New Year's Eve 1904, the year I was born. To celebrate the opening, Ochs threw an all-day street party that concluded with a fireworks display set off from the base of his new tower.

"Anyway, the promotion proved so successful that the area became known as Times Square and immediately replaced City Hall Park as the favorite gathering site for New Yorkers to ring in the New Year. Soon the crowds grew so large that Times Square became recognizable around the world as the official place for America to welcome the arrival of the New Year. To mark the annual occasion, Ochs arranged to have a large illuminated four-hundred-pound glass ball lowered from the tower flagpole precisely at midnight, to signal the end of one year and the beginning of the next. You know the rest of the story, kiddo," Kerby finished, just as Sol pulled up to the curb, exactly fifteen minutes from the time that Penny had called him.

Penny had Sol stop at the New York High School for Science and Technology on their way home. She spoke with the principle of the school, who informed her that, of course, the school kept copies of all of their yearbooks from the time that the school opened to the present. However, she also informed Penny that for liability reasons she could not allow Penny to enter the school library and look through the yearbooks. "Heaven forbid someone were to use the yearbooks in order to target one of our former students for an attack or kidnapping or something," the principle explained. "We've already had our share of misery."

After Sol dropped them off at home, Penny and Kerby went inside so that Penny could get a bite to eat and call Joie Miller to see if it would be convenient for Joie to meet with Penny.

"Sure, sweetie," Joie chirped. "I've been wondering where you've been. You know the rule, just let yourself in and don't be shocked by anything you might see."

Penny tried to convince Kerby that it was best if she met with Joie alone, not being certain whether Joie might be with Sissy Maid or the like, but Kerby insisted that he was a big boy and could deal with any game that Joie Miller might be playing.

♥ ✂ ♟

Penny hit the doorbell before she opened the door and cautiously stuck in her head. Joie was just coming out of one of the side rooms and appeared to be holding a dog leash over her left shoulder, though whatever was on the other end of the leash was out of sight, still within the room that Joie was exiting.

"Come on in, sweetie. Don't be timid," Joie greeted her. Then she looked back into the room from which she had just exited. "Look, Naked Boy! How exciting! We have a visitor!" Joie exclaimed as she tugged on the leash.

At the end of the leash was a large, spiked dog collar wrapped around the neck of a tall, well built young man who was naked, save for the collar and a full face black leather mask. Penny could see the naked guy's eyes through sockets in the mask, but they remained focused on the floor in front of him. The guy made no attempt to cover himself. His arms remained wrapped behind his back as he was led into the room at the end of the leash. Penny did not realize it at first, but the guy's wrists were handcuffed behind him.

"It's double your pleasure, double your fun, Naked Boy. It looks as if you're going to have to pay your Mistress double for today's session," Joie taunted, and the nude guy nodded his head in agreement.

"Don't mind us," Joie said to Penny. "I'm just taking my pet for a little exercise walk around the house. Ordinarily, he'd be on all fours, but I do so like it when his hands are restrained behind him. It leaves him so accessible. Don't you think?"

"Perhaps you were right, kiddo," Kerby said. "I love looking at the naked female form, but I never imagined how uncomfortable I might feel in the presence of a nude guy. I mean, when I was alive I didn't make it a habit to be around naked men, especially not naked men who had all of the hair shaved off their bodies and were attached to dog leashes."

Penny, who had been trying not to look at Naked Boy, suddenly found herself staring up and down at his bare body. She hadn't realized it until Kerby mentioned it, but unlike Sissy Maid's hirsute behind, Naked Boy's body was completely devoid of hair, with the possible exception of his head which was hidden under the leather mask.

"You're uncomfortable! Imagine how I feel," Penny whispered to Kerby.

"Loosen up, kiddo. He's the opposite sex for you. You should be having some fun with this," Kerby teased.

Once inside the library, Joie sat behind her desk and Naked Boy knelt next to her, fully exposed, his hands still cuffed behind him. Joie patted his head and called him a *good boy,* as if he were a dog who had just performed a trick. Penny sat on the other side of the desk and Kerby stood alongside of her.

"I hope you don't think I'm getting on my knees," Kerby joked.

"You know, sweetie, Sol is quite worried about you," Joie started. "He actually comes over here to visit with me all of the time now to tell me about his concerns. And believe me, he must really be worried if he's coming in here. Sol never used to come into my home. For Sol, it used to be like this was the quarantine area of a hospital, and he might catch something if he entered. Fortunately, every time he's come over, I've been alone, so he hasn't seen anything. If he had, his eyes might have fallen out of his head.

"Anyway, Sol seems to think that he saw you levitating above your front porch steps the other day. He also said that he's caught you carrying on conversations with yourself. He told me that lately when you've been in his cab, you've been awfully quiet, but every time he looks into his rearview mirror, you seem to either be hushing someone or whispering to someone."

"Sol's such a sweet man," Penny replied. "But in this case, I'm afraid that he may just be exaggerating things a little bit. I mean, I do my yoga and meditation religiously, but I haven't yet developed an ability to levitate. On the other hand, as far as the allegations that I've been talking to myself, I'm afraid I have to plead guilty. I've had a great deal on my mind lately. You see, at the moment I'm without an income, and it seems that Mags didn't get around to paying off the mortgage on the brownstone before she passed. So I've been trying to figure out a way to turn the bookstore into a profit-maker."

"Sweetie, Mags and I talked about the mortgage on the brownstone lots of times. The last time being only a few days before she died. She found out right before her death that Marky had failed to pay off the mortgage on the home, but it didn't overly concern her. Mags told me that a long time ago she and Marky had figured out a way for her to get you funds outside of the estate, enough money, she said, to pay the mortgage off and then some. Mags didn't give me any details, but she told me how clever she thought Marky was to have come up with the idea. In fact, she said that Marky put everything into motion before her condition even developed. Mags said that even if she had been successful in tearing the building down, the money would have still been a nice windfall for you."

"You call him Marky as if you know him. Did he do legal work for you too?" Penny asked.

"Mark Libby? Do legal work for me? I wouldn't trust the guy in the same room with my pocketbook, though I have to admit that he has a reputation for being a shrewd character when it comes to business. I have my legal work done by the brightest young lawyer in Manhattan. Don't I Naked Boy?" Joie remarked, looking down at the nude guy next her. "In fact, as soon as you leave I'll talk to my attorney about what steps Mags may have taken to get you funds outside of the estate."

"What about Mark Libby? How do you know so much about him?" Penny wondered.

"Let's just say I've had business dealings with Marky on and off over the years," Joie responded cryptically.

"Anyway, even if the mortgage on the brownstone had been paid off, I would still need to turn the bookstore into an income producer," Penny continued. "The idea I've come up with, in order to get more people through the doors, is to add a section on *sex*. I'm even going to change the name of the store from *Ghosts & Gumshoes* to *Sex, Ghosts, and Gumshoes*."

"Now you're talking my language, sweetie. That sounds like a great idea to me. The fact is that I'm in the process of finishing up my memoirs. I have a publisher and everything. In fact, you've already met my publisher. I've been wondering how I was going to get you to stock my book," Joie revealed.

"Wonderful!" Penny exclaimed. "I'll give you a prominent place in the front window as soon as your book comes out. In the interim, there's something I'd really like you to do for me, and it might be a good opportunity for you to start to trumpet the publication of your book. You see, as a way to get people, especially women, into the store, I plan on scheduling talks by different experts in different areas of human sexuality, especially areas of human sexuality of interest to women. I'm going to have a *Grand Opening* of the newly named store as soon as we're stocked. I thought you might be willing to come and give a presentation at the *Grand Opening* on how you do what you do."

"Are you kidding? I would consider it a privilege. Just tell me when. I might even bring along one of my little subbies and put on a demonstration for the crowd. Wouldn't you just love that, Naked Boy?" Joie teased, looking down at Naked Boy who opened his mouth for the first time, but said only, "Yes Mistress."

"I'm also trying to educate *myself* on this stuff," Penny continued. "I wonder if you could answer a few questions for me."

"I told you it would grow on you. If you need some quick cash and you're thinking about becoming a dominatrix in order to earn that money, you've come to the right person. I can put you into a black leather miniskirt and teach you how to use a riding crop this afternoon. Believe me, with your spectacular looks and those legs, by this evening there will be a line of men outside of your door with their pants around their ankles and their wallets open begging you to spank their bare bottoms. Don't you agree, Naked Boy? I'll bet you'd love to have Mistress Penny whip your little naked behind, wouldn't you?"

Again Naked Boy said only, "Yes Mistress," but this time he said it with a great deal more enthusiasm.

"Well, that's not exactly what I had in mind," Penny noted looking at Joie. Then she looked over at Kerby with a smile and continued. "At least not right away. Right now, I'm just looking for a little education. You know, so I'll be able to talk to ladies who come into the store about these things in an informed way."

"Sure, sweetie, sure thing," Joie said, as if she didn't really believe Penny's reasons for wanting to know more about the subject of male sexual domination. "You have questions, let them rip."

"Well . . . mainly . . . I guess I just have some general questions. You know, like are there different areas of expertise in which different Mistresses specialize?" Penny asked, trying to figure out how to delicately get around to the subject of genital mutilation.

Before she started with her answer, Joie excuse Naked Boy from the room by ordering him to go down into the dungeon, stand in the corner, and wait for her to get there. After Naked Boy was gone from the room, Joie explained, "Sweetie, there are all kinds of specialties in this business, usually based upon the nature and severity of the punishment that the slave or submissive is seeking. You see, in many ways, though the male is the slave, he controls the action. It's his fantasy that has to be delivered if the Mistress wants him to come back for more. For most Mistresses, even the 24/7-dominas, like me, it is a business, and we want our subs to come back, not just because we enjoy abusing them, but also because we like their money.

"Certain Mistresses are willing to go to certain extremes or perform certain services that other Mistresses won't. Slaves frequently choose their Mistresses based upon the extremes to which the Mistress will go, or the services that she is willing to provide. You see, even if there is a great deal of money being offered, some Mistresses, again like me, simply find it distasteful to go to certain extremes or perform certain acts on a slave."

"Can you be a little more specific about the nature and severity of the acts that you're talking about?" Penny asked.

"I don't mean to shock you, sweetie, but there are no limitations to the forms of abuse that some men seek out. What I specialize in and what you've seen here is terribly vanilla compared to what some other Mistresses do. Now, I limit my services, for the most part, to two regular and very generous slaves. You've met them both, Sissy Maid and Naked Boy. But even with the other subs that I've seen over the years and those that I still see occasionally, my specialty has always been limited to different forms of humiliation. For instance, forcing a sub to be naked whenever he is in my presence, like Naked Boy. When he comes through that door, he has to remove all of his cloths and stay that way until I allow him to walk back out of the door. Sissy Maid gets off on being forced to put on makeup and dress up like a maid. He gets excited by being made to do things around my house, like clean my toilets. He likes being scolded and punished for not doing a good enough job, which, of course, he never does, or it would take the fun out of it for him.

"But that's just the tip of the iceberg. For example, over the years I've had many slaves who have come here to be treated like a human dog for a few hours, you know, kept in a cage, fed from a dog bowl, walked around with a leash on all fours. Believe it or not, a big thing now is guys who want to be treated as if they were horses, "ponyboys" they call them. They like their Mistresses to put bridles on them and ride around on their shoulders or their backs. The specialty has gotten so big that there are now S&M shops that manufacture bridles and horseshoes for human beings. It was never big in my practice because many of these guys like to be taken outdoors and ridden in a field somewhere. That wouldn't go over too well in Central Park.

"I've had clients who have come here just to be restrained, you know, the bondage thing. They just want to be tied up nude for a while. One of my regulars wanted nothing other than for me to suspend him naked, spread-eagle from the ceiling and make fun of him for how silly he looked. Others were into rubber or latex. They wanted to be confined in tight fitting rubber or latex outfits. Most said that there was something about the smell of the rubber and the claustrophobic feeling that they got when I put them into these outfits that turned them on. In that vein, my favorite was a sub that used to have me strip him naked, slather body lotion all over him and wrap him from head to toe with cellophane. I finally asked him why, and do you know what he told me? He said he got off by imagining himself as a giant penis that had just had an orgasm in a condom. That's why he had to be covered with lotion, because he wanted to feel like a penis that had just had an orgasm. You figure it out.

"I have a whole room downstairs that is filled with man-sized women's clothes. I have man-sized bras, panties, corsets, stockings, high heel shoes, dresses, wigs, you name it. But it's like I told you with Sissy Maid. These guys don't just want to cross-dress, they want to feel as if they're only doing it because their Mistress is forcing them to do it. They want their Mistress to tell them how ridiculous, or maybe how adorable, they look while they're dressing them. They want to be humiliated.

"Naturally, all of my slaves receive some form of punishment, whether it's a bare bottom spanking with a hairbrush or being hung upside down and whipped with a bullwhip, which just happens to be my specialty. Some Mistresses supply their subs with *safe words* that the slave is to use if the pain becomes too severe for him. Others, like me, don't provide our slaves with *safe words*. Our subs are forced to trust us to recognize when they have reached their pain threshold. And believe me when I tell you, we are careful to reach but not exceed that pain threshold. Even with the bullwhip, I was so good that I could sting a man's butt without leaving much of a mark. What I did was not that much more than snapping a towel on someone's behind. It hurt like hell for the minute but there was no serious injury. It was the sense that they were tied helpless at the mercy of this woman with a bullwhip behind them that got most of these guys off.

"On the other hand, there are femdoms who don't give a damn about a sub's pain threshold, and there are men who go to see those Mistresses with the understanding that the Mistress will do entirely as she pleases, and the slave will not be able to do or say anything to stop her until she has satisfied herself. I could show you pictures of slaves whose backs and rear ends have been whipped to gory messes. Yet, once they heal, they go back begging for more from the same merciless Mistress," Joie explained.

"You said that there are particular services that you won't perform. What types of services are you talking about?" Penny wondered, hoping that Joie would get to penis mutilation.

"Again, sweetie, there is no limit to the types of things that subs will seek to have done to them. Like I said, I'm not into any kind of bloodletting, but that's what some Mistresses get off on and what some slaves seek out. Other things that I won't do because I find them distasteful are as mild as a golden shower, you know, peeing on a guy. Lots of slaves are into that, even being forced to drink it. Some, though only a few, want to be defecated on or even vomited on. I would never do anything like that, though I try not to judge the Mistresses who do it, or their slaves.

"The new thing is this asphyxiation or strangulation phenomenon that's going around, where Mistresses are being asked to choke or strangle their subs while the guy masturbates. Supposedly, if you cut off the blood flow to the brain, so that the brain has no oxygen at the time of the climax, it greatly intensifies the orgasm. Some Mistresses have actually devised types of gallows from which they raise their subs off the ground by their necks, let them dangle until they orgasm and then cut them down just before they choke to death. I wouldn't dream of doing anything like that. It's far too dangerous for my tastes. I've heard stories of a number of people who have lost their lives doing similar things.

"Then, of course, there are those subs who want torture heaped upon their phalluses. Mostly all Mistresses will perform some type of abuse on their sub's genitalia. Usually, it's nothing more than tying them up or slapping them, maybe using a riding crop on them. I've done all of the above. But some slaves are not satisfied with that, some slaves want their Mistresses to do everything from piercing their genitals to catheterizing their penises with all kinds of things.

"There's a relatively new dominatrix in Manhattan who is really taking the specialty to an extreme. She's just a kid really, which I think is one of the reasons that she has become so popular in such a short time. Some guys seem to like the idea of being abused by a very young girl. The other reason that she has become so well known so quickly is that this kid has no limitations. I heard that she recently butterflied a guy's penis. You know how you butterfly a shrimp by slicing it down the middle and folding it open. That's what she did, only not to a shrimp," Joie finished, wondering why Penny's head turned suddenly to her left and began nodding up and down while Joie described the young femdom.

"That's our girl," Kerby remarked as Penny nodded in agreement. "See if you can find out how to locate her."

"Who is this girl? Where's she from?" Penny asked.

"I don't know that much about her really. Like I said, she's relatively new to the profession. I did meet her once at one of our Latex and Leather Galas a few months back. I never got her real name, but her professional name is Madame Pain, or something like that. A fitting name, don't you think?" Joie laughed.

"Do you think she has a web site?" Penny asked.

"I don't know. She may be a little too extreme, even for the Internet. If I were her, I wouldn't be advertising what I do too much outside of the femdom community. Why do you ask?" Joie wondered.

"No reason, I was just curious as to how someone like that gets her business. By the way, do the Greek letters Chi, Beta, Theta mean anything in the world of domination?" Penny inquired.

"Not that I know of. What letters do they correspond to in the English alphabet?" Joie asked.

"CBT," Penny answered.

"Sweetie, that's what we were just talking about," Joie chuckled. "The letters stand for Cock and Ball Torture."

As Penny and Kerby headed for the door, a thought occurred to Kerby. "She said she met this girl at one of the S&M community's Latex and Leather Galas," Kerby recalled. "Ask her how often they have these things."

Penny turned back to Joie. "Hey Jo, how frequently does the dominatrix community have a gala like the one you mentioned?"

"I knew you were getting hooked, sweetie. Every third month one of the Mistresses in the city takes responsibility for setting up a gala. In fact, there's one coming up at the end of this month, and it just so happens that it's my responsibility to plan it, and *yes* you are welcome to come. Everything was set, but the place I usually use when it's my responsibility to stage the event is not available. I usually rent out a loft down in SoHo, but the guy who owns the place just baled on me. He said some rapper had already rented the place out for a record release party or something. I'm looking into a warehouse down in Brooklyn that I've used once or twice in the past, but I haven't heard back yet as to whether it's available. I'll call you and let you know as soon as I decide exactly where and when it's going to be," Joie promised.

CHAPTER 9

ALL THAT AND A PIECE OF CHOCOLATE CAKE
JUNE 20, 2003

Carmella showed up for work at nine sharp, expecting that the truckload of new books would be there early. The truck showed up at slightly after eleven, filled almost to capacity with Penny's erotica. Penny decided that she would spend the day with Carmella organizing the books on the shelves in the back of the store. Kerby decided that since he couldn't be of any use to Penny in the bookstore with Carmella around, he would spend the afternoon on the Internet, seeing if he could track down a location for Madame Pain. Sol had agreed to pick Penny up at nightfall, though he seemed confused as to why anyone might want to tour Riverside Park after dark.

It was late afternoon before Kerby finally found the web site that he felt certain was the one for which he was looking. Jean's professional name was not Madame Pain as Joie Miller had suggested, it was Domina Agony. Kerby found her web page at *www.StudioPain.com*. The page was blood red in color. On the top of the page it read simply "Studio Pain" in large black letters. The same black letters on the bottom of the page read "Home of Domina Agony." In the center of the page was an animated grimacing male face. Every three seconds or so the grimace turned into an open mouth and was accompanied by audio of a male voice screaming in pain.

To the right of the face were three buttons. The top button was labeled "Member's Entrance." The second button down was labeled "Join." The third button down said "Preview Tour." The last button read "Coward's Exit." Kerby pushed the button labeled "Preview Tour" and was taken to a second page with the same blood red background. This page was dominated by the figure of a woman dressed in a white lab coat with white rubber gloves. Her face was covered from her eyes down by a white surgical mask, and a white hood of the type used by doctors during surgery covered her hair. A lock of black hair stuck out from under the white hood and curled down onto the woman's forehead. Her right hand was extended upward holding a glistening stainless steel scalpel.

At the bottom of the page were two buttons, one marked "Continue Tour," the other "Coward's Exit." Kerby hit the button labeled "Continue Tour" and was taken to a third page, in the center of which were four digital photographs. On the top of the page it read "Actual Session Photos." The first photograph showed the woman from the second page, wearing the same outfit, leading a clearly nervous man into what appeared to be an examination room in some sort of medical facility. In the center of the room was a hospital bed equipped with stirrups of the type generally seen in gynecologists' offices. Alongside of the bed was a table on which were spread out various kinds of stainless steel surgical tools, including several shiny scalpels.

In the second photograph, the nervous male could be seen removing his clothes while the woman in the lab coat looked on in amusement. In the third photograph, the male was completely naked on the examination table with his feet in the stirrups, his genitals covered with shaving cream. The woman stood between his legs with a straight razor shaving his genital area as if prepping him for surgery. In the final photograph, the male was shown in the same position on the table, except his legs were now manacled to the stirrups and his genitals were completely shaven. The female stood between his legs with the scalpel inches from his groin as if she was about to begin some form of surgical procedure.

Writing on the bottom of the page indicated that the remainder of the scenes from the session above could be viewed in the "Member's Area" along with hundreds of other actual session photos. It was also noted that Domina Agony was in the process of editing several videos filmed during actual sessions with her male subs and that those videos would also soon be available in the "Member's Area." It was also noted that instructions for setting up a live session with Domina Agony could be found in the "Member's Area" only.

Kerby pushed the button below the writing to continue the tour, but the next page was limited to instructions for becoming a member of the web site. For a credit card payment of only $29.95, the user was promised unlimited access to the site for a full one month period. Not having a credit card and feeling certain that he was not going to find any photographs of Domina Agony without her surgical mask on, Kerby exited the web site, feeling almost relieved that he would not have to view the balance of the session photographs.

When Penny came up from the bookstore, Kerby told her what he had found. He thought again about joining the web site for a month, so that he could try to set up a fake session in the hope that they might be able to get a location for *Studio Pain*, but Penny reminded him that she did not own a credit card either.

♥ ⌀ ♣

"You do know that Riverside Park runs from 72nd Street all the way up to 158th Street?" Penny remarked later that evening. "Most of the park is not even visible from the roadway. Riverside Drive is up on a hill and there's a stonewall that runs for a good part of the park, making it impossible to see down into the park. You can't even *see* the Hudson River from most parts of Riverside Drive."

"How do you know so much about the park?" Kerby wondered.

"I used to do my runs up there occasionally when I got bored with Central Park. The bottom line is, we're going to have to spend the night getting in and out of Sol's cab to look down into the park," Penny noted. "This may take all night. I hope Sol has the patience for it."

"I've been thinking about that exact problem," Kerby replied. "These girls are clever young ladies. Where Nick was concerned, they didn't just walk into *Dorrian's* that night by accident. They had a well thought out plan. They took Nick out of that place because it was where Robert Chambers and Jennifer Leven were on the night of her death. They didn't just happen to bring Nick to Central Park either. Central Park meant something to these girls symbolically. I don't think that they just happened into Riverside Park either. There's something up there that had meaning to them, something that in their minds represents the abuse of women by men."

"I'm sure that there have been lots of rapes and attacks on women in Riverside Park over the years," Penny commented.

"That's too general," Kerby replied. "There's something more specific up there that drew them to the spot where they committed the murder. I just can't figure out what the attraction was. The only things that come to my mind when someone mentions Riverside Park are Grant's Tomb and the 79th Street Boat Basin, but a park that big has to have lots of other attractions."

"Sol knows New York better than anybody. When we get into the cab, I'll ask him what there is to see in the park. Perhaps he'll mention something that will strike a cord," Penny suggested.

"I hope so, kiddo. Otherwise, like you said, it's going to be long night," Kerby groaned.

Sol pulled up in front of the brownstone just as darkness seemed to blanket the city. Penny jumped into the back seat and Kerby slid in next to her. Sol looked over his shoulder at Penny and gave her the kind of stern look that a father gives a daughter just before he starts a lecture. Penny assumed that Sol was going to warn her about the dangers of walking around Riverside Park at night, but she was wrong.

"I received a very worrisome telephone call about you today," Sol started. "Mark Libby called me this afternoon and told me that he is in the middle of negotiations with you to purchase your brownstone. He wanted to know if I could be of any help in convincing you that he is a fair man with whom to deal. He's not by the way."

"Mark Libby is delusional," Penny snapped, looking at Kerby who looked baffled by what he had just heard.

"He told me that Mags left you with a huge real estate tax bill, and given your lack of income, you're looking to sell the brownstone to him before the tax people take it from you. He said that he's already retained an appraiser to put a fair market value on the property, but I can assure you that if Libby hired the guy, there will be nothing fair about his appraisal."

"It's not true," Penny assured Sol, still looking at Kerby who still had the befuddled look on his face. "At least, not the part about me negotiating with Libby to buy the brownstone. Apparently, it is true that Mags may have had a large shortfall in her real estate tax payments."

"What real estate tax shortfall?" Kerby asked. "You never said anything to me about a real estate tax deficiency. All you told me about was the mortgage."

"There's that too," Penny responded to Kerby.

"There's what too?" Sol asked, thinking Penny was talking to him.

"There's a mortgage too," Penny said, to Sol now.

"Libby mentioned that," Sol noted. "Anyway, the only reason that I'm bringing this up is to tell you that if you have money issues, just say so, and I'll write you a check. Just tell me how much. The amount is not an issue. Look, honey, I have more money than I know what to do with and very little time left to spend it. Helping you out with your money problems would bring me great joy."

"I couldn't take money from you, Sol, certainly not the kind of money we're talking about here," Penny replied.

"Take the money," Kerby interjected. "Make the old guy happy."

"Like I said, the amount is not an issue," Sol repeated. "But just how much money are we talking about?"

"According to Libby, the tax bill is in the area of $175,000. The mortgage is another $250,000, but I'll figure out how to make those payments."

"When you're talking about money, everything is relative. Trust me, it's not as much as it sounds. Get me your bank account information, and I'll arrange for a transfer. Consider it a loan and a favor to me. The last thing in the world I want is Mark Libby as a next door neighbor for my remaining years," Sol grumbled.

"See, you'd be doing him a favor," Kerby said. "Take the money."

"I couldn't, Sol. I appreciate it, but I really couldn't. I need to work this out on my own. Now let's change the subject. It upsets me to think about it."

"Okay, but if push comes to shove, make sure that you talk to me before you do anything. Now, are you sure that you want to see Riverside Park at night, honey?" Sol asked. "It's a great place, but it's a lot nicer during the daylight hours, not to mention a lot safer."

"I'm sure," Penny responded. "What I'm not sure about is what I should be most interested in seeing. Got any suggestions?"

"Well, you've got to see Grant's Tomb, if you haven't already. That's the most famous monument in the park. Then there's the Soldiers and Sailors Monument, that's dedicated to the New Yorkers who died in the *Civil War*. There's the relatively new Eleanor Roosevelt Monument at the redone entrance to the park down on 72nd Street. I was riding by on the day they dedicated it in 1996. Hillary Rodham Clinton was there.

Penny shot a look at Kerby when Sol mentioned Hillary Rodham Clinton's name, but Kerby just shook his head.

"Then there's the 79th Street Rotunda with the fountain and all. The city uses it occasionally for outdoor celebrations and stuff. Of course, one of my personal favorite places in the city is the Boat Basin, but that's mainly because I keep my boat up there. I haven't been able to get up the energy lately to take it out, but I still love going up there and just sitting on the boat, maybe fishing a little and enjoying the scenery. It's kind of like getting out of the city without ever leaving the city."

"Is that everything?" Penny asked.

"Well, they have some great gardens. There's the Garden for All Seasons and the 91st Street Garden, but you're not going to be able to enjoy them in the dark. Right up the street from the 91st Street Garden, on 93rd Street there's *Joanie on the Pony*.

"Who on the what?" Penny asked.

"It's a bronze sculpture of Joan of Arc on horseback. You get it,

Joanie on the Pony. It's famous because it's the first equestrian sculpture of a woman on horseback done by another woman," Sol explained.

"I should have thought of it," Kerby announced suddenly. "It's the Anna Hyatt Huntington sculpture. She was very famous back in the day for her work in bronze. I was just a kid when the sculpture was dedicated, but it was a big thing back then. It's famous because the pedestal that the bronze is on was made partially from stones taken from the very cathedral in which Joan of Arc was imprisoned."

"It's supposed to be notable because of the authenticity of the armor she's wearing," Sol added.

"It's notable because her left hand is firmly in control of her steed, and her right hand is holding a small, supposedly magical, sword pointing it toward the sky. If there's ever been a historic symbol of a woman abused by men, I guess Joan of Arc would have to be that symbol," Kerby finished.

"Forget about the rest of the tour, Sol. Take me to me to see *Joanie on the Pony*," Penny said.

Penny and Kerby got out of the cab at 93rd Street and Riverside Drive. It took a while for Penny to convince Sol that she would be okay by herself.

"It won't take that long to look at the sculpture, honey. I'll wait right here," Sol insisted.

"No, you go ahead, Sol," Penny replied. "When I'm done, I'm going to take a walk through the park down to the river. I want to see what it looks like at night, in the moonlight."

"Honey, if you're walking through this park at night, I'm walking with you. Just let me find a place to park the cab. At my age, I don't know how much help I'll be to you if there's any trouble, but I could never live with myself if I let you go down there alone and something happened to you."

"It's okay, Sol, you'll be able to protect me a lot better from up here than you could if you were with me. I have you on speed dial on my cell phone. If anything happens, I'll ring your phone and let you know and you can call for help. But I'm certain everything will be just fine," Penny assured him.

After checking out the Joan of Arc statue, Kerby and Penny made their way across the street and found the first entrance that they could into the park. They followed a paved walkway down a hill to a child's playground and then a steep flight of stairs down even further to an underpass that ran beneath the Hudson River Parkway to the Hudson

River side of the park. They wound up on a bench-lined duck walk that seemed to run the length of the park along the river. They looked to their left and then to their right. There was not another human being in sight, but the glow from the spirit sitting on a bench maybe forty feet to their right was unmistakable.

The spirit rose from his sitting position as Kerby and Penny made their way toward him. It was clear that he recognized Kerby as one of his kind, and Penny as not like either of them. As with Nick, the closer that Penny got, the more defined the glow became until she could make out the figure of an unclad man.

"Oh my goodness!" Penny exclaimed. "Look at what they did to this poor guy."

The spirit was literally disemboweled, with a slit running down his torso from his solar plexus to his pubic area. Like Nick, his scrotum had been sliced open from top to bottom. But what caught Penny's eye was the fact that there was a thick curved piece of tubular stainless steel that had to have been twenty gauge thick running through the head of his penis from one side to the other. At either end of the tubular steel was a small ball bearing that made the entire piece of metal look like a tiny, bent barbell.

"Did they send you, pal? I've been waiting an awfully long time," the guy moaned as the duo reached him.

"Who would *they* be?" Kerby wondered.

"I don't know, whoever's in charge of this stuff up there. You know, getting spirits out of this world to wherever they're supposed to go."

"Nobody sent me, but we may just be able to help you in that regard," Kerby remarked. "If I'm right, we just need someone to come and find your body, which I assume is right out there in the river somewhere, and see to it that you get a proper burial."

"If you plan on notifying the authorities of the whereabouts of my body, I'm guessing that she's working with you on this, but how did you get hooked up with a live person? Believe me, I've been trying to get somebody's attention for a couple of years now, but other than scaring the crap out of a few people, I haven't had any success," the spirit groaned.

"Lets just say we met through an Ouija Board," Kerby smiled.

"That's fine with me, pal. As long you can get me on my way, you two can have all of the secrets you want," the spirit replied, clearly not buying the Ouija Board story.

"Getting you on your way is only one of the things we'd like to do," Penny said. "The other is that we'd like to find the girls who did this to you and make them pay for it."

"Sounds as if you're already familiar with these girls, lady. Believe me, there's nobody who would like to see these girls pay for what they did more than I would. Just tell me how I can help you."

"Why don't you start by telling us who you are and how you got here?" Penny suggested, taking out a small pad and getting ready to write down anything of interest that was said.

"My name's Tom Smith. I was from Madison, Wisconsin. This happened on my first trip to New York City. Can you believe it? I had been working in the electronics industry as a salesman for about a year, and they had an industry-wide convention here in the city, down at the Jacob Javits Convention Center. I figured what the heck, I'd get to come to New York City for the first time and write it all off on my taxes.

"My first night here I was looking for a little action, so I stopped at a strip club up on 51st Street, you know, an all nude place. We don't have much of that kind of thing where I came from. Anyway, I'm sitting at the bar, and to my amazement, these two girls come in and sit down next to me. They start tipping the strippers better than I was. They both seemed *two sheets to the wind*, you know, as if they had been drinking all night," Tom explained.

"What did these two girls look like?" Kerby asked.

"One of them was a tall girl. I'm 5'11, and she seemed taller than me, and she didn't even have heels on. The other one was shorter, but she did have heels on, the, long spiky kind. She had muscles too, looked as if she could take most guys in an arm wrestling contest. To tell you the truth, she was the one that caught my eye. I don't really care for girls who are taller than me. But more important, the shorter one had a look about her, like she and I might be into the same kind of things," Tom said without explaining.

"What color hair did they have?" Penny asked, though she felt certain she already knew the answer.

Tom surprised her at first. "When I first saw them, the little one was blonde and the tall one had dark hair, but I could tell by how light her eyebrows were that she was a natural blonde. By the end of the night, they got rid of their wigs and my suspicions were confirmed. The little one was a brunette and the tall one was a blonde.

"Anyway, in the bar, the shorter one started a conversation with me. She said that she could tell that I was an out-of-towner, asked me where I was from and how long I was going to be in the city, that kind of stuff. Then she said that if I was really looking for some fun, she and her girlfriend were in there getting primed for a private party they were going to perform at later. She said that they were strippers too, that they weren't lesbians but they did a lesbian routine as part of their act. She said they made a lot more money that way. She said I struck her as a decent guy and if I wanted to see their act, she could get me into the party. She even said maybe we could get together for a party of our own afterward. To tell you the truth, she didn't strike me as stripper. I've got a sense about girls like her. She seemed like the dominant type, you know, the disciplinarian type. That was what attracted me to her in the first place.

"She said if I was interested, as if any man wouldn't be, the party was going to be out on Long Island. I said sure, and her girlfriend left to get their car. The short one and I left a little later and met the other one around the corner from the strip joint. The short one insisted that as a man I should get in the front seat and she'd ride in the back. Before I had buckled my seatbelt, she reached from behind me and put my head in a vice grip with this medicinal smelling rag over my mouth and nose.

"The next thing I remember, we're pulling off the exit ramp of some highway that leads right through this park. The tall girl pulls over, and they both jumped out of the car. I was still too helpless to do anything, so they pulled me out of the car and dumped me over a guardrail into a grassy area alongside of the exit ramp. The tall girl jumped right back into the car and drove away while the little one dragged me feet first through the brush into the clearing right behind us. When we got there, there was a flat concrete bench that looked like it was set up for the occasion.

"Little by little, I was starting to come out of my fog as the short one undressed me down to my skivvies, plopped me onto the bench, and started tying my hands and feet underneath it. Believe me, she knew how to tie a knot too. I started thinking that my first guess was right; this girl is a dominant, which didn't upset me at first. You see, I'm into that kind of stuff. I've never been with a professional dominatrix, but my wife was what you might call a *domestic goddess*. She ruled the roost in our house, sexually and otherwise, which was fine with me. I liked it that way, especially the sexual part of it.

This news shocked Kerby and Penny to no end because Tom Smith looked like his name sounded, your typical, straight-laced, milk-fed, Midwestern boy. They were even more shocked when Tom went on with his story.

"By now the tall one is running down the trail toward us with a little cooler in her hand, like she's on a pick-nick or something. The short one has got something gleaming in her hand between my legs. The short one said to the tall one, 'You're just in time for the unveiling.' Then she started to cut my underpants off of me, which I've got to tell you was incredibly exciting for me at the time. At first, it was like a fantasy come to life. I was getting hard as rock from the whole scene. Then the little one cut through my underpants and saw my erection and my piercing and she started screaming, 'Damn it, of all the guys in the city to pick from, I go and choose somebody who's into this shit.' Personally, I couldn't see what her problem was. I'm into, she's into, what's she so upset about," Tom continued.

"You said she got upset when she saw your piercing, what do you mean your piercing?" Penny interrupted.

"My piercing," Tom announced proudly, looking down at his manhood and the twenty gauge piece of stainless steel that was running through the head of it.

"You mean, . . . they didn't do that to you?" Penny asked in an astonished tone.

"Oh no!" Tom exclaimed. "This is the little woman's handiwork. She did it right in our kitchen at home with a kit she got for piercing ears, no anesthetic, no nothing, just a little ice and a little peroxide.

"Anyway, the short one was all upset about the fact that I'm into this whole scene that she's set up. The tall one tried to calm her down. She said, 'Don't worry about it, I have the blowtorch. He'll crumple once you start to burn his scrotum.' I still thought it was a game. The idea of her burning my scrotum lightly with a blowtorch didn't sound all that bad to me. The little one fully understood this. 'You don't understand how these guys think,' she howled. 'He'll enjoy it, at least, until the pain gets too bad and then he'll just pass out. I've waited all year for this and I had to pick this idiot. Forget about the blowtorch and the Joan of Arc stuff,' she hollered. I still have no idea what she was talking about as far as Joan of Arc is concerned.

"Then she came over to me and knelt down next to my abdomen with the scalpel still in her hand. She asked me if I knew who Mary Ann Nichols was, and I told her I'd never heard of her. Then she asked me if I knew who Annie Chapman or Elizabeth Stride were, and I told her that I'd never heard of them either. So she asked me if I recognized the names Catherine Eddowes or Mary Jane Kelly. I told her that, as a group, the names sounded familiar to me, but I couldn't quite figure out where I had heard of these women before. She said, 'Perhaps this will jog your memory,' Then she ran the scalpel down my stomach from my chest to my pubic hair. This may sound strange, but it did jog my memory. The names that she asked me about were the names of Jack the Ripper's victims.

"I thought your body was supposed to protect you at times like this, you know, put you into shock, but my body didn't shut down right away. It wasn't until she stuck her hand into my belly and pulled out a handful of intestines that I blacked out."

"Were you able to watch them, listen to them after you were dead?" Penny asked.

"I don't how you would know about that, lady, but yeah I watched them. The little one cut my scrotum open and removed my testicles one at a time. She put them in a sandwich bag and then into a little cooler that the big one brought down with her. Then they each picked up an end of the concrete bench with me on it, as if they were carrying a stretcher. They brought me by the tennis courts down there where there is no fence separating the walkway from the river, then they tossed the bench and me into the Hudson."

"Do you know whether the current has moved your body at all?" Kerby asked.

"No way, pal, that bench weighs a ton. I have no idea how they carried it down there."

After they had finished promising Tom that they would have someone there as soon as possible to retrieve his body, Kerby and Penny went to the water's edge and looked at the moonlight shining across the blackened river. Penny called Sol and told him that she was on her way up. When they turned back toward Tom, Penny looked up, through the trees she saw *Joanie on the Pony,* her magical sword pointed skyward.

After saying their goodbyes to Tom, Kerby and Penny headed down the duck walk and turned left to go back through the tunnel that runs under the Hudson River Parkway. As they made their way into the pitch black tunnel, the silhouettes of three male figures appeared on the other side.

"Hey, baby, you looking for us," a familiar voice echoed from the other side of the underpass. "We been here all night waiting for you. First we gonna--" the voice continued, before it was cut off by another voice.

"Run mother fuckers, that's the fucking voodoo bitch from Central

Park," the other voice screamed as the three silhouettes turned tail and ran in the opposite direction.

♥ ✍ ♟

After the visit to Riverside Park, Kerby and Penny decided to stop at the brownstone so that Penny could freshen up and change before going to *Dorrian's* for a drink and to see if they could find the bartender who was on duty on the night of Nick's disappearance. When they entered the house, Penny saw the message light blinking on the telephone and listened to the message on the speaker. The voice she heard immediately made her feel nauseated. It was Mark Libby.

"Miss Albright, it's Mark Libby," the message started as if Penny might not recognize his voice. "I was just calling to follow-up on our negotiations with regard to my purchasing your brownstone. I hope that you have seriously considered my offer by now. As I pointed out in my office, my offer is a very fair one. By the way, I know I told you that if you don't accept my offer I will still have the brownstone by the end of the year, but I've spoken, hypothetically of course, to some of my friends downtown, and the fact is that if you don't negotiate with me directly, I will probably have your brownstone by the end of the summer. If you don't want my hypothetical discussions with my friends downtown to turn into real conversations about your situation, I suggest that you call me quickly. My patience is wearing a little thin. I look forward to hearing from you."

At the end of the message, a clearly upset Penny started to bang her hand down on the erase button. Kerby caught her hand in mid-swing. "I don't think you want to erase that, kiddo. I think you want to make multiple copies of it."

"And why would I want to do that?" Penny wondered.

"Just trust me on this one for now, kiddo. We have other things on our plate for this evening, and it's getting late. You'd better run up and get ready."

"You don't know how upset I get at the thought that Mark Libby may be able to take this house from me. I'm really concerned, Kerby. Everyone seems to agree that he knows what he's doing when it comes to the law," Penny groaned. "I don't understand why you're not more worried about this. Have you even thought about what it would be like for you living here with Mark Libby as your landlord?"

"Kiddo, I'm a ghost. Mark Libby wouldn't last a night in this house with me. By the time I was done haunting Mark Libby, he'd be in a fetal position with his thumb in his mouth. I would scare Mark Libby back to his mother's womb," Kerby boasted.

"You may be a ghost, but you're about the least scary ghost I've seen since Casper," Penny chuckled.

"Oh really?" Kerby said, smiling now. "It seems to me that I did a pretty good job with you that first night. You have to admit that the Ouija Board was a nice touch, especially with the flickering candle and all. I saw the goose bumps on your arms."

"You didn't see anything, Casper. The fact is that I had on long sleeves."

"We don't have all night," Kerby said. "Are you going up to change or not?"

Penny went upstairs, showered quickly and put on some light makeup. She put her hair up and dressed in her little black dress, the one that every woman has in her closet. She even put on a pair of black suede high heels, which she rarely ever wore. As Penny was coming down the steps toward the front door, Kerby just happened to step out of the sun parlor. He looked up at Penny like she was his prom date and he was seeing her for the first time in her gown.

"What's the matter?" Penny wondered as Kerby continued to stare at her as she made her way down the steps. "Is there something wrong with the way I look?"

"You look incredible, kiddo," Kerby gushed. "My only concern is that you may attract a crowd that might make it difficult for you to talk to this bartender, assuming we find him. Even though you're going be there with me, every guy in the place is going to think that you're alone, and presumably available. We can only hope that the way you look in that dress will so intimidate the men in the place that none of them will think that they're good enough for you."

"I can't remember the last time that I went out for a drink with a man at night. I just wanted to look nice. You don't think I overdid it, do you?"

"If all you were going for was nice, yes you overdid it. Like I said, I think you made it way beyond nice, all the way to incredible," Kerby raved.

There wasn't a guy in the place who didn't do a double take when Penny walked through the door. She honestly did not seem to notice, but Kerby was aware of every male head that turned Penny's way, and it wasn't because he was afraid that somebody might mess up the interview that they were hoping for with the bartender.

There was only one seat left at the bar when they walked in, between a young woman who was chatting with a female friend and an even younger guy, who was by himself and looked like he must have used an older brother's identification in order to get into the place. The young kid was cocky and did not waste any time. He immediately turned and eyed Penny up and down like he was looking at the centerfold in a *Playboy* magazine.

"This little hottie's drink is on me," the kid announced as the bartender made his way toward Penny.

"No, *your* drink is on you," Kerby said as he picked the kid's drink up and poured it over the kid's head.

The bartender, who was looking at Penny, never saw the kid's drink leave the bar by itself. All he saw was the drink pouring down the kid's face. "Look son, if you can't find your mouth with your drink, I'm going to have to throw you out of here," the bartender warned.

The kid did see the drink leave the bar by itself. "You don't need to throw me out of here, Mister. I'm already gone," the kid said, and then he made a beeline for the door.

Penny ordered a shot of tequila, which drew a shocked expression from Kerby. "I thought you were only a social drinker."

"This Libby thing has my nerves on edge. I just need something quick to relax me a little," Penny replied in a hushed tone after the bartender had placed the shot on the bar. "I've never done this before. How do I drink this thing? Don't I need a slice of lime or some salt or something?"

"If you're trying not to taste the tequila, forget about the lime and the salt, that's just Hollywood stuff. Besides, the salt is messy. Just order a glass of grapefruit juice. Take a little sip of the grapefruit juice, gulp down your shot, and follow it with a larger sip of the grapefruit juice. You won't have to hold your nose or anything, that can be embarrassing in a crowded bar," Kerby teased.

"I liked that," Penny remarked, after she finished following Kerby's instructions.

"I've never seen anyone drink tequila that way before," the bartender noted, thinking that Penny's comment was directed at him.

"I'll have another," Penny said.

"Go easy there, kiddo, that's not lemonade you're drinking. Don't forget, you're here to gather information, not drown your sorrows."

The bartender returned with a bottle labeled *Don Julio Anejo 1942*. "It looks like you're a serious tequila drinker, sweetheart," the bartender remarked. "Try some of this stuff. It's the best we've got, really smooth, costs more than a hundred dollars a bottle. I only serve it to people I sense might be true tequila connoisseurs, you know, people like you who can actually tell the difference," the bartender commented as he poured Penny a third shot and left the bottle on the bar in front of her.

"That is really smooth," Penny agreed after she turned up the third shot, but she had no idea what she was talking about. "By the way," Penny said as the bartender poured her a fourth shot. "Just about a year ago, right around this time, a young guy who was an acquaintance of mine went missing. The last place that anyone remembered seeing him was in here on the evening that he disappeared. You wouldn't happen to be familiar with the disappearance, maybe you might know who was on duty that night?"

"You're talking to him, sweetheart," the bartender responded as Penny put down her fourth shot, and he poured her a fifth without being asked.

"I warned you, go easy, kiddo. If he knows about the disappearance, the cops must have interviewed him about it. See if you can find out what they asked him."

"Do you know whether the police have had any success in developing any leads in the case, you know, any suspects or anything?" Penny asked.

"Not that I know of. Two cops came in here a couple of times right after the disappearance. They asked me about the guy, had I ever seen him here before, who did he talk to, did he have any trouble with anybody, did he leave with anybody. You know, that kind of stuff. I remembered the guy as soon as the cops showed me his picture, but I had never seen him in here before that night.

"My recollection is that the guy tried to put a move on this really hot blonde, but she was way out of this guy's league. She let him down easy though. She even bought him a drink before she gave him the brush off. Then she left with a girlfriend. The guy left a little while later and that was the last me or anybody else ever heard from him."

"You say he spoke with a blonde before he left, what was she like?" Penny quizzed.

"I remember she was a very tall girl, gorgeous face, model-type, not stuck up though, a very friendly girl. I mean she talked to the guy for a while before she beat it, and like I said, she even bought the guy a drink before she left. The guy went to the bathroom, and the blonde told me that she was trying to get going because the guy was pressing her for her telephone number and she didn't want to give it to him. Her girlfriend had come in, and the blonde said she was going to use the girlfriend as an excuse to hit the road, but she wanted to ditch the guy in a nice way, so she bought him the drink, waited for him to come out of the bathroom, said goodbye and left with her girlfriend."

"What was the girlfriend like?" Penny wondered.

"I don't recall her that well," the bartender answered. "She was only here for a few minutes. I don't even think that she had a drink. I remember she was a cute girl, darker and shorter than the other one. That's all I really remember about her."

"Had you ever seen either of the two girls here before that night?" Penny asked, but the bartender got called down to the other end of the bar before he could answer.

While Penny waited for the bartender to return, a tall good-looking, professional type sidled up to the bar next to her. "I guess this is my lucky night. Only one seat at the bar and it just happens to be next to the prettiest lady in the place," the guy shmoozed.

"Actually, I'm waiting for someone," Penny responded politely. "I'm kind of trying to save that seat for him until he gets here."

"Well, if you ask me, any man who would make a woman who looks like you sit around and wait for him is unworthy. Let me see if I can show you how a woman like you deserves to be treated. How about if I just have a seat until he gets here?" the professional type suggested, pulling the barstool around him with one hand, his drink in the other, he started to sit down.

"Sure, have a seat," Kerby offered, pulling the barstool out from under the guy just as his behind was about to come to rest on it. The guy fell ass first to the floor. The contents of his drink flew up into the air and rained down all over him, just as the bartender got back to Penny.

"I wouldn't sit there if I was you, buddy, that seems to be an unlucky seat tonight," the bartender commented. The professional type, all embarrassed now, made his way to the bathroom trying his best not to make eye contact with Penny.

"I really wish you wouldn't do things like that," Penny whispered to Kerby before turning her attention back to the bartender.

"To answer your question, no I never saw either one of them in here before that night, and I never saw either one after that night, though I've got to say that the tall one looked awfully familiar," the bartender remarked.

"The cops must have been terribly interested in these two girls.

What kind of questions did they ask you about them?" Penny wondered.

"Actually, not much more than you just did. They didn't seem all that interested in the two girls. They asked a lot of questions about whether we get many gays in here and whether the guy seemed like he might be homosexual, stuff like that," the bartender remembered.

"They asked if he appeared to be homosexual?" Penny asked in a stunned voice.

"Yeah, I wondered about that myself, so asked one of the cops about it while the other one was in the men's room. You see, like I said, there were two cops, a younger one, maybe thirty, and an older guy, probably in his late forties early fifties, but there was no doubt that the younger cop was in charge of the case. He was really closed-mouth about everything, but the older guy, he did a couple of shots of Dewars on the sly while we were talking so I knew if I got him alone, he'd open up a little.

"Anyway, the younger cop goes into the men's room, and the older guy asked me for another quick shot before the young guy gets back. I poured him the shot, and he gulped it down real quick, half of it went down his chin and all over his tie, so I poured him another one and I asked him, 'What's all this stuff about gays?' He said that for four years in a row, on exactly the same date, a young male had disappeared in the city. The cops were thinking maybe there's a serial killer on the loose. Well, since it was guys going missing, and women don't commit serial murders, they were thinking it must be a homosexual male responsible for the disappearances."

"The cop with the whiskey on his chin is, no doubt, our friend from the library. Ask him what the younger cop looked like. At least, we'll know him if we see him following us," Kerby instructed.

"What did this younger cop look like?" Penny asked.

"A good looking young guy," the bartender recalled. "He was Italian looking, with the thick black hair combed straight back on his head, not a one out of place, not greasy looking or anything though. I'll tell you who he looked like. He looked just like that actor from the sixties. I forget his name, the one who was supposed to be the next Cary Grant, but I never saw him in anything other than those *Gidget* movies. You know, he played the boyfriend. His name in the *Gidget* movies was like Moon Doggie or something."

"James Daren, the cop looks like James Daren," Kerby said. "A good-looking actor, but he was never going to be the next Cary Grant, like some people thought. That was like saying that Bobby Murcer was going to the next Mickey Mantle. A nice little ball player in his own right, that Murcer was, but he wasn't ready to walk in the shoes of an immortal, and neither was James Daren. The comparisons weren't fair to either of them."

By now Penny had downed six shots of *Don Julio Anejo 1942.* "I know those movies. I've seen them on television. Moon Doggie *was* cute," Penny giggled, her voice now slurred.

"It's a good thing you don't have to drive home," Kerby admonished. "Come on, let's get going or you won't even be able to *walk* home."

"You know what I feel like?" Penny announced, in her now thoroughly slurred voiced. "I feel like another shot of tequila before we leave."

Penny downed one final shot and headed sideways for the door. As she did so, she stumbled into an obviously inebriated guy who was standing near the exit talking to some friends. "Sorry!" Penny apologized as she tried to straighten her course to the door.

"My pleasure, in fact, here let me give you a hand," the drunk guy said, letting his hand slip down Penny's back toward her bottom.

Kerby grabbed the guy's hand before it got to its intended destination and twisted it up behind the guy's back. The drunk guy howled and arched his back as if somebody had stuck something up his behind.

"Let me give *you* a hand," Kerby snarled, taking a handful of the drunk guy's hair with his free hand and forced his face down into a nearby table. The drinks on the table flew all over the group that was sitting there, and a small riot erupted. Fists and drinks were flying everywhere by the time Penny finally found the door and exited into the evening air, oblivious to what was happening behind her.

♥ ☄ ♟

"That was fun! We should do this more often," Penny slurred as they made their way slowly down Second Avenue, with Penny weaving from one side of the sidewalk to the other.

"Talk to me in the morning, kiddo, and we'll see how soon you want to do this again," Kerby replied.

"You know what I'm going to call you from now on?" Penny slurred. "Casper?" Kerby guessed.

"No, but that's a good one too," Penny said. "I'm going to call you

Archie. Archibald Leach, that was Cary Grant's real name, and from now on I'm going to call you Archie."

"Archie Leach is what Cary Grant named his dog," Kerby noted. "Grant buried Archie Leach in the movie *Arsenic and Old Lace*. If you look in the cemetery outside of the aunts' house, you'll see a headstone with the name Archie Leach on it. Later in life, Grant owned a Sealyham Terrier, and he named the dog Archie Leach.

"Do you know how they picked the name Cary Grant for him?" Kerby continued. "He went to work for Paramount Studios in 1931 to do his first movie, *Singapore Sue*. It was only a ten minute short. At the time, the studio's biggest star was Gary Cooper, so they took Cooper's initials, reversed them and came up with a name that was different but similar."

"Well, as of today, I'm changing your name to Archie," Penny repeated as they made their turn down East 80th Street toward home.

Halfway down the block, a still weaving Penny stopped suddenly and wobbled in place. "Do you know what I feel like, Archie?"

"Another shot of tequila?" Kerby guessed.

"That too," Penny said. "But what I really feel like is a *tingle*. Give me a *tingle,* Archie."

Kerby reached and took Penny's hand in his. "I don't want a little *tingle,* Archie. I want a big *tingle*, like the one you gave me when I was about to fall down the stairs," Penny insisted. Then she closed her eyes and held her arms out as if waiting for a big hug.

"All right, kiddo, but if anyone is looking, and I suspect someone is, they're going to think you've lost it, standing here hugging the air," Kerby warned as he wrapped his arms snugly around Penny's midsection and she wrapped her arms tightly around his neck.

"Aaaaah," Penny sighed as she felt the gentle, warm current run through her body. "You have no idea how good this feels, Archie."

"I do know that this is neither the time nor the place for this," Kerby replied, easing Penny's hands down from around his neck.

"Party-pooper," Penny bawled as she started down East 80th Street again. "And you're the one who's always telling me that I need to loosen up."

When they reached the front of the brownstone, Penny stopped to admire the new sign over the bookstore. *Sex, Ghosts, and Gumshoes,* the neon sign read, with *Sex* in magenta colored letters, *Ghosts* in blue and *Gumshoes* in yellow.

"Look, Archie! Doesn't the new sign look great? Add *sex* to anything and it makes it better. Right, Archie, isn't that what you say?" Penny slurred. "I have to trust you on that stuff, Archie. I really don't know that much about the subject. Do you know how many times I've had sex, Archie? Once, with an icky, little nerd. He slipped me that date rape drug and had sex with me while I was unconscious. Does that count as sex, Archie? Do you think that being raped while you're unconscious counts as sex?"

"No, kiddo," Kerby said softly, taking Penny back in his arms. "That doesn't count as making love."

"Aaaaah that feels sooo good, Archie," Penny sighed again. "Then I guess I've never had sex. If that doesn't count as sex, I guess I'm still a virgin, Archie."

Kerby helped Penny up the stairs with his arm around her waist. At the top of the stairs, Penny began fishing around in her pocketbook for her keys. As she did so, she caught sight of man emerging from the shadows on the other side of the street.

"Don't look now, Archie, but I think Officer Moon Doggie is across the street watching us," Penny giggled.

"He's watching you, kiddo. He can't see me. He's been following us since we left the bar," Kerby noted.

"You mean he saw me hugging the air back there? He's going to think I'm nuts."

"His thinking you're nuts is not what you have to worry about. What you should be concerned about is the fact that he thinks you're a murderer."

After Penny finally found her keys and got the brownstone door open, she turned and waved at the good-looking guy on the other side of the street. "Good night, Officer Moon Doggie," Penny hollered. The good-looking guy just nodded his head.

"I have got to get these shoes off," Penny groaned as the door slammed shut and she kicked her shoes into the sun parlor. "You know what I feel like, Archie?" Penny asked.

"A tingle," Kerby guessed.

"That too, but first I feel like a glass of wine," Penny slurred.

"Don't you think perhaps you've had enough for the night?" Kerby chided. "It's way beyond your bedtime, isn't it?"

"If you'll get me one glass of wine, I swear to you I'll go right up to bed when I finish it," Penny promised.

"Fine, but you'll be sorry in the morning. Mixing tequila and white wine is not a good idea," Kerby cautioned. Then he disappeared into the kitchen and returned with a glass of white wine.

Penny was sitting with her back against the arm of Aunt Mags's heavily cushioned sofa. Her legs and feet were stretched out the length of the sofa. "Sit there, Archie," Penny demanded, pointing at her feet as Kerby reached toward her with the glass of wine.

After Penny had taken the wine, Kerby lifted Penny's feet and sat down on the other side of the sofa. Penny plopped her feet down onto Kerby's lap. "My feet are killing me, Archie, but I bet that a *tingle* would make them feel all better. *Tingle* my sore *tootsies* for me, Archie, *pleeese*?" Penny whined.

Without saying a word, Kerby took Penny's right foot into his two hands and started to gently massage the soles of her feet. Penny laid her head back, sipped her wine and moaned. When Kerby had finished with the right foot, he moved to the left and gave it the same treatment that he had the right. By the time he had finished massaging each foot, Penny had finished her wine.

"Thank you, Archie, that was delicious," Penny sighed.

"You mean the wine?" Kerby asked.

"That too, but I was talking about the foot massage," Penny replied.

"Good, now let's get you up to bed before I wind up having to carry you up the stairs."

At the stairs, Kerby got behind Penny, put his hands around the small of her back and guided her up the steps. She continued to sigh in satisfaction the entire way up. In her bedroom, Penny fell backwards onto the bed. Kerby made his way to the dresser and pulled out an oversized cotton pajama top.

"Oh good! Are you going to undress me and put my pajamas on me now?" Penny giggled.

"No, I'm going downstairs, and you're going to undress yourself and put your own pajamas on."

"That doesn't sound like as much fun as what I suggested," Penny pouted, jumping up into a standing position on the bed as Kerby headed for the door.

"Okay, if you want me to. I'll undress myself," Penny shouted. Then she pulled down the zipper on the back of her little black dress and let it slip to her feet. "Ooooh, Kerrrr-by, are you sure you don't want to give me a hand?" Penny teased, drawing Kerby's attention back to her.

When Kerby turned, he could not help but stare in awe at Penny's flawless body. She wore only a pair of black lace bikini panties and a black lace bra. Her dress was still wrapped around her ankles. Her sinewy body was lightly bouncing up and down on the bed, causing her breasts to heave upward and almost out of her bra every time her body went up. Then she stopped jumping and playfully kicked her dress at Kerby, causing it to land over his head, covering his face.

As Kerby took the dress from his head and tossed it onto the dresser, he sternly admonished Penny, "Be careful up there or you're going to fall off and hurt yourself. Now, put your pajamas on, lay down, put out the light, and go to sleep."

"Don't be embarrassed. I'm not ashamed of my body. In fact, I'm quite proud of my body," Penny announced.

"You got that from your Aunt Brit, didn't you? She used to run around here naked all the time saying exactly the same thing," Kerby recalled. "Now, put your pajamas on and go to sleep."

"What's the matter, my body not good enough for you? I guess I'm no Helen Rose. Or maybe in order to impress *you*, I need to show you the rest of my body," Penny taunted, her hands slowly moving to her waistline as she began to ease her panties down.

"Don't do that, kiddo. You're already going to hate yourself in the morning. Don't make it any worse," Kerby warned, flipping Penny's pajama top up to her. Penny reached for the pajama top, but seemed to lose her balance in the process and began stumbling toward the end of the bed. Kerby reached her just as she flopped forward off the bed, landing right in Kerby's outstretched arms. He held her more tightly than he needed to.

"I told you to be careful or you would fall," Kerby said softly into Penny's ear.

"I didn't really fall," Penny whispered back with a giggle. "I did it on purpose, so that I could wind up right where I am."

Starting to feel a bit uncomfortable with the situation, Kerby tried to ease Penny away from him, but she pulled him back to her and nuzzled her head into his chest. She said softly, "Don't push me away. I just want to feel like I'm as much of an incentive object as that piece of chocolate cake you told me about. You can't tell me that when you look at me, the memories don't flood back in. You can't tell me that the desire isn't flowing within you right now. You can't tell me that the longing isn't there. I can see it in your eyes every time you look at me. I want you to make love to me, Kerby. Don't they say that sex is mostly in the mind anyway? Let's take a chance and see just how fulfilling it can be for each of us."

"Kiddo, I don't think that's such a good idea right now, not in the condition that you're in. The fact that I'm a spirit has nothing to do with it. I'd be happy to please you, sexually or otherwise, regardless of whether there's anything in it for me at the end. But the truth is that even if I were flesh and blood, I still wouldn't allow anything sexual to happen between us tonight. I'd need to know you were in a position to make a decision you wouldn't regret in the morning. Tonight, I'd be too afraid that the tequila might be making your mind up for you," Kerby breathed into the top of Penny's head. "I don't ever want you lumping me in with the icky little nerd."

After Kerby had finished saying what he had to say, he waited for a response but none came. Then he looked down and realized that Penny had fallen asleep in his arms. There was no way for Kerby to be certain how much of his speech Penny had even heard.

Kerby pulled the blankets back and laid Penny on the bed, still clad only in her bra and panties. He stood at the base of the bed and stared at her for several seconds, amazed at just how sensuous her body was.

"Kiddo, you're all that and a piece of chocolate cake too," Kerby whispered, pulling the blanket up to Penny's chin and tucking her in.

CHAPTER 10

WHEN PIGS FLY
JUNE 21, 2003

Kerby was not in the least bit surprised when Penny did not come down for breakfast at her usual time. It wasn't until almost nine o'clock that Kerby heard any sign of life coming from Penny's bedroom. The sign he heard was a repeated moaning that, ironically, sounded like a ghost trying to scare someone out of the house. Still, Kerby waited for a while before going up to investigate. When he finally did go up the stairs, the moaning stopped momentarily, so Kerby put his ear to the door to see if perhaps Penny had fallen back asleep. The instant that his ear came to rest on the door, he was startled when the moaning started again, only louder this time.

Kerby eased the door open slightly and peeked in. Penny was in the bed with the blanket pulled up to her neck and a pillow resting on top of her head, covering her face from her nostrils up. Kerby pushed the door open further and entered the room without Penny becoming aware that he was there. Once inside, Kerby loudly cleared his throat in order to alert Penny to the fact that he was in the room with her.

Penny peeked out from under her pillow with one eye. "How did you get in here?" Penny whimpered.

"Well, the door was closed, so I turned the knob, opened the door, and came in," Kerby answered flippantly.

"That's not what I meant," Penny groaned. "You know what I meant to say. I meant to say, what are you doing in here?"

"I couldn't help but hear you moaning," Kerby responded.

"What do you mean, you couldn't help but hear me moaning?" Penny persisted.

"I had my ear to the door," Kerby said smiling.

"Are these original lines, or are you quoting from some Cary Grant movie?" Penny wondered, finally coming out from under the pillow but holding her right arm up over her face to allow her eyes to adjust gradually to the light in the room.

"*The Bachelor and the Bobby-Soxer,*" Kerby admitted, a bit chagrined. "Cary Grant, Myrna Loy, Shirley Temple and Rudy Vallee."

"I never heard of it," Penny grumbled.

"Not one of my favorites either," Kerby replied. "Temple plays a high school girl who has a crush on Grant's character, a playboy artist. Loy plays Temple's sister who happens to be a judge. Grant gets into trouble, and as his punishment Loy makes him squire Temple around town until her crush is over. Of course, Grant ends up with Loy in the end."

"Is that why you came up here, to tell me the plot of *The Bachelor and the Bobby-Soxer*?" Penny groused, putting her head back under the pillow.

"No, I came up to tell you that you remind me of a woman."

"I know, Helen Rose," Penny said.

"No, not her. You remind me of the women with the power."

"What power?" Penny asked, taking her head back out from under the pillow as if she were now interested in what Kerby had to say.

"The power of hoodoo."

"Hoodoo?" Penny asked, now totally befuddled.

"You do." Kerby answered.

"I do what?" Penny asked, clearly growing impatient.

"Remind me of a woman," Kerby said with a big smile. "That's the most famous exchange in the movie."

"No wonder it's not one of your favorites," an annoyed Penny replied, not smiling at all. "So what you really came up here for was to torture a woman who is already on her deathbed?"

"What I *really* came up here for is to tell you that I think you should probably get up and get yourself ready to face the day. I'm expecting visitors soon," Kerby said.

"Oh really, are some of your ghost friends coming to see you, perhaps to play some hide and seek, or something?" Penny responded, putting her head back under the pillow.

"The visitors I'm expecting aren't coming to see me. They're coming to see you, to question you about a murder."

Penny flipped the pillow off of her head and shot upright, holding the blanket to her chest. "What makes you think that today is the day they're going to introduce themselves to me?"

"Well, for one thing they've been standing outside of their car all morning staring over here as if they're waiting for some sign of life in the house. For another thing, they have to question you at some point in time, and given the fact that they now know that their cover has been blown, there's not much point in continuing to follow you around. So, if my guess is right, today is the day, and I can't think of any reason why if they're going to do it, they would put it off until later. As soon as they're sure that you're up and about, they'll be over."

"What makes you so sure that they know that I'm onto them?" Penny asked.

"Mostly it's the fact that you waved a goodnight to one of them last night when we got home. Let's see, if I recall right, what you hollered to him while you were waving was, 'Goodnight, Officer Moon Doggie,'" Kerby laughed.

"I didn't! I called him Officer Moon Doggie? Are you certain that he heard me?" a chagrined Penny asked.

"He certainly acknowledged you."

"I can't believe that I did that and I can't even remember it," Penny said, her face scrunched up as if she were trying to recall the previous evening. "The last thing that I remember about last night is getting out of my seat at the bar and heading for the door. I hope I didn't do anything else to embarrass myself," Penny continued, staring at Kerby as if she was waiting for him to confirm that nothing else embarrassing had happened.

"Nothing that I can think of," Kerby said with a grin. "Unless you'd consider jumping up and down on the bed in your undies something to be embarrassed about."

"I didn't do that. Please tell me I didn't do that," Penny pleaded.

"Okay, if that's what you want to hear, then I guess I must be mistaken. It probably wasn't you who was jumping up and down on the bed in her black lace bra and matching bikini panties," Kerby taunted.

Penny peeked under the blankets hoping that her underwear wouldn't match Kerby's description, but knowing that they would. After she confirmed her belief, Penny pulled the blankets up over her head. From under the blankets she said, "You'd better leave now, so that I can get into the shower and get ready before they ring the bell."

"Why do I have to leave?" Kerby asked sarcastically. "After all, you're not ashamed of your naked body. In fact, as I recall, last night you said that you're quite proud of your naked body. You sounded just like your Aunt Brit."

"Out! Now!" Penny shouted from under the blankets.

♥ ✂ ♣

Penny had just finished her last swallow of coffee when Kerby hollered, "Showtime, kiddo!"

Penny raced into the sun parlor, and found Kerby standing at the window looking out between the curtains. When she peered out of the window, Penny saw two men crossing the street approaching her brownstone. The one guy she recognized from the library. It was the guy with the wrinkled suit and stains on his tie. The suit he had on looked like the same one he had on at the library, wrinkles and all. Penny did not recognize the other guy from sight, though she had seen him the night before. She did, however, recognize him from the description that the bartender had given her. The bartender was right. The guy looked a whole lot like Moon Doggie from the *Gidget* movies, except he wasn't wearing a bathing suit. To the contrary, he was impeccably dressed in a blue suit and red tie that made him look like he had just come from *Barney's of New York.*

What was that actor's name from the movie? Penny asked herself. *Oh yeah, James Daren,* she remembered. *He does, he looks just like James Daren,* she concluded.

"What do I say?" Penny asked Kerby as the two cops neared the top of her stairs.

"Tell them that your Aunt Mags was a recognized clairvoyant, and the first night that you stayed here you found her Ouija Board and decided to play around with it. To your amazement, the Ouija Board talked to you, and you wound up communicating with the spirit of Nicholas Demopolous."

"They're not going to buy that," Penny replied after the doorbell rang. "It's way too farfetched."

"It's not that far from the truth," Kerby reminded her. "On the other hand, if you have a better idea, go with it."

"Hi! Can I help you?" Penny greeted the officers as she opened the door.

"Good morning, Ms Albright. My name is Rocco Francona," the good-looking cop said. "This is my partner, Stan Slowinski. We're officers with the Homicide Division of the New York City Police Department. I wonder if we might have a few words with you?"

"Of course, come in," Penny replied, leading them into the dining room where they all took seats at the dining room table, the two officers opposite Penny and Kerby. "Why in the world would you want to speak to me?" Penny asked, feigning surprise .

"We're not here to answer questions, Ms Albright. We're here to ask them," Slowinski snapped in response to Penny's question.

"Calm down, Stan," Francona said, putting his right hand on Slowinski's left arm as if holding him back from a fight.

"Look, Roc, if it was up to me, we'd be asking these questions downtown. We've got enough to bring her in, at least, as a material witness, if not enough to prosecute for obstruction of justice, so let's not mince words here," Slowinski barked, after which he and Francona went into a private huddle.

"It looks as if they're going to play good-cop, bad-cop with you," Kerby predicted. "Mr. Wrinkles over there is going to be the bad-cop. He's going to keep threatening to bring you downtown, maybe lock you up. Officer Moon Doggie is going to keep acting as if he has to calm Wrinkles down, hold him back to protect you from him. Let's surprise them, see if we can cut through all the games by just cooperating. Tell them everything you know."

"Ms Albright, I'm going to be candid with you," Francona started. "A couple of days ago a young woman matching your description made a 911 telephone call from a payphone not too far from here. She informed the emergency operator that there was a body in Turtle Pond in Central Park. Because of other information that was provided by the caller, we immediately dispatched a squad car to the payphone. Unfortunately, by the time our people got there, the caller had hung up and left. Fortunately, at least from our perspective, a grocer with a store just a few doors down from the payphone recalled a woman who had used the phone just a few minutes before our squad car arrived. The grocer described a woman who looked very much like you. In fact, his description was a perfect match for you.

"More important, the grocer said that a taxi had waited for the woman, and not only that, but for reasons of which we are not certain, the grocer had written down the license plate number for the taxi. We found out that the cabbie lives right next door. That evening, we showed up to see what information the cab driver might be able to provide us, but before we could exit our vehicle, you came out of your home in a pair of jogging shorts and sneakers, like I said, a perfect match for the woman described by the grocer. Needless to say, we decided not to talk with your next door neighbor and possibly tip you off.

"Instead, we chose to follow you for a few days and see where it might lead us. Ms Albright, I have to be frank with you, it led us to places that we never imagined it might. Now, before we go any further, I feel like I have to tell you that last night we took your fingerprints off a glass in *Dorrian's The Red Hand*. We are currently processing those fingerprints in order to compare them with prints taken off the payphone from which the emergency call was made. We'll have the results by later in the day. That said, Ms Albright, are you, in fact, the woman who made the 911 call?"

"Yes," Penny answered bluntly.

"Would you like to tell me how you came by the information that you provided to the emergency operator?" Francona asked.

"Officer Francona, I'm afraid that you are not going to believe this, but this home was left to me by my aunt who passed away recently. My aunt was a well recognized clairvoyant and medium. You know, she held séances and stuff. On my first night sleeping in the home, I found an Ouija Board and started playing with it. To my surprise, the board started talking to me. To make a long story short, the information that I gave the emergency operator is information that I got directly from the deceased's spirit."

"I told you, Roc, why are we wasting our time up here trying to be nice? Let's bring her downtown and do this in a cell. I'll bet she gets honest in hurry," Slowinski groused.

"Relax, Stan," Francona said, before turning his attention back to Penny. "It appears that my partner doesn't believe in psychics. Personally, I have an open mind on the subject. I even used one in a case once. A little girl went missing, and her mother had seen this clairvoyant on *Oprah* or something. The mother actually hired the woman, but we cooperated with her. I mean, a mother loses a child, you do what you can to help her get through it.

"Anyway, do you know what the psychic said? She said that the little girl was dead, and we would find her body in a white box in a field on the same street as a school. She said the street name started with a P, but for some reason she couldn't see any other letters in the name. Do you know where we found that little girl's body? It had been stuffed in an abandoned refrigerator in a lot next to a preschool. Do you know what street the lot was on? It was on Avenue P in Brooklyn."

"I take it that the clairvoyant did not become a suspect in the murder case," Penny commented, glaring at Slowinski.

"No, but as you can see there's a big difference between the information that you provided with regard to the murder of Nicholas Demopolous and the information that our psychic provided in the case of the little girl," Francona noted. "You see Ms Albright, psychics are rarely specific and never detailed in the information that they provide. She said it was a white box, not a refrigerator, and she said it was on a street that started with a P, not specifically Avenue P. She was good, but not that good.

"In contrast, the information that you provided was incredibly specific and detailed. You didn't just know exactly where the body was, you knew the victim's name. You knew the manner of death and the nature of the injuries that he had suffered. And Ms Albright I have to tell you, in all of my years as a police officer, I have never before seen or heard of injuries of the type we're talking about in this case."

"All I can tell you, Officer Francona is that the spirit provided me with that information," Penny insisted.

"Somebody provided you with the information, Ms Albright, but it wasn't any spirit. Eventually, you're going to tell us who it was or you are going to be trading this million-dollar brownstone you just inherited for a lockup downtown that's not nearly so comfortable," Slowinski threatened.

"They're not taking you downtown, kiddo," Kerby remarked. "If they were going to take you anywhere they would have done it already. I get the feeling that they know something that we don't."

"Did the spirit also tell you about the Sizemore kid and the O'Brien kid?" Francona quizzed. "We know that the other day you just happened to go down to the library and look through newspapers for the months that those two kids went missing. We also know that when you left the library, you just happened to stop at the high school that both boys attended, and when you got there you asked to look at yearbooks for years that they were there. What did the spirit of Nicholas Demopolous tell you about the Sizemore and O'Brien kids?"

"He told me that they had been killed in the same way that he was, only they were both killed in a warehouse in Staten Island. He said that the boys' bodies were somewhere in the water near where the warehouse is located."

"Isn't that a coincidence, all of a sudden your information is vague and unspecific, like a psychic's information is supposed to be? Too bad the spirit wasn't as specific with regard to where the two kids were murdered as he was with regard to his own murder. I've got two mothers who would very much like to have the bodies of their sons so that they might give them proper burials," Slowinski said sarcastically.

"Mr. Demopolous wasn't there when either boy was killed, like he was for his own murder," Penny explained.

"Did Mr. Demopolous's spirit happen to mention any other murders?" Francona continued with his interrogation.

"He said that exactly one year before his murder, a guy was killed in Riverside Park in the same way that he was murdered and by the same people."

"Which I guess brings us to why you happened to visit Riverside Park last night," Francona said with a smiled.

"Yes," Penny answered.

"You didn't just happen to locate the body of this guy while you were there, did you?" Slowinski interjected smugly.

"Yes, it just so happens that I did," Penny replied. "His body is in the Hudson River, just opposite the tennis courts."

"And just why did the murderers decide to dump the body opposite the tennis courts?" Slowinski wondered.

"Because opposite the tennis courts there is no fence separating the walkway from the river. The body is weighted down by a concrete bench that the killers could not lift over the fence."

"Again back to the specifics," Slowinski laughed mockingly. "You wouldn't happen to know who this Riverside Park victim is, would you?"

"His name is Tom Smith. He's from Madison, Wisconsin."

Slowinski's mouth dropped open, and he turned to Francona who also had a stunned expression on his face.

"From the looks on their faces, I'd say that they put the four disappearances together a long time ago," Kerby commented. "They can't say you're not cooperating now, kiddo."

"I told you we should have sent a diver down first thing this morning," Slowinski said to Francona. "Murderers always return to the scene of their crime."

"Look, Stan, you know as well I do that Ms Albright could not have committed these murders, so be careful how you go about describing her," Francona barked sharply to his partner.

"You may not realize it, kiddo, but you have a rock solid alibi for one or more of these murders that we hadn't even thought about," Kerby remarked. "That's why they haven't taken you in."

"That's four murders so far, Ms. Albright. Did the spirit of Mr. Demopolous tell you about any other murders?" Francona asked.

"That's it, just four so far. But the killers apparently have plans to keep killing one guy a year, every year, on the same date each year, until they either grow tired of it or you catch them."

"Ms Albright, I don't know whether it has been intentional or not, but you've been using the plural to describe the person or persons who committed these crimes. Are you telling me that Mr. Demopolous's spirit told you who committed these murders?" Francona wondered.

"Not specifically, but he did describe the murderers. They're two young females. Apparently, they were schoolmates of the first two boys killed. One is a tall attractive blonde. She may be a model. The other is a shorter brunette. She's muscular and may work as a dominatrix here in the city, but I'm not certain about that yet."

"Here we go again with the ambiguities . . . " Slowinski cracked.

"Where'd he learn that word?" Kerby joked, as Slowinski continued.

"One minute she can tell us specifically the name of the guy who was killed, how he was murdered, exactly where the body is and even that the body is weighted down with a concrete bench. But when it comes to the killers, all she knows is that one is a blonde and might be a model, and the other is a brunette who might work in the S&M community.

"It's time to cut to the chase, Ms Albright," Slowinski bellowed in a threatening tone. "Let me explain something to you, so that you don't think you're fooling anybody. First off, I personally spoke to the bartender at *Dorrian's* last night after you left, while Roc here was following you home. The bartender told me that he gave you descriptions of the two girls that Nick Demopolous spoke to on the evening that he disappeared, and ain't it a coincidence that you just described to us the same two girls that the bartender described to you last night.

"Second, in case you haven't heard, men are from Mars and women are from Venus. You know something about Venus, Ms Albright? There are no serial killers on Venus. Women don't do that kind of thing. I think you already know this, but I'm going to tell you anyway. What we're looking for here is probably a crazed gay guy who hates himself for being gay and is killing these guys because he can't stand the fact that he's physically attracted to them. You got any male homosexual friends, Ms Albright?"

"I don't ask my friends what their sexual preferences are," Penny answered calmly.

"Well, if it wasn't a crazed gay guy, then something else occurred to me just this morning while I was sitting here listening to you describe the way these murders were committed. Once a year, every year, the same time each year, each of these guys being sexually mutilated, isn't that what you described? It sounds to me like we might be talking about some kind of ritual murders here. You know, devil worshipers, sacrifices, that kind of thing. You say you're into Ouija Boards and stuff, contacting dead people. Do you know any devil worshipers, Ms Albright? Or perhaps you have some friends or relatives who are witches?" Slowinski asked with a sly smile.

Francona sat forward in his seat as if maybe Slowinski had hit on something.

"Kerby sat back in his seat, waiting for Penny to offer an emphatic *no*, then it dawned on him. *Oh no, Beth O'Malley is a Wiccan,* Kerby remembered. Then he said, "You'd better tell them the truth, kiddo. The way Officer Moon Doggie is chomping at the bit over there, I'm thinking he already knows about your Aunt Beth anyway. It's better not to get caught in a lie. I don't mind him thinking you're crazy, but I don't want him thinking you're a liar."

"Not the kind of witch you're talking about," Penny finally answered.

In the O'Malley clan, Aunt Beth was the middle sister. Next to Mags, Aunt Beth was Penny's favorite. Penny chose to go to New Mexico State University partly because Aunt Beth lived in Santa Fe, not far from Penny's campus in Alamogordo. During her years in college, Penny spent much of her off time in the summers living with Aunt Beth. After college, Penny lived with Aunt Beth again for over a year before Penny went to work at New Mexico State, as an Adjunct Professor in the English Department.

Like many people today, at some point in her life Aunt Beth grew disenchanted with the established religions and decided to seek out something that she felt was spiritually more fulfilling. In the eighties, Aunt Beth got involved in the New Age Spirituality Movement and even moved to Santa Fe, New Mexico because the movement seemed to be centered in that area. However, Aunt Beth began drifting away from New Age Spirituality when the movement became increasingly involved with the power of crystals, channelers (most of whom were found to be over-the-top frauds) and even out-of-body astral travel.

In search of an alternative religion that centered itself in personal spirituality, Aunt Beth found herself attracted to Wicca, which she attempted to blend with the Christianity on which she had been raised. Aunt Beth found that Wicca, which she sometimes called "White Witchcraft" or "The Craft of the Wise," was nothing more than an earth-based religion, similar to Native American Spirituality. She also found that, contrary to popular belief, Wicca is as far removed from Satanism as any religion could get, even though, like many other religions, both use forms of pentacles or pentagrams in their religious ceremonies.

Aunt Beth was attracted to the Wicca belief in a deity that is largely unknowable, which she referred to as "The All" or "The One." She also liked the fact that the Wicca religion is gender neutral in that Wiccans believe they can comprehend and commune with either the male or female aspects of the deity, whom Aunt Beth called "The God" and "The Goddess."

But most of all, Aunt Beth was impressed by the Wiccans' reliance upon the *Threefold Law* and the *Wiccan Rede* in the way that they live their lives. The *Threefold Law* provides simply that, "All good that a person does to another returns threefold in this life; harm is also returned threefold." The *Wiccan Rede* simply says, "An it harm none, do what thou wilt," meaning that as long as it harms no one, including oneself, one is free to do what they wish. Aunt Beth viewed the credos as an obligation on the part of each Wiccan to carefully review the implications of each action or non action in their life. It was important to her that domination, manipulation, and control were particularly and specifically prohibited by the Wiccan convictions.

Beyond all of that, Aunt Beth found the Wiccan rituals to be generally more interesting and fun than those of the established religions. She liked the fact that when possible Wiccans held their rituals outdoors. Aunt Beth also enjoyed the casting of spells, which many Wiccans do, though they are strictly prohibited by their belief system from engaging in spells or other activities that harm others, a logical result of their belief in the *Threefold Law*, and their commitment to following the *Wiccan Rede*.

As a result, Aunt Beth was always careful before performing a spell to think through all of the possible repercussions that the spell might have, in order to make certain that it would not have a manipulative component. Like most Wiccans, Aunt Beth believed that spells alter the course of the universe and are not to be entered into without thoroughly considering all of their possible effects. Nevertheless, once she had thought her spells through, Aunt Beth loved casting them.

It wasn't long before Aunt Beth had formed her own Wicca coven in Santa Fe, comprised primarily of New Agers who had become disenchanted with the New Age Movement. Though Aunt Beth was careful not to force it on her, as a little girl Penny loved the rituals and watching Aunt Beth prepare and cast spells. When Penny turned sixteen, she expressed an interest in becoming a Wiccan and even went through the "Initiation Ritual" with Aunt Beth's coven. Penny never cast a spell and gave up the Wiccan rituals before she turned twenty, but she remained a staunch supporter of the right of others to practice Wicca, and she even wrote a college paper her senior year comparing the practice of Wicca favorably with the way that some of the established religions are practiced today.

"Why don't you tell us about how some witchcraft is not as bad as others, or maybe you've already written something on the subject?" Slowinski challenged, leaving no doubt that he was already aware of Penny's paper.

"Ms Albright, I sense that you are doing your best to cooperate here without hurting someone else. I mean, I'm not buying into the Ouija Board story just yet," Francona explained. "But given the information that you've already provided, I feel as if it's only fair to be honest with you. You see, we know a great deal more about you than you might think. We know that you could not have committed any of these murders because we have determined that at the time of each abduction you were at New Mexico State University in Alamogordo, New Mexico, teaching summer courses in English 101 to students who were struggling with the subject.

"We have also had an opportunity to review your background with the school administrators and even to look at some of the papers that you did while you were a student there. We know that you lived at various times with an aunt in Santa Fe, New Mexico who runs a coven for so-called *White Witches*. We believe that you were a member of that coven for a period of time, and we know that you were a staunch supporter of the right of individuals to practice the Wicca religion without prejudice," Francona finished.

"I believe that the freedom to practice the religion of one's choice, *without prejudice,* as you say, is written into our constitution, Officer Francona. If you knew anything about my Aunt Beth or the ethics of the Wicca religion, you would know that any suggestion that these murders might in someway be related to Wiccan rituals is ludicrous," Penny retorted angrily.

"Unlike my partner here, I have read your paper on the subject, and I fully understand your position. But to some people, witchcraft is witchcraft and something to be feared. You know more than anyone possibly could about these murders, unless of course that person was there when the murders were committed, or had a conversation with someone who was there. Since we know that you could not have been there when any of these crimes occurred, we have to assume that you know someone who was there and that they described to you what happened. We have no alternative but to believe that for some reason you are trying to protect the person or persons who committed these crimes. That is, unless you can convince us that you really can communicate with spirits. I think you can appreciate our position," Francona explained.

"I do appreciate your position," Penny responded, much more calmly now. "I'm just not certain how to prove to you that I have had communications with spirits."

"Do you know when you'll convince me of that, Ms Albright?" Slowinski interrupted. "When pigs fly!"

"Thank you for your time, Ms Albright. I'm sure we'll be talking again very soon," Francona said, lightly shaking Penny's hand before he and Slowinski made their way to the door.

"He likes you," Kerby noted.

"Who?" Penny asked as if she did not know to whom Kerby was referring.

"Officer Moon Doggie, he likes you. I could see it in his eyes," Kerby said.

♥ 🚫 🎩

"Where are we going?" Penny wondered, slipping on her shoes outside the sun parlor early that evening.

"You'll see soon enough," Kerby answered.

"Are we going to see if we can find the two boys?" Penny persisted.

"Not tonight, but I have a plan for that too, if Sol will cooperate," Kerby replied.

"Then where are we going tonight?" Penny asked again.

"Hopefully, we're going to eliminate one of your worries before it turns you into an alcoholic," Kerby smiled.

"I may never drink again, at least not tequila," Penny groaned. Then she had an image of Kerby tossing Mark Libby out of a window. "I hope that when you said *eliminate* you didn't mean what came to my mind."

"I'm not that kind of a guy," Kerby assured her, after thinking about what images Penny might have conjured as a result of his use of the word *eliminate*.

Sol pulled up in front of the brownstone just as Penny and Kerby exited. Kerby looked to his left and saw Stan Slowinski sitting alone his vehicle. Slowinski began to fidget nervously when he saw Sol pull up in front of the brownstone.

"When we get into the cab, tell Sol that all you want him to do is take you to Lexington Avenue and drop you off at the subway station. Tell him you're really sorry for inconveniencing him, but if you stay in the cab, the guy back there in the car is going to follow you, and you don't want to be followed tonight. We can't have Stan Slowinski with us for what I plan on doing this evening."

When they got into the cab, Penny informed Sol of her concerns. Sol initially told Penny not to worry because he would have no trouble losing the guy, but he changed his mind when Penny told him that the guy in the car was a cop. Sol drove up to Lexington Avenue and took a left turn. Stan Slowinski's car pulled out directly behind Sol, but by the time both vehicles had turned onto Lexington Avenue, Slowinski's vehicle was two cars back. It wasn't because Slowinski was trying to be clandestine. He was making no attempt to hide the fact that he was behind Penny, and intended to be with her for the evening.

Penny had Sol drive past the first subway station at 86th Street when she noticed that there were several open parking spaces in the area of the subway entrance. At the 96th Street Station, there were no open parking spaces, so Penny instructed Sol to slow to a stop without pulling over. Once Sol had come to a complete stop, Penny and Kerby jumped out of the cab and headed for the stairs leading underground. Penny made an effort not to make eye contact with Slowinski, but Kerby made a point of looking for the surprise and disappointment on Slowinski's face. When Kerby looked back, Slowinski was banging his steering wheel with the base of his palm like a pizza maker kneading his dough. He was repeatedly mouthing the word *damn*.

Kerby and Penny raced down the stairs and directly toward the turnstiles. Penny was able to skip having to stop at the token booth because she had her extra token from a few days earlier in her pocket. As a Transit Officer eyed her suspiciously, Penny flew through the turnstile as if she were late for an appointment. Once on the platform for the downtown trains, Penny looked up anxiously and saw Slowinski hitting the bottom of the stairs at the same time that she saw the light from a Number 4 Express Train coming down the tunnel toward her.

Slowinski hit the turnstile just as the train screeched to a stop. He placed his hands on the turnstile and hurdled his feet over just as the train's doors began to open. He would have made it to the train in time too, if it weren't for the fact that as he started toward the platform, the Transit Officer caught him by his collar and yanked him back. As the train pulled away from the station, Penny and Kerby watched an angry Stan Slowinski digging through his jacket pocket looking for his badge to show the Transit Officer.

Kerby popped out of his seat at the 33rd Street Station and Penny followed him out of the subway car, up the stairs, and onto 33rd Street at Lexington Avenue. Kerby then headed east with Penny behind him still demanding to know where he was taking her. At the corner of 33rd Street and Second Avenue, Kerby stopped and looked up admiringly at an office building on the corner.

"I'm not taking another step unless you tell me where we are going," Penny said adamantly.

"We're not going anywhere, kiddo. We're here," Kerby smiled, opening the door to the building and gesturing for Penny to enter.

A security guard, who looked to be a septuagenarian, sat behind a counter in the center of the lobby. A listing of the occupants of the building was on a large board behind him.

"They didn't have security when I was here last," Kerby recollected as they approached the old security guard. "Just pick any company on the twenty-first floor and tell him you have an appointment."

Penny looked up at the board and then down at the security guard. "Hi, I'm looking for the Law Office of Dempsey and Santucci," Penny said.

"They're on twenty-one, lady, but I'm quite sure they're all gone for the night," the old guard rasped.

"That's strange," Penny countered. "Mr. Dempsey assured me he would be here late this evening. I came in all the way from New Jersey."

"I'm sure I saw Mr. Dempsey leave earlier, but I just went to take a leak, and he may have come back while I was gone. You can go ahead on up and see whether he's up there if you want, just as long as you sign in first," the old guard coughed.

Penny signed in and they made their way around to a bank of elevators. "This better be good," Penny snarled, glaring at Kerby.

"You're either going to love me or hate me, kiddo, and it's all going to depend upon what kind of renovations they've done to this old building over the years," Kerby replied as the elevator sped up to the twenty-first floor and the doors sprang open.

Once out of the elevator, Kerby led Penny to the west side of the building and down a corridor lined with offices with wooden doors and frosted glass windows, most of which had company names painted on them.

"It looks pretty much as I remember it," Kerby reminisced, stopping in front a door with no writing on it. "Except it looks vacant, which is good for us."

"Do you want to fill me in now on what we're doing here?" Penny grumbled.

"This is my old office. It used to say 'Kerby Brewster, Private Investigator' right there," Kerby said proudly, pointing to the frosted glass window.

"You brought me all the way down here on a subway and had me run from a police officer so that you could wax nostalgic outside of your old office?" Penny complained in an outraged tone. "I mean, you can't even get inside there."

"Why not?" Kerby asked, taking an old key out of his pocket. "The door sure looks the same," Kerby continued as he stuck the key in, and to Penny's surprise it turned.

"What were you going to do if it was a different lock?"

"Then I would have used a paperclip," Kerby said, taking a paper clip out of his pocket. "Tricks of the trade, you know. I used to be good at this stuff."

Kerby led Penny into the dimly lit, vacant office and over to a large window where he looked up at the lights on top of the Empire State Building. "Nice view, isn't it?'

"It's very nice. Now can we get out of here before I get arrested for breaking and entering?"

Penny started for the door, but Kerby caught her by her arm and pulled her back. "This way, kiddo," he instructed, looking up toward the ceiling while leading Penny to a corner of the office. "The ceiling looks the same too."

"Great, the door is the same, the ceiling is the same, isn't that all nice. They just don't make things like they used to. Can we go now?" Penny asked impatiently.

"I'm going to lift you onto my shoulders, so that you can reach the ceiling. When you get up there, I want you to remove the ceiling tile there in the corner. Look into the wall space and let me know if you see anything interesting," Kerby instructed, after which he placed his hands around Penny's waist and began to lift her.

"You're going to do what?" Penny asked incredulously, just before she felt Kerby's hands around her waistline. Then she started to moan lightly as the current from Kerby's fingers started to tingle her sides. Kerby bent his head and hoisted Penny onto his shoulders, so that her legs straddled his neck and hung down on either side of his chest. Her groin and the bottom of her backside rested firmly on the back of Kerby's neck. The tingling sensation spread up the back of Penny's legs and into her behind and groin, causing her whole body to begin to shudder.

Penny started making noises as if she were in the throes of lovemaking. "Jeeezzuss, wait, wait, wait, this is not a good idea," Penny gasped when she first felt the tingling start to run up into her loins. "Mmmmph, put me down, put me down," Penny panted as the current ran up inside of her. "Ooh, ooh, ooh, that area is too sensitive for this," Penny grunted, and then she let out a long aaaaahh.

"This will only take a minute, and I'm not putting you down until you do what I asked, so get on with it. In fact, if you'd loosen up, you might enjoy this," Kerby chided.

Penny squirmed on Kerby's shoulders trying to keep her bottom off of Kerby as much as possible while she reached for the ceiling tile he had pointed to and removed it from its space, then she saw the safe on top of the wallboards. "Ooohmygod, theeere's a saaaafe in theeere," Penny squealed, through a strained voice.

"No kidding! If my memory hasn't failed me, the code is 36, 22, 34," Kerby remembered.

"Penny continued to swivel about on Kerby's shoulders as she turned the dial of the safe and it popped open. "Theeere's lotssss ooof moooneeey in theeere," Penny shrieked as if the sight of the money had sent her over the edge.

Two hundred thousand dollars if I'm not mistaken," Kerby said calmly. "Now come on down."

"Uuummm, what's your hurry," Penny moaned. "I'm starting to enjoy it up heeere. I think I should count the money before I geeet downnn."

"If you think you've found yourself a ponyboy, you're mistaken," Kerby joked. "Now, give me the money and come on down."

Penny dropped the wad of money down to Kerby who in turn dropped it into Penny's pocketbook. Penny let out another "Ooohmygod" as Kerby began to lift her from his shoulders. Kerby stopped when the door to the office suddenly popped open. The old security guard stuck his head in tentatively.

"I don't know what kind of perverted stuff you're up to in there, lady, but this is not the place for it," the old guy rasped. He stepped into the office and his eyes searched the darkened room for the source of the noises. Finally he saw Penny, apparently floating in midair in the corner of the room, still oooohing and aaaahing.

Kerby lifted Penny from his shoulders as quickly as he could and placed her on the ground. "Jeezzuss *that* was intense," Penny wailed to Kerby, but loud enough for the old guy to hear. "I've never felt *anything* like *that* in my *life*."

The old guy was staring at Penny, his mouth wide open. "Thanks for sharing, lady. I'm not even going to ask how you did that, but I've got a wife at home who would love to know your secrets," the old guy wheezed.

♥ ♦ ♣

After the old guy had escorted Penny out of the building, Kerby tried to convince her that since they were so close, they should take a trip down the block and visit the top of the Empire State Building. Penny was reluctant at first, mainly because she didn't like the idea of sightseeing with $200,000 in her purse. Kerby finally convinced her by telling her that even though his office was right up the street, the Empire State Building had only been built shortly before he was killed, and he had never had the opportunity to travel up to the observatory.

When they reached the base of the Empire State Building at 350 Fifth Avenue between 33rd and 34th Streets, Penny called Sol and told him where she was. She asked him to pick her up in about forty-five minutes. Sol told Penny that he was concerned because Stan Slowinski had been following him around all night and would probably follow him down to the Empire State Building too. Penny told Sol not to worry because once he picked her up, she was going home for the night and Slowinski was welcome to follow her there if he wanted to.

Penny paid for her ticket, and she and Kerby took the elevator up to the 86th Floor Observatory and then to the Observatory on the 102nd floor. A light breeze blew through Penny's hair as they made their way around the observatory deck. "They say that on a clear day you can see five different states from up here," Kerby commented, marveling at the lights of the city.

Kerby stopped on the northeast corner of the building and pointed toward the ornate Art Deco spire of the Chrysler Building with its metal stylized eagle gargoyles, winged hood ornaments, and sunburst crown. "The Chrysler building was finished less than a year before the Empire State Building," Kerby recalled. "They were in a competition to see who would have the tallest building in the world when they were both done. The Chrysler Building wound up being the tallest building in the world, but for less than a year, until they finished this one.

"See that television tower up there," Kerby continued, pointing up now. "That was originally supposed to be a dirigible mast, you know, for blimps to be moored to, so that passengers could disembark up here. I was watching from the ground the day they successfully attached a privately owned blimp in 1931, but it was only for about three minutes. On the second attempt a short time later, a Navy Blimp was almost upended and nearly swept away a bunch of celebrities who were attending the event. That was the end of that idea.

"Then in 1945 at the end of World War II, in the fog an Army Air Corps B-25 twin-engine bomber crashed into the 79th floor. It killed fourteen people and caused $1 million worth of damage, but the structural integrity of the building was unaffected," Kerby finished.

Penny knew most of the facts that Kerby had recited about the building, but she kept nodding her head and saying "Really!" as if she wasn't aware of any of the building's history. "It's been said that this is the closest thing we have to Heaven in New York City," Penny remarked.

"That's very good, kiddo. That line is from *An Affair to Remember,* Cary Grant and Deborah Kerr," Kerby smiled.

"Just testing you," Penny responded, also with a smile. "Put aside the films he did with Hitchcock, and that's my favorite Cary Grant movie."

"Really! Why is that?" Kerby wondered.

"It's very romantic. You know, a real tear-jerker, the kind of film that women usually like."

"Tell me about it," Kerby said, testing Penny's recollection of the movie.

"Grant plays a suave, well-bred playboy, living the good life by charming wealthy women with his good looks and sophistication. Kerr plays the girl next door from Boston with a dream of going to New York City and making it as a singer. They meet while sailing back from Europe, both on their way home to their intended fiances, but they fall in love with each other along the way. Then, on the last night of the cruise, they make a pact to meet in exactly six months at the top of the Empire State Building at exactly 5:00 P.M. That's when Kerr says, 'It's the closest thing to Heaven we have in New York City.'

"As you well know, Kerr has an accident that leaves her crippled just as she gets out of her cab at the Empire State Building because she's in a rush to meet Grant on time. Grant spends the night up here hoping that Kerr will show up and feeling deserted when she doesn't. Kerr can't bring herself to explain because she doesn't want to burden Grant with her condition as an invalid. Of course, in the end Grant finds her and love wins out," Penny recalled, as she glanced down at her watch. "We'd better get going. Sol is probably already downstairs waiting for us."

As they made their way past a souvenir stand, Kerby watched as the doors of the elevator to the observatory opened. The elevator was filled to capacity with a group of Japanese tourists who exited the elevator like a stampede. In the center of the group, doing his best to look inconspicuous but standing out like a sore thumb, was Stan Slowinski.

Kerby looked up at the souvenir stand and then, without alerting Penny to Slowinski's presence, said, "I think I'd like a keepsake. Buy me the pink stuffed pig that says 'Oink if you love New York,'" Kerby requested, as the Japanese tourists and Stan Slowinski with his head down made their way out onto the observatory deck.

"I didn't figure you for the souvenir type, at least, not a stuffed animal," Penny noted, holding the pig in her arm.

"Perhaps you're right, kiddo," Kerby replied, and then he stunned Penny by taking the pig out of her hand, so that it looked to everyone else as if the pig were floating in midair. "I think this guy might appreciate it more than me," Kerby said, lifting the pig high over his head and starting back out onto the observatory deck with Penny close behind.

One of the Japanese tourists was the first to spot the pig, which appeared to flying on its own toward the group. The tourist started pointing at the pig and shouting excitedly causing the rest of the group and Stan Slowinski to look up. Penny remained stunned by Kerby's actions until she saw Slowinski in the midst of the group, staring up in astonishment at the flying pig.

"What was that you said, pal? Oh yeah, *When pigs fly*," Kerby recalled, extending his arm up over the awed tourists and dropping the pink pig down onto Slowinski's upturned head.

CHAPTER 11

ROLLIN' ON THE RIVER
JUNE 22, 2003

*P*enny was surprised when Sol rang the doorbell as early as he did. She was expecting him, but not until nine, and where time was concerned, Sol was usually as dependable as a Swiss watch. Penny knew it had to be something important if Sol was at her door more than an hour earlier than expected.

"Good morning Sol. Come on in. I'm not quite ready yet. Would you like some coffee?" Penny asked, leading Sol into the kitchen where Kerby was waiting, also curious about Sol's early arrival.

"Sure," Sol said as Penny poured him a cup of coffee. "I take it you haven't seen the newspaper yet this morning. Has it been on the television news? Once I saw the headline, I couldn't wait to get here to ask you about it," Sol continued excitedly.

"What headline?" Penny asked.

Sol flipped his *New York Daily News* onto the kitchen table. The headline read "Clairvoyant Leads Police to Bodies of Missing Men."

"That didn't take long," Kerby remarked, after reading the headline to himself.

"My goodness! I don't know what to say," a stunned Penny said.

"Is it true?" Sol asked. "Did you actually tell them exactly where the bodies were? How did you know the victims' names and the details of their murders? No wonder you have police following you around the city."

Penny read the entire article before responding to any of Sol's questions. The article indicated that Penny was the niece of "world renowned medium, Mags O'Malley." It stated that Penny had informed police that she was contacted by one of the murder victims through an Ouija Board and that the spirit of the victim had provided her with the location of the bodies, the identity of both murder victims, and certain details with regard to their deaths, which the police were not at liberty to divulge. The article also indicated that Penny had solid alibis for her whereabouts at the time of both murders, and could prove that she was not even in the State of New York at or near the time of the disappearances of either of the murdered men.

However, the article also stated that Homicide Detective Stan Slowinski had informed the reporter that police were investigating the possibility that the murders might be ritual sacrifices related to some form of devil worship. He also stated that Penny was a known member of a witch's coven in Santa Fe, New Mexico and, given the detail of the information that she had provided, police were not ruling out the possibility that Penny might be involved in the crimes in some way. There was no mention of the disappearances of Peter Sizemore or Danny O'Brien in the article.

"Mags must be having a good laugh up there in Heaven at the fact that the article identifies her as a 'world renowned medium,'" Penny chuckled. "As far as the rest of the article is concerned, let's just say it's basically true, up until it starts to discuss Officer Slowinski's statements about the possibility that the murders might be ritual sacrifices and that I'm a witch who might be involved with the people who committed the murders," Penny explained.

"I never believed that part anyway. But are you telling me that you are actually communicating with dead people through an Ouija Board?" Sol asked in a disbelieving voice.

"Not exactly. But that is what I told them. Between you and me, for now, let's just say that Mags wasn't as crazy as people thought when she said she had a conduit to the other side."

"Actually, it's kind of a relief having some explanation for your recent behavior. I was really starting to worry about you. I mean, a young lady walking through Riverside Park at night by herself is not a good idea," Sol pointed out. "By the way," Sol continued. "I stopped by to see Joie Miller yesterday to talk to her about your problems with Mark Libby. Like me, Joie does not want to spend her remaining days with Libby as her next door neighbor. As a result, Joie and I are going to make you an offer that you cannot refuse, and please believe me when I tell you that we are not just doing this because of our love for you. There's a lot of self-interest involved here as well."

"Thanks Sol, but the Libby problem is a thing of the past. In fact, the reason I need a ride this morning is to go and take care of that issue. For better or worse, it looks like you have me as your next door neighbor for the foreseeable future," Penny smiled.

"Joie also told me that when you get a chance she would like to talk to you about Libby. She wouldn't discuss it with me, but she said that you would be very interested in hearing about her past dealings with Libby. She also said she needed to talk to you about some party or something that you two are planning to attend together. It looks like it may have to be canceled."

"I'll call her as soon as we get back. Knowing Joie, I doubt that she's even up yet," Penny laughed as the group started for the door.

As they reached the door, the telephone rang and Penny stopped to listen to the message. "Ms Albright, my name is Tori O'Brien. I was wondering if you might have the time to--" the message started, before Penny got to the telephone and picked it up.

"Ms O'Brien, this is Penny Albright. I guess you've seen the newspapers this morning."

"Yes, I have," O'Brien answered. "But, actually, I got your name and telephone number from Rocco Francona last night. He called to forewarn me about the article, and he suggested that I might want to speak with you about my son's disappearance."

"If you've seen the article, you know that I have not been completely ruled out as an accomplice of some kind in the disappearances. Doesn't that concern you?" Penny wondered.

"Officer Francona also forewarned me about the quotes that Stan Slowinski had given the paper, but Fancona said that he did not believe for a minute that the murders were in any way related to devil worshipers or witches or ritual sacrifices.

"Officer Slowinski's not a bad man, Ms Albright. He's been very cooperative with me where my son's disappearance is concerned, and I know that he has been working as hard as anyone to get the case solved. But he tends to have an overactive imagination sometimes. When it comes to which one has the better judgment, especially judgment of a person's character, I have to go with Officer Francona, and not just because he's cuter either."

"Great!" Penny said. "Then I would love to meet with you, though I'm afraid that what I have to tell you may not be what you are hoping to hear."

"Officer Francona has already given me that impression, without telling me exactly what you know, or what you believe that you know, about Danny's fate. The truth is that I had pretty much resigned myself a long time ago to the fact that Danny is dead. Whatever hope I had vanished when I heard that Nicholas Demopolous's body had been found. I assume you know that the police linked my son's disappearance and the disappearance of Peter Sizemore almost immediately. The other two disappearances were linked as well because they occurred on the same date, each only one year apart.

"The fact that Danny may be dead, however, does not change the fact that I want my son home. I am a devout Catholic, Ms Albright. I need to know that Danny has received a proper burial before I can have some form of closure with this thing. I also need to know that whoever is responsible for these murders has been stopped and punished for the harm they have done."

"I need to make a trip to Brooklyn this morning," Penny noted. "I should be back by noon, if that's good for you."

"Perfect," O'Brien responded.

"Tell her that if she has a copy of her son's high school yearbook, she should bring it with her," Kerby reminded Penny.

"Ms O'Brien," Penny said, just before Tori O'Brien hung up her telephone. "I was wondering if maybe you have a copy of your son's high school yearbook around."

"Certainly, I haven't touched his room since he went missing. The yearbook has been sitting on his dresser since a few days before he disappeared. Danny told me that he took it out because he had run into a friend a few days earlier whom he hadn't seen since high school, and she had changed so drastically that he wanted to refresh his recollection as to what she looked like in high school."

"Could you bring the yearbook with you when you come?" Penny asked.

"I'd be happy to," O'Brien responded. "There's nothing that a mother enjoys more than showing off her son."

♥ ✄ ♟

Penny had Sol take her to the bank first, with Rocco Francona and Stan Slowinski not far behind them the whole way. Sol informed Penny as soon as he noticed the unmarked police car behind them, but Penny let Sol know that where she was going she was not concerned about being followed by the officers.

At the bank, Penny shocked the teller by pulling the $200,000 in cash out of her pocketbook and seeking to deposit it into her account. The teller was even more shocked when she noticed that though all of the bills were incredibly old, they still had a crispness to them. Fortunately, the money that Renata D'arcy gave Kerby was all in $100 bills. Up until 1946, the Federal Reserve was still issuing bills ranging from $1 to $10,000. It wasn't until after 1946 that the Federal Reserve stopped printing bills in excess of $100, and it wasn't until 1969 that the Federal Reserve retired all bills in excess of the $100 bill.

It was also fortunate that all of the bills that Kerby had been given postdated 1929, when the Federal Reserve changed the size and style of its bills to what we are familiar with today. Nevertheless, after noticing that the bills lacked the inscription *In God We Trust,* the teller decided that she had better talk to the bank manager before accepting the deposit. The bank manager was delighted to have the old bills just the way they were, after Penny informed him that she had inherited the money from an aunt who did not believe in banks.

After the money was deposited, Penny had Sol take her to the New York Department of Taxation and Finance in downtown Brooklyn. Sol took the Brooklyn Bridge, at Penny's request, which had actually come from Kerby.

"It may not be the biggest anymore," Kerby commented as they started over the bridge. "But it's still the prettiest and the most impressive. It was the brainchild of a guy named John Augustus Roebling back in the1860s. It took him years to get the authority to build it. Unfortunately, he died before the towers were even erected. While he was setting the location for the tower on the Brooklyn side, a ferryboat crashed into the pier he was standing on and crushed his foot. He developed tetanus poisoning from the injury and died.

"His son, Washington Roebling, took over as chief engineer, but the son suffered a crippling attack of decompression sickness during construction of the Manhattan caisson. He was down in the caisson at the time, seventy-eight feet beneath the surface of the East River. The disease left the younger Roebling paralyzed, partly blind, deaf, and mute, but he refused to give up or turn the project over to someone else. Instead, he took an apartment on the East River in the Columbia Heights section of Brooklyn and directed construction by observing the building of the bridge through field glasses.

"Twenty-seven men died during its construction, but when it was done, it was one of the great engineering marvels of the world. Before they started building skyscrapers, the towers of the bridge were the tallest structures in the city," Kerby finished, looking back admiringly at the bridge as they reached the Brooklyn side.

Once inside of the Department of Taxation and Finance, Penny asked if she could speak to a manager. When Penny introduced herself, the manager acted as if they were old friends. "Ms Albright, so nice to finally meet you personally. Heaven knows we have seen enough of your attorney lately," the manager greeted Penny. "Of course, down here we are used to seeing a great deal of Lawyer Libby."

"So I hear," Penny commented. "I understand that Mr. Libby has lots of friends down here."

"Friends? Down here?" the manager asked in a disbelieving voice. "Ms Albright, Lawyer Libby has lots of acquaintances down here, but only because he spends so much time down here annoying people for favors. I don't think there is anyone in this department who would appreciate your calling them a friend of Mark Libby."

"So it wouldn't be correct to say that Mr. Libby has some clout with your superiors?" Penny wondered.

"If I were to allow Mark Libby in to see any of my superiors, it would probably cost me my job. You must have misheard Mr. Libby. He isn't considered to have clout down here, he's considered to be a lout down here. Especially lately, since he brought your problem to our attention. It seems he's here daily."

"Well, I'm hopeful that I'm going to be able to eliminate that problem for you this morning. If you could have someone calculate my aunt's tax shortfall, I'll cut you a check this morning to correct the deficiency."

"Fine, if you'd like," the manager said. "But as we've repeatedly told Lawyer Libby, there is no urgency with regard to your case. I mean it's clear that nothing your aunt did was fraudulent or criminal. The whole thing is probably our fault for not catching the fact that she never changed the classification of her brownstone when our reclassification went into effect. As soon as the shortfall is calculated, we'd be more than happy to work out a payment plan with you. It shouldn't come to more than a hundred dollars or so a month."

"I would think that at a hundred dollars or so a month, I would be paying this thing off for the rest of my life," Penny remarked. "As I understand it, we're talking about something close to $200,000 here, aren't we?"

"Ms Albright, I don't know what Lawyer Libby has told you about our position on your case, but we have been very clear in letting him know that most of the shortfall in your aunt's case is well beyond any statute of limitations we might apply. We are only looking to recoup the deficiency over the last few years. It will probably total something in the area of $15,000, and, as I noted, we would be willing to work out a payment plan for that amount," the manager explained.

"Are you telling me that Mark Libby was aware of all this?" Penny asked, with a bewildered look.

"Oh, he's been aware of it for some time now. In fact, because he had been spending so much time here discussing your case, we sent him a certified letter setting forth the department's position, hoping that it might keep him away for a while," the manager laughed.

"Good thing you didn't delete Libby's voice message. I suspect that the New York State Lawyer's Ethics Commission will be interested in having a copy of that tape as well as a copy of the department's letter. Let's make sure we get a certified copy of the letter before we leave," Kerby suggested

♥ ☠ ♣

On the way home, Penny noticed that Sol was driving somewhat faster than usual and dodging in and out of traffic in a way that was atypical for him. "Easy Sol," Penny said. "No need to lose these guys. We're only going home."

"If I heard you right, you're meeting with someone at your house at noon. I intend to have you there on time," Sol replied, looking down at his watch.

"Ask him now, kiddo," Kerby urged, nudging Penny.

"I don't know if I'm comfortable with this," Penny mouthed silently to Kerby.

"Don't be silly. He thinks of you as his granddaughter. A grandfather can't refuse a granddaughter anything she asks," Kerby noted.

Penny shot Kerby an evil glare but then spoke to Sol. "Sol, I was wondering if I could maybe borrow your boat this evening," Penny asked sheepishly.

"Gee, I don't know, honey. Do you even know how to drive a boat?" Sol asked.

"Sure," Penny answered. "You don't think I'd ask to use your boat if I didn't know how to drive one, do you? Mags's sister Brit in Florida had a boat that she kept at the restaurant at which she worked. Aunt Brit taught me how drive a boat when I was just a little girl. I still renew my license every year."

"Well, you know I can't refuse you anything," Sol conceded. "Especially now, given that my guess is your need for the boat is related to those murders and your attempt to identify the killers. I'll pick you up at six, so that I can show you around the boat before you take it out."

"You're too good Sol," Penny said, smiling at Kerby who smiled back and said, "I told you so."

Sol pulled in front of Penny's brownstone at exactly noon. As he pulled up, an attractive, well-dressed woman, who appeared to be in her mid-forties started up the stairs to the brownstone. She carried a large black book in her right hand.

"Good afternoon, Ms O'Brien?" Penny called out, causing the lady to stop on the upper landing of the stairs and turn to look down at Penny.

"Good afternoon, Ms Albright, or may I call you Penny?"

"Penny is fine, as long as I can call you Tori."

"I wouldn't have it any other way. Calling me Ms O'Brien makes me feel my age, which is not a good thing," O'Brien said with a smile.

At the top of the stairs, the two women embraced before Penny turned to open the door. Once inside, Penny led Tori O'Brien into the dining room just as she had Francona and Slowinski, only this time she sat on the same side of the table, directly next to her. Kerby sat on O'Brien's other side, so that he would be able to view the yearbook that sat in front of her once it was opened.

"Tori, I don't know exactly what Officer Francona told you about my conversation with him and Officer Slowinski. I'm certain you must have some doubts about how I came by my information," Penny surmised.

"If you can help me to find my son and stop these murders, I'm not sure I care what the source of your information is. Officer Francona told me that if I looked into your eyes when we met, it would eliminate any doubt I might have about you being involved in these crimes in some way. You made quite an impression on him, and I can see why. I'm a very good judge of character myself, Penny. I knew the minute we were face to face and embraced that I wasn't hugging an accomplice to murder," O'Brien said firmly.

Penny reached for O'Brien's hand and held it gently as she spoke. "Your son is dead, Tori," Penny said softly. "I'm not certain yet exactly where his body is, but it's somewhere in the water off Staten Island. He was murdered in the same location as Peter Sizemore, and his body was put in the same place as Peter's body. If it's any comfort to you, I have strong reason to believe that the spirits of the two boys are together waiting for their bodies to be found. By the end of this evening, I hope to know the exact location of the bodies."

Tori O'Brien placed her head on Penny's shoulder and sobbed softly for several seconds before speaking. "How can I help you to find them?" she said, dabbing her eyes with a tissue. "Do you know that there is still a $25,000 reward outstanding for anyone who provides information leading to the location of Danny's body or the arrest of his murderer? If you need anything, money is not an issue."

"There is nothing that you can or need to do in order to help me find Danny and Peter. Money is *not* an issue, and I could never accept a reward for helping a mother to find her son's body," Penny explained. "The reason that I wanted to meet with you is because I believe that you may be able to help me find the people who committed these murders and stop them from doing it again."

"How can I help?" O'Brien asked eagerly. "Before this devil worship thing came up, the police were working under the assumption that the crimes were being committed by some crazed homosexual male, but Danny had no contacts with homosexuals of which I was aware. He was a real man's man, you know, an athlete with a very pretty girlfriend. Danny went to college in California on a baseball scholarship just to be near his girlfriend when she got accepted into UCLA."

"These crimes were not committed by a gay male," Penny replied. "They were committed by two young ladies who I believe attended the same high school as Danny and Peter."

"I'm afraid you're losing me now," O'Brien responded. "I made it a point to know all of Danny's close friends in high school. Believe me, none of them were capable of this kind of thing. Certainly none of the girls that Danny knew could have done anything like this."

"Find out what the girlfriend looked like," Kerby suggested. "Where was she when all of this was going down?"

"What did Danny's girlfriend look like?" Penny asked.

"She was very pretty, a brunette, medium height. For lack of a better word, let's just say she was voluptuous, you know what I mean, she was quite large on top. She could not have been involved in Danny's disappearance. She was in Los Angeles at the time that he went missing. I called her there as soon as I suspected that something was wrong," O'Brien recalled.

"Let's look at the yearbook," Kerby said. "The two girls that we're looking for shouldn't be too hard to pick out."

"Can I look through Danny's yearbook?" Penny asked.

"Certainly, I have markers on the pages with Danny's pictures on them. He's in a lot of pictures because he was on several of the athletic teams," O'Brien said proudly, opening the yearbook to the page with Danny's class picture on it.

Penny waited patiently while the proud mother went through every picture of her handsome son before she began leafing through the yearbook on her own, looking for a picture of a tall attractive blonde or a shorter muscular brunette. It didn't take long before Penny stopped at the picture of Nikita Bach. Even though it was not a good likeness of Niki, there was no mistaking her classic beauty.

"Did you ever meet this girl?" Penny asked, pointing a finger down at Niki's picture.

"Niki Bach?" O'Brien responded in an astonished tone. "Of course, Danny dated her for a short period of time during a temporary break up with his girlfriend. If it had been up to me, he would have stayed with Niki. She's a really sweet girl, very smart too. Her mother and I have developed a bit of a friendship since she divorced Niki's father. The mother is a very talented violinist.

"This picture really doesn't do Niki justice. In real life she's an absolute stunner, long legs, natural blonde hair that most women would die for, and a perfectly symmetrical face. If she looks familiar to you, it should be no surprise. She's a fashion model now. She's been on the covers of most of the important glamour magazines. But if you're thinking that Niki Bach might be involved in this in some way, you're way off base."

Penny looked beyond Tori O'Brien to Kerby on the other side. "We've got one," Kerby noted confidently. "Now let's find our femdom."

Penny continued to go through the yearbook, stopping at every page that had a picture of a brunette on it. She spent several minutes looking at the team pictures for each of the girls' athletic teams to see whether any of the girls had particularly well defined muscles, but none of the girls in the graduating class seemed a match for the description that both Nick Demopolous and Tom Smith had given for the other girl.

"Ask her if Niki had any very close friends in high school," Kerby suggested.

"Tori, do you know if Niki Bach had any girlfriends in high school with whom she was particularly close?" Penny asked.

"Yeah," O'Brien answered without missing a beat, taking the yearbook and flipping quickly through the pages until she got to the pictures of students whose names started with an "M." Then she slowed down until she reached the page with Jeannie McCloone's picture on it. "Here, Jeannie McCloone, she and Niki have been inseparable since grade school. Jean lived right upstairs from Niki. They were the two smartest kids in the high school. Jean was the valedictorian of Danny's graduating class. From what Niki's mom tells me, Jean is up at Columbia now. She just finished her exams to see if she'll be accepted into their medical school. Medical school seems to run in her family. Jean's mom is a very highly regarded surgeon at Sloan Kettering."

Penny and Kerby looked hard at Jean's picture and then at each other. At first, Kerby shook his head. Jean was a far cry from the description of the ruthless, muscular, little femdom they had been given by the murder victims.

"She's going to medical school and the mother is a doctor, that would explain the scalpels that were used on both victims and the chloroform that was used on Tom Smith. It would also explain her skills in her chosen profession, if you know what I mean. The woman on the web site I found was wearing surgeon's garb and holding a scalpel," Kerby recalled. "But, if she's the other murderer, Demopolous and Smith were way off in their descriptions of her."

Penny did not even seem to hear what Kerby had said. Something that Tori O'Brien had said puzzled Penny, and she was deep in thought of her own. Finally it hit her, and she looked up at Tori O'Brien. "Did you say that this girl was the valedictorian of Danny's class?"

"Yes, she was smart as whip, still is."

"But I've looked through old newspaper articles dealing with the boys' disappearances, and the class valedictorian was quoted in one of the articles. As I recall, there was a picture of the girl's face along with the quote. The girl in the picture didn't look anything like this girl," Penny remembered.

"In high school, Jean was kind of a chubby, mousy-looking girl, but she apparently went through a metamorphosis during her first at college. She came back from her first year away at school looking as if she had just finished basic training with the Marines. Her hair was cut short and dyed black and she had lost all of her baby fat. She suddenly had the body of a Russian gymnast.

"Do you remember that I told you Danny had taken out his yearbook a few days before his disappearance because he wanted to take a look at someone he knew from high school who had gone through a major change in appearance? He was looking for Jeannie McCloone's picture," O'Brien said.

"We've got her!" Kerby exclaimed. "She's our dominatrix."

"You've been a great help, Tori," Penny said as the two ladies got up from the table. "I think that by the end of the night we'll know the exact location of your son's body."

"One more thing," Kerby added as the two women reached the

door. "Ask her if she knows whether the parents of either of the two girls owned a business or other property on Staten Island."

Penny repeated the question to Tori O'Brien who responded with an amazed look. "How did you know that? Niki's father was a Russian furrier. Before the divorce, he owned a warehouse on Staten Island where he stored some of his merchandise. I only know that because after Niki's mother filed for divorce, the father went back to Russia and was never heard from again. Niki's mom had trouble getting rid of the warehouse and asked me if I knew anyone who might be interested in buying it."

"You wouldn't happen to have an address for the warehouse, would you?" Penny wondered.

"All that I know is that it's on Staten Island's north shore somewhere," O'Brien said.

"That narrows things considerably. Our night might not be as long as I thought it was going to be," Kerby remarked.

Penny and Tori O'Brien embraced tightly on the top of the stairs again before O'Brien started down. She stopped at the bottom of the steps and looked back up at Penny. "Penny, if your sense is that Niki and Jean may have been involved in these disappearances, you're wrong. These are two very intelligent young ladies we're talking about. Both are from upper-class backgrounds, and their mothers are refined, highly respected women. These kinds of kids are not capable of murder," O'Brien assured Penny, before turning to start down the street.

"She's obviously never of Leopold and Loeb," Kerby noted.

♥ 🐾 ♣

Penny didn't bother going back into the house after Tori O'Brien departed. Instead, Penny went straight over to Joie Miller's brownstone. At the top of the stairs, Penny reached for the door, but as she reached for it, the door opened inward. On the other side of the door was a male face that was very familiar to Penny, but she couldn't remember the name that went with the face. The face flashed by Penny quickly with its eyes looking downward the entire time. Penny's eyes followed the guy down the stairs and then she looked back to see Joie standing in the doorway.

"Wasn't that . . . what's his name . . . the anchor man from the evening news? What network is he on?" Penny asked.

"Don't ask, I can't tell you anyway," Joie answered.

"You mean *he* is a client of yours?" Penny continued in an astonished tone.

"Sweetie, if you knew the movers and shakers who used to visit me on a regular basis, you would be astounded. But so far as *he* is concerned, you did not just see him leaving my home on his way to work," Joie laughed. "On the other hand, as far as Marky Libby is concerned, let's talk, lady." Joie snickered, after which she led Penny into the library.

"I don't know whether you spoke with Sol today or not, but the Libby thing is over, though I have decided to bring an ethics complaint against him. It turns out that Libby was not being entirely truthful with regard to the tax situation related to the brownstone or with regard to the tax department's intention to foreclose on the property. It seems that Libby wanted the brownstone for himself and was trying to scare me into selling it to him before I found out that it was not really in jeopardy at all," Penny explained.

"Good!" Joie exclaimed. "Then I don't have to feel guilty about what I did."

"I am almost afraid to ask," Penny responded.

"I told you sweetie, Marky and I had dealings going way back. In fact, before I *semi-retired,* Marky was one of my regular clients. As I understand it, he still sees the Mistress that I referred him to after I decided not to practice full-time anymore," Joie said, before Penny cut her off.

"Joie, I don't want you divulging client confidences to me, just so that I can get even with Mark Libby."

"Look, sweetie, when a submissive male walks through that door, he's mine to do with as I please. I don't sign any agreements with anybody. The confidences that I keep, I keep because I choose to and because it used to be good for business. After what Marky did to you, I wouldn't accept business from him now under any circumstances. Anyway, that's water over the dam. It's too late to change what's already been done," Joie chuckled.

"What did you do?" Penny asked, afraid of what the answer might be.

"Marky was an unusual client for me. His fetish was infantilism. He got off on, and from what I have been told he still gets off on, dressing as and being treated like a baby. I never did much of that stuff, but in my early days I thought it might help business, so I took Baby Libby on as a client. In return, Baby Libby agreed to let me videotape his sessions for use on my web site. At the time, I blanked out his face before I ran the tapes to protect his anonymity, but, of course, I kept copies of the videos with Baby Libby's face visible."

"You didn't!" Penny gasped.

"What Mark Libby tried to do to you was a lot more horrendous than what I have done to him," Joie insisted. "I've just given the Mistress who purchased my web site permission to republish Baby Libby's tapes with his face fully exposed. I've also sent copies of the tapes to the New York City Bar Association and the New York State Bar Association, with Baby Libby's face fully exposed," Joie laughed.

"Joie you shouldn't have," Penny groaned, but with a smile on her face. "What did the tapes show?"

"Just Baby Libby dressed in a diaper and bonnet, crawling around the floor, being fed on my lap with a baby bottle in his mouth, having his diaper changed and being spanked on his bottom for misbehaving," Joie giggled.

"I don't belief you did that."

"Like I said, after what Mark Libby tried to do to you, he earned that and a whole lot more. Now on to less pleasant news. I know you were looking forward to this month's Latex and Leather Gala. I also know I told you the loft that I usually use in SoHo was already rented out. Well, I set up the gala for a warehouse in Brooklyn for this coming Friday night, June 24th, but yesterday I heard that there had been a suspicious fire in the warehouse. Personally, I think we're talking about an insurance fire since the warehouse has been vacant since the last time that I rented it. In any event, I had gotten a great response from the other Mistresses in the area. As usual, everyone was looking forward to the event. Unfortunately, if I don't find a place to hold it by morning, I'm going to have to cancel. I mean, I need time to either let everyone know that the location has been changed or that the gala is off."

"June 24th is the girls' anniversary," Kerby remarked. "Ask her if Domina Agony had indicated whether she planned on attending."

"Just out of curiosity Joie, did Domina Agony accept your invitation?" Penny asked.

"Yes, in fact, she said that she would be there with another dominant female and a submissive male. Apparently, the sub is new to the scene and has a fetish for foot worship. Unusual for Domina Agony, like I told you, her specialty is extreme genital torture. I can only guess that the other dominatrix who is coming with her is into foot worship and trampling. They've even offered to put on a demonstration at the gala, if we have it."

"Do you think you'll be able to find a replacement site in time?" Penny wondered, sounding as if she were upset at the fact that the gala might be canceled.

"I doubt it," Joie remarked. "Time is running short, and like I said, if I don't find a place by tomorrow morning I won't have time to alert the Mistresses who plan on attending of the change in location."

"If you should find a place, feel free to use Carmella to help you get the word out," Penny offered. "I'll let her know that you might be calling."

"I knew this stuff would grow on you," Joie smiled. "You are going to make an incredible femdom. Any man would consider himself lucky to worship at the feet of someone like you, sweetie."

♥ ✄ ♣

Sol was double parked outside the brownstone when Penny and Kerby came out at six o'clock sharp. Slowinski was sitting in his car on the other side of the street. Francona was not with him. When Penny and Kerby hit the bottom of the stairs, instead of getting into Sol's cab, they crossed the street to Slowinski who looked surprised to see them approaching. He rolled down his window but did not get out of his car.

"Is Officer Francona around?" Penny asked.

"No, but if you have something to say, you can talk to me," Slowinski grumbled.

"I believe I know who committed these murders," Penny said.

"I've always said that you know who did it," Slowinski cracked.

"No, I mean, I met with Danny O'Brien's mother earlier today, and I believe that I was able to pick out the girls who did this from pictures in Danny's high school yearbook," Penny explained.

"If you want to give me some names, I'll pass them on to Roc, but I'm not buying into it," Slowinski said.

"I thought he said he would believe you when pigs fly. What does he want, a real pig?" Kerby grinned.

"One of the girls is a fashion model. Her name is Nikita Bach. I still believe the other girl is a dominatrix. Her professional name may be Domina Agony, but her real name is Jean McCloone."

"Like I said, I'll pass the names on to Roc. If he feels like chasing wild geese, that's his prerogative--" Slowinski was saying when Kerby cut in.

"Where does he learn these words?" Kerby wondered.

"Personally, I plan on staying with *you* until the deadline passes," Slowinski finished.

"I'm afraid that won't be possible tonight," Penny informed Slowinski, without explaining as she and Kerby started for Sol's cab.

"If you think the geezer can lose me, you're mistaken," Slowinski hollered.

"Oh, yeah" Penny hollered back to Slowinski. "Tell Officer Francona I'll let him know by tomorrow morning where the bodies of Peter Sizemore and Danny O'Brien are located."

"I'd like to see his face when we pull away on the boat," Kerby laughed.

Penny's jaw dropped when she saw Sol's boat which was actually a 36' Sabreline Cruiser with a forward cabin done in teak wood. Bigger and more comfortable than many of New York City's studio apartments, the yacht was about twice the size of Aunt Brit's puddle jumper back in Key West.

"It has a 315 horse power engine and a cruising speed of about twenty to twenty-two knots, a top speed of about twenty-seven knots," Sol explained, leading Penny to the helm of the boat and sitting her down in the captain's chair. Kerby sat next to Penny in the mate's seat while Sol directed Penny's attention to the helm pod and explained the engine controls, the ship's compass, and navigational electronics.

"Are you sure you can handle this, honey?" Sol asked, sounding slightly worried.

"It's a little bigger than Aunt Brit's boat--" Penny was saying when she heard Kerby's voice.

"Sure you can, kiddo. I have confidence in you."

"But I guess I can handle it," Penny finished.

Sol started the boat's engine and listened to it roar for a second before he made his way toward the dock, leaving the yacht idling. Once off the boat, Sol slipped the ropes from their moorings, tossed them onto the boat, and wished Penny a *bon voyage*.

As Penny eased the yacht out from its slip, she hollered back to Sol. "Just out of curiosity, Sol, how much is this thing worth?"

"It's a couple of years old now," Sol hollered back. "But I guess it's still worth about $250,000."

Penny shuddered at the thought that she had taken responsibility for someone else's quarter of a million-dollar plaything. "Relax, it has to be insured," Kerby assumed.

Out in the Hudson, the boat traffic was quiet, and Penny made a point of staying as far away as possible from any other boats that she saw. As they made their way south on the Hudson toward midtown, Penny's confidence in her ability to handle the yacht grew to the point that she started to thoroughly enjoy the ride.

"I never imagined how peaceful it might be out here in the water, only a stone's throw from the clamor of midtown," Penny remarked as the yacht sailed by the aircraft carrier USS Intrepid, which along with the destroyer USS Edson and the submarine USS Growler had been turned into an air, sea, and space museum.

Once at Battery Park, at the southern most tip of Manhattan, Kerby directed Penny toward the Statue of Liberty. "Now how did I know that you would want to get as close as possible to the statue?" Penny smiled.

"The statue is great, but what I'm really looking to get close to is Ellis Island," Kerby corrected Penny.

Penny steered the yacht to the west side of the Statue of Liberty toward the massive old red brick building that dominates Ellis Island. She slowed her cruising speed as the yacht made its way past the island with Kerby standing at the rail staring.

"I was only ten years old when my family came through Ellis Island in 1914, but I remember it as if it were yesterday. We had been at sea for three full weeks, and we weren't even certain that we would be allowed to enter the country. World War I had just started and there had been talk about ending immigration until the war was over. When we got off the boat, we were led into a cafeteria with foods unlike anything I had ever tasted before. I ate ice cream for the first time that day.

"After we ate, my family and thousands of other hopefuls were led into a huge room that they called the Great Hall. We stood in line for hours waiting for an interview with an inspector who would decide our future. Once we were processed, they led us like cattle up a broad set of stairs that they called the Stairs of Separation. As we made our way up the stairs, Public Health physicians watched from the landing above to see if any of the immigrants showed signs of disease or insanity. Those who did were weeded out and taken away, some separated from their families.

"The rest of us were taken for less-intrusive medical examinations. After we were approved for admission, we were led down another flight of stairs to a place where families were reunited with family members who had been admitted earlier. They called that spot the Kissing Post because of the hugging and kissing that resulted from the happy reunions that took place there," Kerby reminisced as the island grew smaller behind them.

Darkness had set in, and Penny had put her running lights on as the craft made its way south through Upper New York Bay and took a right-hand turn down the Kill Van Kull along the north shore of Staten Island. She slowed her cruising speed and moved as close to the Staten Island shoreline as possible. As they coasted down the river, both she and Kerby kept their eyes glued to the coastline looking for the spirits of Peter Sizemore and Danny O'Brien.

Only a short way down the river, Penny saw something glowing on the shoreline. She directed Kerby's attention to the glow, and both stared as Penny put the boat into neutral, bringing it to an almost complete stop.

"It's a spirit, but it's only one and it's neither of our boys," Kerby said dejectedly.

"It's a fat guy in a suit," Penny added.

"I don't know how well you can make out his features," Kerby commented. "But that guy looks just like Jimmy Hoffa. We need to make a note of the location of that body. Your Officer Francona may be in for a promotion."

Penny and Kerby spotted several other well dressed, Mediterranean-looking, male ghosts sitting on the shoreline of the Kill Van Kull as they slowly made their way down the river. They charted each spirit on a map before continuing their search for the spirits of the boys.

Penny was the first to spot the two spirits, about a third of the way down the river toward New Jersey. "Look, there's two together," Penny pointed out. "Can you tell if they're young?"

"They're young, and they're male, and they're naked, and they're sitting on a bulkhead outside of a warehouse. They're our boys!" Kerby exclaimed. "Can you get close enough so that we can tie off to the bulkhead?"

Penny slowed the yacht down even more and eased her way toward the shoreline. As the yacht got closer and closer to shore, the two spirits grew more interested. They rose from their sitting positions on the bulkhead and stared intently at the boat as it got nearer to them. When the boat was close enough, Kerby tossed one of the yacht's lines to one of the boys, but the spirit seemed dumbfounded and did not react. The rope hit him in the head and fell to the ground as the other spirit watched, equally befuddled by what was happening.

"Don't just stand there, pull us in and tie us off to the bulkhead," Kerby shouted.

When the boy who had been hit with the rope realized that Kerby was one of them, he looked at the other spirit and broke into a huge grin. Both boys reached down for the rope at the same time, clanging their heads in the process. One of the boys finally got hold of the rope and started pulling the boat toward the shore as Penny cut the engine.

"Toss me the other rope, Mister," the second spirit shouted to Kerby, and Kerby flung the yacht's other line to the other boy. By the time they were finished pulling it in and securing the yacht, the side of the boat was resting firmly against the bulkhead. Kerby and Penny jumped to shore.

"You're Danny, aren't you?" Penny asked, looking at the spirit of Danny O'Brien.

"That's right," Danny answered, realizing that Penny could see them. "Whoa, she can see us too, Mister?" Danny asked as both he and Peter quickly covered their exposed genitals with their hands.

"It's okay, fellas. You're basically just a blur to her. She can't see any details," Kerby lied to ease the boys' embarrassment.

"How did you know my name?" Danny questioned Penny, after relaxing about his nudity.

"I was with your mom just this afternoon. She showed me your pictures in your yearbook," Penny responded. "She sends her love."

"My mom, you know my mom?" Danny asked incredulously.

"It's a long story," Kerby chimed in, after which he explained the long story in most of its detail to Danny and Peter.

"So, you mean you got Niki and Jean. They've been arrested?" Danny asked hopefully, when Kerby had finished telling his story.

"Not yet," Kerby replied. "We know that they committed these murders, and we've let the police know that they committed these murders too, but so far we don't know whether we have any believers in the police department. The problem is that up until tonight we didn't have any evidence linking the girls to the crimes. It's not as if you can go into court and testify. And the testimony of a self-proclaimed psychic, who says she got her information from ghosts, is not going to fly in a courtroom. Once we let the police know that your bodies are here, and they determine that Niki Bach's family owns this place, they'll have some connection, but certainly not enough to arrest either girl."

"So what do we do?" Pete wondered. "I mean, I want to get out of here as quickly as possible, but I'd like to know that those two are paying for what they did."

"Like I told you, the girls have been committing a murder every year on the anniversary of Peter's murder. We're two days away from that date. If Penny can convince the police of the girls' guilt, maybe the police can catch them red-handed trying to commit this year's murder," Kerby explained.

"If the police don't believe me, we'll have to be there ourselves to make sure that we at least try to stop these two from committing another murder. But the questions remain, how do we find out where they're going to commit the next murder and how do we stop them," Penny added.

When Penny looked toward Kerby for some suggestions, he seemed more interested in the warehouse than in what she was saying. Above the large metal bay door in the center of the front of the warehouse was a sign with big red letters that read, "For Sale or Lease." Beneath the printed words was a telephone number in large black letters.

"How long has the warehouse been vacant?" Kerby asked.

"I guess since about a year after Danny's murder, so about two years," Pete answered.

"Give Joie a call on your cell phone," Kerby instructed Penny. "Tell her that maybe you have a place for her Latex and Leather Gala. Give her the number on the sign and tell her to call and see whether she can work something out with the realtor. If the place has been vacant for two years, I'm guessing they'd be happy to make some kind of arrangement with her."

Penny called Joie immediately and gave her the information. Joie thought the location on the water sounded ideal. She even said she would rent a spotlight, like the kind used for grand openings, to put in the parking lot in order to make it easier for the other Mistresses to find the place.

"I know you boys are about ready to get out of here, and if that's what you'd like, Penny can have a police diver here by tomorrow," Kerby told the boys. "On the other hand, if you don't mind hanging around for another couple of days, you might just be able to renew old acquaintances with Niki Bach and Jeannie McCloone. I have a feeling that they might be showing up here for a party on Friday night. You boys might even be instrumental in helping to insure that they pay for their crimes."

"Mr. Brewster, I have no idea what you're talking about, but if there's any possibility of my being helpful in getting Niki and Mean Jean arrested, you can count me in," Danny asserted firmly.

"Like you said, Mr. Brewster, I'm about ready to get out of here, but I've never been one to miss a party, so count me in too," Peter added.

"If things work out the way I'm hoping they do, we'll see you boys on Friday night. If my plan falls apart, Penny will get a police diver here as soon as possible," Kerby assured them as he and Penny made their way for the boat while Danny and Peter talked privately to each other.

"Mr. Brewster," Danny called to Kerby as he and Penny jumped onto the boat. "I'm sure you folks are in a hurry, but how about a short ride on your yacht before you two head home?"

"I take it that you two haven't found your portals yet. If you move to far from this spot, you'll wind up someplace that you don't want to be," Kerby warned. "We don't want to lose you boys now."

"Believe me, we found out about that place a long time ago," Peter replied.

"The thing is though, there's some benefit to having your body dumped in the water," Danny explained. "As long as you stay on the water, you can go anywhere you want without winding up in that place you're talking about."

"How would you know that?" Penny wondered.

"That guy keeps his fishing boat here all season," Peter noted, pointing down to the end of the bulkhead where a small fishing boat was tied up. "He doesn't know it, but every time he goes out, we go out. It kills the boredom."

Penny called Sol to tell him that everything was fine, but she would be a little late getting home. Kerby and Penny spent the next two hours touring the New York waterways with two very enthusiastic passengers.

CHAPTER 12

SEAMS THAT DRIVE MEN WILD
JUNE 23, 2003

*A*fter her morning workout, Penny called Joie to see if she had any success in scheduling the Latex and Leather Gala at the Staten Island warehouse. To Penny's surprise, Joie was not only up and about but invited Penny over for coffee, so that she could tell her what had happened. Penny threw on a pair of sweats, and with Kerby at her side they headed out the door to Joie's brownstone.

"Don't these guys have homes?" Kerby wondered, after spotting Francona and Slowinski already parked in front of Joie's house.

"Should I tell them now that I've located the boys' bodies and that I think the murderers are going to be at the gala tomorrow night?" Penny asked.

"Tell them that you believe you've located the boys' bodies, but you won't be sure until tomorrow night," Kerby suggested. "I think we owe it to Danny and Peter to let them be a part of what's going on here if that's what they want. As far as the murderers being at the gala, I would make sure that Domina Agony and friends still plan on attending this thing before I let these guys in on that information. Besides, if you tell them too soon where the gala is, Francona may put two and two together and send a diver down today to look for the boys. We can tell them where the gala is, and the fact that the murderers are going to be there tomorrow afternoon. They'll still have plenty of time to prepare, but we won't have to worry about them starting a search for the boys."

Before heading up Joie's stairs, Penny stopped at the unmarked police car. Francona, looking as if he were dressed for court, immediately stepped out of the car with a broad smile on his face. Slowinski remained in the passenger seat of the car.

"Good morning, Ms. Albright," Francona said cheerfully, taking Penny's hand. "Stan tells me that you believe you've identified the two girls responsible for these murders. We're in the process of checking them out. I'd say that within a day or so we should have a very good read on who these girls are and whether they may have been involved in these crimes."

"Regardless of what your investigation shows today, whatever you do, don't let them out of your sight tomorrow," Penny warned. "I believe I know where they're going to be tomorrow evening. I'll let you know as soon as I'm certain. By the way, I also have a good idea precisely where the bodies of the two boys are located, but again I want to be absolutely certain before I say anything. I don't want you sending divers down too soon."

Slowinski finally acknowledged Penny's presence. He leaned over and looked up at Penny. "I'm sure the boys' mothers will be happy to know that you've located their sons' bodies, but you're not prepared to share that information with them just yet," Slowinski remarked snidely. "I guess they haven't been waiting long enough."

After a brief glare at Slowinski, Penny looked back at Francona and said, "Believe me when I tell you that I have my reasons for not providing you with that information just yet. I believe that the boys understand exactly what it is I'm doing and that they are on board with it. I'll talk to Tori O'Brien later this morning and let her know what's going on."

Penny and Kerby started up the stairs but turned around midway up and headed back to the police car. Penny pulled a piece of paper out of the pocket of her sweat suit. "It's a map of the north shore of Staten Island. The four red Xs indicate spots at which I located bodies within the water. All of the bodies appear to be those of well-dressed, Mediterranean-looking men, except for one who looks a whole lot like somebody you guys have been looking for for quite some time now," Penny remarked, handing the map to a surprised Rocco Francona before she started back up the stairs.

"I hope you're not buying into this stuff, Roc. Don't be fooled by those baby blues or the killer legs either. She's up to something. She wants us out of her hair, chasing these little girls around or maybe trying to find missing mob hits, so she and her friends are free do their thing," Slowinski snarled.

"It doesn't make sense, Stan. Why would she have given us the information that she's already provided if she's involved in the murders in some way?"

"Don't forget, pal, she tried to provide that information anonymously. We had to track her down. She didn't come to us," Slowinski reminded Francona.

"Even still, why give us the information at all? If she hadn't made that phone call who knows if we would have ever found those bodies?

And she didn't have to tell us about Tom Smith or the two kids. I don't know how she does it, but I think she's legit. I'll bet you that we find bodies at each and every one of the locations on this map. What are you going to say then, that she's a hit woman for the mob in her spare time, when she's not out committing ritual sacrifices with her devil worshiping friends?"

"I don't know how or why she does some of the things she does, but that just makes me more suspicious. She's got powers that normal, God-fearing people, aren't supposed to have. As far as the information that she's provided, I think she just likes toying with us. This is all a cat and mouse game to her, but I plan on being the cat.

"What I do know is this, she lost me last night on purpose when she got on that boat, so that she would be free to do whatever she wanted to do without me being aware of it. But she also freed me up to do a few things that I needed to, and I spent my time constructively too. I went right to Tori O'Brien's apartment. Tori told me that she and Albright went through Danny's yearbook yesterday afternoon. Albright stopped at the first good-looking blonde she saw and asked about her. It was one of the same girls whose names Albright gave me after she met with Tori. The kid's name is Nikita Bach.

"After Albright asked about the Bach kid, she went through the rest of the album, but she couldn't find anybody that met the description of the other girl, so she asked Tori if this Nikita Bach had any close friends in high school. Tori pointed out Bach's best friend in high school, and she just happens to be the other girl that Albright identified to me. Her name is Jean McCloone. The problem is, I looked at Jean McCloone's picture in the yearbook. It is as far from the description that Albright gave us as you could possibly get. She's a dowdy-looking little thing, real collegiate type. Beyond that, she doesn't look like she's had an athletic day in her life. She looks as if she has problems carrying her own weight, never mind lifting weights."

"Did you ask Tori whether or not she's seen this girl recently? Maybe the girl has changed," Francona noted.

"If she was one of the murderers, she would have done Nicholas Demopolous only a few years after the picture in the yearbook was taken. There's no way that this girl could have made that kind of change that quickly. We're talking about a caterpillar to a butterfly here, only it doesn't happen that way with humans.

"I'll tell you what I did ask Tori O'Brien. I asked her what she thought about the suggestion that these girls might have been involved in the murders. Tori told me that, like you, she doesn't think that Albright had anything to do with the crimes, but she's *absolutely certain* that these two girls are not capable of murder. Tori said that both girls come from broken, but very privileged homes. She said that she kind a knows both girls' mothers, and they're great role models. One's a concert violinist and the other is surgical oncologist, at Sloan Kettering no less. These two girls were the two smartest kids in the school the year that Danny graduated. The McCloone kid was the class valedictorian for crying out loud. I agree with Tori, no way two kids from backgrounds like these girls could possibly be involved with murder."

"Did you ever hear of Leopold and Loeb?" Francona asked.

"Sure I've heard of them, but there's a difference here. They were boys; these are girls we're talking about. Girls are not capable of this sick stuff."

"So that was the end of your investigation?" Francona wondered.

"It would have been. I mean, I was satisfied, but I knew you'd ask that question, so I dug deeper. I took the yearbook over to *Dorrian's* and showed it to our friend the barkeep. He looked at this Nikita Bach's picture and said that there is some similarity between her and the woman who was in the bar with Nick Demopolous the night he disappeared, but the bartender remembered the girl in the bar that night as being prettier than the girl in the picture. I showed him Jean McCloone's picture, and he said, *no way.* He said he didn't see the other girl for that long, but he's certain that the girl in the bar that night didn't look anything like the girl in the picture."

"So-- " Francona began to ask before Slowinski cut him off.

"Nope, that's not the end of it either. Tori told me that this Nikita Bach is a model now, which fits with what Albright said, so before I left for *Dorrian's,* I got Tori to call the girl's mom and get her agency's number. Then I called the agency and pretended that I was interested in hiring her for some advertising work. Well, guess where this Nikita Bach is right now," Slowinski said with a big smile on his face.

"I have no idea," Francona muttered.

"She's in Marakesh, Morocco on a photo shoot. Actually, the shoot ended yesterday, so I asked her agent when she would be available again. It seems that the Bach kid decided to take a vacation for a few days after the shoot. Apparently, a bunch of the models that were on the shoot together decided that after the shoot was over, they were going to stay in Morocco for an extra couple of days to see the country. The agency was 99% certain that our girl was part of the group that was staying because she had told them not to book her for a few days after the shoot was over."

"Did you check with the airlines to see if perhaps the agency was wrong, and Bach is on her way home?" Francona asked.

"You're really pushing it here, pal, but if it'll make you happy, I'll call the office and get them on it," Slowinski said.

"It can't hurt," Francona replied.

"What I did do is I talked to the new kid, you know the one who's supposed to be the computer whiz, and I had him look up Domina Agony on the Internet. I gave him the yearbook, so that he could compare Jean McCloone's picture with any pictures of this dominatrix that he found on the web. He found her right away. He said that the dominatrix on the web site has most of her face covered in all of her pictures, but from what he could see, there's absolutely no similarity between the two females," Slowinski noted, with an *I told you so* smile.

"What kind of dominatrix are we talking about here? I mean, is she the vanilla type, like Albright's neighbor, or is she into the more serious stuff?" Francona asked.

"It's interesting that you ask that, Roc. The computer geek said that he couldn't even look at some of the pictures on this web site because they were so disturbing. He said that this dominatrix is into some serious male genital mutilation. He wondered if what she was doing is legal, even if she does have the okay of the guys she's doing it to. He said it's *that* gruesome."

"Didn't that pique your interest?" Francona wondered.

"I have to admit that it would have, if it wasn't for the fact that Albright's good friend and next door neighbor just happens to be in the business. Albright could have easily found out about this dominatrix from her neighbor and offered her to us, believing that it would get our juices flowing, and take the heat off her. I'm telling you, this is all a cat and mouse game for her, Roc. If you want to be the mouse go ahead, but I know where I'm going to be tomorrow night and that's going to be right in the White Witch's back pocket."

♥ ✂ ♛

When Penny and Kerby entered Joie's brownstone, they found Joie sitting in her dining room sipping coffee and nibbling a croissant. She was wearing a black-velvet, leopard-trimmed robe and black high-heel slippers, also leopard-trimmed. She had a telephone tucked between her left shoulder and her ear. What struck Penny the most about Joie's appearance, however, was the fact that her hair and makeup looked as if she had just come from the beauty parlor.

"That's wonderful darling. Keep me posted if you have any problems," Joie sang into the telephone before hanging it up.

"How did you make out, Jo?" Penny asked.

"Super, you are a life saver, sweetie," Joie said, pouring Penny a cup of coffee from a sterling silver pot that sat on the dining room table. "I called the realtor as soon as I hung up with you last night, and though it took a little convincing, he went for it. They're really looking to sell the warehouse or lease it out on a long term basis, but it's taking them so long to move the place that I think they were just happy to be making some money on it. Of course, I'm paying top dollar, but it's only money.

"That was my party planner that I just hung up with. He's at the place right now. He said that the place is dirty, but ideal for what we want. It's out of the way, so we won't have complaints from nosey neighbors. It's plenty large enough for the crowd that I'm expecting, and it has a large parking lot, so there will be plenty of parking without anyone having to leave their limo on the street. My planner will spend the day having his people clean the place up, and tomorrow morning he'll start setting up for the party. There's a lot to do, but it looks like it's a done deal. All I have to do is make about a hundred or so telephone calls today and let the other Mistresses know about the change of location."

"Like I said, feel free to have Carmella make some calls for you. The bookstore is closed until the Grand Opening next Friday night, and Carmella's just about got everything done as far as that's concerned. She's putting an announcement in the newspapers this morning that will include the fact that you will be giving a presentation on 'Training the Recalcitrant Male,'" Penny smiled.

"I am so looking forward to that too, sweetie," Joie chuckled. "The only problem is that both Naked Boy and Sissy Maid are going to be busy that night, so I'm still looking for a submissive to use for demonstration purposes."

"Nothing too outrageous I hope," Penny commented.

"Just outrageous enough to keep the girls amused," Joie replied.

"Ask her if she's called Domina Agony to let her know of the change in location," Kerby suggested. "If she hasn't, see if you can get her to do it before we leave."

"Joie, have you called any of the other Mistresses yet?" Penny asked.

"I was just about to start," Joie remarked, holding up a small personal telephone book, black leather of course.

"I wonder if you could make Domina Agony your first call," Penny asked.

"I understand your growing fascination with male sexual domination, but I'm surprised by your interest in what Domina Agony does. Believe me, sweetie, when you see what she does up close, you'll know that it's not for you," Joie assured Penny, as she began to dial her telephone.

♥ 🐍 ♟

Jeannie McCloone was standing outside of the custom's gate at the International Arrivals Terminal at New York's Kennedy Airport waiting impatiently for Niki, whose plane from Morocco had just landed. As Jean paced about nervously, her cell phone rang. When she heard the ringing, Jean reached into her left pocket and pulled out a cell phone before realizing that the ringing was coming from her right pocket. It wasn't Jean McCloone's cell phone that was ringing; it was the business cell phone of Domina Agony.

"Studio Pain," Jean answered.

"Hello dear," Joie chirped. "It's Maitresse Joie. I'm sorry to bother you so early, but I know you had indicated that you planned on attending the Latex and Leather Gala tomorrow night with some friends. I just wanted to let you know that I've been forced to change the location. I wanted to make certain that you still plan on attending. The gala is being moved to a place on the north shore in Staten Island, right on the water. My party planner will be setting up a spotlight, so it should be easy to find."

"Thank you so much for calling, Mistress, but I am afraid that I may have to change my plans. Some unforeseen circumstances have arisen since I accepted your invitation. In fact, I'm waiting right now to speak with the dominant who was going to accompany me, to see whether or not she is still available. Would it be all right if I call you back in about an hour or so to let you know what my intentions are?" Jean asked, just as she saw Niki come into sight.

"No problem, dear, I'll be around all day. You have my number," Joie said into the telephone before turning to Penny. "Too bad, Domina

Agony and friends might not make it," Joie said, hanging up her phone. "She's going to call back and let me know in an hour or so."

As she cleared customs, Niki spotted Jean and started racing toward her, grinning from ear to ear. She slowed her gait when she realized that Jean was not returning the smile. Jean, who was holding a *New York Post* newspaper in her right hand, had a worried looked on her face as she waited for Niki to reach her.

"What's the matter, babe? You don't look happy to see me," Niki commented. "I thought you'd be all excited with our anniversary so close and all."

"You know I'm always happy to see you, but I'm afraid that our anniversary celebration may have to be canceled. I don't suppose that you had an opportunity to see any of yesterday's New York papers while you were in Morocco. Take a look at this," Jean said, handing the *Post* to Niki. Niki looked stunned by the headline, and she immediately began reading the article as they made their way through the airport. That is, until she spotted an espresso bar out of the corner of her eye as she was walking through the terminal.

"I slept most of the flight, but I still have a horrible case of jet-lag. I could really use a little pick-me-up," Niki noted, pulling Jean into the coffee bar by her arm.

"Do you see what that says?" Jean asked in a disbelieving voice. "You don't seem terribly concerned."

"It's fascinating," Niki responded, after sitting down at a table and ordering grande cappuccinos for each of them. "But do you really think this lady gave the police the names of the victims and the nature of their injuries before they found the bodies? I would bet that they stumbled onto the body in Turtle Pond and, coincidentally, around the same time, some fisherman probably came up with some part of the body in the Hudson. Once they saw the similarities and put the dates together, they probably related the killings."

"You think this is all made up?" Jean asked incredulously.

"Come on, Jean, you're smarter than I am. You can't believe that this lady is really talking to dead people through an Ouija Board. I'm betting that she's a police officer, and they concocted this story in order to try to get the killers to go after her. I think it's a setup. If she really is a psychic, why hasn't she found the bodies of Danny and Peter? Those are the only ones that really count. They have no way to link us to the Demopolous or Smith murders, and our only link to the other murders is that we happen to know the boys and the bodies happen to be in the water near my family's warehouse. There's no physical evidence linking us to the murders.

"Besides, I would be willing to bet that even if they found the bodies there, they'd never put it all together. I mean why would they even be concerned about who owned the warehouse? To me, this is much ado about nothing. I think we should just ignore it and go ahead with our plans. There's one thing I can tell you for certain. With what I have planned for the disposal of Damian Bradford's body, the only way this psychic is going to find it is if she communicates telepathically with fish. Even then she won't be able to lead the police to an exact location in the Atlantic Ocean."

"You don't think that maybe we should forget about it this year?" Jean suggested.

"After all of the trouble I've gone through setting this thing up? I just confirmed everything with Damian on the flight home. We flew back early just for the occasion, only he doesn't know exactly what the occasion is. His girlfriend, who was on the shoot with me, is still in Morocco sightseeing or something. Do you know that asshole flew all the way to Morocco just to be with his girlfriend, but every time she looked the other way, he was asking me about the Latex and Leather Gala? I told you he was kinky. You have no idea how into this thing he is. If it weren't for the gala, I don't think I could have ever pried him away from that girlfriend.

"He's *really* into her. When I first tried to lure him in, he was insistent that there was no way he was going to cheat on the girlfriend. I told you that the threesome thing wouldn't work with him. He's already done that loads of times with groupies. When I suggested that if he didn't come around I might mention our relationship to his girlfriend, it didn't faze him in the least. It seems he's already confessed all of his past dalliances. The girlfriend not only knows that before her he made love with lots of other women, he even told her the details of his lovemaking sessions with some of those women. In fact, she apparently gets all hot hearing about that stuff, as long as he assures her that he'll never do it again.

"Anyway, when I wasn't able to lure him with the threat, I started trying to figure out how to use his foot fetish to get him interested. I thought about the last time you and I went to one of these S&M galas. You remember, one of the Mistresses did a foot worship and trampling demonstration. Then, when I realized that the gala was on our anniversary, I thought, *What the heck?* And I mentioned it to him in passing, just to see if it drew any interest. The next thing I knew, he was following me all over the place, asking me how he could get an invitation to this thing. When I told him that you could get him in, he was the one who came up with the idea of us doing a foot worship and trampling demonstration with him as the foot sucking doormat.

"It could not have worked out better. We can take him to the gala and make his last night on earth fun for him. After the party, I'll suggest a midnight boat ride around New York Harbor, where he can fantasize about the evening while we make love on the water under the moonlight. We won't even have to knock him out. I told you he's into the whole bondage thing. I can guarantee you that he will be more than happy to let us tie him up him up once we get him on the boat. The only thing is, once you get him secured, the boat ride won't be quite what he expected."

"Isn't he afraid of being recognized at this thing? I mean, for that matter, aren't you afraid somebody might recognize him? We can't be seen with him on the night that he disappears from the face of the earth," Jean pointed out.

"That's the beauty of the whole thing. He's into this stuff, but it would be disastrous for his career if the tabloids ever got hold of it. That was his only concern. I relieved that concern by explaining to him that most of the submissives at these things want their anonymity protected, so it's usual for guys to wear full-face leather masks. He liked the idea. He thought it would make the evening that much more fun. The only way that anybody is going to recognize him is if they recognize his body, which though incredible, is not so unique that somebody is going to know it's Damian Bradford under the mask."

"Then it's decided," Jean conceded. "We go through with it as planned. I'll let the Mistress who's throwing the gala know that we will be there."

"I thought that was already taken care of," Niki said.

"It was, but I just spoke with the Mistress and the location has been changed. It's being held at a warehouse on Staten Island's north shore, right on the water. She said that they would have one of those spotlights out so that the place would be easy to find."

"It's right on the water?" Niki asked. "When you call her, find out if there's a place that we might dock a boat for the evening. If we can take the boat down to Staten Island, we won't even have to drive back into the city. It would work out perfectly."

"I'll find out right now," Jean responded, pulling out her cell phone.

Penny was still sipping her coffee and chatting with Joie about the gala and the bookstore's Grand Opening when Joie's telephone rang. "Maitresse Joie," Joie crooned into the phone.

"Mistress, it's Domina Agony. I just wanted to let you know that I've spoken with my friend, and we will be joining you for the Latex and Leather Gala after all. You said that the new location is on the water in Staten Island. My friend and I are considering the possibility of taking her boat there. I wonder if you know whether there might be a place nearby at which we could dock the boat for the evening?"

"One second, dear," Joie answered into the phone and then cupped her hand over the mouthpiece. "Good news," Joie announced to Penny. "Domina Agony and friends will be attending. She wants to know if there is a place nearby that she might dock her boat."

"Dock her boat?" Penny asked in a surprised tone. "Yeah, tell her that there is a bulkhead right at the warehouse that she can tie up to."

"Yes, dear," Joie said into the phone. "Apparently there is a bulkhead at the site that you can tie up to for the evening."

"Wonderful! I look forward to seeing you," Jean said, after which she clicked off her cell phone and turned to Niki. "Perfect, there's a bulkhead at the warehouse that we can dock at for the night."

"It's amazing how things seem to fall into place for us. I'm telling you that Nemesis, the goddess of destiny and inevitability is watching over us," Niki said.

"Niki," Jean replied. "You do know that Nemesis is also the goddess of retribution, don't you? She ensures that nobody has too much good fortune, and it's her job to ensure repayment for sin and crime."

♥ ⚘ ♟

"We need to pick out an outfit for you, sweetie, but it's going to have to wait until later. Even with Carmella's help, I'm going to be busy for the rest of the morning making these calls. You have no idea how these dominatrices love to tell war stories," Joie laughed, handing Penny a list of names and telephone numbers for Carmella. "And later this afternoon I have a very special newby coming in for a session that I am really looking forward to."

"A newby?" Penny asked.

"You know, a novice, someone who has never done this type of thing before," Joie explained.

"I thought you had stopped taking on new clients?" Penny remarked.

"I have, but like I said, this is a special case," Joie replied with a smile. "Anyway, if you stop back this evening after I'm done with him, we can go through my wardrobe and pick something out for you."

"Don't be silly," Penny replied. "I have clothes that I can wear."

"Sweetie, they don't call this the Latex and Leather Gala for nothing. Since I'm guessing that you don't have any latex in your wardrobe, unless you have something in your closet that's black, leather, and fits like skin, come over later and we'll go through my outfits. And don't be looking at my behind thinking I can't have anything in my closet that's going to fit you like a glove. I'm a woman. I don't throw anything away. I've convinced myself that I'm going to fit into all of it again someday. I have outfits from the day I started this stuff, and the good thing is that in this business as long as it's tight and black and leather, it never goes out of style."

"Okay, sounds like fun. I mean, what girl doesn't like playing dress up. I'll see you later," Penny said, making her way to the door.

Rocco Francona was still standing outside of his car as Penny made her way down the stairs of Joie's brownstone. He was talking with an attractive, doe-eyed, cocoa-skinned woman wearing a tight skirt and blouse that showed off a very curvaceous figure. Slowinski was still sitting in the passenger seat of the car.

Penny smiled at Francona and the woman as Penny started to make her way past the vehicle. Francona approached Penny with a strained look on his face while the cocoa-skinned woman waited at the car.

"Ms Albright, I'm not sure how to tell you this, but while I was busy testifying in court yesterday afternoon in another matter, Stan had our office seek a warrant to search your home. Apparently, they found a judge who felt that we have probable cause to do such a search." Francona explained, handing Penny a copy of the warrant.

Penny did not even look at the official looking sheet of a paper that Francona handed her. "No problem. You could have saved yourselves a little time and a lot of trouble if you had just asked for permission to search the house the other day while you were there. I have nothing to hide. In fact, I'll put on a pot of coffee for you and whoever else is planning to help you with the search," Penny offered, starting for her home.

Stan Slowinski had finally stepped out of his vehicle and began hurriedly following Penny toward the brownstone, as if he did not want her to have any time in the house by herself before they started their search. He stopped when his cell phone rang, and he had a short conversation on the phone before he changed direction and approached Francona.

"According to a representative of *Royal Air Moroc,* Nikita Bach just got off a plane from Marakesh at Kennedy Airport," Slowinski said, sounding almost disappointed at the news.

"Like I said, it couldn't hurt to check," Francona said as both officers and the female detective started behind Penny.

"I wish you had told me that you were going to do this, Stan," Francona added.

"Look, Roc, whoever is doing this stuff is taking trophies, souvenirs. It's classic behavior for these kinds of criminals. I know she couldn't have been present when the murders were committed, but that doesn't mean that she might not be the keeper of the trophies. I don't know whether we're going to find any of these souvenirs in there or not. I really don't think we will, but like you say, it couldn't hurt to check."

"I'm not saying it was the wrong thing," Francona conceded. "I'm just saying I would have liked to have known about it."

Inside of the brownstone, Francona introduced the female officer as Regina Jackson, but she made a point of noting that everyone called her Reggie. While Penny put the coffee on, the officers had what they thought was a private meeting in the sun parlor before beginning their search. They didn't realize that Kerby was standing in the center of the group and listening, in an amused fashion, while Francona gave the others instructions.

"Reg, I want you to look through any dressers, closets, or bathroom cabinets that may have female items of a personal nature in them. That means that you get her bedroom and bathroom. Stan, there's an attic up there. I want you to start there. I'm going to start on this floor and keep an eye on Ms Albright while you're doing what you have to do. We'll do the bookstore together. I kind of doubt that if she has something to hide, she'd hide it in a place that's open to the public."

As the officers exited the sun parlor, Penny entered the dining room and put a tray containing a coffee pot, small milk jug, sugar bowl, and four cups on the dining room table. "There's coffee if anyone would like before you start. Or, you're welcome to take a cup with you while you're looking around," Penny offered to no one in particular, though she was looking at Reggie.

"At least he's respecting your dignity. He's having the female officer go through your dressers and stuff. The only thing is, if anyone ever asks, you're going to have to admit that Reggie Jackson has been in your panties," Kerby said with a smile, which Penny returned with a grimace.

"Not surprisingly, Francona is going to search this floor, so that he can keep an eye on you. The truth is, he hasn't taken his eyes off you since he met you. I'm telling you, he likes you, kiddo," Kerby insisted. Penny just shook her head in response.

"Stan is going up to the attic to look around," Kerby continued as Slowinski started up the stairs with a cup of coffee in his hand. "I think I'll join *him*," Kerby smiled, following Slowinski up the steps.

"Behave yourself," Penny blurted out to Kerby, without thinking before she said it.

The three officers looked at an embarrassed Penny with surprised expressions on their faces. "It's not like television, Ms Albright. We'll put everything back the way we found it," Francona assured her.

Once on the second level of the home, Slowinski followed a narrow flight of stairs that led up from the end of the hallway outside of Penny's bedroom. At the top of the stairs, he eased open a door allowing a stream of light into a large, dark room. The only other light in the room came from a small, round, stained-glass window that faced the East 80th Street side of the building. Slowinski used his free hand to search the wall alongside the door for a light switch but found none. As his eyes adjusted to the darkness, Slowinski spotted a chain hanging from an uncovered light in the center of the room. He made his way to the middle of the room and pulled the chain, but he was disappointed at how little light the naked bulb provided.

The only furniture in the room was an overstuffed, weather-beaten, leather chair that sat between two end tables beneath the stained glass window. Three old trunks, all of which looked like treasure chests, sat against each of the remaining walls, leaving the center of the room bare. Slowinski took a sip of his coffee before placing the cup on the end table to the left of the leather chair. Then he made his way to the far side of the room and dragged the trunk that was against that wall back to the chair, so that he could relax in the chair as he went through the chest. As Slowinski pulled the heavy chest across the room, Kerby moved Slowinski's coffee cup from the end table on the left side of the chair to the end table on the right side of the chair.

After struggling to get the trunk in front of the chair, Slowinski plopped himself down into the comfortable seat and reached for his coffee cup. At first startled by the missing cup, Slowinski swiveled his head nervously around the room looking for the coffee cup before spotting it on the other table. Confused, but willing to accept the fact that he was mistaken about which table he had placed the cup on, Slowinski reached for his coffee, took another sip and placed the cup back down on the table to his right. Then he opened the chest to find it neatly stacked full with folders, each stuffed with papers. Each of the folders was labeled with a black magic marker identifying the subject of the documents inside.

Slowinski reached for a folder marked "Brownstone," took out his glasses, and began perusing some of the documents. As he did so, Kerby moved to the center of the room and pulled the chain, turning the light off and leaving Slowinski sitting in the dark. At the click of the chain, Slowinski's head shot up in time to see the chain swinging as the light went out. He jumped up from his chair and raced to the chain in order to get the light back on as quickly as he could. When the room was illuminated again, Slowinski went back to his chair and sat down, looking at the chain to make sure that it did not click off.

After waiting several seconds to assure himself that the light was going to stay lit, Slowinski reached to his right where he was certain he would find his coffee cup, but it wasn't there. He looked to his left to find that Kerby had moved the cup back to where he had initially placed it. *What the fuck?* Slowinski thought to himself.

He leafed through papers in the chest quickly and then just as quickly pushed the trunk back to where he had found it. Once the trunk was back in place, Slowinski looked back to the other side of the room, half expecting to see the coffee cup back on the table to the right of the chair. He wasn't disappointed. Kerby had switched it again.

Slowinski kept his eye on the table as he slowly walked to the trunk on the left side of the room. He continued to keep watch the cup out of the corner of his eye as he rummaged quickly through the trunk, which was loaded with various memorabilia. Slowinski had one eye on the contents of the chest and the other on his coffee cup when he heard the click of the light behind him, and the room went dark again.

"Holy shit!" Slowinski exclaimed, out loud this time, as he moved quickly to the light chain and pulled it back on. When he could see again, Slowinski looked back to the chair and tables. The cup was back on the left end table.

Slowinski almost jumped out of his skin when the attic door flew open. "Geez, why so jumpy, Stan?" Reggie asked, realizing that she had startled him. "No testicles down there. You find anything interesting up here."

"Stay right there and watch this. You are not going to belief this shit. You see where my coffee cup is now? Well watch it," Slowinski instructed Reggie excitedly. Then he clicked the light off, leaving them in the dark for several seconds. After giving the cup plenty of time to make its move, Slowinski pulled the chain and lit up the room again.

"Ta da!" Slowinski sang out, pointing toward the table to the left, but the cup had not moved this time.

"I'm watching," Reggie said with a bewildered look on her face. "What am I supposed to see?"

"Never mind," a disappointed Slowinski mumbled. "Forget it. Just do me a favor. Stay right here while I go through this last trunk."

"Something got you spooked up here, Stan? You don't look right." Reggie opined.

"Forget about it," Slowinski grumbled, quickly moving about some old clothes with which the last trunk was stuffed.

When he was satisfied that there was nothing of interest in the trunk, Slowinski retrieved his coffee cup from the table and the two started down the stairs. Near the bottom of the stairs, Reggie looked back and said, "You left the light on, Stan."

Reggie continued down toward the first floor as Slowinski headed nervously back to the attic. He pushed the door open tentatively this time and started to enter the room. He was about two feet from the light when he saw the chain yank downward and the room went dark again.

"Find anything interesting?" Francona asked when everyone was back in the dining room.

"Not me," Reggie replied.

"Nothing," Slowinski muttered, heading for the door.

"What about the bookstore?" Francona hollered to Slowinski.

"I'm satisfied," Slowinski mumbled, making his way out into the sunlight and taking a deep breath. "You want to search the bookstore, be my guest. I'll be out here waiting."

"This was your gig, pal," Francona responded. "If you're satisfied, then I guess we're done. Thanks again," Francona said to Penny as he followed Slowinski out the door with Reggie at his side.

"That's one strange partner you've got there, Francona," Reggie remarked. "When I found him up in the attic, the poor guy looked scared out of his wits."

Once they were all together at the car, Francona gave out assignments for the next day. "Okay, Stan, you said you want Albright, tomorrow she's yours for the day. Reggie, you're into the fashionista stuff. Nikita Bach is yours. Be at her apartment at sunrise and don't let her out of your sight. I'll take the McCloone girl. We'll find out tomorrow whether she's really an evil femdom, or still the sweet valedictorian from the yearbook.

"These girls can't know that we're following them, Reg, so be careful. And I want constant communication. Anything unusual happens, I want to know about it." Francona ordered as Reggie headed for her own car and Slowinski got into Francona's.

"You okay, Stan? You don't look well," Francona noted, once he was in the driver's seat of the car.

"If I told you, you wouldn't believe me anyway. In fact, I'm not even sure that I believe it myself," Slowinski murmured.

♥ ⚔ ♟

It was early evening when Penny and Kerby made their way back to Joie's house. Joie did not answer the bell immediately, so they entered slowly, hoping that she had completed her session. Once they were in the foyer, Joie appeared from within the library.

"Sorry, sweetie, this one is running a little longer than I had expected it would. My newby has more staying power than most novices."

"I'll come back later when you're through," Penny offered.

"No, it's okay, sweetie. He's not going anywhere. He's tied up downstairs, both literally and figuratively," Joie laughed. "But this one has a special concern about his anonymity being protected, so let me get you upstairs and into my wardrobe room, so I can get him out of here privately."

Joie led Penny and Kerby up the stairs and through her bedroom, into a separate inner room that was connected to the bedroom. The inner room was perfectly round with no windows or corners. The wall on half of the room was covered with mirrors. The other half of the circle was lined with Joie's all black, mostly leather, outfits hanging from a stainless steel bar. Though there was no outside light in the room, the room was quite bright, partly because of the interior lighting and partly because the room was done entirely in white, except for Joie's clothes. The lone piece of furniture in the room was a large circular divan, which sat in the center of the room, covered by a white fur blanket. A white shag carpet covered the floor.

"Basically, I keep my outfits in chronological order based on the date I bought them. The one's to the far left are the oldest. Not surprisingly, they're also the smallest in size. That's where you'll want to start going through things and trying them on," Joie instructed.

"Have fun, sweetie, and take anything you like. I have to run. I don't want to leave my newby hanging around too long by himself. If you don't mind, I'm going to lock this door behind me to make sure that you two don't run into each other by accident. Like I said, this one is particularly concerned about remaining anonymous," Joie repeated, after which she pulled the door closed behind her, and Penny heard the lock click shut.

"How am I supposed to try on clothes with you in here with me?" Penny asked.

"I'll face the wall," Kerby offered, looking back at the mirror lined wall behind him.

"A lot of good that will do," Penny groaned, making her way to the outfits on the other side of the room.

"It's not as if I haven't already seen you in your undies," Kerby smiled.

"And less," Penny added, thinking back to that first morning in the shower.

"The bottom line is that with the way you take care of your body, you *really* don't have anything to be ashamed of," Kerby remarked.

Penny ignored the comment and began working her way through the outfits on the wall. "I can't wear any of these things. I'll look ridiculous," Penny complained.

"Where we're going, you'll look ridiculous in anything but one of those outfits," Kerby opined, making his way alongside Penny. "Here, try this one," Kerby suggested, taking a black leather mini dress with a sleeveless mock turtle neck top down from its hanger and handing it to Penny. But Penny ignored the offer, opting instead to try on a black leather pants outfit, with a connecting top.

"All right, close your eyes," Penny ordered. Then she dropped her jeans and slipped off the tee shirt she was wearing, so that she was standing before the mirror in only a pair of white cotton panties and a sports bra. She looked into the mirror and admired her body for a second, thinking about what Kerby had said about her not being ashamed of her naked body. She started to pull the pants outfit on when she looked into the mirror again and saw Kerby leaning back on the divan, watching her with the smile of an owl that had just spotted a mouse.

"You're supposed to have your eyes closed," Penny said, although she was flattered that he didn't.

After Penny had pulled on the pants outfit, she turned her back to the mirror and smoothed the pants across her rear end. They fit so snugly that the contours of her behind were clearly visible through the shiny, black leather.

"What do you think?" Penny asked, looking at Kerby in the mirror.

"It looks nice, kiddo, but it covers too much. It's summertime, and it's going to be a little hot for that. Anyway, you should be showing off those legs, not hiding them. Try this one," Kerby suggested, again pushing his choice of the mini dress.

Penny stepped out of the pants suit, this time without asking Kerby to turn his head or close his eyes. She unashamedly strolled by Kerby in her bra and panties. She never looked at him as she passed by, but Penny could feel his eyes following her as she went by. She could still feel his eyes burning into her behind as she reached up to hang up the pants suit, and went through several more outfits before taking down a mid-length black leather dress which was slit all the way up the right leg.

With the dress held up in front of her, Penny finally turned to look at Kerby who was suddenly looking a bit uncomfortable at Penny's newfound boldness. "What do you think of this one?" Penny asked, smiling at the thought that her ghost was blushing slightly red.

"I can't tell like that," Kerby answered, stammering slightly. "Maybe if you try it on."

Penny pulled the dress on and made her way by Kerby again to the mirror. As she checked the slit that ran all the way up her right thigh, Penny turned back to Kerby. "Do you think this is a bit too much?" Penny wondered, toying with Kerby and excited by the fact that she was able to do so.

"It's very nice," Kerby responded, again stammering slightly and still looking a tad embarrassed. "But you've got a great *pair* of legs. Why show off just one? I still like this one," Kerby insisted, offering the mini dress yet again.

"Okay, you win. I guess there's no harm in trying it on," Penny acquiesced, unsnapping the dress and letting it slip to her ankles before she stepped out of it and headed toward Kerby, this time looking into his eyes as she made her way to him. Kerby looked like a deer caught in the headlights. He wanted to scan Penny's entire body as she closed in on him, but he felt obligated to maintain eye contact.

When she reached him, Penny took the dress from him, stepped into it, and pulled it up, struggling to get the mock turtleneck top over her breasts. "There, are you happy now?" Penny asked, spinning and making her way back to the mirror. "Maybe you were right after all. I think I like this one best. How do you think it looks?" Penny asked, looking at Kerby in the mirror, but this time the eye contact was not returned. Kerby's eyes were staring at Penny's behind.

Kerby finally looked up and met Penny's eyes. "I think it fits you in more ways than one," Kerby smiled.

"Good, then we agree. I'll wear this one, but I'll need a pair of stockings to match. None of the hosiery in my drawers is going to fit with this thing," Penny remarked, making her way to a rack of rolled up nylons and high heel shoes that ran beneath the outfits. She pulled out a pair of fishnet stockings and spiky, black heels, sat down next to Kerby, and slowly pulled the stockings up one leg at a time, smoothing each one the length of each leg as she did so.

As Penny spun in front of the mirror checking her legs from every angle, Kerby watched, feeling as if his head was spinning with Penny's body. "A little too sleazy I think," Penny noted, making her way back to the hosiery rack. She pulled out a pair of black nylons with a thick, black seam running up the back of the legs, made her way back to Kerby and again sat next to him as she again eased the stockings slowly up each leg one at a time.

Kerby now had an ache inside of him that was growing by the second. Penny knew it and was thoroughly enjoying it as she stepped into her heels, got up from the divan, and started to walk lasciviously on her heels toward the mirror. Kerby looked down at the spiky, black heels and then his eyes followed the seams of the stockings up to Penny's thighs. The image brought back memories that Kerby could not control.

When Penny turned to ask for Kerby's opinion on the stockings, she found herself staring directly into his eyes. Without uttering a word, he wrapped his arms around her and pulled her to him. Penny felt as if her body was melting into Kerby's as the tiny surges of electricity started pulsing through every pore of her skin. Kerby kissed her mouth lightly, and Penny's lips parted immediately. As their tongues met, Penny felt as if a small fireworks display had been set off inside her head. She could not stop herself from wondering what the same thing would feel like down below.

Penny stepped back and pulled the mini dress down as quickly as she could. Then she reached for Kerby's belt and began unbuckling it. With the belt loosened, Penny stuck her hands into the top off Kerby's pants in order to lower them, but as she did so she heard the click of a lock and the door to Joie's bedroom suddenly flung open.

"How did you make out, sweetie?" Joie asked, looking across into Penny's flushed face and glazed-over eyes.

"Good . . . I think . . . I like this one," Penny stuttered, trying to compose herself, as she picked the mini dress up from the floor.

"From the looks of you, sweetie, I'd say you *really* like that one,"

Joie smiled. "By the way, those old-fashion nylons with the seams are my favorites too. I don't know what it is about them, but those seams drive men wild."

"I'll say they do!" Penny exclaimed to Joie, but she was looking at Kerby.

CHAPTER 13

SUGAR AND SPICE BUT NOT SO NICE
JUNE 24, 2003

It was 11:30 A.M. when Rocco Francona's voice crackled over the two-way radio in Stan Slowinski's car. "Anything happening there yet, Stan?"

"She came out in her running clothes about an hour ago and went right to the cab driver's house to talk to him. That was a little strange, only because when I came back last night, she went back to the femdom's home. The old guy was already in there and the three met for about an hour. The old guy came out and Albright followed him out about fifteen minutes later. It's kind of strange that she's with the cabbie for an hour last night, yet she's got to see him about something first thing this morning," Slowinski opined.

"After she talked with the cab driver, she started jogging toward Central Park. It's her normal route and she's in her running clothes, so I let her go, even though this is not her normal time to go running. To be safe, I called our guy down in the park just to make certain that she showed up there. The last I heard, she had just finished doing her laps around the reservoir, and was heading back this way. How about you, anything interesting on your end?"

"Reggie's up here with me now. She started out this morning at Nikita Bach's apartment down in Greenwich Village, but she determined pretty quickly that Bach wasn't in there. Reg talked with a neighbor who told her that Bach spends a lot of time at her mom's apartment and slept there last night. You know that Bach's mom lives right above McCloone's mother's apartment? Jean McCloone still lives with her mother, but from what we've been able to find out, the mother spends most of her time at a girlfriend's apartment on the other side of the park.

"Anyway, a little earlier, Bach came out of the building on a coffee run to the Starbucks down the street. There's no mistaking that one. Even in a Yankee cap and oversized sweats, you can see why she's on the cover of glamour magazines. She was with a girl who was a perfect match for the description that Albright gave us for the other murderer, but we couldn't be certain at first who she was. I have a blow up of McCloone's yearbook picture, and I had the computer geek print out a copy of this Domina Agony's picture from the web site. Guess who the other female looks just like. Even with the face covered in the picture, you can tell that this girl and Domina Agony are one and the same. She has this unmistakable little curl that hangs down on her forehead.

"We still couldn't be certain that McCloone and this dominatrix were the same person. Like you said, the dominatrix doesn't look anything like the girl in the yearbook picture. So Reggie followed them down to the coffee shop. On the way, the girls stopped at a newsstand. Bach bought a bunch of glamour magazines, including one with her face on the cover, and the other girl bought a couple of newspapers.

"Reggie stopped at the same stand and bought a copy of the magazine with Bach's picture on the cover. She followed them into the Starbucks, pretended that she was a big fan of Bach's and asked her to autograph the magazine. Bach was very flattered and very gracious. She even asked Reggie to sit with them, and she bought her a coffee. Reg says that the other girl didn't say much. She had her nose buried in a newspaper most of the time, but Bach eventually introduced the other girl as 'her friend Jeannie.'"

"No shit!" Slowinski exclaimed.

"That's right, pal, your caterpillar is now a butterfly. Only this butterfly looks like she could do more pushups than you and me put together," Francona noted.

"Where are they now?" Slowinski asked.

"After the coffee, they went back into the apartment building and haven't come out since," Francona answered.

In the middle of Francona's last sentence, Slowinski looked into his rearview mirror and saw Penny jogging into view. "It looks like Albright is done with her run," Slowinski said into the two-way radio.

"She's stretching her leg muscles out now," Slowinski continued, as he watched Penny stop in front of her apartment, place her right leg up on the stair rail, and bend her head down to her knee like a ballet dancer limbering up. "She's got *some* flexibility. I'm starting to understand what it is you see in her," Slowinski finished, while watching Penny's running shorts tighten across her butt as she leaned forward into her stretch. When she was finished stretching, Penny jogged up the steps with Slowinski eyeing her, all the way up, without saying a word.

"Are you still there, Stan?" Francona finally asked.

"Yeah, I'm here, but not for long. She's gone into the house, and my guess is that she won't be out for a while. I'm heading up the street to get myself a sandwich while I know where she is," Slowinski responded, before signing off and heading to the deli up the street.

Kerby was waiting at the door when Penny walked in. "Did you speak with Sol about using his boat again tonight?" Kerby asked.

"Yup, he said no problem, any time. I apparently proved my nautical skills to him last time out," Penny answered proudly.

"Did you stop over and fill Slowinski in on what we know about tonight?" Kerby continued.

"I don't like talking to that guy," Penny complained. "He has a sarcastic remark no matter what I say to him."

"I know, but it's not as if I can do it, and we don't know whether Francona is going to show up here at all today. If he's smart, and I think he is, he's parked outside of one of those girls' homes right now, and he'll be there until she makes a move. You have to let someone know where the party is and that these girls are apparently planning on traveling there by boat. Francona is not going to be able to stick with them unless he has some advance warning that he is going to need water transportation."

"Fine, I'll tell him," Penny groaned.

Penny started back out of the door but stopped at the landing on top of the stairs when she realized that Slowinski was not in his car. "It figures, the one time you need him, and he's not here. I'll leave him a note. That way he gets the message, and I don't have to see his smiling face up close," Penny said cheerfully, heading back to the kitchen to write the note.

"Just make sure you leave it where he can't miss it," Kerby instructed.

"I'll leave it in plain view, on his windshield, under the wiper on the driver's side, so he has to see it."

"Sounds good," Kerby replied, as Penny finished her note.

The note read:

Officer Slowinski:

Please inform Officer Francona that I am now certain that the murderers you are looking for are Nikita Bach and Jean McCloone. Both girls will be attending an S&M party in Staten Island this evening. The party will be held at a warehouse on the north shore of Staten Island. The warehouse, which coincidently is owned by Nikita Bach's mother, will be easily identifiable because a spotlight will be set up in its parking lot to alert partygoers to the location

The girls will be attending the party with a male whose identity I do not know. But I am certain that if these girls are not stopped this evening, this male will be their fifth victim. It is my understanding that the murderers plan on traveling to Staten Island from Manhattan by boat. I do not know to whom the boat belongs or where it is docked. I do know that in order to follow these girls throughout the evening, you must make arrangements for some type of water transportation.

Since I assume that you also intend to follow me throughout the evening, this is also to alert you to the fact that I too will be attending the party in Staten Island, and I too plan on traveling there by boat. I will be using the same craft that I took out of the 79th Street Boat Basin two days ago.

Finally, I will give you an exact location for the bodies of the two boys in the morning. I have spoken with Tori O'Brien, and she is okay with this. Tori is going to inform Peter Sizemore's mother that the location of the boys' bodies will be known tomorrow and that the bodies will be retrieved within the next few days. Please do not hazard any guesses as to where the bodies may be located. I assure you that you will have that information by tomorrow morning.

If you or Officer Francona have any questions, I will be home until early evening.

Penny Albright

When Penny exited the house, she was relieved that Slowinski had not yet returned to his car, which sat alone at the curb on the opposite side of the street. Friday was street sweeping day on East 80th Street, and all of the other cars on the south side of the street had been moved to avoid being ticketed. Penny rushed to the other side of the street and placed the note under the windshield wiper on the driver's side of Solwinski's vehicle. Once certain that there was no way Slowinski could miss seeing the note, Penny raced back to the brownstone. As she made her way across the street, Penny noticed a traffic officer placing a ticket on the windshield of a vehicle halfway down the block, but it meant nothing to her.

"It's done," Penny shouted to Kerby, making her way up the stairs toward her bedroom. "I'm taking my shower now. I'll be down in a while."

As Penny undressed for her shower, the traffic officer had just finished writing out a ticket for Stan Slowinski's vehicle and was placing the ticket on Slowinski's windshield. He stopped when he heard Slowinski cursing at him from up the street. With his head turned in Slowinski's direction, the traffic cop lifted the wiper and placed the ticket on top of Penny's note, without ever realizing that the note was there.

"What are you doing, asshole?" Slowinski shouted at the traffic officer when he reached the car. "That's a police vehicle on official police duty."

"How am I supposed to know that? The car is unmarked, and you left it without putting your 'Official Police Duty' placard in the window. So who's the asshole?" the traffic cop shouted back.

"Thanks a lot. Now I've got to have someone downtown take care of this for me," Slowinski hollered, still glaring at the traffic cop. Slowinski snatched the ticket from the window, grabbing Penny's note with the ticket, without realizing that the note was in his hand.

"You'd think you were going to have to pay the damn thing," the traffic cop shouted back, as Slowinski stepped into his car and threw the ticket and note onto the front seat, unaware that the note had slipped free from underneath the ticket. It landed right next to Slowinski's bottom as he plopped into his seat.

Wrapped in a towel, Penny headed straight for the bedroom window as soon as she got out of the shower. The traffic cop was just pulling away from Slowinski's car. Slowinski was sitting in the vehicle. The note was gone from the windshield.

Penny stuck her head out of the bedroom door. "He didn't ring the bell while I was in the shower, did he?" Penny shouted down to Kerby.

"Nope, I didn't hear any bell," Kerby shouted back.

"Good, it worked out perfectly. He has the information and no questions, so for the time being, I don't have to deal with Officer Slowinski's pleasant demeanor," Penny sang out cheerfully.

♥ ⚒ ♣

It was nearly 8:00 P.M. when Rocco Francona's voice finally crackled over the two-way radio in Slowinski's vehicle again with something positive to report. "It looks as if we've finally got something going on up here, Stan. The girls came out of the apartment building together a few minutes ago, each of them carrying an overnight bag. They went into an underground parking facility around the corner from the apartment. We're waiting for them to come up now. Anything happening there yet?"

"Albright hasn't been out of the house since her jog. But some guy went into the femdom's house a little while ago and a few minutes later a limo pulled up. The dominatrix and the guy came out and left in the limo. She was dressed in full femdom attire, black leather from head to toe. The guy had on something that looked like an opera cape with a hood and all, it covered him right down to his shoes. It was the weirdest damn thing I've ever seen."

"You know what they say, 'Different strokes for different folks.' But that's not our concern," Francona responded.

"I thought Albright said she was going to give you the heads up on where these girls were supposed to be tonight. She didn't say *boo* to me all day," Slowinski grumbled.

"I think that what she said was that she had an idea where the girls were going to be but she wasn't certain. Maybe she didn't want to risk sending us on one of those wild goose chases you're always talking about," Francona replied.

"She could have at least said something so as not to leave us hanging," Slowinski grunted.

"Here we go, Reg," Francona announced when he saw a red Jaguar XK8 Convertible exit the parking garage with its top down. Niki Bach was behind the steering wheel, and Jean McCloone was in the passenger seat.

"Got to go, Stan. They're on the move. Keep me posted," Francona ordered, before clicking off his two-way radio.

Niki turned to Jean as she started out of the parking lot. "Damian lives in a loft at the tip of Trinity Place just below the bottom of the Tribeca triangle, but there's a Bruce Springsteen concert at Madison Square Garden tonight, and I don't want to chance traffic on the West Side Highway. I'm going to cut through Central Park, take the FDR Drive downtown and swing around."

"She's out," Slowinski announced excitedly into his radio, as Francona pulled his car out behind the Jaguar. "The cabbie pulled up and a second later Albright's out of the door. Roc, you've got to see what she's got on. I just caught a glimpse of her before she buttoned up her raincoat, but she took my breath away for a second. She's wearing a black leather mini dress with a slit on the side that goes up to the whazoo. It's so tight I don't know how she's able to breathe. And she's wearing some of the highest high heels I've ever seen, with those sexy black stockings with the seams running up the back of the legs. Roc, she looked more like a dominatrix than the neighbor did."

"That doesn't sound like her," Francona remarked.

"Maybe it's her devil worshiping outfit. Who knows, maybe the next door neighbor is in on this stuff too, and they're meeting for their annual bloodletting ritual somewhere. One thing I do know, wherever she's going, I'm going too," Slowinski assured Francona as he pulled out behind Sol's cab.

As Sol drove around the corner and headed west on East 79th Street, Niki Bach was entering Central Park at 81st Street. Once in the park, the Jaguar sped around a curve, passing the Shakespeare Garden on its left, before ending up on the 79th Street Transverse, crossing Central Park from west to east. As the Jaguar raced past Turtle Pond and the Belvidere Castle on its right, with Francona on its tail, Sol Hirsh's cab was just passing through the light at Central Park East and East 79th Street entering into the park from east to west. Nearing the exit to the park on Central Park East, Niki Bach stepped hard on the gas to make certain she made it through that same light before it turned red. If Penny had looked to her left as Sol's cab entered Central Park, she would have seen Nikita Bach and Jeannie McCloone speeding past her in the opposite direction, their hair blowing wildly in the wind.

"Was that Stan?" Francona asked as the unmarked police cars zipped by each other in opposite directions.

"I didn't notice," Reggie answered. "Call him and see."

"Stan what's your location?" Francona asked Slowinski on the two-way radio.

"I'm on the 79th Street Transverse heading west through Central Park. Why do you ask?"

"We just went by you going in the opposite direction," Francona replied.

"Well, at least now we know that Albright and the two girls are not going to the same place," Slowinski figured.

"Apparently not," Francona agreed.

As they exited the park, Penny looked behind her and eyed Slowinski who appeared to be talking to himself. "He must not have believed what I wrote in the note. If he had, he could have just met us at the Boat Basin instead of following us around. I assume he has a boat there waiting for him just in case."

After looking back at Slowinski for several seconds, Penny turned her head forward just in time to see a New York City Transit Authority Bus pull out from the curb and bump into the right front corner panel of Sol's cab.

"Damn it!" Sol exclaimed as the bus pulled to the curb and Sol followed suit. "This won't take too long. It's just a scratch, but I'm sure he's going to want to exchange insurance information. By the time he gets back to the garage, everybody on that bus will have complained of a backache or neck pain, and by tomorrow morning people who weren't even on the bus will be filing claims with the city's insurance carrier," Sol predicted, getting out of his vehicle.

While Sol spoke with the bus driver and exchanged insurance information, Officer Slowinski sat double parked several cars behind. He never got out of his car to investigate the accident. "We've got a little delay here," Slowinski informed Francona over the two-way radio in an annoyed tone. "The cab driver just had a fender-bender."

At the time of Slowinski's call, Francona was doing his best just to keep the Jaguar in sight as it sped south down the FDR Drive. "The way this girl is driving, wherever she's going she'll be lucky to make it there alive," Francona noted. "Let me know when you're moving again Stan."

♥ ♒ ♟

By the time the bus driver checked his passengers for injuries and exchanged insurance information with Sol, the Jaguar was pulling to the side of the road on Battery Place, between Trinity Place and State Street in downtown Manhattan. The car was parked right outside of Battery Park, just opposite the damaged *Sphere Sculpture* from the World Trade Center which had been placed in Battery Park as a temporary memorial to the World Trade Center tragedy. Francona pulled over about a block behind the Jaguar, near Pier A, the departure point for the ferry to the Statue of Liberty.

"He lives up the street on Trinity Place, but I told him to meet us at the park, so that no one from his apartment building would see him getting into the car. I used the excuse that I'm never able to find a parking space in front of his building," Niki informed Jean.

Less than a minute later, the girls saw Damian Bradford with a knapsack flung over his shoulder making his way down Trinity Place toward the car. When Bradford reached Battery Place, Reggie noticed him crossing the street in the direction of the Jaguar.

"Ooooh my goodness!" Reggie exclaimed. "Do you see who that is, Roc?"

"I see who it is, but I don't know who it is," Francona replied, about the tall handsome guy who was headed for the Jaguar.

"That's because you're not a female. Every woman in this city knows that face, and the body that goes with it too. If you want to see what he looks like without those clothes on, just go up to Times Square and look up. He's on a billboard up there that's as big as a building, and all he's got on is a pair of tight fitting briefs," Reggie said.

"I think I'll pass," Francona replied.

"Like I said, that's because you're a man, but I know women who have skipped lunch just to travel up to midtown to stare at his billboard for a few minutes."

"So are you going to tell me his name or leave me in suspense?" Francona wondered, while watching Bradford jump over the side of the convertible and land in the back seat.

"That guy is none other than Damian Bradford," Reggie announced. "There are very few male models who have been deemed worthy of the term "super model," but he's one of them, and deservedly so I might add. If these girls were planning on making Damian Bradford disappear, they were about to disappoint a whole lot of women in this world."

Once Bradford was in the vehicle, Niki headed east to State Street and then down past the Staten Island Ferry Terminal to South Street, where she turned north again, toward the South Street Seaport. About two blocks before the Seaport, Niki took a quick right and stopped in front of a chain link gate that led into a local marina at which a number of very expensive yachts were docked.

Francona pulled to the curb on South Street, about a block before the marina. He watched as the gate to the marina rolled to its left and the Jaguar drove through, with the gate closing behind it. "What the heck is she doing now?" Francona wondered.

"Stay here," Francona instructed Reggie. Then he made his way to the fence where he watched Niki Bach exit the vehicle, put up the ragtop on her car, and make her way to a sleek, futuristic looking 32' Doral Cruiser. She was met at the boat by a dockhand who hugged her lightly and spoke with her briefly before making his way back to a small building within the marina property.

After the dockhand entered the building, Niki waved for Jean and Damian to come over. As Francona watched, Jean and Damian made their way to the yacht and the three boarded. Francona remained frozen at the gate, not believing what he was seeing, until he heard the engines of the boat start to rev, at which point he raced back to his car.

"We're screwed! Wherever they're going, they're going by water. We need to get the Harbor Unit on the radio. We need a boat to pick us up and a chopper on standby just in case," Francona shouted urgently.

Reggie reached for the radio, but before she could pick it up, they heard Stan Slowinski's static written voice coming through. "I'm fucked up here, Roc. You're not going to believe this, but Albright just took off on that boat again. The way she was dressed, I never thought in my wildest dreams she'd be going for a boat ride," Slowinski said from the parking lot of the *79th Street Boat Basin*. "I'm not sure what you want me to do. I was tempted to arrest her, but I've got no probable cause. I didn't know how else to stop her."

"Just sit tight," Francona ordered. "We have the same problem down here that you have up there. The model and the femdom just pulled out of a marina down by the Seaport on a yacht that looked like something out of *Star Wars*. They have a guy on the boat with them. It looks as if either Albright has some connection to these girls, or it's an awfully big coincidence that everybody picked tonight to go out for a moonlight cruise around New York Harbor."

"No wonder she didn't let us in on their plans," Slowinski grumbled.

"We're going to call the NYPD Harbor Unit and have them send a boat over to pick us up. We'll swing around and pick you up there while we look around for any sign of the girls' yacht or Albright's boat. I'm going to talk to the guy from the marina and see whether or not Bach left a travel plan with him, but at this point, there's no telling where they may be headed," Francona said dejectedly, before signing off with Slowinski.

Francona made his way to the marina while Reggie called the Harbor Unit, explained their problem, had them send a boat to pick them up and had them put a helicopter on standby. Francona rang a bell at the gate of the marina and an annoyed voice came over the intercom. The tone of the voice changed and the gate rolled open as soon as Francona identified himself.

"She said she's on her way to a party tonight," the marina guy said, after Francona explained why he was there. "When the party's over, she's following the coastline down to Cape May to her aunt's beach house. She said the guy with her is her cousin. This was his first time in the Big Apple, and she's taking him to the party tonight and then dropping him home in Cape May. She and her girlfriend are going to spend the weekend down there, catch some sun and maybe go to Atlantic City and do some gambling. She told me not to expect her back until Monday or Tuesday. She also told me not to bother calling her because her receiver is out."

"She didn't give you a location for the party, did she?" Francona asked.

"She just said it was local. I'd guess Long Island or Northern Jersey, maybe one of the other boroughs. It wouldn't make much sense to take a boat if the party is in Manhattan."

"We need that Harbor Unit boat in a hurry, Reg," Francona yelled, racing back to his car. "Wherever they're going, they're not planning on bringing Damian Bradford home with them."

♥ ∅ ♣

"The poor guy looked like the kid who got left home from the party, standing there on the dock watching us pull away," Kerby laughed, speaking of Stan Slowinski, as Penny steered a course down the Hudson River toward Upper New York Bay.

"I don't get it. Why didn't he have a boat there waiting? He had to have seen my note."

"I'm not worried about him. He knows where the party is. Maybe he's decided to drive there. It's Francona who better have made arrangements for a boat," Kerby noted.

Penny maintained a constant speed as she cruised through the confluence of the Hudson River and East River and then between Liberty Island and Governor's Island. But she slowed considerably just outside the turnoff for the Kill Van Kull where she saw a sleek new yacht that seemed to be drifting about aimlessly.

"That's strange," Penny pointed out as she coasted up to the yacht. "There's no one at the helm, but they're not anchored. They're just drifting. I wonder if they need help?"

In the ultramodern cabin of the Doral Cruiser, Damian Bradford sat on a customized queen size berth that occupied the entire front of the cabin. "Here, baby," Niki hollered to Damian, tossing him a black leather bikini bottom. "That's your outfit for this evening."

"Is that it?" Damian asked, dangling the tiny bikini bottom up in front of his face from his index finger.

"Don't forget you're here as a foot slave. That's what slaves wear, baby. Anyway what are you worried about, you have the body for it, and you know you love showing it off," Niki cracked.

"Where do I go to change?" Damian wondered.

"Change right there, baby. It's not as if I haven't seen it before," Niki noted, looking down at Damian's crotch. "And I told you what Jeannie does for a living, so you haven't got anything that she hasn't seen a thousand times over. Stop being a wimp and get into your slave suit," Niki ordered.

The girls gawked in titillated amusement as Damian stripped down to nothing and pulled on his tiny, leather bikini bottom. When Damian was done, the girls put on their outfits. Niki dressed in a black latex outfit that clung to her body from just above her ankles to just above her breasts, looking as if it had been glued on. Jean put on a black leather miniskirt and black leather corset top. By the time Niki had finished lacing up Jean's top, Jean looked like she had no waist at all, and her breasts looked like they were doing their best to burst free from their bindings. Both girls wore black patent leather high heels.

"Oh yeah, I almost forgot. You do get to cover up more than that. Here, baby," Niki mocked, flipping Damian a full face leather mask with cut outs for the eyes, mouth, and nose.

"Look, baby, my mask almost matches yours," Niki noted, pulling a black latex mask over her head and hair until it stopped on either side of her nose. Niki stared out at Damian through large eye slots as she adjusted two cat ears that sat on the top of her mask, pointing them straight up in the air.

"Have you ever seen a cat torment a mouse before it eats it, baby?" Niki taunted. "Well tonight I'm the cat and you're the mouse and that's what I'm going to do to you, except I probably won't eat you when I'm done, at least, not all of you," Niki said with a wicked laugh before she started up the stairs for the deck of the boat.

Penny was just about to pull away from the Doral Cruiser and call the Coast Guard to come and check it out when she saw a head emerge from the cabin onto the deck.

"Ahoy, is everything all right over there?" Penny hollered.

As Penny watched, whoever it was that had come out from below-deck snatched something from the top of her head and approached the rail. "Everything's fine," Niki hollered back, smiling across at Penny. "We just went below for a second. I thought I had set my anchor, but I guess it didn't catch."

"That's Nikita Bach," Kerby announced with assuredness as he eyed the gorgeous face, blonde hair, and skin-tight latex outfit. "If there's a guy down in that cabin, I hope he's still breathing."

As Kerby finished his statement, Penny started to slowly pull away. When she looked back, she saw a second and then a third head emerge from below-deck on the Doral Cruiser. The third person out was a male who appeared to be almost naked. Penny could see the guy's muscles rippling in the moonlight. She continued to look backward as she headed for the Kill Van Kull. The sleek looking yacht took a course directly behind her larger Sabreline Cruiser.

"He's still alive," Penny noted. "It looks like they're waiting until after the party to take care of him."

"That's a relief, but what concerns me is where the heck is Francona?" Kerby replied.

"Maybe he's already in Staten Island," Penny suggested.

"It wouldn't have done that guy any good if they had decided to kill him before the party," Kerby pointed out, keeping an eye on the Doral Cruiser just to make certain that it stayed on a course for the warehouse.

At the entrance to the Kill Van Kull, Penny looked up and saw the beam of the spotlight swaying back and forth across the sky. She directed Kerby's attention to the spotlight, and then she followed the beam directly to the warehouse, with Niki's yacht following not far behind. At the warehouse bulkhead, Kerby spotted Danny and Peter waving excitedly. Behind them, the parking lot was crowded with black limousines.

"Hey, Mr. Brewster! Hey, Ms. Albright!" Danny yelled as Penny eased the boat to the bulkhead and Kerby tossed the lines ashore to the boys.

"You are not going to believe what's going on in there, Mr. Brewster. It's like a masquerade party for sex freaks," Peter shouted as Penny took off her raincoat revealing her outfit and slipped into her high heels.

"Whoooa, Ms. Albright! Look at you! Are you into that stuff too?" Danny asked in a surprised tone.

"This is just for this evening," Penny responded quickly. "So that I don't stand out from the crowd."

"Don't believe her, fellas. She likes that ponyboy stuff, where the woman rides around on the man's shoulders and treats the guy as if he's her horse," Kerby teased, but with a straight face.

"Don't listen to him. He thinks he's funny," Penny muttered, looking back to see the Doral Cruiser coasting toward the bulkhead.

"I don't believe this. Do you realize where we are?" Jean asked with her mouth agape as Niki's eyes followed the spotlight beam down to her mother's warehouse.

"I told you Nemesis is guiding our every move. It's a poetic coincidence that we would wind up here tonight on our fifth anniversary," Niki insisted.

"It's a *bizarre* coincidence," Jean shot back. "In fact, it's almost too bizarre to be a coincidence."

"What are you ladies taking about? What's a coincidence?" Damian inquired.

"Nothing, baby, nothing you would understand anyway," Niki answered. "You just flex your muscles and look good. Get ready to suck a few toes."

"Would you mind grabbing our line?" Niki hollered to Penny as Jean tossed the line ashore. Penny pulled the idling boat in and held it in place while Damian jumped from the boat, clad only in his leather bikini bottom and leather face mask, he secured the boat in place.

"I'd recognize that voice anywhere," Danny announced, staring through the darkness, looking at Niki and totally ignoring Damian, despite his unusual and revealing outfit.

"I thought Mean Jean was going to be with her," Peter said.

"That's right," Danny remembered. "They did you before Jean changed her look. Believe it or not, that's Mean Jean right next to Niki on the boat."

"You've got to be kidding me. She looks like she's doing more steroids than I did," Peter commented as Damian helped Jean and then Niki off the boat in their high heels.

"Thanks so much, and thanks for the offer of help back in the bay," Niki said to Penny. "With the raincoat on I couldn't tell that you were on your way here too. I was afraid that you might think I was some kind of a nut, riding around New York Harbor in a latex cat suit with a naked man onboard," Niki finished, laughing.

"I wish I could have pushed her into the water," a disappointed Danny said to Kerby. "I'll bet it would have really freaked her out knowing that she was in the water with me and Peter right below her."

"The evening's not over yet, son," Kerby reminded Danny. "Don't give up hope."

"We'd better get inside before my *foot sucker* here catches a chill. We don't want any shrinkage of that bulge now do we, baby?" Niki taunted Damian.

"I don't believe that we've ever met," Jean said to Penny, eyeing her suspiciously, as the group made its way to the warehouse entrance. "I'm Domina Agony and this is my friend, Lady Kat. Are you new to the business?"

The question caught Penny by surprise. "Very new," Penny stammered. "My name is Mistress Penelope. I'm a friend of Maitresse Joie. You might say that she's my mentor."

"You couldn't have picked a better teacher. Do you have a specialty, you know, a way of punishing a man that turns you on more than anything else?" Jean asked, sounding almost as if she were quizzing Penny on her knowledge of the profession.

"Actually, I'm a . . . a Riding Mistress," Penny blurted, expressing the first thought that came to her mind. I'm into the human equine thing, you know, the ponyboy stuff. To be totally honest with you, nothing gets me hotter than stripping a man naked, putting a harness in his mouth, and riding around on his shoulders while I whip his bare ass with a riding crop," Penny continued, trying to sound as convincing as possible.

"See, I told you," Kerby cracked to Danny and Peter, but loud enough for Penny to hear. The three looked over at Penny and chuckled. Penny looked embarrassed while shooting Kerby a stern look and shaking her head.

"No offense, Mr. Brewster, but if stripping me naked and riding around on my shoulders would make *her* happy, I'd be whinnying around the room like Trigger every night," Peter said enthusiastically.

"Settle down, son, she already has a pony," Kerby replied.

Penny stopped and stared in amazement as the group entered the warehouse. "Is this your first time at a gala? They're quite spectacular, don't you think?" Jean asked as they made their way into the building.

"I'm speechless!" Penny exclaimed.

Inside, the warehouse looked like a cross between a medieval torture chamber and an S&M industry convention. The room was crowded with women, all dressed in black leather or black latex, and men, all of who were in various stages of undress. The only male that Penny spotted who was more covered than not was a guy wrapped in a tight-fitting latex outfit that covered him from head to toe, including his eyes and nose. It appeared that the only thing preventing the guy from suffocating to death was a breathing tube which had been stuck into an opening near his mouth.

Almost all of the men in the room wore thick leather dog collars around their necks, and many wore shackles around their ankles or handcuffs on their wrists. Almost all of the females carried whips or riding crops or wooden switches with them and most seemed to look for any excuse to use them.

The only male subs that Penny saw who were not being led around naked by their Mistresses, were restrained in one way or another in various places throughout the warehouse. Two male slaves were secured naked to St. Andrew's crosses at the far end of the room. Two others were restrained spread-eagle on bondage tables on either side of the room, one face up and the other face down. In the far left corner of the room, a nude male was secured to a whipping post and in the corner opposite him was a naked man with his arms and head locked in a stockade, both were in the process of receiving demonstration lashings from their Mistresses. In the near left corner of the building opposite the entrance, Penny saw a naked man standing up in a cage that was just big enough to fit his body. Opposite the caged guy, in the other near corner was a nude male hung from the ceiling in a bungee-cord-like sling that ensured that his arms and legs remained spread outward and upward.

"I told you it was weird in here," Danny commented.

"Why am I not surprised that Mean Jean and Niki would be invited to something like this?" Peter added.

Maitresse Joie rushed to the door as soon as she saw Penny enter with Niki and Jean. "You look incredible, sweetie," Joie gushed. "And I see you've already met Domina Agony and friends after all of your inquiries."

Penny looked stunned by the comment from Joie and waited nervously for Jean to say something. "Inquiries about me? From where do you know me?" Jean quizzed Penny in a very serious tone.

"Your reputation precedes you," Penny responded.

"She has a real fascination with your specialty," Joie chimed in. "I've told her all about you, but the truth is that I think that when she sees what you actually do, she'll find it a little extreme for her tastes, at least this early in her career."

"I don't believe that it's an acquired taste. You're either born with a love for it or you're not. Regardless, you are welcome to come up to *Studio Pain* and see it up close and personal any time you'd like," Jean offered, now with less concern in her voice. "But I have to warn you that it is not for the squeamish."

"I'll say it's not," Danny cracked.

"I'd love to catch you at work," Penny said smiling.

"Yeah, like maybe tonight," Kerby added.

"Like I said, any time," Jean repeated.

"Too bad, Domina Agony was going to demonstrate some CBT tonight, but she had a change in plans. She and her friend are going to be using this fine looking specimen for a foot worship and trampling demonstration instead. Isn't that right, deary?" Joie said to Jean, while eyeing Damian as if he were a special dessert.

"They're saving the CBT for later," Peter noted before Jean or Niki could answer.

"That's right, and I think I could use a little refreshment before we start," Niki announced as the trio headed for a bar and buffet table that had been set up along the left sidewall.

"I think I could use a drink too," Penny whispered to Kerby. "I think the McCloone girl is suspicious for some reason. She's making me nervous."

"Go right ahead, have one to calm your nerves," Kerby suggested. "Just do me a favor and stay away from the tequila."

The evening moved by quickly with hardly a dull moment. An all-female heavy-metal rock band dressed in black leather played rock music on and off throughout the evening. Before the band started, a slave auction was held, during which several Mistresses paraded their naked slaves on a makeshift stage and offered them up for an evening of enjoyment to the highest bidder. Joie was insistent on bidding for one particularly well built slave and giving him to Penny for the night, but Penny finally convinced Joie that she planned on limiting her first experience to that of spectator.

Throughout the evening, Kerby and Penny, along with Danny and Peter, kept close watch on Niki, Jean, and Damian while the festivities and demonstrations went on. About an hour into the evening, Danny and Peter begged out, first indicating that it was all a little too bizarre for them, but finally admitting that the reason they really wanted to get outside was to get onto Niki's ultramodern yacht and see what the cabin looked like.

Shortly after Danny and Peter left the warehouse, Niki and Jean stripped Damian of his leather bikini and did their trampling and foot worshiping thing with him. First, they laid him down on the floor in front of the crowd of envious Mistresses who had been admiring his flawless, heavily muscled body all night and were even more jealous now that his sizable package was on full display. Then, together they walked up and down Damian's prone and willing body from his groin to his neck. They even took turns standing on his face with their bare feet, each helping to balance the other when it was her turn.

Finally, they had Damian get on all fours while they placed one chair in front of him and another behind him. While Damian massaged and licked and sucked the feet and toes of the one who sat in front of him, the other sat behind him and rubbed his scrotum and manhood with her feet from underneath. When one was done, they switched places. Damian was a more than willing participant for the entire demonstration, at times growling like a wild man on the verge of orgasm, but neither girl would let him off the hook. "You're going to have to wait until later for that, baby," Niki whispered into Damian's ear as they finished their performance.

After the foot worshiping demonstration, Joie approached Penny just as a real "collaring ceremony" was about to be performed. "Watch, you'll enjoy this, sweetie," Joie alerted Penny.

"What's a *collaring ceremony*?" Penny asked.

The collar that you see the male submissives wearing means they are owned by their Mistresses. There is nothing more significant in this lifestyle than the collar worn by an owned submissive. It's the outward symbol of the commitments made by the dominant and submissive and marks the submissive as the property of the dominant, kind of like a wedding ring is for our counterparts in the real world. You see, the collaring ceremony is like a wedding ceremony, except in the collaring ceremony the submissive agrees to become the property of the dominant."

Penny was fascinated by the ceremony which played out at an altar in the front part of the warehouse. A woman stood at the altar dressed in a black leather wedding gown, carrying a short whip in her left hand and a thick leather dog collar in her right. On either side of her were two women wearing black leather bridesmaids' gowns. A man wearing a hooded white cotton robe approached the woman in the center. He carried a leash in his right hand and a single red rose in his left.

When the male reached the altar, the bridesmaids approached him from either side and together removed the robe from his body, leaving him stark naked in front of the gathering. The now naked man then knelt before the woman, offered her the leash, and in an elaborate speech expressed his desire to belong to the woman, which she in turn accepted. The woman then expressed her desire for ownership of the male and asked whether he would agree to wear her collar as a symbol of the fact that he was now her property. The naked male agreed and lowered his head so that the female could place the collar around his neck.

When he raised his head, the woman attached the leash to the male's collar and said, "You now belong to me, and with this leash I will lead you wherever I choose and you will obediently follow." The male then offered the woman the red rose and said, "I kneel naked before you as a sign of my submission to you, and I willingly accept the symbol of your ownership that you place around my neck. I will wear it proudly, for I now belong to you." When the ceremony was over, the female led the naked male away at the end of the leash.

"That was sweet. I liked that," Penny smiled, looking at Kerby who stuck his finger down his throat as if he were about to make himself vomit.

"I can tell you one thing," Joie said. "A smaller percentage of people who take these vows break them than do people who take marriage vows."

Penny suddenly realized that during the collaring ceremony she had completely lost track of Niki, Jean, and Damian. When she looked around the room, she spotted them at the bar with a bottle of champagne.

"Don't worry, I was watching them the whole time you were getting misty-eyed watching the lady put the dog collar and leash on the guy," Kerby joked.

"There's something about her," Jean said to Niki, referring to Penny. "She doesn't look like a femdom to me, and every time I look over there, she has her eye on me."

"You're too paranoid. You heard what Joie said about her being fascinated with what you do. Maybe she likes you. She's awfully pretty. You know what the rules of our relationship are. I wouldn't be jealous if you wanted to make a move on her," Niki assured Jean. "Why don't you ask her for her phone number?"

"You're right, she is beautiful, but it's not that I'm attracted to her. There's something about her that's just not right," Jean said suspiciously. "I'm going to talk to the Maitresse and see whether she knows any more about her."

"The last thing on the schedule is the human animal demonstration," Joie said to Penny.

"Oh good, I bet you'll love this one," Kerby commented, smiling as he and Penny started toward the corner of the warehouse where people were gathering for the last demonstration. Joie, who had seen Jean waving for her, headed in the opposite direction toward the bar.

When they got to the corner of the warehouse where the demonstration was starting, Kerby stood to the right of a tall, attractive, redheaded Mistress, and Penny stood directly to Kerby's right. On the far side of the demonstration area they could see a naked guy kneeling in a dog cage, sipping water out of a dog bowl. A dominatrix was sitting on top of the cage with her long legs crossed. In the center of the demonstration area, another femdom, dressed in black riding clothes, complete with black leather riding boots and a black velveteen riding helmet, was placing an undersized horse bridal on a naked man.

"Where the heck did she get a thing like that to fit a human being?" Kerby wondered, watching in fascination as the dominatrix placed her foot into a stirrup and raised herself onto the guy's shoulders as if mounting a real horse.

While Kerby watched the human equine demonstration, Joie pulled Penny by her arm to get her attention. "Did you and Domina Agony have words or something?" Joie asked.

"Of course not," Penny assured Joie. "Why do you ask?"

"She asked me a bunch of questions about how I knew you and what you were like, and when I mentioned that you were the psychic who had located those missing bodies, she got all red in the face, grabbed her friends, and left in a huff," Joie explained.

"She left? You mean she's gone?" Penny asked, looking around the room frantically to see if she could find them.

"All three of them just ran out the door," Joie answered.

"Oh no!" Penny exclaimed, turning and running for the door as fast as she could. Outside, Penny looked toward the bulkhead and saw Damian Bradford jumping onto the Doral Cruiser with a baffled look on his face. Niki and Jean were standing in their high heels on the bulkhead waiting for Damian to help them aboard.

Penny turned suddenly after realizing that Kerby was not with her. She stuck her head back into the warehouse. "Kerby, let's go, they're getting away." Penny screamed. Then she turned and ran toward the Doral Cruiser, hoping she could delay the girls until Kerby got there.

Nearing the yacht, Penny spotted Danny and Peter sitting on the rail of the boat with their feet resting on the bulkhead. By now, Damian had each girl by an arm and started to assist them onto the boat together, but as he did so, the boys stretched their legs, pushing the boat away from the bulkhead with their feet. As the two girls jumped for the boat in their heels, the yacht suddenly drifted away from them, and they both plunged into the filthy, smelly, murky water of the Kill Van Kull.

"I told you loosening the lines would work," Danny said proudly to Peter as they looked down at the girls whose heads had just broken the surface, each spitting out a large mouthful of the filthy water.

"Get me out of here!" Niki screamed, reaching her arms up to Damian who was hanging over the rail.

"Get me up! Get me up!" Jean wailed while fighting Niki to see who would be the first one pulled into the boat.

Then, as if both girls had the same thought at exactly the same moment in time, they turned and stared into each other's eyes. "This is right where we dumped the bodies," Jean gasped. "They're right beneath us."

"I felt something on my leg." Niki cried out in a panicked voice. "Do you feel that? There's something touching my leg."

"I feel it! I feel it! Get us out of here!" Jean shrieked, again reaching for Damian to pull her up.

"Would you two relax and try to help me?" Damian said calmly, grabbing each girl by the arm and trying to pull them up together. "You don't have to be afraid. There's nothing down there except maybe some raw sewage," Damian continued, still in a calm voice as if he saw nothing wrong with swimming in a pool of raw sewage

While the girls were fighting each other to get into the boat, Penny stopped short of the bulkhead and looked back for Kerby. *Where the heck is he?* Penny wondered before it dawned on her. *Oh no, I've gotten too far away from him. I've put him in purgatory*, Penny realized, turning and running back to the warehouse as fast as she could.

At the warehouse door, Penny looked back toward Niki's yacht and saw Damian pulling the girls up to the top of the rail, where they pulled themselves over and onto the boat. Danny and Peter were in the boat laughing the entire time. As she barged into the warehouse, Penny heard the engine of the Doral Cruiser roar and the boat speed away from the shoreline.

CHAPTER 14

A DATE WITH A LADY
JUNE 25, 2003

*O*ne instant Kerby Brewster was minding his own business watching some guy being whipped and ridden like a horse, the next he was standing in the middle of a desolate wasteland, that he had come to call purgatory. *Don't move,* Kerby thought to himself. *If she remembers exactly where you were when she left and she comes back soon enough, who knows, maybe there's still a chance you will get out of here.* But as the seconds ticked by with no sign of Penny, Kerby felt less and less hope that he would ever find his way out of the wasteland.

Penny searched the room urgently with her eyes, but Kerby was nowhere to be found. *Dear God, don't let him be gone,* Penny prayed to herself, making her way quickly to the human equine demonstration without seeing any sign of Kerby. *Where was he when I last saw him?* Penny wondered, looking around for something to jog her memory. *There, he was standing right there next to the redhead when Joie pulled my arm,* Penny remembered, and she raced for the spot.

Penny was in mid-stride when she hit the spot next to the redhead and found herself nose to nose with Kerby. Kerby caught her in his arms and she felt a huge sense of relief along with the warm electricity that pulsed through her body. Kerby felt the same sense of relief when he found himself back in the warehouse with Penny snug in his embrace.

"Are you trying to get rid of me, kiddo?" Kerby whispered. "Because if you are, I'm going to have to hold on to you like this all the time to make sure you don't get away."

"No way! I don't want to lose you already. I'm just starting to like you," Penny replied, as people around her began staring in her direction, wondering to whom she was talking and why she was hugging the air.

"You'd better keep it down, kiddo. People are starting to stare. You don't want these nice people to think there is something weird about you, do you?" Kerby remarked with a smile.

Penny explained what had happened as they made their way out of the warehouse and onto Sol's yacht.

"Where are the boys?" Kerby asked.

"They were on the boat with the girls when I saw them last," Penny replied.

"Good, then even if the girls haven't changed their minds about what they plan on doing to the masked man, he's still got a chance if the boys are with him."

"You don't think that they would go ahead with their plans, do you?" Penny asked.

"Serial killers become more and more narcissistic with each kill. No matter how careful they are when they first start, as time goes by without them being caught, they start believing that they have some kind of protection from above and that they can't be caught. Laymen believe that serial killers keep doing what they do and start taking greater risks because they really want to get caught. But the experts will tell you that the reason serial killers get sloppy is because they start believing that they can't be caught," Kerby explained. "If our girls are true narcissists, and I believe that they are, they'll go ahead with what they had planned."

Niki left her running lights off as she made her way full throttle down the Kill Van Kull. She was hoping to prevent Penny from being able to tell whether she had turned north or south as she entered Upper New York Bay. Approaching the mouth of the bay, Niki found another reason to be happy that she had left her lights off. A large blue and white vessel from the NYPD Harbor Unit was cutting across the mouth of the river heading north toward Manhattan. Niki cut her speed to give the Harbor Unit boat time to clear and then increased her speed again.

Upon entering the bay, Niki turned south toward New Jersey and opened up the throttle to its top speed again. Within minutes they were passing under the span of the Verrazano Narrows Bridge into Lower New York Bay, and heading directly for the Sandy Hook area of Gateway National Park.

"North or south?" Penny asked, exiting the Kill Van Kull, just as Niki's boat had cleared the Verrazano Narrows Bridge into Lower New York Bay.

Before Kerby could answer, Penny looked to the north and saw the large blue NYPD letters on the stern of the Harbor Unit vessel as it finished its circle of Governor's Island and started cruising north again. Without saying a word, Penny blasted her trumpet horn and started behind the Harbor Unit boat. The police boat dropped its speed immediately, and Penny closed in on it quickly. As she neared the boat's stern, Penny was able to make out Francona, Slowinski, and Reggie at the back rail of the boat. Penny shifted her boat into neutral and drifted alongside the Harbor Unit vessel.

"Where the heck have you been?" Penny shouted.

"We've been cruising around the New York area waterways all night looking for and your friends," Francona hollered back. "The question is where have you been?"

"I left a detailed note on Stan's windshield telling him exactly where we would be and even letting him know that you would need a boat in order to follow the girls," Penny answered.

Francona looked at Stan who looked confused. "There was nothing on my windshield," Slowinski asserted adamantly. Then he remembered the parking ticket. "Except . . . I did get a parking ticket. I guess her note could have been under the ticket when I lifted it off the windshield, but I never saw it."

"That's spilt milk now," Francona said, turning back to Penny. "Do you have any idea where they may be now?"

"I was at a party with them at a warehouse on the Kill Van Kull in Staten Island. The warehouse at which the party was held belongs to Nikita Bach's mother. The bodies of the boys are in the river alongside the warehouse. Someone at the party told the girls I was the clairvoyant who had located the bodies in Turtle Pond and the Hudson River, and they apparently put two and two together and made a run for it in their boat."

"The guy at the marina where Bach's boat was docked told me that after the party the girls were going to Cape May for the weekend. But we just finished searching the coastline in Central Jersey and the Sandy Hook and Raritan Bays looking for their boat, and we didn't see them. If they had headed south recently, they would have had to have gone by us," Francona opined, not knowing that he had just missed the girls as they exited the Kill Van Kull.

"If somehow we missed them, we have a chopper flying down the rest of the Jersey coastline to Cape May and back. The chopper should spot them if they're headed that way. But my guess is that they must have changed plans and headed north, either up the Hudson River or the East River. We'll run up the East River and see if we spot them. Why don't you take Stan and look for them up the Hudson?" Francona suggested.

"Why don't I take Reggie and look for them up the Hudson?" Penny responded.

"Fine with me," Francona replied as Reggie balanced herself on the port rail of the Harbor Unit boat and then leapt agilely onto Penny's boat.

♥ ⚓ ♟

At the moment that Penny's vessel and Francona's vessel split at the confluence of the Hudson River and the East River, the Doral Cruiser was just reaching the tip of the Sandy Hook peninsula. Niki Bach turned right, away from the open ocean and into Sandy Hook Bay. She rode the west coast of the Sandy Hook peninsula down to an area known as Horseshoe Cove, where she swung around the curved lip of the cove, so that the boat could not be seen from the bay. Then she cut her engine and anchored.

"Great! Can we do this now?" Damian asked urgently. "I could really use some relief."

"We need to get this muck off us first. Strip, get on the bed and get ready while Jean and I shower. We have something special planned for you, baby," Niki promised, struggling out of her gooey, wet, latex outfit.

In an instant, Damian was on the bed naked with his manhood standing at full attention. Jean, who had already taken off her corset and skirt and was wrapped in a towel, handcuffed Damian's wrists to the posts on either side of the top of the bed while she waited for Niki to finish undressing.

"We need to talk about this," Jean insisted, when she was done securing Damian to the bedposts.

"Calm down! We'll talk in the shower. Unless you'd prefer to talk in front of him," Niki whispered, nodding her head in Damian's direction.

"It doesn't matter, it's not as if he's going anywhere now," Jean pointed out.

"She looks even better than she used to," Danny remarked to Peter, referring to Niki's now naked body. "She's put on a little weight up on top."

"I wouldn't know. I never got that far," Peter replied as he and Danny followed the girls into a small bathroom on the right side of the cabin.

One side of the bathroom was occupied by a shower stall that was just big enough for two people. Opposite the shower stall was a sink, and on the far wall was a toilet. Niki reached in and turned the water on in the shower. Then she checked to make sure that the water was just hot enough without being too hot before she stepped in. Jean followed immediately behind Niki, pulling the doors to the shower stall closed behind her. Their bodies rubbed against each other as they jostled for space under the showerhead in the cramped stall.

"We can't go through with this now," Jean said. "As much as I would like to after seeing him naked and bound on that bed with a full blown erection, we cannot go through with this after what just happened!"

"Relax, babe! If you think about it, nothing just happened, except that we panicked for no good reason. I admit that it's all a little too much to be coincidence, but so what if this self-proclaimed psychic set up the evening? At this point, we don't even know if she knows that Danny and Peter are down there. If she knows where *their* bodies are, why hasn't she told the police yet? If she's established some credibility with the police, based upon her locating the other bodies, the police would have been in that water in a minute, and you know that we would have heard about it right away. Danny's mom would have had it in the newspapers the next day. If the psychic said anything to the police about the bodies or suspicions about us being involved, why weren't the police there tonight? Believe me if they had been, we would have never gotten out of there as easily as we did," Niki noted, massaging Jean's scalp, in part to shampoo the gunk out of her hair and in part to soothe her nerves.

"Okay, so she hasn't said anything to the police yet about Danny and Peter or about us, and they haven't located the boys' bodies yet. What if she goes to the police tonight and tells them where the bodies are and that she suspects us? What if a diver goes down tomorrow and finds the bodies? What do we do then?"

"It's like I said yesterday, even if they find the boys' bodies, they have no physical evidence linking us to the murders. It's a weak circumstantial evidence case, at best, that no prosecutor in her right mind would ever bring before a jury," Niki assured Jean.

"Okay, if they can't prove anything based upon what's already happened, then explain to me why we should put ourselves in jeopardy by risking something new tonight?"

"Because there is no real risk involved. My plan is to prepare Damian right here, while things quiet down up above in Upper New York Bay. I mean, it's not as if the psychic is going to be cruising around all night by herself looking for us. It's clear that the police are not involved in this thing yet, so doing Damian tonight, even in the shadow of the Statue of Liberty, is really not a risk at all."

"But what about tomorrow, when people start to wonder where Damian Bradford is?" Jean asked.

"So what, nobody knows that Damian Bradford is with us," Niki reminded Jean. "The beauty of the whole thing is that nobody knows who it was that was with us tonight, and given the circumstances of the evening, people will certainly understand why we would want to keep that person anonymous. More important, they are not going to find Damian Bradford's body, and there is no way that they are going to try anyone for Damian Bradford's murder without a body."

"We can't have any of his blood on the boat, or they may be able to match his DNA," Jean said after a long pause, making it clear that she was coming along on the idea of going through with the murder.

"You said yourself that your needle plan will not cause much blood. But you'll need to be extra careful when you make your incision in the scrotum. Once he's dead, I plan on cruising out into the Atlantic and dumping his body out where they'll never find it. Then we'll head down to Cape May. We can have dinner right on the boat tonight, and we'll have all weekend and then some to clean up the boat before we start home. Bleach destroys DNA evidence," Niki explained.

"All right then, if you're up for it, so am I," Jean relented.

"I'm more than up for it. My adrenalin is pumping like mad. I'm almost glad it's happening this way. It makes it that much more exciting. I was actually starting to get bored with the whole thing. I know that the genital torture is what turns you on, but what I have enjoyed most has been committing the perfect murders. The thrill of the chase just adds to the excitement for me." Niki explained. "I don't worry about getting caught because I know Nemesis is watching over us."

"Did you hear all that?" Peter asked Danny.

"I sure did," Danny answered.

"What do you think we should do?" Peter wondered.

"I think we should start by prolonging their shower a little bit and making sure that the water stays hot enough for them. My dad used have a fishing boat, and I can tell you that there is a limited amount of water pressure on a boat. Do you know what happens on a boat when someone's taking a hot shower and somebody else turns on the cold water?" Danny asked.

"I can imagine," Peter answered, making his way out to the kitchen area to turn on the cold water.

Once Peter was in the kitchen, Danny took the toilet paper holder from its spot and placed it through the door handles where the doors to the shower stall met. When he heard Peter turn the water on in the kitchen sink, Danny turned the water on in the bathroom sink.

Almost immediately both girls began screaming frantically. The scalding hot water poured down onto the two girls who had no room within the tight shower stall to avoid the spray. Jean threw her body at the shower stall doors, but they opened only slightly before closing shut again.

"Turn off that fucking cold water you fucking half-wit," Niki screamed at the top of her lungs, reaching desperately to turn the water off, while at the same time trying her best to avoid the stinging spray.

"It can't be him. He's handcuffed to the bed," Jean shouted, throwing her body at the shower stall doors again, this time with Niki following right behind her. The toilet paper holder slipped free and both girls flew headfirst into the sink opposite the shower before falling hard to the floor of the bathroom which was now filling with steam.

Niki got up from the floor and reached in carefully to turn off the hot water in the shower. Then she turned off the water in the bathroom sink. "How the hell did this get on?" Niki snarled.

As Jean sat on the floor tending to her severely bruised knees and elbows, Niki looked up from the sink and found herself staring at her reflection in the mirror above the sink. She saw a huge bump forming on the right side of her head just above her eye, where her forehead had crashed into the base of the sink. By the time she stopped watching, the bump was the size of a fist and a nasty yellowish purple in color.

Both girls wrapped towels around themselves and rushed into the cabin, half expecting to find Damian Bradford at the kitchen sink, but when they got there, he was still handcuffed to the bed with a huge grin and an erection to match.

"Are you two ready now?" Damian smiled before he saw Niki's eye. "Holey shit, Niki! What happened to you? That is one ugly bump you got there."

"Don't worry about what happened to me. It's what's going to happen to you that you need worry about," Niki growled, glaring at Damian before turning to Jean. "Get your needles, let's give him a little taste of what's in store for him later."

"Just give me a second. I think I may have fractured my left knee cap," Jean moaned, easing herself down onto a cushioned bench that ran alongside the dinette table nearest the wall.

Jean felt the pinch of the needle entering into her right buttock the minute that she started to sit down, but it was too late to stop. The momentum from her body weight forced her down onto the bench and the nine-inch needle made its way all the way up into her right butt cheek before she was able to jump back up, howling in pain. When she reached a standing position, her knee gave out and she collapsed to the floor in agony.

"Get it out! Get it out!" Jean screeched to Niki, kneeling on all fours despite the agonizing pain in her knee.

"Good placement," Danny complimented Peter with a smile.

"I assumed one of them would sit there eventually," Peter replied.

"Get what out?" Niki asked when she reached Jean.

"That asshole must have been fooling around with my needles," Jean squealed through gnashed teeth as she pointed Niki to the needle that was nine inches into her ass cheek.

"Oh my goodness! That must hurt!" Niki exclaimed while slowly easing the needle out of Jean's behind.

"Give it to me," Jean demanded, snatching the needle out of Niki's hand and hobbling over to Damian on the bed. "You like playing with these things?" Jean screamed, her face only inches from Damian's face.

"I didn't touch the damn thing. I haven't gotten off this freaking bed. How could I?" Damian shouted back.

But it was too late for explanations. Jean had Damian's penis in one hand and the needle in the other, and she jammed the needle right through the head of Damian's organ from back to front. Damian was shocked by the sight of the needle entering into one side of his manhood and coming out the other, but the needle was so fine and Jean had jabbed it through so quickly that, other than the initial pinch, there was very little sensation.

Damian waited for a second, expecting an excruciating pain and lots of blood, but neither came. He finally looked up at Niki. "Is that going to cause a scar?" Damian asked. "That better not cause a scar, Niki."

"You don't have to worry about scarring, baby. As of tomorrow, the only ones seeing your penis will be the fish in the Atlantic Ocean," Niki hollered.

Damian was looking back and forth from Niki to his penis, which was still erect and only stinging slightly. "Why, are we going to skinny dip off the boat tomorrow?" Damian asked.

"You fucking dolt, don't you get it yet?" Jean screamed.

"What did you call me, a colt?" Damian asked.

"No, I didn't call you a colt. I called you a fucking dolt, an idiot," Jean blared.

"Calm down, I only asked because I used to have a girlfriend who called me her stallion," Damian explained. "I thought maybe you were thinking the same way."

"You have no idea how much I am going to enjoy the next few hours," Jean shrieked, staring into Damian's eyes threateningly.

"Great! Are you girls finally ready to get started? I know I am, but you had better pull that thing out first," Damian said. "Otherwise this is not going to work."

Exhausted, Jean ignored the comment, hobbled back to the bench and checked for more needles before she sat down again.

"It's been long enough, let's cruise up to the Statue of Liberty and do this," Niki hissed, making her way to the stairs out of the cabin.

"Here we go," Danny said as the boys followed Niki to the stairs staring down at her bare feet as she started up the steps.

"Damn, a near miss," Peter groaned, after watching Niki bring her left foot down inches away from another one of Jean's needles which Danny had secured point upward into a slat in the third stair.

"She still has to come down," Danny pointed out.

"Don't start until I come back down," Niki hollered into the cabin as she set course for the Statue of Liberty. Jean had just finished tying Damian's ankles to the bottom corners of the bed.

♥ ⚡ ⚓

A short time later, Niki was pulling her boat around to the front of the Statue of Liberty, so that Lady Liberty appeared to be looking down into the boat. She anchored the boat at the center point between Ellis Island and Governor's Island, about three quarters of the way from the tip of Manhattan to Liberty Island.

When Jean felt the boat come to a stop, she hobbled to the top of the stairs, missing the needle on the third step by a hair.

"You can't get any closer than that," a dejected Peter said.

"It's magnificent," Jean exclaimed, looking up at Lady Liberty. "It's so much bigger in real life than it looks in pictures."

"I didn't want to get too close. With the 9/11 tragedy, I'm sure there's lots of security on Liberty Island. I don't want anyone thinking that we may be terrorists or they'll search the boat," Niki explained as the girls finished admiring the statue and headed for the stairs.

"We wouldn't want that to happen," Danny said to Peter as the girls started down the stairs one at a time, the boys following close behind in anticipation of one of the two girls stepping on the needle. Jean's right foot landed just to the right of the needle, and Niki's left foot followed just to the left of it.

"Do you think maybe we should have put it to one side or the other instead of right in the middle?" Peter wondered.

"It's sure starting to look that way," a disappointed Danny muttered as the boys followed Niki and Jean into the cabin.

"Do you think you could take that thing out now?" Damian asked Niki who was approaching the bed while Jean went to get the rest of her needles. "I mean, were not going to be able to do anything with that thing in there, and it is starting to sting."

"Get this through that fucking airhead of yours. Any pleasures that you've had in life are over. What little time you have left on this planet is going to be spent in pain that will be excruciating for you and exquisite for us," Niki snarled.

"Is this all part of the game?" Damian asked.

"Yes, but you are no longer an active participant in the game. From here on in we are the players, and you are nothing more than a toy for us to play with," Jean answered, hoping to finally strike fear into Damian.

Instead, Damian gave her back a blank stare. "All right, as long as it's all part of the game," Damian replied. "I don't know whether Niki told you or not, but I'm always up for new sexual experiences."

"Fuckhead!" Niki screamed into Damian's face. "This is not going to be a new sexual experience for you. Do you see those needles? Jean is going to skewer your dick with every one of them and then she's going to heat them and burn your cock from the inside out."

"That sounds as if it's going to hurt, Niki. I told you this one is starting to sting really badly," Damian said "And I don't want anything that's going to cause any scarring."

Exasperated, Niki turned to Jean. "Just do it. He'll start to understand once you get started."

"Is this guy for real?" Danny wondered as Jean put a ball gag into Damian's mouth.

"I don't know, but either way, we can't let them use his manhood as a pincushion," Peter said, making his way out of the cabin.

As Jean finished securing the ball gag and hobbling back to the table to get her needles, wincing all the way, Danny was in the process of raising the anchor on the boat. Once he had it up, he signaled to Peter, who wedged a pencil into the lever for the boat's electronic signal horn.

Jean was just about to pierce Damian's member with her second needle when she was startled by the incredibly loud horn which broke the silence of the New York night, echoing in a cacophony around New York Harbor. The girls stared at each other, stunned by the piercing sound of the horn.

"What the hell is that now?" Niki shouted before she raced toward the stairs.

This time when Niki's bare left foot came down onto the third step she felt the needle enter the bottom of her foot and slide up into the arch until it hit the talus bone. On impact with the bottom of the talus bone, the needle snapped off inside Niki's foot. Her scream was almost as loud as the horn as her body toppled backwards down the steps, with Niki hopping on her right foot, trying desperately not to put the left foot down. At the bottom of the steps, Niki continued to hop backwards for several feet before finally losing her balance completely and falling ass first to the floor. She slammed her left elbow against the kitchen sink as she crashed to the floor, then she slid backward until the back of her head smashed into the baseboard of the berth.

Though neither boy saw what had happened, both knew immediately the cause of Niki's squealing. "Bulls-eye!" Peter shouted to Danny, and they raced for the cabin so as not to miss the fun below.

Niki lay at the base of the bed screaming in pain while a confused Jean was trying to get off of the bed without stepping on Niki. When she was finally down from the bed, Jean began hobbling toward the cabin exit.

"Where the fuck are you going?" Niki screamed at Jean.

Jean stopped at the bottom of the stairs leading out of the cabin and turned back to Niki. "I'm going to try to turn the horn off," Jean said.

"Fuck the horn! Get this fucking thing out of me!" Niki demanded. "You're the one who's dropping these fucking needles all over the place."

"I didn't drop anything. Your meathead boyfriend there must have been playing with the damn things," Jean insisted, trying to find a piece of the needle in Niki's foot that was big enough to grab hold of. The boat horn continued to blare outside.

"I see it but I need tweezers," Jean noted.

"Well, then get a pair of fucking tweezers out of your bag and get it the fuck out of me," Niki hissed.

"Don't you think I should turn the horn off first?" Jean asked, taking a pair of tweezers out of her bag.

"It's killing me! Fuck the horn! Get it out! Get it out now!" Niki shrieked as the color drained from her face and beads of cold sweat began to form on her forehead.

"Fine!" Jean relented, sitting back on the floor and squinting as she aimed the tweezers for the tiny piece of needle sticking out of the arch of Niki's foot.

Jean had finally gotten hold of the needle with the tweezers and began slowly easing it out of Niki's foot when the boat crashed into the boulder strewn shoreline that surrounds Liberty Island. Jean's body lunged forward, pushing the needle and the tweezers deeper into Niki's foot, causing her to wail even louder.

Niki stopped howling suddenly when she heard the sound of sirens and helicopter blades drowning out the screeching horn.

"Come out of the cabin with your hands up," a barely audible voice shouted through a megaphone.

"We're heeere!" Danny announced.

"Historic Liberty Island," Peter added.

"Oh shit!" Niki whimpered.

"I knew I should I should have turned off that horn first," Jean sniveled.

Jean and Niki exited the cabin, but not with their hands up. They needed their hands and arms to hold onto the walls and then the rails of the boat to prevent themselves from falling down. Once out of the cabin, the girls were met by swirling spotlights from Liberty Island, a Coast Guard Cutter that sat off their port side and a NYPD helicopter that was hovering above the boat. Several armed officers were on shore with automatic weapons aimed at the girls, believing that they might be terrorists. Several seamen on board the Coast Guard cutter also had automatic weapons pointed at them.

Penny's Sabreline Cruiser sat to the starboard side of the Doral Cruiser with Penny, Kerby, and Reggie at the rail. Reggie had her badge high in the air and had just finished explaining to the Coast Guard Captain what was going on.

Danny and Peter came out from the cabin directly behind the girls. "Have you boys been misbehaving?" Kerby asked with a smile.

"You know what they say, Mr. Brewster, 'Boys will be boys,'" Danny answered, also with a smile.

"How's the masked man?" Kerby wondered. "Did he make it?"

"He made it all right, but he's a little tied up down there, if you know what I mean?" Danny replied.

"And he does have what looks to me like a very painful injury, though he's taking it like a man," Peter added.

"Damian Bradford's below deck. He's alive, but he's hurt," Penny told Reggie.

"Now how would you know that?" Reggie wondered, climbing to the top of the rail.

"Don't forget, I'm psychic," Penny reminded Reggie as Reggie leapt onto the Doral Cruiser.

Below-deck, Reggie's eyes bulged from her head and her jaw dropped open when she saw Damian Bradford totally naked and bound to the bed with the ball gag in his mouth, the needle still through the head of his manhood.

Reggie took the ball gag out of Damian's mouth first. "That must really hurt, honey. Let me see if I can help you," Reggie offered, gently taking Damian's now flaccid organ in one hand and easing the needle out with the other. "Does that feel better, baby?" Reggie asked, still holding Damian's manhood gently in her hand.

"Yeah, that feels good," Damian said softly, laying his head back and sighing as if he had just slid into a hot bath.

"Oops!" Reggie gasped, dropping Damian's penis from her hand when she realized she was suddenly holding an erection. "Now is not the time for that, baby," Reggie giggled, after which she released Damian's binds and wrapped him in a sheet before helping him out of the cabin and onto the deck.

By the time Damian and Reggie exited the cabin, the NYPD Harbor Unit boat had pulled next to the Coast Cutter alongside the Doral Cruiser. Francona and Slowinski were in the process of leading Niki and Jean in handcuffs across a plank onto the Harbor Unit boat. Reggie followed, her arm wrapped around Damian's waist.

"You boys did good tonight," Kerby remarked. Then he looked at the damage to the Doral Cruiser. "You'd better jump over. You're going to be needing a lift home."

Danny and Peter looked at each other. "Mr. Brewster, we were wondering, since they're going to get our bodies out of the river tomorrow anyway, would it be all right if we just stayed onboard here for the night?" Danny asked.

"It's a lot more comfortable in here than it is on the bulkhead. She even has some kind of satellite television on board," Peter noted.

"They probably won't tow you out of here until sunrise anyway, and I'm sure they're not going to take the boat out of the water for a while, so I don't see why not," Kerby said. "By the way, good luck tomorrow, fellas."

"Good luck, Danny! Good luck, Peter!" Penny mouthed to the boys, a tear trickling down her right cheek.

With everything settled, Penny waved goodbye to Francona, Slowinski, and Reggie and aimed her boat for the Hudson River while the Harbor Unit boat started back toward the East River.

♥

After passing the tip of Manhattan, with the Harbor Unit boat now out of sight, Penny shifted her boat into the lowest possible cruising speed and put the boat on automatic pilot. She turned to Kerby who looked at her curiously.

"This is romantic! Don't you think?" Penny sighed, looking out into the black water with the lights from the city skyscrapers sparkling on it like stars. "It kind of reminds me of that scene in *Charade* where Cary Grant and Audrey Hepburn are cruising down the Seine at night with the lights of Paris all around them. He takes her in his arms--" Penny began before Kerby interrupted her.

"I know the scene. It goes like this," Kerby whispered, taking Penny into his arms and squeezing her tightly to him.

As their mouths came together, their lips parted and Kerby eased his tongue into Penny's mouth. She immediately felt the tiny fireworks display exploding in her head again. After several seconds, their mouths parted and Penny looked into Kerby's eyes. "I think I know now why Hitchcock always cut to fireworks when his leading characters were about to make love," Penny whispered before pulling Kerby back to her.

Penny was lost in a moment that she had never before experienced when the siren from the Harbor Unit boat blasted her back into reality.

"Are you okay?" Rocco Francona shouted to Penny.

"Sure . . . I'm . . . uh . . . fine," Penny stammered, trying to compose herself.

"I'm glad I caught you before you got too far up the river. It occurred to me that Stan's car is still up at the Boat Basin. I was thinking that maybe if I rode up with you, it might save Stan and me a little time and provide you with a little company for the trip up," Francona said.

Penny looked to Kerby for an excuse to say no. "How could you say no? What could you possibly tell him?" Kerby wondered.

"Sure," Penny murmured dejectedly to Francona. "I can't think of a reason why not."

EPILOGUE

A GRAND OPENING
JULY 1, 2003

The crowd that showed up for the grand opening of *Sex, Ghosts, and Gumshoes* was larger than Penny had dared to dream it might be. Carmella and Penny had moved all of the reading tables to the walls in the front of the store. Hors d'oeuvres and buckets filled with ice and magnums of champagne sat atop tables covered with crisp white linen table clothes. They also set folding chairs up in the center of the room, causing the front of the store to look like a small auditorium.

By the time scheduled for Maitresse Joie's presentation, the room was filled to capacity with women of all shapes and sizes, but Joie was nowhere to be seen. Penny started next door to see what was holding Joie up. At the base of the stairs to Joie's brownstone, Penny looked up to see Sol Hirsh coming out of Joie's front door rubbing his behind. Joie, who was a step behind Sol with a huge grin on her face, spotted Penny starting up the steps.

"I haven't forgotten you, sweetie," Joie hollered down to Penny as a sheepish Sol sped by a confused Penny on his way to the bookstore. "I just wanted to make certain that everyone was there before I came over. I do have to make an entrance, you know. Just let me get my *plaything* from downstairs and I'll be right over."

When Joie said she had to make an entrance, she wasn't kidding. Maitresse Joie strutted into the bookstore in a black leather dress that looked as if it had been painted on and was slit up to the top of her thigh on one side. Penny was certain that had it not been for the slit, Joie would not have been able to take a step in the dress. She had a long dog leash slung over her shoulder, one end of which was in her left hand, with the other end attached around the neck of someone who was walking behind Joie wearing a hooded black cloak that covered him from head to toe. Joie stopped at her position in front of the fascinated women who had filled the place. After holding the crowd in suspense for several seconds, Joie whipped the cloak off her *plaything*.

Underneath the cloak was an extremely well muscled young man dressed in nothing but tight fitting black leather shorts and a black leather hood that covered his entire head and face. The guy's body had been oiled to better show off the cuts of his muscles.

"My hard-bodied slave," Joie announced to the gasping ladies. "Every woman should own one."

The hard-body lifted Joie into a sitting position on the counter, which had been cleared for the evening, and as Joie began her talk on training the recalcitrant husband or boyfriend, the hard-body went down on one knee and eased off her leather boots. While Joie gave her talk with a riding crop in her right hand, the hard-body proceeded to paint her toenails, getting a swift snap with her riding crop every time he painted anything other than a nail.

By the time the evening ended, pretty much every woman in the place had made a point of touching one or another of the oily muscles on the hard-body's frame, but Penny was quite certain that no one in the room, other than Joie, Penny, and Kerby that is, recognized that under the full face mask was none other than Damian Bradford.

Though the bookstore was filled throughout the night mostly with women, Damian and Kerby were not the only men to make an appearance. Of course Sol was there, though Penny noticed that he did not sit down for the entire evening. Early in the evening, Penny noticed Sol with another distinguished looking elderly gentleman wearing a gray *Brooks Brothers* suit. Sol waved for Penny to come over.

"This is my good friend Morris Titlebaum," Sol said. "Morris and I started in the insurance business at about the same time. I've known him for years. I don't know whether you're aware of this, but Mags used Morris as her insurance agent ever since I recommended him to her years ago. If you have a second, Morris has something he'd like to discuss with you."

"As you can see, I'm kind of occupied at the moment," Penny said politely to Titlebaum. "But I can assure you that if you're a friend of Sol's, and Mags used you for all of these years as her insurance agent, then I certainly intend to use you as well. If it's okay with you, I'll call your office in the morning and set up something for a more convenient time."

"Oh, I'm not here looking for business," Titlebaum responded. "Actually, I have some news for you which I had assumed you would be eagerly anticipating, but after speaking with Sol, I'm not so sure anymore."

"I have no idea what you are talking about," Penny said.

"If that's the case, then I think it best that you have a seat while I explain," Titlebaum replied. "I had assumed that you were aware of what was going on because I had heard from your lawyer, Mark Libby, on several occasions on the subject. He asked that, given that I knew him to be your lawyer, I keep him posted on everything that was transpiring, and of course I did. Apparently, Mr. Libby has not been transmitting my messages with regard to this matter on to you.

"You see, Ms Albright, shortly before your Aunt Mags was diagnosed with cancer, she met with Mark Libby to devise a plan to make certain that you would be well-taken care of after her death. She wanted to make certain that you received a substantial amount of money outside of her estate, so that there would be no estate tax on the money that you received. Mr. Libby suggested that your aunt purchase a life insurance policy on *her* life, but in *your* name. That is, you were to be both the owner and beneficiary on the policy.

"Because of your aunt's age, at the time that the policy was purchased, it took me some time to find an insurance company willing to underwrite the risk, and it cost Mags a small fortune to purchase the policy, but I was eventually able to place the insurance. When Mags died, the insurance company commenced a fraud investigation. Not surprising really, given that Mags was diagnosed with cancer almost immediately after the policy was written. The company wanted to make certain that your aunt was not aware of the cancer before she purchased the policy, and had failed to include the diagnosis in her application. Had that been the case, the insurance company would have been in a position to disclaim on the policy based upon the misrepresentation.

"The reason I'm here tonight is to tell that the insurance company has completed its fraud investigation and determined that Mags had no reason to believe that she was suffering from cancer at the time she applied for the insurance. In fact, the physical exam that the company's own doctor did on Mags showed her to be free of any signs of cancer. The bottom line is that the insurance company is ready to transfer the money to you. I just need your bank account information to facilitate the transfer," Titlebaum finished.

"Just how much money are we talking about?" Penny asked.

"That's why I suggested that you take a seat, Ms Albright. It's also why I'm somewhat amazed that Mr. Libby never discussed this matter with you. You see, your Aunt Mags had purchased a $2 million insurance policy on her life in your name. That money is yours now."

When she heard the amount of the policy, an astounded Penny was happy that Morris Titlebaum had recommended that she take a seat. She still might have fallen off that seat had Kerby not steadied her.

"She always told me that she had you covered, kiddo. She just never told me how or how much," Kerby said.

Before Penny had fully recovered from the shock of hearing about the insurance money, she spotted yet another male milling among the throng of females in the store. It was Rocco Francona. Smartly dressed and looking as debonaire as always, Penny wasn't the only female to check out Francona as he roamed about the store as if he were looking for someone in particular. Lots of female eyes followed Francona around the room before he spotted Penny and made his way to her. Kerby's eyes followed Francona too.

"Hello, Mr. Francona," Penny said. "I have to say, I'm a bit surprised to see you here tonight. I didn't think you would have any interest in the subject matter."

"I'd appreciate it if you would call me Rocco from now on or maybe just Roc, if you'd like, and if it's okay with you I'll call you Penny," Francona suggested. "To be totally honest with you, the subject matter of the discussion is not what brought me here tonight, though I have no doubt that the right woman can train any man.

"I'm here because I wanted to properly thank you for the assistance you gave us in solving these crimes and arresting the murderers. I also wanted to apologize on behalf of the New York City Police Department for the way that my partner treated you at times, though I think you can understand why he felt certain that you were covering up for someone.

"Personally, I'm still not sure how you came up with the information that you provided us. It's still a little difficult for me to believe that you have these detailed conversations with dead people. I can, however, tell you that you've made a believer out of Stan Slowinski. He now has fewer doubts about your supernatural abilities than I do. Of course, I never did get to see the *flying pig trick*, like he did," Francona said with a smile. "Stan is still talking about that one."

"I'll have to show it to you some time," Penny said, returning the smile.

"That brings me to the real reason that I'm here tonight. I thought maybe . . . you know . . . you might like to go out for dinner some night . . . maybe a movie or something," Francona offered nervously.

Penny looked at Kerby who said, "Go for it, kiddo."

"That sounds nice," Penny said, still looking at Kerby before turning back to Francona. "But would you mind if I took some time to think about it? I have a great deal going on in my life at the moment, and I'd like for things to settle down a little before I start any kind of a relationship."

"Take your time," Francona replied, starting for the door. "I have to run, but when you feel like you're ready, you know how to reach me."

"I told you he liked you, kiddo," Kerby said. "But what's this stuff about taking some time to think about it? I mean, he's no Cary Grant, but James Daren's not a bad catch by most women's standards."

"I couldn't tell him, but I already have my hands full with one man in my life. Anyway, why would I settle for a Cary Grant *wanna be*, when I already have a clone of the real thing?" Penny whispered.

"Everybody wants to be Cary Grant, kiddo. Even Cary Grant wanted to be Cary Grant," Kerby replied, recalling a famous Grant quote. "But what Officer Moon Doggie has that I don't is flesh and blood, and don't fool yourself, kiddo, every woman needs a warm-blooded man in her life."

"Flesh and warm blood is nice, I guess," Penny responded, still in a hushed tone. "But I'll bet he can't *tingle* the way you do," she finished with a smile.

The only other male to enter the bookstore that night showed up just as the party was ending. Penny didn't recognize him, but she approached him, with Kerby right behind her, as soon as she saw him walk into the bookstore.

"You're a little late," Penny greeted the guy with a smile. "How can I help you?"

"I'm sorry to bother you, Ms Albright. I came by earlier, but you were very busy. I've been waiting across the street for things to settle down a little. Ms Albright, I've been reading a great deal about you in the papers lately. Maybe you've read some things about me as well. My name is Paul Richards. I'm from New Jersey. My wife was brutally raped and murdered recently. At the time that the killer took my wife, he also took my twin girls. The man that the police believe killed my wife died later in a car accident. My girls are still missing. Ms Albright, the police feel certain that my girls are dead, and I've come to accept that. Nevertheless, I want their bodies to receive a proper burial next to their mother. I need you to help me find them, Ms Albright," Richards pleaded.

Penny looked at Kerby. "Tell him you'll meet with him in the morning at his home to gather whatever information he has," Kerby instructed. "Then talk to Sol, tell him you're going to need a ride to New Jersey in the morning. The spirits of two little girls are out there somewhere looking for their mother, and we're going to reunite them."